WOLF BY
WOLF

WOLF BY WOLF

RYAN GRAUDIN

LITTLE, BROWN AND COMPANY
NEW YORK BOSTON

Copyright © 2015 by Ryan Graudin
Excerpt from *Blood for Blood* copyright © 2016 by Ryan Graudin

Cover art by Jeff Miller/Faceout Studio. Cover design by Marcie Lawrence. Cover photography © 2018: Girl - Arcangel Images; Motorcycle - Getty Images; Nazi Imagery - Alamy; Blimp - Wikimedia Commons; Clouds, Map/Graph, and Paper Texture - Shutterstock.com. Cover © 2018 Hachette Book Group, Inc.

Little, Brown and Company

Hachette Book Group
1290 Avenue of the Americas, New York, NY 10104
Visit us at LBYR.com

Little, Brown and Company is a division of Hachette Book Group, Inc.
The Little, Brown name and logo are trademarks of Hachette Book Group, Inc.

The publisher is not responsible for websites (or their content) that are not owned by the publisher.

First Paperback Edition: October 2016
First published in hardcover in October 2015 by Little, Brown and Company

The Library of Congress has cataloged the hardcover edition as follows:

Graudin, Ryan.
  Wolf by wolf / by Ryan Graudin. — First edition.
     pages cm
  Summary: "The first book in a duology about an alternate version of 1956 where the Axis powers won WWII, and hold an annual motorcycle race across their conjoined continents to commemorate their victory"— Provided by publisher.
  ISBN 978-0-316-40512-6 (hardcover) — ISBN 978-0-316-40510-2 (ebook) — ISBN 978-0-316-40511-9 (library edition ebook) [1. Motorcycle racing—Fiction. 2. Government, Resistance to—Fiction.] I. Title.
  PZ7.G7724Wo 2015
  [Fic]—dc23

2014044026

ISBNs: 978-0-316-40508-9 (pbk.), 978-0-316-40510-2 (ebook)

10 9 8 7 6 5

LSC-C

Printed in the United States of America

TO DAVID, FOR BEING BY MY SIDE AND
SHARING MY MOST IMPORTANT JOURNEYS

THE ROTTEN BONES ARE TREMBLING,
OF THE WORLD BEFORE THE RED WAR.
—FROM THE OFFICIAL SONG OF THE HITLER YOUTH

Once upon a different time, there was a girl who lived in a kingdom of death. Wolves howled up her arm. A whole pack of them—made of tattoo ink and pain, memory and loss. It was the only thing about her that ever stayed the same.

Her story begins on a train.

CHAPTER 1

THEN

THE NUMBERS
AUTUMN 1944

There were five thousand souls stuffed into the train cars—thick and deep like cattle. The train groaned and bent under their weight, weary from all of its many trips. (Five thousand times five thousand. Again and again. So many, so many.)

No room to sit, no air to breathe, no food to eat. Yael leaned on her mother and strangers alike until her knees ached (and long, long after). She choked in the smell of waste and took gulps from the needle-cold buckets of water that were shoved through the door by screaming guards. Far below the tracks, a slow, shuddering groan whispered her name, over and over: *yah-ell, yah-ell, yah-ell.*

"You won't have to stand much longer. We're almost there," Yael's mother kept saying as she smoothed her daughter's hair.

But *almost there* kept stretching on and on. One day rolled into two, into three. Endless hours of swaying kilometers and slats of sunlight that cut like knives through the car's shoddy planks and across the passengers' gray faces. Yael huddled against her mother's taffeta-silk skirt and tried not to listen to the crying. Sobs so loud her name almost drowned in them. But no matter how loud the sadness got, she could still hear the whisper. *Yah-ell, yah-ell, yah-ell.* Constant, steady, always. A secret under everything.

Three days of this.

Yah-ell, yah-ell, yah—squeal!

Stop.

Nothing.

And then the doors opened.

"Get out! Hurry!" a man—bald, thin, dressed in clothes like pajamas—yelled, and kept yelling. Even after they started spilling out of the train car. He yelled and yelled in a way that made Yael shrink close against her mother. "Hurry! Hurry!"

All around was darkness and glare. Night and spotlights. The cold air was sharpened by the screams of guards, snarling dogs, and snapping whips.

"Men on one side! Women on the other!"

Push, push, jostle, push, screams. There was a sea of wool and shuffling. Everyone seemed lost. Moving and pushing and crying and not knowing. Yael's fingers clenched the edge of her mother's coat, so tight they could have been seams of their own.

*—HURRY HURRY MOVE—*an iron voice inside Yael fought and pushed and cried*—DON'T GET WASHED AWAY—*

They were all flowing in one direction. Away from whip-lash and dog fangs. Toward a man who stood on an overturned apple crate, looking out across the platform's dark, milling crowd. A floodlight bathed him. The pure white fabric of his lab coat glowed and his arms were stretched wide, like wings.

He looked like an angel.

Every face that passed he measured and judged. Male and female. Old and young. The man in the glowing lab coat plucked and sifted and pointed them into lines.

"Too small! Too ill! Too weak! Too short! Too old!" He barked out characteristics like ingredients for some twisted recipe, sweeping away their offenders with a wave of his hand. Those he approved of received a passing nod.

When he saw Yael, he neither barked nor nodded. He squinted at first—eyes serpent sharp behind his glasses.

Yael squinted back. There was a sharpness in her eyes, too, whetted by three days of fear and too-bright lights. Her knees ached and wobbled, but she tried her best to stand straight. She did not want to be too small, too weak, too short.

The man stepped down from the crate and walked toward Yael's mother, who shifted just-so against her daughter as if to shield her. But there was no defense from this man's gaze. He saw all, staring at Yael and her mother as if they were suits that needed tailoring. Taking measurements with his eyes, imagining what a few stitches and tucks might do.

Yael stared back, taking measurements of her own. The man looked different up close. Out of the light, with the shad-ows pressed in. (They seemed extra dark on him, as if making up for that first glowing impression.) He smelled different, too. Clean, but not. Harsh, peeling scents Yael later learned to associate with bleach and blood and uncareful scalpels.

This man did not trade in heralds or blessings or miracles.

He was an angel of a different kind.

Yael's knees ached, ached, ached. Her eyes stung and watered. She kept standing. Kept staring. Clenching her mother's skirt with stubborn fingers.

The man in the white coat glanced at the guard next to him, who was busy inscribing notes onto a clipboard. "Reserve this girl for Experiment Eighty-Five. It's long-term, so she should be housed in the inmate barracks. And make certain her hair is only cut. Not shorn. I'll need strands for samples."

"Yes, Dr. Geyer." The guard grabbed Yael's hand, snapped his pen across her skin in two quick strikes. *X* marks the survivor. "What about the mother?"

The man shrugged. "She seems strong enough," was all he said before he walked back to the crate, back to the light that made him dazzle and glow.

———

Yael never did find out why Dr. Geyer chose her. Why she— out of all the young children who stumbled out of the train cars and clung to their mothers' coats that night—was placed in the line of the living.

But it did not take her long to discover what she'd been marked for.

6

This was Experiment 85: Every other morning, at the end of the four-hour roll call, a guard shouted out Yael's number. Every other morning, she had to follow him through two sets of barbed-wire gates and over the train tracks, all the way to the doctor's office.

The nurse always strapped Yael down to the gurney before the injections. She never really looked at Yael, even when she turned the girl's arm over to check the numbers stamped there. Those water-weak eyes always focused on the inanimate. Things like the not-quite-dry bloodstains on the floor tiles or flecked across the pristine white of her apron. The shiny black leather of her shoes. The clipboard she scrawled Yael's information on.

INMATE: 121358ΔX
AGE: 6 YEARS
EXPERIMENT: #85 MELANIN MANIPULATION
SESSION: 38

Dr. Geyer was different. From the moment he stepped across the threshold, his eyes never left Yael. He sat on his rolling stool, arms folded over his chest. Leaned slightly back. Examining the little girl in front of him. There were no wrinkles on his face—no weary frown or weight of the world sagging his skin.

He even smiled when he asked his questions. Yael could see all of his white, white teeth, cut apart by the tiny black gap where his two front incisors didn't quite meet. It was this part of his face she always focused on when he spoke. The gap. The not-quite-fullness of his soft words. The single break in his paternal mirage.

"How are you feeling?" he'd ask her, leaning forward on his toadstool seat.

Yael never really knew the answer to this question. What exactly it was that Dr. Geyer expected her to say when the bunk she shared with her mother and Miriam and three other women was infested with lice; when the night temperatures dropped so low that the straw in their mattress stabbed her skin like knitting needles; when she was hungry, always hungry, even though the Babushka in the bunk across from her snuck her extra bread rations every night.

—DON'T LOOK AT THE KNIVES TELL HIM WHAT HE WANTS TO HEAR—

She wanted to be strong, brave, so she offered the one word a strong, brave girl might say: "Fine."

The doctor's smile always grew wider when she said this. Yael wanted to keep him happy. She didn't want the bloodstains on the floor to be hers.

Every session he examined her skin. Shone a dazzling penlight into her eyes. Tugged out a few of her stubby hairs for color analysis. When the string of questions and answers ended, Dr. Geyer took the clipboard from the nurse stationed in the corner. Always he flipped through the pages, his brown hair tumbling to his eyes as he deciphered the nurse's crude writing.

"'Melanin production seems to be on a steady decline.... Note paler patches on skin as well as slight change in subject's iris pigmentation. Eumelanin is also decreasing—as can be seen by subject's hair coloration.'"

They never called Yael by her name. She was always *subject*. Or if they needed to be more specific: Inmate 121358ΔX.

"We're making progress." Dr. Geyer's smile stretched, as if his lips were being held open by tenterhooks. He handed the clipboard back to the nurse, rolled his seat to the sterling tray table, where the needles sat in a neat row. Straight silver fangs, waiting to sink poison into Yael's skin. Fill her with another two days of fire and agony. Change her from within. Take all the colors and feelings and human inside. Drain, drain, drain until nothing was left.

Just a ghost of a girl. A nothing shell.

Progress.

CHAPTER 2

NOW

MARCH 9, 1956
GERMANIA, CAPITAL OF THE THIRD REICH

The sun was a low orange threat in the sky as Yael stepped out the flat door onto Luisen Street—an asphalt artery at the heart of the city once called Berlin. She'd lingered too long in the tattoo artist's chair, bearing the needle and the sting and the memories. Watching him put the final black touches on the final black wolf.

It had been her fifth and last visit to the tiny back closet, with its ink bottles and cracked leather chair. Five visits to cover up the crooked numbers on her left arm. Five visits for five wolves. They swooped and jostled and howled up her arm, all the way to her elbow. Black and always running, striving against her skin.

Babushka, Mama, Miriam, Aaron-Klaus, Vlad.

Five names, five stories, five souls.

Or, a different way to do the math: four memories and a reminder.

But Vlad's wolf *needed* to be as perfect as the others, which meant Yael pushed her luck to the edge, watching the clock on the far wall tick its way toward sundown. In the end Vlad's wolf was a flawless open wound—throbbing under hastily wrapped gauze.

Yael was late.

Germania was a dangerous place after dark. Official curfew was not for a few more hours, but that didn't stop patrols from lurking on the capital's street corners. Checking the papers of random souls who passed. Ready to arrest at the slightest aberration.

Nothing good happened at night, the National Socialists reasoned. Honest *Volk* had no reason to be out once the shops and beer halls locked their doors. The only people desperate enough to do business under high moon and heavy shadows were resistance conspirators, black-market scoundrels, and Jews in disguise.

Yael happened to be all three.

The resistance leaders were going to have her head. Henryka especially. The tiny Polish woman with too-bleached frizz springing from every direction of her scalp was far more fearsome than these features credited her for. Yael would've preferred Reiniger's stern National Socialist army commander voice to the whirlwind/Mama Bear/spitfire that was Henryka.

More than likely they would both give her a talking-to. (Henryka: *How could you stay out so late! We thought you were dead or worse!* Reiniger: *Do you realize how selfish you were being? You could have compromised the resistance. We're close. So close.*) If the patrols didn't catch her first.

Luisen Street was empty as Yael walked under its brightening streetlamps. A long row of Volkswagens—identical but for their plate numbers—fortified the curbs. The grocery down the block was already locked tight, windows dark. Propaganda posters—some tattered and curled, others still fresh with paste—lined the walls between flat doors, reminding strong blond Aryan children to attend Hitler Youth. Reminding their mothers to produce more strong blond Aryan children to attend Hitler Youth.

Yael did not have far to walk, just a few blocks to the safety of the beer hall's hidden basement. But all it took was one encounter. One too-hurried answer.

The necessity to move quickly and avoid detection beat high in Yael's throat as she tore past the rows of posters, turning a corner onto a sequestered side street.

And came face-to-face with a patrol.

It was a standard unit: two young men with Mauser Kar.98Ks strapped over their shoulders. The soldiers were leaning against a wall, trading a single black-market cigarette between them. Illegal smoke curled from their lips like dozens of phantom tongues. White—not black like the billows of Yael's childhood. The ones that poured, day and night, out of tall smokestacks. When Yael was very little, she'd thought a monster lived inside those sooty brick walls. (She knew the truth now. Saw the photos and endless lists of the dead. Rows and rows of numbers like the ones her wolves hid. There was a monster, but it didn't live inside the death camp's crematorium. Its den was much finer—a Chancellery full of stolen art, and doors with iron locks.)

This smoke, the white smoke, vanished quickly when the soldiers caught sight of her. The first tossed the cigarette down, crushing it under his heel. The second called to her in a rough voice, "You there! Fräulein!"

There was no turning back now.

—WALK STRAIGHT SHOW NO FEAR NO FEAR—

When Yael reached the pair, she offered a mandatory, unflinching salute. *"Heil Hitler!"*

Both soldiers mumbled it back. The first pulverized the tobacco further into the cracked sidewalk with his heel. The second held out his hand.

It took Yael an extra beat of a moment to realize what he was asking for. She'd been through this dance with patrols before (more than she'd ever admit to Henryka and Reiniger), but the sight of smoke, plus hours in the artist's back closet, had rattled her. Sessions under the needle always left Yael feeling raw. It wasn't the ink and pain so much as the needle itself. The memories of needles. What they could do. What they did.

Even at their most basic function, needles do two things: They give and they take away. The tattoo artist's needles took white skin and numbers, gave her wolves. Dr. Geyer's needles had taken so much more. But what they gave…

Yael had many faces. Many names. Many sets of papers. Because the chemicals the Angel of Death had crammed into Yael's veins had changed her.

"Papers," the second soldier demanded.

Yael knew better than to argue. Her fingers fluttered to the pocket of her leather jacket, pulled out the tattered booklet that belonged to today's face.

" 'Mina Jager,' " the soldier read aloud. Looking from picture to face to picture again. He flipped to the next yellowed page, taking in Mina's unremarkable history: Germania-born. Blond. Member of the Hitler Youth. The rough biography of every adolescent within a sixteen-kilometer radius.

"What are you doing out so late, Fräulein Jager?" the first soldier asked while the other read.

The real answer? *Getting a black-market tattoo to hide my Jewish numbers before I go on a top secret mission for the resistance to bring an end to the New Order.* A truth so absurd the soldiers might even laugh it off if Yael voiced it. A small, contrary sliver of her wanted to try, but she settled with the best answer. The boring one. "I was hoping to reach the grocery before it closed. My mother ran out of eggs and sent me to fetch more."

"Eggs . . ." The first soldier frowned and nodded at her arm. "What's that?"

Yael followed his gaze to the cuff of her left sleeve. Her gauze wrapping had been too hasty. Its netted white tail peeked out from under the leather.

"A bandage," she told him.

He leaned in. Closer, curious. His breath was stale with smoke. "Let's have a look."

Flash, *thud*, *verdammt*, went Yael's heart.

Yael could manipulate her appearance the way other people might change clothes. These skinshifts could modify many things: her height, weight, coloring, the length of her hair, the sound of her voice. But some things could not be altered: gender, wounds, tattoo ink.

14

These things stayed.

The wolves were her constant, the single thing about her that was solid and sure. Months ago, when Yael had returned to the resistance headquarters with her first, fresh wolf, Henryka had several peevish words to offer on the matter (the foremost among them being "dead giveaway"). The Polish woman even went so far as to point out that the religious laws of Yael's people forbade the practice.

But what was done was done. Ink had been under Yael's skin for more than a decade. By adding the wolves she'd simply made it her own. These new markings were far, far better than the National Socialists' numbers. Their presence alone was not enough to condemn Yael, but they would raise questions if the patrol saw them. Enough suspicions to get her detained.

The only thing that would raise more questions would be for Yael to refuse the soldier's request. Slowly, slowly she lifted her sleeve. The gauze went all the way up her arm. Flecked in rust spots and frayed at the edges.

The soldier squinted at it. "What happened?"

Yael's heart was louder now (FLASH, *THUD, VERDAMMT.* FLASH, *THUD, VERDAMMT*), pumping hard with the knowledge that only a few threads stood between her and disaster. All the soldier had to do was reach out and tug. See the ink and the raw and the blood.

What then?

There was always a way out. Vlad had taught her that, along with so many other things. These two men and their

15

two rifles were no match for the skills she'd learned, even in this seventeen-year-old girl's body. She could knock them out cold, disappear in twenty seconds flat.

Yael could, but she wouldn't. An incident so close to the resistance's headquarters, on the eve of her first mission, was far too risky. It would draw the eyes and the wrath of the Gestapo to the neighborhood. Expose the resistance. Ruin everything.

There was always a way out, but tonight (tonight of all nights) it had to be clean.

"It's a dog bite," Yael answered. "A stray attacked me a few days ago."

The soldier assessed the bandage for another moment. His stance slacked from aggressive to conversational.

"Was it bad?" he asked.

Was it bad? Yael would take a thousand and one of Mina's dog bites in place of what had really happened. Trains and barbed-wire fences. Death and pain and death.

"I survived," she said with a smile.

"Stray bitches make good target practice. Almost as much as commies and Jews." The soldier laughed and slapped the butt of his Mauser. "Next one I see I'll shoot in your honor."

Yael kept her lips drawn up in Mina's meek, demure fashion. The mask of a good little Reichling. It was only in the unseen places she raged. Her toes curled hard inside her boots. Her fingers slid back to her jacket pocket, where her trusted Walther P38 handgun nestled.

The second soldier shut the book, so all Yael could see was the Reich stamp on the front. The eagle's wings were rigid: a double salute. The wreath and twisted cross hung effortlessly from its talons. All as black as that monstrous smoke. The same blackness that grew inside Yael if she let the memories billow back.

"Everything seems to be in order, Fräulein Jager." He held Mina's book out to her.

The lining of Yael's throat tasted sooty. Her toes were cracking—*pop, pop, pop*—tiny, quiet gunshots inside her boots.

There was a time and a place for remembering. There was a target waiting for her rage, her revenge. This evening, this street, these men were not it.

Her touch slipped off the gun. Yael reached out and grabbed the papers instead.

"Thank you," she said as she tucked the pages of another girl's life deep into her jacket. "I must go. My mother will be worried."

The second soldier nodded. "Of course, Fräulein Jager. Sorry to delay you."

She started walking, her fist shoved into one of the jacket's normal pockets, clenching the talismans she kept there: a blunted thumbtack, a pea-sized wooden doll with its face worried off. One by one her toes uncurled. Bit by bit the blackness retreated, back to its uneasy sleep.

"Watch out for the strays!" the first soldier called after her.

Yael held up a hand to acknowledge him but did not turn. She was done with soldiers and strays.

She had much worse things to face.

CHAPTER 3

NOW

MARCH 9, 1956
GERMANIA, THIRD REICH

Yael held her breath when she entered Henryka's office—
expecting a barrage of mother-hen clucking and pecks of
guilt (*Where were you? I was so worried! I thought you'd been
discovered/killed/[insert disaster here]!*). But the basement door
swung open to a Henryka-less room.

Perhaps she had not been missed after all.

Yael let her breath leak out and stepped into the office. It
was not the fanciest of spaces, its smallness made even more
cramped by the shelves upon shelves, the military-grade desk,
and the card table petaled by mismatched chairs. Paper was
everywhere. Forests' worth, covering the walls, sticking wayward out of drawers, stacked in files all across Henryka's
desk. Documents of old operations, reams of intelligence on
the National Socialist government's top officials, and rescued
books. (Yael had read her way through Henryka's library

at least six times, learning about the *Biology of Desert Wildlife* and the *History of Western Civilization* and *Advanced Calculus* and everything else the battered encyclopedia sets had to offer.)

But one piece of paper in particular always drew Yael's eye: the operations map that took up the far wall. The whole of Europe was stained in red. A crimson tide rolled over the Ural Mountains, bleeding into Asia. Scarlet spilled through the Mediterranean Sea and dripped down the crown of Africa.

Red: the color of battle wounds and the Third Reich. Bitter, bright death.

Whenever Yael studied this map, she couldn't help but be amazed at the scale of Hitler's victory. According to the stories, when the Führer first announced his vision of an occupied Africa and Europe to his generals, some of them had laughed. "Impossible," they'd said. "It can't be done."

But the word *impossible* held no sway over a man like Hitler. He sent his armies marching across Europe anyway; his ruthless SS troops ignored all "civilized" rules of war, mowing down soldiers and civilians alike.

Some countries, such as Italy and Japan, joined Hitler's annexing rampage, hungry for territories of their own. Other countries, too scarred by the war that ravaged the world two decades before, refused to fight. It didn't take much persuading for them to sign a nonaggression pact with the Axis. "Peace at all costs" was the isolationist catchphrase in the American newspapers. The Soviet Union put its pen to the pact as well, for all was not right in its lands. Localized uprisings against

Stalin's ethnic purges and dissension within the government were chipping away at the great Communist war machine. It was far from battle-ready.

Britain was the sole great power that did not collaborate or stand by. It was also the first of the great powers to fall. Its planes and pluck could not stop Operation Sea Lion. After the National Socialists hung their flags over the stones of a broken Parliament, Hitler bided his time, solidifying his hold on the conquered countries as he kept his calculating gaze to the east.

The Soviet Union was fracturing under the stress of itself. Stalin's naysayers rose out of the woodwork, decrying his alliance with the Germans. Entire regions of the country splintered off into rebellions. By the time the Führer finally broke his nonaggression pact in 1942, Stalin's armies were too diminished from within to fight a two-front war. The National Socialists and Italians beat down the Soviets' European border while Japanese soldiers edged their way into Siberia.

Once Hitler was assured of the Soviets' defeat, he turned his sights back on his Italian allies (whose newly acquired territories happened to be in Europe and Africa). After using his spies to assassinate the Italian leader, Mussolini, and blaming the murder on Italian partisans, Hitler moved his armies into Italy and its territories to "stabilize the region."

They never left.

The red lands of Europe and Africa were claimed as Lebensraum, living space for the Aryan people. Their native populations were reduced to second-class citizens; any who resisted were shipped off to labor camps. Jews, Romani, Slavs, and all others the Führer considered to be *Untermenschen* were rounded up. Taken to camps of a different kind.

Crimson wasn't the only color on Henryka's operations map. Two distinct empires made up the Axis: the Third Reich and Japan, which helmed the Greater East Asia Co-Prosperity Sphere. The Führer and Emperor Hirohito had halved the Asian continent like a Christmas pie, straight down the Seventieth Meridian. Henryka had chosen an ominous gray to color the Emperor's territory.

At the top of the map, hanging in the high north, there was no color at all. Just a vast white stretch of winter lands, where echoes of Stalin's army lived on. Too fractured, too underresourced, and too cold for the Axis forces to bother with.

For over a decade these colors stayed the same. Settling in, deeper, dye strong. (Though according to the resistance's intelligence, Hitler's ambitions for the National Socialists and the Aryan race were on a global scale. It didn't matter that he'd signed nonaggression pacts with the Americas or that he was sworn allies with Emperor Hirohito. Intrigue and political backstabbing were Hitler's specialty. Besides, why else would the Reich's hundreds of labor camps be dedicated to churning out war materials?)

But as Yael stared at the map this time, she wasn't looking at colors or the lack of them. She was not counting the coded operative pins that dotted the Reich's major cities—Germania, London, Cairo, Rome, Baghdad, Paris.

Yael was looking at the road ahead.

The Axis Tour.

The long-distance race had started its life as a Hitler Youth activity, training for boys who wanted to join the Kradschützen motorcycle troop. It was so popular it evolved into a race. Once the war was won, Joseph Goebbels—the Reich's propaganda minister—decided to televise the competition, to show off the two Axis empires' conquered territories, commemorate their victory, and promote their alliance. Teenagers from the Hitler Youth and the Great Japan Sincerity Association competed every year, racing their motorcycles from capital to capital. A journey that captured the attention of the Axis's entire population for the better part of a month.

Henryka had marked the tour's path as a dotted black line that spanned three continents in a crooked U. Yael traced the path with her forefinger. Starting in Germania, down the boot that was once Italy, across the sea, along the Sahara's sands, through the Middle East's rugged mountains, into the jungles of Indochina, up to the port of Shanghai, over another sea, all the way to Tokyo. It was 20,780 kilometers divided into nine legs, traveled by twenty racers all fighting for victory via the lowest cumulative time.

This was the journey she had to take. This was the race she had to win.

The basement door swung open to reveal Henryka, wide-eyed, cradling armfuls of documents.

"Yael?" The older woman always greeted Yael with a question mark when she wore sleeves. There were, Henryka sometimes complained, too many faces in Yael's repertoire for her to keep track of. (To be fair, the faces looked very similar: oval shaped, light hair, bright eyes, long nose, straight white teeth. Yael often had trouble keeping all the aliases straight herself. They were almost, awfully, interchangeable.)

Yael's finger dropped away from Tokyo. She dropped Mina's face at the same time, letting Fräulein Jager's soft features slough away. There was a new face in her mind, just as Aryan but sharper. Yael sculpted it in practiced seconds. The process of stretching skin, shifting bone, and warping cartilage was always painful, but it was quick: *snap, snap, snap*. New pieces, new girl.

Henryka watched Yael's transformation through strands of brittle, home-bleached frizz, a scowl growing on her face. "Where have you been?"

Here we go. Yael could feel the rant whipping up in the woman's tiny body. It almost made her smile—Henryka still fussing over her like some sort of ugly duckling, even after years of the girl's own scrappy survival and Vlad's intense operative training.

"You were due here over a quarter of an hour ago! Kasper has been waiting with the truck, and I've been half out of my mind with worry! I was five minutes away from notifying Reiniger and sending out a search party! He could have canceled the mission altogether! So much depends on you."

This lecture held too much truth for Yael to smile at.

"I'm sorry, Henryka." She paused, trying to think of what else to say that wouldn't add another worry line to the woman's aging skin. "I am."

23

Henryka's anger wilted in a heart's space. Ten seconds of yelling seemed to be all she had the energy for. Yael wondered how long she'd been awake. Stretches of sleepless days weren't rare for the older woman, who spent most of them in this hidden office—coordinating drops for operatives and decoding messages from cells all across the Axis territories. This place and this indomitable Polish woman were the brain stem of the resistance. Collecting information, dispersing it through the many nerve endings, causing movement.

Henryka's workload had been especially heavy lately, with the upcoming Axis Tour. She had to make sure the world was ready for what was about to happen if Yael completed her mission: a complete uprising. Operation Valkyrie reborn.

Henryka moved over to her desk, tucking the new documents into the avalanche of manila folders. In the far corner, behind the mass of files and a worn typewriter, a television whined out high, grainy frequencies. Its black-and-white pictures flickered strange light off the peeling ceiling paint. Henryka paused to watch it. Old footage was playing, a montage of last year's Axis Tour. Short clips of motorcycles filmed from the roadside were interspersed with shots of the racers' official times being recorded on the checkpoint cities' chalkboards. But the real meat of the coverage were the interviews conducted at each checkpoint. Conversations with the racers who'd clawed their way to the top of this list. There were a slew of *Mein Kampf*–quoting German boys, proud and puffed. There were glossy-haired Japanese boys, serious and honor-heavy.

And then there was Adele Wolfe. The girl who used her

twin brother's papers so she could enter the all-male race. Who cut her hair and taped her breasts and raced like all the rest. The only girl who had ever competed. The victor of the ninth Axis Tour.

Victor Adele Wolfe was a classic Reich beauty—pale, pale, pale—with corn-silk hair and Nordic eyes. This face was aired all over the Reichssender (the television's only state-approved channel) just days after her victory and astonishing confession that she was not actually Felix Wolfe but his sister. (Her Iron Cross had almost been revoked by racing officials, but the Führer had taken a liking to the svelte blond. She was, he said, a perfect example of Aryan splendor and strength. No one dared argue with him.) The cameras followed her everywhere, documenting dozens of press interviews, an awards ceremony in view of Mount Fuji, the traditional Victor's Ball at the Imperial Palace in Tokyo.

Out of her racing gear and wrapped up in a silk kimono, Adele Wolfe almost appeared delicate. It was hard to imagine exactly *how* a girl who looked like a forest fairy straight out of the Grimm Brothers' storybooks had beaten out nineteen burly boys under such grueling conditions. Even after ten months of studying the race footage and mastering the maneuvers and speed of her own Zündapp KS 601 motorcycle on countryside autobahns, Yael still wasn't quite sure how Adele had managed the feat.

But she was about to find out.

Henryka turned away from the screen, eyes back to Yael's freshly changed face. "You look just like her."

Exact impersonations usually took days of study. Even then they weren't always accurate. There were always adjustments to be made, minute details to fix. The exact color of eyes and hair. A missed freckle. The precise angle of the nose. Scars deep and wide and worrying over skin.

Yael had perfected Adele Wolfe's appearance in a single week. She was tall (175 centimeters) with white-blond hair and three very distinct freckles on the left cheek. Unreal blue eyes—like ribboning layers of glacier ice, or tropical shallows. Replicating Adele Wolfe's features was the easy part. It was every other aspect of the ninth victor's life that was the challenge.

Yael had been studying Adele Wolfe for nearly a year. Breathing, sleeping, eating, living everything Adele. Observing the girl from close and far. Perfecting the way she walked (as if she were being pulled on silk strings). Noting how she twisted the ends of her hair when she was nervous. Memorizing every strange, seemingly useless fact from Adele's past.

Yael knew the following: Adele Wolfe had been born to a mechanic and a housewife in the outskirts of Frankfurt, Germany, on May 2, 1938. Her two brothers—Martin (older) and Felix (twin)—taught her boxing and wrestling. Her mother taught her knitting (not so successfully—the socks always came out warped and unraveling), and her father taught her racing (rather successfully, even though girls weren't allowed to compete in formal races). She hated beets and fish with livid passion. Her favorite color was yellow, but she always told people it was red because it seemed fiercer.

Adele Wolfe wanted, more than anything, to be someone.

She started racing under her twin brother's name at the age of ten. At first it was just a race or two. But then she kept winning. Felix Wolfe rose to the top of his age rank and even had his name and photograph printed in the newspaper *Das Reich*. Adele raced and won, raced and won, and there seemed to be nothing that could stop her.

Until the day of Martin's racetrack accident. The day the Wolfe family broke in a way that could never be fixed. The day Adele's parents swore off racing altogether—banning their remaining children from even watching the Nürburgring races.

But Adele's fear of the road was no match for her fear of being lost. Swallowed into the Führer's breeding systems to mother a whole nation of blonds. Doomed to years of swollen ankles, a body run down, and breasts sucked dry.

That would not be her fate. So, five years after her older brother's death, she took Felix Wolfe's papers, entered the largest race in the Reich, and won.

As if on cue, the most popular film clip of Adele Wolfe's racing career flickered across the bubble screen. It was from the Victor's Ball of 1955—a party held for the winner of the Axis Tour, attended by Tokyo's high society and the Reich's highest officials. Adele had shocked the world at the finish line by revealing her true identity as a girl, but what happened during the ball stunned some Reichssender viewers even more.

Adolf Hitler—a man notorious for being a stick-in-the-mud at parties—asked Adele Wolfe to dance. The Führer, who left the Chancellery's great iron-bolted doors only twice a year (and when he did, swarmed himself thick with the crisp black uniforms of the SS), let Adele's skin collide with his for a five-minute, televised waltz.

It was one of the many reasons Reiniger—the National Socialist general and secret leader of the resistance—placed Adele Wolfe's file in Yael's hands. Hitler had the girl close enough for her to slide a knife blade between his ribs. If he did it once, he'd do it again.

And this time, the weapon would be ready.

But to attend the Victor's Ball in Tokyo, Yael had to win the race. To win the Axis Tour, she had to enter as Adele Wolfe. To enter as Adele Wolfe, she had to take the real girl's place. To take the real Adele's place, she would have to carry out the kidnapping and retrieval before curfew set in. Soon.

Yael glanced around the office. It seemed too small, too quiet for everything that was about to happen. "Where's Reiniger?"

"Erwin wanted to be here to see you off, but he had… other obligations." This was Henryka's code for National Socialist duties. Yael knew that even when Reiniger was with the National Socialists, he was doing the resistance's work— infiltrating the party for its secrets, converting officers whose sense of horror and morality was somehow still intact after all these New Order years, preparing great chunks of the army for the upcoming putsch—but the thought of him sitting in meetings with men who danced in her people's ashes and blood always twisted her stomach.

"He wanted me to give you this." Henryka plucked a folded sheet from the new papers and handed it to Yael. It was a list of addresses and contact protocol, written in code. There was one for each of the nine checkpoint cities along the dotted black line.

Prague. Rome. Cairo. Baghdad. New Delhi. Dhaka. Hanoi. Shanghai. Tokyo.

"If you need anything on the road, these cells should be able to help you. Just be certain you've lost any tails before you pay them a visit."

Yael refolded the paper into eighths and put it away. "Anything else?"

The older woman's lip trembled. Even her fingers were shaky as she tucked her bleached hairs behind her ear. When she shook her head, the wisps sprang back to their wild selves.

"I'll be watching you." Henryka nodded at the screen. Her eyes were wet and there was a weight in her whisper. A sadness full of the years they'd spent together: baking and reading and spying on beer hall customers through a knothole in the old headquarters. Years where Yael had almost felt like a normal adolescent.

"Do what needs to be done, then come back." The way the older woman said this made Yael think of all the operatives who hadn't returned. The pins that were taken off the map. Leaving trails of tiny holes all over the crimson paper world.

Yael hugged Henryka, burying her face in the woman's blouse. Its thin fabric held an odd mixture of smells: butter and flour, old papers and typewriter ink. Henryka's arms were much stronger than their scrawniness suggested, vising Yael's ribs until a mist sprang in her eyes. Yael rested in the tears and the holding for several seconds. Then she took one final, deep breath—libraries, bakeries, *home*—and pulled away.

Neither of them said good-bye. It was too hard a thing to voice. Too final and damning in times like these.

Yael walked to the door and gave one final glance at the far wall. Where hole-riddled continents bled red, smoked gray.

This was the last time she'd see the map like this.

Because tomorrow the end began. She was going to race from Germania to Tokyo. She was going to win the Axis Tour and earn an invitation to the Victor's Ball. She was going to kill the Führer and spark the death of the Third Reich.

She was going to cross the world and change it.

Or die trying.

CHAPTER 4

NOW

MARCH 9, 1956
GERMANIA, THIRD REICH

Adele Wolfe lived alone on the outskirts of Germania. Hers was the highest flat in the building, with a brilliant view of the capital's winking lights. It had been bought and paid for in full a year ago, with a chunk of the prize money from her Axis Tour victory.

Just one of hundreds of facts from Adele's file. Though Yael knew every meter of the victor's living space through surveillance and studying the old building's blueprints, she'd never been inside the flat herself.

That was about to change.

Yael crouched in the back of the shiny laundry truck (the one the resistance never actually used for laundry, just stakeouts and courier errands), watching the entrance to the building. It was quiet, weighted with the stillness of almost curfew. In the past five minutes only one middle-aged man had been out, tugging a reluctant bulldog, urging it to relieve itself as he stamped and grumbled under the orange lamplight. Now he was gone and the way was clear: empty streets and Gestapo-less cars. High, high above, the windows of Adele Wolfe's flat shone bright.

"You ready?" Kasper, driver and fellow operative, looked at her around the cracked leather headrest.

A laugh bubbled in Yael's esophagus. *Ready?* Her readiness was years in the forging. What had started in the death camp as stubborn survival had bloomed into something far more lethal. Vlad's training left her brutal in hand-to-hand combat. Bull's-eye deadly with every weapon she fired. Henryka's books left her with a buffet of languages and information at her disposal. In the camp she'd picked up Russian to add to her native German. Japanese, Italian, and English came later, along with smatterings of Arabic. She'd learned all she could about Zündapp KS 601 motorcycles. She'd studied the other qualifying racers, memorizing biographies and favorite cheating tactics. To cram all this into a word as short and simple as *ready* seemed . . . well, funny.

Hence the laugh.

"More than," she told Kasper. "I'll signal from the window when the target is secured. Be ready to help load her up."

Kasper nodded. "Don't push it too long. Curfew's in an hour. I want to have Victor Wolfe back at Henryka's well before then."

Yael made certain her face looked like Mina Jager's again. After one last sweep of the street (still empty, eyeless), she slipped out of the truck, through the cold night, and into the building's marble foyer. At the end sat a shiny brass lift gate, covered in a lattice of bright X's. It was the easiest way up, but too much like a cage. Too many X's to cross over her face. Cross her out.

Never again.

She took the stairs instead.

Yael wasted no time when she reached the door to Adele's flat. Her heart rattled in time with her knock. *Tap, tap, tap, tap...*

...

There was no answer. Just the flat's heavy silence leaking out into the hall. Accenting the sharp of her own heartbeat.

Adele Wolfe was not home.

Yael's fingers flew up to Mina's hair, fished out two bobby pins, and bent them straight. It took only seconds to coax apart the lock, swing the door open, and enter.

Inside held a mess that put Henryka's office to shame. Yael was, admittedly, not the cleanest person (it had taken Vlad three months to break her habit of leaving dirty glasses in the sink when she lived on his farm), but the state of Adele Wolfe's flat made her cringe. Clothes were everywhere. Strewn over armchairs. Crumpled against the baseboards. The walls were cluttered with Reich-approved art and photographs of Adele at the Victor's Ball, dressed in an elaborate kimono and sandwiched ceremoniously between the Führer and the Emperor. Giants of the East and West, smiling at the camera.

Yael's skin crawled, drawing tight over her bones. She

couldn't look at their faces for long, so her eyes skated to other pictures: the ones in frames scattered between long-standing, half-finished mugs of creamless coffee.

The largest picture sat by the turntable. It sported a much younger Adele: face sullen and arms crossed. Her hair was the brightest thing in the picture, done up in pigtail braids. Her brothers each held one; their expressions full of tease. Felix and Martin were handsome (Yael had noted this fact long before, when she first opened Adele's file), though it was hard to tell in this photo.

The crawling. It wasn't in her skin this time, but her heart. Yael looked at the faces of Adele's brothers—her *family*—and thought of the wolves on her arm. That lonely, lost pack.

Yael turned her back on all this and pushed the door shut. From the looks of things, Adele was still packing. A quick glance into the kitchen showed her that a kettle of water sat on a lit burner. (Had she stepped outside to meet someone? She must have used the lift.) She'd be back soon—or else the place would burn down.

Sure enough, the kettle was howling steam when the front door rattled open. Yael hung back, out of sight in the scratchy fabric shadows of the coat closet.

"*Scheisse!*" was the first word out of Adele Wolfe's mouth. Yael watched through the crack in the closet door as the girl dashed across the flat. She flicked the flame off, muttering more curses and a loud yelp as she tried to yank the hot kettle off the burner.

The girl was distracted and frantic. Waving her burned

fingers in the air. Her curses had disintegrated from *Scheisse*s to *verdammt*s to other colorful verbiage.

Now was the time to strike.

The crawl of Yael's skin met the crawl of her heart. Her fingers latched on to her gun. She started to step out of the closet.

"I see some things haven't changed," a voice—deep and male—spoke just a meter from her, freezing Yael midstep. Her free fingers hovered over the closet door's wood, too stunned to pull back.

This isn't right. For months Yael had staked out the victor's flat. Watching her go in and out. Sometimes Adele lugged armfuls of brown grocery bags; other times she was dressed in biking gear, ready to ride. Always she was alone.

But not tonight.

Yael gritted her teeth and sank back into the forest of winter coats. The strip of door light darkened as the visitor stepped past. His back was to the closet, but Yael could see he was tall, lean, strong, with muscles that made themselves known even under his jacket's bulky fabric. He stood like a fighter—legs planted apart. Even if she caught him unawares, she didn't think she could overpower him *and* Adele.

Not quietly. Not bloodlessly.

Besides, if this strange boy went missing (last seen in the company of Adele Wolfe), the authorities would get suspicious. Something this mission could not afford.

"*Scheisse*, that hurt!" Adele hissed, blowing on her burned fingers.

"So I've gathered." The boy moved to the freezer and

pulled out a handful of ice. "Germania's done wonders for your vocabulary."

Adele's swears drifted off. She accepted the ice warily, as if she expected the boy to lunge at any moment. "We both know you didn't come all the way here to criticize my manners."

The boy said nothing. His shoulders had gone strangely tense, as if *he* was expecting *her* to lunge.

"Let's have it, then," Adele sighed.

"You can't race tomorrow," the boy told her.

Adele's glare could have cut steel. She crossed her arms and set her jaw to one side. Her hurt fist crushed tight over the ice cubes. "Why not?"

"I can think of about a thousand reasons: motorcycle sabotage, dehydration, road rash, flooded river crossings...Luka Löwe."

The girl's jaw tightened along with her fist. Melting ice seeped through the cracks in her knuckles like tears.

"And for what?" The boy's voice sounded as hot as the kettle. Hissing syllables. Boiling consonants. "Another Iron Cross? More profiles on the Reichssender? More money?"

"I sent most of my winnings back to Frankfurt. You know that."

"We don't need your money, Ad. We need you. Please. It's time to come home."

Home. This wasn't just any boy, Yael realized. This was Adele's *brother.* Her *twin* brother. Of course. His hair was the same silk-fine, bitter-blond as that of the girl who clutched the ice. There were other similarities: their stance, their fists curled to the same tempered tempo.

36

Adele shook her head. Her arms crossed tight.

"We're almost eighteen, Felix. The worst that can happen to you is that you'll be conscripted as a mechanic for one of the Lebensraum settlements. But I'll be married off or put into the Lebensborn." Adele's fist grew even tighter when she talked about the breeding programs. An ice cube she held slipped out, spinning across tiles and floorboards. It came to rest by the closet door. "This race is my last chance to escape that fate. To prove that I can serve the Reich as well as any man."

"I thought that's what you were doing last year," Felix said.

Adele Wolfe's lip twitched. "One win isn't enough. I can't be as good as the men. I have to be better than them. No racer has ever earned two Iron Crosses before."

Not, Yael knew, for lack of trying. The Double Cross was elusive, which made both participating empires salivate for it.

Over the years the Axis Tour—officially a celebration of the Axis's continued alliance—had devolved into what Reiniger called a pissing contest. The Third Reich and the Greater East Asia Co-Prosperity Sphere's partnership was tenuous, crumbling a bit more with each passing year. They were a long, long way from all-out war, but these tensions played out every tour through the riders and their victories.

Win one race in the name of the Reich and you received cash, fame, your choice of a Lebensraum assignment. Win a second and you'd have the Führer himself in your debt. The proverbial world was yours.

"Luka Löwe and Tsuda Katsuo will be fighting for that same privilege," Adele's brother reminded her. "It's their last year of racing, too. They're going to be out for blood, and it's your throat they'll go for first."

Adele said nothing. Her lips were pressed so tight they were white.

"How can you do this to Papa and Mama? After what happened to Martin…"

Martin. The other brother. The one who snapped his neck on the Nürburgring racetrack on the twins' twelfth birthday. They were supposed to go home from the race and eat cake. They went to the morgue instead.

All these memories played across Adele's face: ugly shadow puppets. The white of her lips spread to her cheeks. Anger past red. "It's not the same."

Felix's hands knotted, anxious behind his back. "You're right," he told her. "What you're doing is far more dangerous."

Cramps were starting to vine up Yael's thighs. She shifted as silently as she could and thought of Kasper in the laundry truck, watching the window. Waiting.

"The other riders fight dirty, but so do I." Adele said this with her arms still crossed. "I know what I signed up for. Besides, the Führer himself gave me a special blessing to race. He even sent me a telegram that said he'd be cheering for me."

Felix's head turned oh-so-slightly, so that Yael could see the boy's profile. His features looked apprehensive and pressed, like his sister's. *Exactly* like his sister's. But for his slightly stronger jawline, her three freckles, and a few centimeters in height, the siblings were almost identical.

"I always sat back; I always kept your secret, always let you compete under my name," Felix reminded her. "You know I wouldn't be asking you to drop out unless I meant it. Trust me on this, Ad. Please."

Adele Wolfe was silent for such a long moment that Yael started to fear she might say yes. (Then what? Burst out of the closet and say boo? Kidnap them both?)

But Adele did speak. Her words were slow, determined. "I'm racing under my own name this time."

Felix's fists gripped tighter, cracking his knuckles with his thumb. Five *pops* for the right hand, five for the left. The sounds made Adele scowl. "Go back to Frankfurt, Felix."

"Not without you."

Stubbornness, it seemed, ran deep in the Wolfe family. Yael would fit right in.

Adele shook her head. "I'm racing tomorrow and you can't stop me."

If the twins had been rams, they'd be clashing heads, tangling horns. Instead they just stood, engaged in an invisible battle of wills. It was silent, all in their eyes and history.

A winner emerged. Victor Adele Wolfe cleared her throat and spoke. "It's almost curfew. You should go."

Felix's hand fished into his jacket pocket, came back with a pocket watch. It was a cheap, dented thing, making a tinny sound as he snapped it open. The time was right: *almost curfew.* He broke his wide-leg fighter stance and retreated to the door. Adele followed him—both moving out of Yael's slim vision. The only thing left for her to watch was the ice cube, melting into nothing.

The door clicked open and shut. If there was any good-bye between the twins, it was wordless. The flat fell silent and the ice chip disappeared altogether.

Finally, Adele's footsteps creaked across the room. The whine of a television sprang to life. Familiar sounds of the Reichssender floated through the flat.

"We now join our beloved and honored Führer on the eve of the Axis Tour for a very special *Chancellery Chat*," a generic male voice droned.

It felt as if ants were marching up and down Yael's arms. Henryka loved her television; it stayed on for hours straight, lighting up her office into the evening hours with news propaganda from all the Axis territories and stilted shows about perfect Aryan families. But even Henryka couldn't stomach a full *Chancellery Chat*.

The Führer was known for his speeches. His voice turned words into living, breathing things that snaked under skins, lit fires inside even the dullest minds. Many years ago—before the Great Victory, before the war stretched its long shadow across the world—he'd spoken everywhere. Pubs. Theaters. Stages. Letting his bright red words wash over a whole nation.

He didn't appear in public anymore. He didn't have to, when his words could be transmitted through wires and speakers from the comfort of his own Chancellery. After forty-nine assassination attempts, the Führer hardly ever stepped past the threshold of his hermitage.

There were two exceptions to this rule. The beginning of the Axis Tour. And the end.

"Ten. That, my fellow countrymen, is the number of years we've dwelt in a land of peace. A world of purity. The Aryan race has risen to its God-granted station. We have tamed the wilds of the East and Africa, scoured the filth of lesser races from the crevices of our own continent."

Words from a monster's mouth. Aged, but still evil red, intoxicating the masses like some potent wine. They made Yael hot and twitchy and *ready*.

It was time. Now or never.

Yael pulled her P38 handgun out of her jacket, flicked up the safety, and stepped out of the closet.

Adele stood in front of the television, watching the old man behind the glass—his silvering mustache quivered as he spit out words, words, and more words. "The Axis Tour is how we remember our Great Victory. We see the drive and resilience of our race in our prized young racers. We watch them travel through the lands we've conquered and purified. We are the audience to our own progress."

Progress. Yael steadied her gun hand. She swallowed back the anger. Deep, deep in her bones. Where it had to stay.

Adele still hadn't turned. Hitler's words were too loud, too enveloping for her to notice the danger. Yael crept—closer, closer.

A loose floorboard betrayed her, letting out a noise when Yael stepped on it. Victor Adele Wolfe snapped around to face her.

Though she still wore Mina's face and form, Yael felt as if she were staring into a mirror. It was all so familiar. The platinum hair barely long enough to pull back, tied into a twig of a ponytail. The eyebrows so pale they were nearly invisible, afterthoughts over her dagger-blue eyes. A bone structure that belonged to a Viking queen.

They looked at each other for a long, still second. The gun between them.

"Sit on the couch." Yael's pistol flashed against the lamplight as she waved it toward the dark red upholstery. She tucked her free hand into her pocket, where the tranquilizer pills nestled beside the doll and the thumbtack. "Now!"

Adele's eyes weren't shirking or scared. Just...wary. They never left Yael as she stepped around the coffee table, plowing through mountains of discarded clothes. When she got to the couch, she stood. Her stance was the same as her brother's. Wide, ready for a fight.

"I don't want to hurt you." Even though these words were true, Yael regretted them as soon as they left her mouth. They made her sound weak, less-than, out of control.

Everything she could not be. Refused to be.

"Sit," Yael barked again.

The girl's movements were lightning quick. She grabbed a half-empty mug of coffee, threw it at Yael's face, and lunged.

The liquid was cold, harmless. But the mug was not. It clipped past Yael's jaw, shattered against the far wall. Fifty-nine kilograms of fingernail and kick barreled into her chest. Sent her world flying.

The pistol tumbled to the floor. Adele dove for it with hungry hands. Yael's limbs lashed out. They seemed to move apart from her, guided by hours and hours of Vlad's combat training. Painful, sweaty, bloody years all culminating in this single chop to Adele's half-bent wrist.

The other girl's cry turned into something savage as Adele's elbow met Yael's rib cage. Hurt sang under her skin—fresh and winter-bright. Yael didn't scream. She gathered the pain close, harnessed its energy, and hit back.

Adele's body stretched long across the Turkish rug, fingers straining for the butt of the P38. Yael lunged for her hand, digging Mina's nails deep into Adele's wrist, until she felt the wet of blood seeping to the quick. She snatched the pistol from the other girl's reach, pointing it straight at Victor Wolfe's forehead in a swift, trained motion.

All went still. Silent except for their geyser-hiss breaths and the Führer's spinning-silk lies from the television: "Our racers are pure. Our racers are strong. They are the next generation, bearers of light into the still-dark continents of this world."

Adele didn't beg. Her eyes were ice and slit. She stared past the gun, straight at Yael. "Who are you?"

Not *What do you want?* or *What are you doing here?*

Who are you? Who? Who? Who?

Why, of all questions, this one?

Yael did not answer. She held the pistol tight and brought it down in a quick, blunt move to Victor Wolfe's skull.

CHAPTER 5

NOW

MARCH 9, 1956
GERMANIA, THIRD REICH

Germania's night sky was not deep. Not the way it was in the mountains. Where you could stare up through the snow-stung air and feel like you were falling. Tumbling into endless voids of black and stars.

There was no black to this night as Yael stood at Adele Wolfe's window—just a mix of orange and gray and almost-sleet. Storm lights. Adele's reflection hovered in the glass in front of her. Staring at Yael with the same ferocity as the real Victor Wolfe.

Who are you?

Once, just once, Henryka had been thoughtful enough to ask Yael what she really looked like. Before Dr. Geyer's needles. Before the burn and the bleach and the skinshifts. Before the many scores of other girls' faces. (*I'll bet you had the most beautiful dark hair*, she'd said. *You seem like a girl who would have had curls. Long, gorgeous curls.*) Yael opened her mouth to answer and realized, with a start, that she did not remember.

She did not remember.

She did not remember.

What kind of person forgets her own face?

(*It's okay*, Henryka had told her. *It's what's on the inside that matters*.)

But what *was* inside? An invasive cocktail of chemicals. Something she did not completely trust. (Could anything *good* come out of those needles?) Chain reactions in Yael's body that she'd tried to research, grasp, understand. But nothing in Henryka's volumes on biology and organic chemistry could explain her skinshifting.

Whatever lurked within Yael was new. Revolutionary.

The sky lit bright, clouds webbed with lightning. The flash erased Adele's face. Erased her. All Yael could see was the storm—roiling black over the flats of Germania—and the silhouette of the Volkshalle, a grand building Hitler commissioned after the Axis's Great Victory. (Its dome, at 290 meters high, was the only thing wandering eyes saw if they looked to Germania's skyline.) She wondered if the weather would last through tomorrow. If the beginning of the Axis Tour would be full of dripping reporters and sopping pomp and circumstance.

Drops of sleet slapped against the glass. As if to answer.

Yael pulled the curtain tight across the window and turned back to the bed. She'd cleaned up nicely. Kasper had been quick to retrieve Victor Wolfe's unconscious form, tucking her into a laundry bag and taking her back to the truck, back to Henryka's beer hall basement, where Adele would be held until the end of the Axis Tour.

The bloodstains were harder to get rid of than the girl. It wasn't until the real Adele had been carted away and Yael was alone in her flat that she realized how much red her nails had spilled. Enough to notice from the doorway. Even with towels, powders, and a scrub brush, it took her over an hour to hide the stains.

But now all was ready. She wore Adele's skin, spoke with Adele's voice, slept in Adele's bed.

Yael sat down on the mattress, rolled up her left sleeve, and unraveled the gauze where the wolf pack lunged against her skin. Vlad's was still raw and puffed. Too tender to touch.

She traced the others with a soft finger, let the syllables of their names linger on the tip of her tongue. "Babushka, Mama, Miriam…"

The ones the ash ate.

"Aaron-Klaus, Vlad." Yael swallowed. Five wolves. Four memories and a reminder.

Her loss was larger than that…but four + one was a number she could remember. A number she could handle without letting the vastness of it pick her to pieces like a crab's ragged claws. Scavenging death on the ocean floor. Sometimes (usually) there was nothing left for the grief to feed on. Yael was a barebones blank slate. A hanger that held a cloth of pretty skin.

Who are you? (On the inside?)

The answer to this question was something Yael had to fight for. Her self-reflection was no reflection at all. It was a shattered mirror. Something she had to piece together, over and over again. Memory by memory. Loss by loss. Wolf by wolf.

It was easy—too easy—to pretend. To fill that empty space inside her with other lives. Bernice Vogt. Mina Jager. Adele Wolfe. Girls who never had to face the smoke or watch the syringes slide under their skin. Girls who never had to stare into the eyes of the Angel of Death. Again and again and again.

It was too easy to get lost.

This was why, every night before she fell asleep, she peeled back her sleeve, traced the wolves, and said their names. Because somewhere in there—in those fragments of gone souls and memories—was Yael.

Not chemicals, but essence. The real Yael.

She'd already lost her face. She could not let the rest of herself (however dark, however broken) slip away. So she traced and she named. She hurt and she raged.

She remembered.

———

THEN
THE FIRST WOLF: THE BABUSHKA
AUTUMN 1944

The Babushka was Yael's oldest friend. Older than most of the women who slept in Barrack 7. Her hair was silver, and deep lines swooped past the end of her eyes. (*Crow's-feet*, she called them, in that heavy, chopping language of hers.)

She was a miracle, Yael's mother said. Her wrinkles alone should have been enough for the guards to sort her into the *too weak!* line. But they let her keep walking through the gates. They let her live.

She was old, but she was strong. Every morning, in the cruel cold of the predawn, the Babushka rose with the others. She slipped wooden clogs over her feet, walked to the morning roll call, where she stood under spotlights and stars for hours on end. Then she followed the others to the sorting hall. There her fingers threaded through many things: gold rings, sooty dresses, boots that would not give her blisters. The belongings of the dead (or soon-to-be) were piled in mountains and moved by the women of Barrack 7, to be looted by the SS men's magpie greed.

After the long day, the weary trudge back (under more glaring bulbs, a callous moon), the soup of withered vegetables and spoiled meat, the Babushka sat in the corner of her bunk. Those brown eyes were drained and glazed, but she always smiled when she caught Yael peeking across the way. None of her teeth seemed the same color. They held the gray of shadows, the black of night. A very few were yellowed white. They reminded Yael of old piano keys.

"Volchitsa," she whispered Yael's nickname—*she-wolf* in Russian, a stubborn, fierce creature for a stubborn, fierce girl—and waved. "I have something for you. Come."

Yael picked her way through the bodies of her bunkmates

(her mother, an older girl named Miriam, and three other women who never spoke to her). Mattress straws raked up her legs as she slid to the floor.

The Babushka's bunk was just as crowded. Yael climbed through the jumble of bony, inked limbs, and bristle-hair scalps. There was a small patch of mattress by the Babushka's hip. Enough for her to nestle in.

The older woman smiled and dipped her hand into the thin fabric of her dress. Magic or miracle—somehow her fingers came back wrapped around a piece of bread. Crumbling, so hard that the edges of crust cut into Yael's gums, but *bread*. Something to make her forget the dull gnaw of her insides.

"Eat," the Babushka commanded.

Yael's eyes fluttered guiltily across the way, where Miriam and her mother slept on. She crammed the food into her mouth anyway, a few more mealy ounces to stick to her sparrow bones.

"Did you see the doctor today?"

Yael's mouth was too full. She shook her head.

The older woman grunted. "You're lucky, Volchitsa. Most of the children who go into his office do not come back again."

A sharp jag of crust caught in Yael's throat. She thought of the instruments on Dr. Geyer's silver tray. Not the needles but the crueler ones. The scalpels and wide knives—things he never used on her.

An angel of a different kind.

"He must think you're special," the Babushka went on. "He's saving you. Passing you over."

"I hate him." Yael swallowed the final crumb. Her last

injection was over a day ago, but her arm still felt like it was on fire. So much hot and pain in such a small body. She gathered it all up and crammed it into words. "I wish the smoke would eat him."

The Babushka did not tell her to hush, the way Yael's mother did whenever she said these things. Instead her eyes were sad and knowing. Flooded with smoke-monsters of their own.

"I've made you something." The straw beneath the Babushka rustled as she fished through the mattress innards. Cradled in the callused, canyon skin of her hands was something that reminded Yael of a misshapen egg. A crude line wrapped through its center.

"It's a matryoshka doll." The old woman placed it in Yael's hands. Now that it was closer, she could see the lump was doll-shaped. With awled, colorless eyes. A scratch of a smile.

"Open it."

Yael obeyed. The wood split apart like a nutshell. Something spilled out. Another doll. Smaller. It, too, had a crack down its center.

Another doll. And another. Each one smaller. Each one with a different face. A half-moon smile, a shepherd's crook smirk. Eyes both squinting and wide. When Yael got to the end there were so many pieces. Tops and bottoms piled like tiny wooden cups on her bare legs.

Yael's fingers closed over the last, a pea-sized matryoshka. She tried to think of where the Babushka might have found wood in a place like this. Much less something to carve it with.

Magic or miracle? Whichever it was, the Babushka was full of them.

"My husband was a woodworker. Before everything," the old woman explained. "He used to carve them for our children. They always loved the dolls. Such bright, happy things. Full of color—so many colors. Ruby red, grass green, blue so deep you think you're looking at the sky. Yellow like butter. Or the sun."

Yael knew red. Red was the color of the wet patches on Dr. Geyer's floor. The color of the guards' armbands.

It was the other shades Yael had a hard time imagining. There was no grass inside the barbed-wire confines of the camp. Sometimes weeds sprouted from the cracks in the dormitory bricks. But these were usually coated in ash and withered into quick, drab deaths. And blue—that was the color the doctor wanted her eyes to be. The reason he kept sinking needle after needle into her skin.

She supposed that when she was younger—before all the grimy grays of the camp, the train, the ghetto—she'd seen all these shades. But these memories were like photographs: rare, blurred around the edges, black and white.

The colors had been taken. Bled out.

The Babushka plucked the wooden pea child from Yael's palm and started putting the dolls back together. They swallowed each other with *snaps*. Yael watched with wide eyes as the pieces became whole again.

"There," the Babushka said after the final *snap*. "The little one stays safe."

"This is for me? To keep?"

The old woman nodded.

"Why me?" Yael stole another glance over at Miriam, so still in her sleep. She gripped the dolls-within-dolls to her chest, breathing light against the precious wood. She knew she should share it—but there was a hardness in her heart that kept her clenching.

"The doctor is right. You are special, Volchitsa." She said this with a *knowing* voice. "You are going to change things."

Yael squeezed the dolls even tighter and wondered exactly why the old woman sounded so solid, so sure. So full of magic, miracle words. Yael knew she was different. Dr. Geyer's injections had already set her apart. Splotched, flaking skin stretched over Yael's toothpick bones. Her boy-short hair could not decide what color it was (some bristled light, others dark). Even Yael's eyes were mutt-mixed—one brighter than the other, almost glowing—such a far cry from her mother's steady brown.

Different, yes. But special?

"Now, off to bed with you," the Babushka *tutt*ed, and waved over the pile of her long-collapsed bunkmates. "Tomorrow will not be forgiving."

The next day, Yael would remember those words—those last, ominous words—after roll call, when she watched the others leave through a crack in the barrack's tired doors. They marched as they always did: strung out like dull beads on a string, wooden clogs crunching through piles of gravel and ice.

Tomorrow will not be forgiving.

Yael did not blink when she watched her old friend crumple into the dirt and snow and shoes. She watched with both eyes (the bright and the dark) as the Babushka fell. It was a strange collapse, more like a kneel: gentle, willing.

She did not get up again. Even when the guard yelled and kicked. The other women shuffled on, none daring to look back. Yael felt a hard knot growing in her chest, as if the matryoshka doll were still pressed against it.

When the guard was done kicking, he looked up. Met her strange gaze. His eyes were flat gray—like a winter horizon. He almost looked as if he was the one who died. Not the pile of fabric and skin, so still at his feet.

The guard trudged over to the barrack door, his hand gripping his rifle strap. "Why aren't you with the others?" he barked.

Yael's mouth was too dry to tell him that Dr. Geyer ordered her not to work in the sorting hall, in case the extra stress interfered with whatever chemical reaction he was trying to coax out of her body.

She could not speak, but her instincts did. They shouted inside her—iron-loud and clanging—the way they always did when danger drew close. —*X MARKS THE SURVIVOR SHOW HIM SHOW HIM*—

Yael offered her arm.

"'121358ΔX'?" He read the numbers out loud. "Geyer's pet. Should've known from the look of you."

The guard spit into the leftover snow.

—*DON'T MOVE HE MIGHT STRIKE*—

53

Yael's back was to the door, braced for whatever came next. She felt every one of the wood's splinters digging into her rib cage, her spine. Over the shambly, slanting roofs she watched the smoke spewing, blotting out the sun.

But the guard did not slap or kick. He did not catch her by the scruff and drag her to those brick buildings no one returned from. Instead his hand slipped away from his rifle strap. "The doctor will see you now. Follow me."

Yael trailed him with quick steps. Away from what-was-once-the-Babushka, away from the hungry black smoke.

But there were some things that would not be left behind. Her friend's magic, miracle words haunted her ears. Rolled inside the knot of her chest. Burned in her veins.

You are special.

You are going to change things.

When she came back, with Dr. Geyer's wicked concoction roiling beneath her skin, the Babushka's body was gone. But the doll was still there, safely nestled in the straw of her mattress. When all the others were finally asleep, Yael took it out and pressed it to her chest. For the whole night.

And every dark night to come.

CHAPTER 6

NOW

MARCH 10, 1956
OLYMPIASTADION
GERMANIA, THIRD REICH
KILOMETER 0

The stadium was full and roaring. Yells, one hundred thousand strong, wove together to drown out the once-morning-sleet, now-afternoon-rain. Yael stood at the center of it all, her heart dancing hard to the tempo of the crowd's excitement. Drops rolled down her suit of treated leather, gathering into her armband. The crimson fabric swelled like a bandage heavy with blood. It started a long, slow slip down Yael's sleeve.

She didn't bother fixing it.

The crowd was wet, too, but its cheers were on fire, pouring over Yael and the other racers. They stood in a straight line. Twenty faces—German and Japanese, ages thirteen to seventeen, mostly male—turned up into the storm, toward the Führer's box.

The man who made this world was barely visible. A silhouette etched behind tempest-glazed glass. Yael stared hard at the figure. Toes popping, black rising, hate eating her veins like battery acid.

Half a field of grass, track, and seats. A centimeter of glass. These were the only things that separated the Führer from Yael (and the blade slipped inside her boot—weapons were forbidden on the Axis Tour, yet everyone carried them because everyone else carried them). But there was no getting up there. If there was a way, Reiniger would've found it. He'd spent hours hunched over roster lists and blueprints, trying to find cracks in the armor of the Führer's SS security detail. She'd spent almost as many hours helping him, elbows pinning down the curls of thin paper, her neck sweating as she leaned under the hot lamp.

"Why can't I just dress up as a maid and infiltrate the Chancellery?" she'd asked after a particularly frustrating training session on the Zündapp. Her leg wept from road rash, and her heart quivered at the thought of 20,780 more kilometers on the contraption. "Wouldn't that be simpler?"

Reiniger didn't even glance up at her. He flipped to the next blueprint. "It has to be in public. In front of the cameras. With lots of witnesses."

"Why?"

"This isn't an assassination." Reiniger's beard stubble glistened silver in the harsh carve of lamplight. "It's an execution. If Hitler dies behind the walls of the Chancellery, it will be covered up. Made to look like a sudden illness or a bad fall down the stairs. Another will just take his place. Nothing will change. The National Socialists will keep grinding the bones of innocents through labor camps to feed their future war machine. People need to be watching when the Führer dies. They need to know the resistance is out there. They need to know they're not alone."

Not alone. It was a cruel irony that this was the message she had been chosen to deliver. She, the loneliest of all. The girl without a people. Without a face. The girl who was no one. Who could be everyone.

But she knew Reiniger was right. There would be no dressing up as a maid. No cyanide slipped into his crystal glass of mineral water. The Führer's death was to be a loud, scream-ing thing. A broadcast of blood over the Reichssender.

"But what about during *Chancellery Chat?*" she pressed. (The road rash really hurt.) "There are cameras then."

"Prerecorded. They'd never air it." He waved his hand. "It needs to be live. His death is the signal all the resistance cells will be watching for. The moment you strike is the moment we mobilize."

This—winning the Axis Tour, attending the Victor's Ball in Tokyo—was the only way.

Rain smeared Yael's vision as she watched the box. The Führer's outline melted, indistinguishable from the glass. All she could see were the colors of the Axis banners, draped over the balcony. Emperor Hirohito's rising sun, red and white. Hitler's swastika watched back through the storm, an unblinking eye.

"Welcome!" a male voice belted through the stadium. The crowd's cheers fell to a chatter, then a hush. Air sizzled with the power of the speakers. The soothe of rain.

"Our honored Führer and the Emperor Hirohito welcome you to the tenth Axis Tour. Ten of the Fatherland's finest youths have been selected from our most rigorous training programs. They will race alongside Japan's ten strongest. These racers will endure the desert sands of Africa, the jagged peaks of the Indian subcontinent, the tangled jungles of Asia, the waves of the Pacific. Only the hardiest and purest will survive. Only the strongest will win."

More cheers. More rain. The medal of Adele's past victory hung heavy around Yael's neck. She stood straight, didn't take her eyes off the Reich banner's twisted cross.

"Racing in the name of the Fatherland, we have Victor Adele Wolfe."

Yael stepped forward. She smiled with her cheekbones, the way Adele always did in the newsreels, her right arm hinging up in an automatic *"Heil Hitler!"* Her fingertips pointed toward the box.

The voice went on, crackling above the roar of the crowd. "Victor Luka Löwe."

A tall, powerful frame joined Yael's left side, his own arm snapping into a plank-straight *"Heil Hitler!"* He'd stood apart from the other racers even before he stepped out. His jacket was brown, where all others were black, and battered, where all others were new. It was the same jacket he'd worn in the last two Axis Tours. His signature look.

Luka Löwe. The boy in the brown jacket. The most threatening of her competition. Yael had spent more than a few weeks mulling over his file. Copies of school records, his birth certificate, his Hitler Youth performance booklet, a complete history of racing times, family genealogy, transcripts of his many Reichssender interviews. Luka Löwe's life inked onto paper and into her memory.

```
Name: Luka Wotan Löwe
Age: 17
Height: 185 cm
Weight: 92 kg
Bio: Born in Hamburg, Germany, to Kurt
and Nina Löwe. His father served in
the Reich's elite motorcycle troop, the
Kradschützen. Luka joined the Hitler Youth
at age ten and dedicated his passions to
learning all he could about motorcycles.
He has competed in the Axis Tour for the
past four years, with one win at the age
of fourteen. He is the youngest victor in
the history of the race.
```

The boy's shoulder was mere centimeters away. Though they weren't touching, Yael could feel the tense of Luka's muscles. His breath sounded the same: stretched, ready to snap.

"Victor Löwe," she muttered through the edge of her lips.

Luka did not turn, but she felt his eyes peel over her anyway. "Fräulein."

Fräulein. That word—the weight behind it—whet Yael's own blade-breath. Her armband kept slipping down her forearm, sliding over the covered ink wolves. Coming to rest around her wrist. A fabric manacle.

More, victor-less German names were called. As they stepped forward, their files flashed through Yael's memory. Pages and pages of perfect childhoods. Boys born in the Fatherland. All of them Aryan, most of them fatherless (the cost of victory is always high). Loyal members of the Hitler Youth.

Even their names blended together: Kurt and Karl. Lars and Hans. Rolf and Ralf and Dolf. Only one stood out: `Hans Muller: 15. Placed fifth in last year's Axis Tour. His times have drastically improved in the qualifying races. Possibly dangerous underdog.` By the time the final Reich name was called, Yael was only half listening.

"Felix—"

Yael started. That name wasn't in the racers' files. Except for . . .

"—Wolfe, who has recently joined our roster due to Dirk Hermann's unfortunate accident."

This time she actually turned her head and looked—down the line of rain-jeweled noses and chins. Felix was staring back. He was the same person from the photographs: square jaw, prism-pale hair, an extra bump on the bridge of his nose. But in those pictures—the ones Adele framed in silver and displayed in her flat—Felix was always happy. Always smiling.

Now his mouth was pinched, the same way his sister's had been during their standoff the night before. His eyes—the same death-cold Wolfe blue—cut through the rain. Into Yael.

Not without you.

This was why he'd left so easily the night before....

Yael tore her gaze from his. Back to the wet, wet banners.

The announcer moved on. "Racing for the glory of Imperial Japan, we have Victor Tsuda Katsuo."

```
Name: Tsuda Katsuo
Age: 17
Height: 173 cm
Weight: 66 kg
Bio: Sent by his parents to a training
camp outside Tokyo once they realized
his talent for motorcycle racing. His
abilities attracted the attention of
his peers and instructors alike. He is
rarely seen without a group of followers.
Won his first Axis Tour at age fifteen. He
is now facing immense pressure in the
homeland to win the Double Cross.
```

Katsuo stepped forward and gave a stiff bow; flecks of rain burst fast from his jet-black hair. His own Iron Cross swung out, landing with an audible thud to his chest when he straightened again.

Katsuo. The third and final victor in this score line. In his final year of racing, vying for the Double Cross and whatever favors Emperor Hirohito dangled before him like a carrot on a stick. He was another racer Yael would have to watch closely.

More names. More highlights from Henryka's files on files.

    Ono Ryoko: 16. The only other girl in the
    race. Emerged on Japan's racing circuit
    after Adele's victory.

    Watabe Takeo: 16. Placed third in last
    year's Axis Tour. Attended the same
    training camp as Katsuo and seems to
    defer to the victor. Hides a Higonokami
    blade on his person and has a reputation
    for slashing contestants' tires.

    Oguri Iwao: 16. Second year in the Axis
    Tour. Has a fondness for drugging food
    and drink. Guard your provisions with
    care. Also attended Katsuo's training
    camp and seems devoted to him.

Yamato. Taro. Hiraku. Isamu. Masaru. Norio.
Most of them were younger. First-years. No threat.

"Racers, proceed to your vehicles."

The Zündapps sat half a field away. Custom-fitted bikes straight from the factory (to ensure quality and prevent any illegal modifications): shiny chrome, slick slate-colored paint, panniers packed with camping supplies for the nights between checkpoints. Yael's motorcycle was parked ahead of the others, followed closely by Luka's and Katsuo's bikes. A head start for the victors. (Nothing more than a formality. A few meters hardly made a difference when one had thousands of kilometers to endure.)

It took Luka only half a stride to catch up to Yael as she crossed the grass. She could hear his Iron Cross beating against his chest as he drew close. *Thud, thud, thud, thud.* Constant as a heartbeat. Deep as drums of war.

"Making this a family affair, Fräulein?"

Yael—uncertain how to answer—pinched her lips and kept walking. Her boots left scars of mud in the sopping field.

"Don't think I've forgotten," Luka went on, "what you did."

Yael had no idea what Luka was talking about. But she was supposed to. She read that much on the boy's face.

Adele Wolfe and Luka Löwe shared a history. One the newsreels never managed to catch. One that never made it into the wide-spaced type of Henryka's transcriptions. And from the sound of Luka's voice—the stab in his stare—it wasn't a pretty one.

Yael pressed her lips harder, walked faster. As if she could escape it. As if she weren't about to ride neck and neck with it across entire continents.

Slosh, slosh, slosh, slosh. Another racer was beside her, wallowing through mud of his own. Not Luka. He'd fallen behind, taken her silence for what it was.

"Ad…" Felix's voice was as crooked as his twice-broken nose as he caught her by the elbow. "Please—for the love of God—forget this, come home."

"Why are you here?" Yael hissed under her breath. Luka, Katsuo, the others—she was prepared to deal with them. But Felix—Felix was a footnote. A few estranged paragraphs in the novel of Adele's past. She hadn't planned for him to show up again.

"You know why." His fingers grew tight, just under her armband. Her skin-wolves cried under pinching leather.

"Then *how* are you here?" she asked. "You weren't even in the qualifying races."

"You have nothing left to prove. Everything to lose," said Felix the footnote. Felix: who knew Adele's past better than libraries of pages could fill. Felix: now the most dangerous face in this race.

Yael wrenched her elbow away. She was walking on asphalt now, trailing mud in the shape of her boot soles. She grabbed her helmet from the seat, cinched its strap under her chin, fitted her goggles, and mounted the bike. This Zündapp felt almost like the KS 601 she'd used for training. Just sharper, fresher, stronger.

The motorcycle's engine purred as she kicked it to life. During training, this sound had always centered her, brought her mission, the road ahead, into focus. But today even the hum of her bike's gears didn't put Yael at ease. Every eye in the stadium was on her. Girl: glossy with rain and black leather riding gear. Her boots heavy on the gears. Eager. Ready.

Every eye was on her, but she felt only two pairs. The ones that were digging, digging, digging at her back. Mining a past she didn't hold inside her memories. Creating holes she couldn't fill.

Don't think I've forgotten what you did.

You have nothing left to prove. Everything to lose.

She might look like Adele. But she could never *be* Adele. Yael was a cobweb version, composed of gaps and strings and fragile nothings.

A different voice slid through the speakers now—*his* voice. The one that raised armies, toppled kingdoms. The one that sent the entire stadium into a hush. Even the raindrops hung back in the sky; the air cleared into a spitting drizzle.

There was only *him.* The voice she had to silence.

She hadn't just been born to do it. She'd been *created* to. By *his* needles. *His* men.

"Take your marks."

The Führer didn't know it yet, but he was about to sign his own death warrant. (And cheer while doing it.) Yael gripped the handlebars so tight her gloves felt about to split.

"Get set."

Behind her the nineteen motorcycles revved and roared.

"Go!"

Yael went.

The wind tore ice across her cheeks. Her face was so numb, so cold, but the wolves burned under her skin. Howling secrets. Hidden things anyone could pick up if they listened closely enough.

Felix and Luka...they had sharp ears.

Yael would not let them hear.

CHAPTER 7

NOW

The rain kept falling in hard, relentless sheets, hounding the racers all the way through Germania, past lines of drenched spectators and limp Axis flags, down the autobahn. Yael's fist gripped the throttle. Tighter. Faster than she probably should have been going on such slick roads.

But the others behind her were going just as fast. A glance over her shoulder showed them looming. Luka and Katsuo fanned out like unwanted wings. Their leather and chrome shredding through her rear tire spray. And beyond them—seventeen hungry faces.

All of them out for blood, like Felix said, and hers was the first throat.

Causing deliberate harm to racers was forbidden in the Axis Tour's rules (to keep it from turning into a bloodbath), but this never really seemed to stop harm from happening.

Every year, racers dropped out with stab wounds, mysterious cases of food poisoning, road rash via bike sabotage. The officials usually turned a blind eye, writing *accident* on the incident reports. After all, this was a race of tooth and claw. Only the strongest survived. Only the vicious could win.

But there was a line. Five years ago a boy was disqualified from the tour because he'd been foolish enough to stab another racer in front of a Reichssender camera. (Film evidence wasn't something the race officials could brush under the rug.) Any attacks witnessed by officials or Reichssender cameras demanded retribution. In extreme cases—such as the stabbing—the attacker was disqualified. Most of the time, however, offending racers were penalized an extra hour. This never stopped the backbiting, just pushed it under the surface, where it lurked, hidden until just the right moment.

Yael could not let her guard down.

To her right—a shadow. It crept forward until Yael didn't even have to turn her head to see Luka. He was close. Too close. Crouched on his bike like a lion about to spring. His tires drew level with hers, flaying mist.

"Let's...ha...fun, Fräulein!" Yael only heard snatches of Luka's words through the rush and storm, but his meaning was clear. His arms jerked and his Zündapp careered toward hers. Tires chewing away the scarce space between them.

Yael's heart sat at the top of her throat. She almost thought she could taste blood, weeping iron and salt between her teeth. From the corner of her eye, she glimpsed Luka smiling:

a hook-cheeked expression. He was playing with her. Just playing.

She wouldn't give him the satisfaction of her fear. She kept her eyes on the road.

He pulled away in the last of final moments. It was a stupid stunt, oozing pride. Fueled by the Iron Cross still hanging from his neck. If Yael wanted to, she could've dragged him off the seat by the sleeve of his jacket, skinned him alive on the autobahn's asphalt.

And to her left—another shadow. Katsuo closing in. This boy wasn't smiling. The edge of his mouth was hard. The veer of his bike—aggressive.

He did not seem too concerned with the rules.

Luka moved toward her again, in time to Katsuo's descent. A pincer movement, trapping her between the tip of their metallic claw. They held her tight in a gridlock of gears, caught up in the smell of peeling rubber.

Dangerous, stupid, reckless. There weren't enough words in any of Yael's languages to describe this maneuver. Any turn, any jerk, would end in a tangle of engines and flesh on the road. Their race would be over before it had really begun.

Yael kept her eyes on the road's white dash lines. If she kept going straight, they'd lose interest. Pull away.

But then Katsuo's gloved hand crept into Yael's vision. Reaching for her wrist, the handlebar. He was going to wreck her, send her bike spinning into Luka's, and edge off his biggest competition before they were even beyond the borders of Germania.

She couldn't fend off his hand. Not without veering, causing a tangle of her own. And Luka still hung close, riding high on his game of dare. Oblivious to the wreck only seconds away.

Yael did the only thing she could.

Both brakes squealed with wet as she pumped them. The wheels wavered beneath her and Katsuo's fingers tore ahead—just centimeters from the chrome gleam of her handlebars—pointing toward Luka instead.

Yael's boots flurried as she downshifted, eased up on the brakes. Her bike crawled, so the raindrops against her cheeks were more lull than sting. She was shaking, her motorcycle was sputtering, and Luka and Katsuo were gone. Two fading plumes of rear-wheel mist. The others were at Yael's heels now, ripping past in twos and ones, giving her bike a wide berth. Lightning jagged the sky—fury white—spotlighting all the racers. Most were ahead of her now, darting off into the distance like minnow shadows.

Yael gritted her teeth. She had to pull herself together, shove the stun, scare, shake of her almost-wreck away. Dive back into the fray.

Another Zündapp slowed. Drew even with her.

Felix wasn't even *trying* to race. His eyes were on her, all concern through his rain-flecked goggles. "You all right?"

"Fine." She was. She should be. It was just a scare. A brush with death. She'd had so many crammed into her short years. It shouldn't bother her, stick to the roof of her mouth the way it did. Because *she* was the predator this time. Not the prey.

Never again.

The tremble had not quite left Yael's fingers when she revved her engine and shot forward. Away from Adele's brother, back into the race.

━━━

PRAGUE CHECKPOINT
KILOMETER 347

In the evening the sky peeled back, layers of storm dissolving under a dying sun. Color seized the western horizon with clouds like claws. Flaring red, pulling true night over the ragged steeples of Prague.

Yael watched the day end through the checkpoint's many-paned windows. She hadn't spent much time at all on the bike (two hours and forty minutes according to the official scoreboard). Germania to Prague was by far the shortest leg of the race, but the road had worn her.

Chill settled under Yael's skin, to a depth even the roaring hearth fire could not reach. Adele's hair hung translucent in front of her eyes, as limp as the rest of her felt, after plowing through 347 kilometers in the mid-March storm, fighting to earn back the seconds Luka's and Katsuo's stunts had cost her.

The race was tight. It always was the first few days—burning fuel on Europe's smooth autobahns, through quaint villages lined with shiny-eyed Hitler Youth, past rolling pastures of cows munching contentedly on their own cud.

71

Katsuo had reached the Prague checkpoint first. Mere meters and seconds before Luka's wheels skidded over the white line. Their names and times clustered at the top of the board, written in an official's runelike script. Yael had fought her way back to the middle of the pack. *Adele Wolfe* was chalked ninth on the list, seconds between Yamato's eighth and Hans's tenth. Felix had hung back behind her, finishing in twelfth place. The next leg of the tour—Prague to Rome— would be just as tight. Barring any engine troubles, the standings wouldn't change much.

"Did you name your bike yet?"

Yael's limp muscles went stiff. Her eyes broke away from the slipping sky to see Felix standing by the fire. Sparklight glinted off his pale hair. A bowl of soup was cupped in his hands.

Name her bike? What was he talking about?

Yael's thoughts riffled through pages of file facts. But this tidbit of information wasn't in Adele's novel. Or Felix's footnote. It was a living, breathing memory, something only the twins shared.

A cobweb gap.

"Remember that BMW R35 you had that always fish-tailed? *Whiplash*?" The corner of Felix's lip twitched with nostalgia. "*Grim* was my favorite, though. Had the best rpm, smoothest gearshift. Nothing quite like it."

Whiplash? Grim? What the *Scheisse* was she supposed to say?

Felix, it seemed, didn't need her to say anything. He

was still talking. "These Zündapps are solid. A lot of engine power. I was thinking of naming mine something like Thor. Or Loki?"

"Whatever you want." Yael's words hung on that spider's thread, tense, angry. Not unlike the tone Adele used the night before in her flat.

Adele's brother sighed. "Look, I know you don't want me here. But if you're going to be bullheaded enough to go through with this, the least I can do is make sure you don't starve."

At this, Felix stretched out his soup bowl offering. Its steam spun into her face, prickling her nostrils with rich scents of oxtail soup. Cloves, bay leaves, and pepper. Thyme, parsley, and juniper. Tender hunks of meat. Yael's mouth went heavy with hunger, but she made no move to take the meal. "It's a rookie mistake, you know, accepting food from other racers."

"I'm not some other racer. I'm your brother."

Brother. The term was supposed to hold some weight between them. Some code of honor Yael could not navigate. Not when her own family was long ash—spread to the wind.

"Now, stop being stupid." Felix pushed the bowl of soup into Yael's hands. "Eat up. I'm going to get us some water."

She wanted to. The time on the road had been too short for the refueling pit stops where riders usually crammed their mouths with jerky and protein bars, and it had been long hours since the plate of eggs she'd helped herself to in Adele's flat that morning. Hollow, hollow hunger edged Yael like a shadow. Reminding her she wasn't full.

But something was off. His tone was too cozy, too light, compared with the pleas he'd made last night. This afternoon. Yael knew he hadn't given up that easily. (She wouldn't.)

She watched Adele's twin brother weave through the gaping dining hall. He moved with explosive elegance past the eighteen other riders huddled over their own meals. They'd clustered off into groups around oak tables. It was as if the Seventieth Meridian had been ripped off Henryka's map and pasted over the room. German faces on one side of the room. Japanese on the other. Restless, uneasy neighbors. Just like the empires they rode for.

Most wore this tension on their faces. The only soft expression in the room was Ryoko's. The girl sat elbow-to-elbow with Nagao Yamato, who was reading a book of poetry. Ryoko had tried speaking to him a few times, but the boy kept shrugging his shoulders, never tearing his eyes from the pages. Ryoko's fingers fiddled with her napkin; her stare wandered, met Yael's. The girl's expression—lonely eyes, borderline smile—was so honest that Yael (despite knowing that Adele's grins were usually reserved for cameras) smiled back.

"Still don't scare easy, I see."

Yael turned toward the fire to find Luka Löwe mere steps from her. He was still wearing his trademark jacket. It hadn't been treated like the others, and it was soaked. She wondered why he didn't just take it off.

"Is that what you call your little stunt today? A scare?"

Yael didn't take her eyes off the boy. According to one of his many *Das Reich* profiles, the victor's face was handsome enough to snare the hearts of ten thousand German maidens at first sight. Even Yael had to admit that the boy was attractive. The lines of his face were strong, not harsh, highlighting sea-storm eyes. Stubble, darker than the rest of his golden hair, swathed his jaw like dusk.

(*Ten thousand* maidens, though? That seemed like a bit much.)

"Just some fun to spice things up. The first day is always so dull." Luka sighed. "So...tame. You always did appreciate getting a bit wild."

The comment was bait, meant to rile her (Adele). Yael could see that much in the boy's crooked lip and proud-set shoulders.

Anger wasn't an act she had to dig for. All Yael had to do was stare at the Iron Cross hanging from Luka's throat. At the swastika around his arm. At the blue irises and blond hair that kept him alive when so many others were not. It didn't matter that she also wore these heavy, heavy things. This boy meant them all.

It was so easy to hate him.

So easy to take the furnace in her bones and let the molten marrow leak into her words: burn, burn, sear. "Your dummkopf driving almost got us both killed!"

Luka just shrugged. "*I* had everything under control, but it seems Katsuo's not in the mood for games this time around."

Yael glanced back to Katsuo's table. It was crowded with his training camp clan: Takeo was using his sharp-as-song folding blade to make notches in the tabletop. Iwao and Hiraku nodded with religious fervor at everything Katsuo said. The victor was reenacting the morning's almost-wreck, diagramming the pincer movement and mimicking Yael's shrieking brakes in a way that made his listeners laugh.

Katsuo fell silent when he caught her staring. His gaze speared through Yael, into Luka. Speaking histories, calling for war.

"At least he's quick," Yael said. "Easy to read."

"You mean boring." Luka snorted and leaned back on his heels, as if he were shifting the gears of an imaginary bike. "I quite enjoy our dance, Fräulein. Always have."

Our dance. What was he talking about? What was Yael supposed to say next? And *how* was she supposed to say it? Would Adele stay angry? Would she ignore the boy altogether?

There was too much about Luka (and Felix, for that matter) that Yael didn't know. For a while on the road, when it was just herself and asphalt and hissing mist, she'd hoped that she could avoid them. But that tactic clearly wasn't working— Yael's fingers itched for the list of Reiniger's coded addresses tucked inside her undershirt. Soon, very soon, she was going to have to pay one of them a visit.

"Get away from my sister." Felix had returned. The too-light of his tone had vanished. The glasses of water in his hands trembled.

Luka's eyebrows rose. They were the same dark shade as his stubble, Yael noted. A color most would try to bleach. "No need to get snippy, Herr Wolfe."

"Snippy?" Felix's knuckles tightened around the glasses. Yael kept waiting for cracks to appear, glass to shatter, and Felix's hands to dissolve into blood. "You almost killed her on the road today!"

"Not to worry, Herr Wolfe. I plan on keeping your sister around for a while. It's a long race yet. God knows, I could use the entertainment."

The shatter came, but not in the way Yael expected. Felix dropped the glasses, his hands closing into fists. Just in time to throw his first punch.

It was a solid hit, cracking against Luka Löwe's cheekbone. Bending into the cartilage of his aquiline nose. The blood flowed fast—a crooked ruby trail spilling over Luka's mouth, down his chin. As the boy bowed in pain, something silver slipped out of his shirt, tangling with his Iron Cross. His hands fished for it quickly, tucking it back where Yael could not see.

"Good punch for a grease monkey." Luka was still smirking when he straightened. "I'll give you that one, Herr Wolfe. But hit me again and I will wreck you."

Yael's ankle throbbed against the blade sheathed inside her boot. She watched the two boys face off in front of the fire: Felix in his boxing stance, Luka glowering through the red smear on his face.

The air between them was charged: tingling with heat and the sudden silence that had washed over the room. Everyone watched, breaths held, food forgotten. Waiting for the second hit.

It was coming. Yael could see it in the throb of Felix's temple vein, the cording of his jaw muscles. The next punch was about to jag through the air between them. Start a bloodbath.

They were going to tear each other to pieces.

The boys were an even match—made of the same strength and speed. Neither of them would be walking away from a serious fight. Not well enough to ride. Yael wanted to sit back and let it happen. But Adele...she would spare her brother. She'd stop this.

Yael set the bowl of soup on the floor and walked over to Adele's brother. She locked her hand around his trembling arm. "Felix."

He looked over at her; a white mop of hair bristled over his face. His eyes were piercing, tinged with feral. She could feel Felix's heart thrumming through his jacket. His muscles danced to the rhythm, eager, angry.

"Let it be," she said. "He's not worth it."

Luka flinched, a twitch of the cheek that spoke of pain. He brought an arm up to his face, daubing the blood across his cheek and jacket. Red dripped to the floor.

"I know you want to protect me." Yael's grip tightened as she said this. "But this isn't the way."

Slowly, slowly, Adele's brother began to unwind. The *something to prove* faded from his pulse.

Blood was still leaking from Luka's nose. It burbled and gleamed as he spoke. "Don't trust your guard dog too much. I saw him slip a little something into your soup."

"He's lying." Felix's voice was flat, but Yael felt the extra leap of his brachioradialis under her fingers. Saw his pupils flare, pinholes to fear. Signs Vlad had trained Yael to look for in others and hide in herself.

"Maybe I am. Or maybe I just don't want to see our dance cut short." Luka winked—actually *winked*—at her, and Yael entertained a fleeting fantasy of throwing a punch of her own. "Your call, Fräulein."

With that, Luka spun on his heels and swaggered out of the dining hall.

"I still don't understand why you didn't report that cocky son of a..." The last of Felix's insults mumbled away as he tore out of Yael's grip. Broken glass snapped under his boots. "I'll go get us some more water. You should eat."

Yael eyed the soup. Still on the floor where she'd set it. All simmer, steam, and sabotage. So many good ingredients gone to waste.

"Only if you take a bite first," she said.

Felix scowled. "C'mon, Ad, you can't seriously believe him. After everything that happened between you two...Luka's trying to get in your head."

Everything that happened. Adele's brother said these words with such heat. The vein on his temple was rising again, snaking into his hairline. Yael sensed there was something more to his temper—not just the words Luka Löwe had spit across the room, but some deeper story. The same one she'd glimpsed in Luka's face in the stadium.

What was everything? What didn't Adele report? The secrets of Adele and Luka, coming around again. Wrapping another noose-coil around her neck.

She should have let them fight.

"One bite." Yael held up a finger. "That's all I ask."

Felix didn't speak. Didn't move. The red crept down his cheeks, around his neck. His black-hole pupils swallowed the firelight: big and round and full of lies.

It was all the answer Yael needed. She turned around and started walking.

"Where are you going?" he called after Yael—desperate— as she stomped on, her boot clipping the edge of the soup bowl. Chunks of oxtail spun out, mixed with traces of Luka's nosebleed. It looked . . . wrong. All that meat and blood. Together.

"I'm getting my own soup," she said, and walked away.

CHAPTER 8

NOW

MARCH 10, 1956
PRAGUE CHECKPOINT

There would be no visiting the Prague address. Not with
Felix watching her the way he was—all glower and guilt
from the spilled soup fireside. There was only one way out of
the checkpoint, and Yael had no doubt that if she tried to use
it, he'd ask her where she was going and try to stop her. Or
worse, follow her.

She had to shake him, but it wouldn't be here. She'd only
really escaped his stare by locking herself in the washroom.
After she'd changed the gauze on Vlad's still raw wolf, Yael
sat on the covered toilet, fished the wad of addresses out of her
undershirt, and set about decoding and memorizing the numbers for Rome. Tomorrow she'd pull ahead. Jump from ninth
place to first and ride, ride, ride until she reached Rome. She
would go to the resistance address, request the files on Felix
and Luka, and cross the second Axis Tour checkpoint before
Adele's brother (or any of the other racers) appeared.

That was the plan, anyway. Tomorrow would be a long day.

When Yael lifted the pillow of her assigned communal bunk, she found a lone star made of folded propaganda paper. It was carefully constructed, with a smallness that made her smile. It would've been easy to toss away, but she tucked it into her pocket instead and put her boot-knife under the pillow in its place. Many of the other riders were already asleep. Bare-chested, their snores as rough as their Zündapp engines. A racing official sat in the corner, playing chaperone, looking close to slumber himself.

Yael slept with her jacket on. The smallest doll, the thumb-tack, the paper star, and her gun lumped in its pockets. Her wolves hid under its sleeve. She traced them by memory over the leather, named them in silence.

Babushka, Mama, Miriam, Aaron-Klaus, Vlad.
Good night. Good night. Good night. Good night. Good night.

——

THEN

THE SECOND WOLF: MAMA

WINTER 1945

Time between sessions whittled away, shedding off like scales of Yael's skin. There were no more days of rest. Every single morning, Dr. Geyer punched needles into Yael's arm. Pushing in more poison than her body could bear.

She was a raw pink thing. The color of a newborn, arms

peeling and glossy under the electric light of Dr. Geyer's office. The doctor's eyes were shining, too. Invisible hooks pried his grin wider every time he examined her. He even joked with the nurse, who never smiled back even though her shoes were soled and there was a cushion of fat under her pasty skin.

"The compound is working!"

Progress. Progress. Progress.

The stab and slide of needles didn't hurt as much as what came after: a coal-glow burn that spread from Yael's arm to every part of her. There was no relief—even when the evening's cold slunk into Barrack 7. Her skin itched, fell in flakes like snow. Searing to the touch.

The pain she could handle. It was the stares that punched through Yael's soul. The same sight that made Dr. Geyer's teeth split into what he called a smile summoned blank horror from others. Women whispered about the strange blaze of her eyes, the phantom-wash of her skin and hair. A girl who was disappearing right before their sight…being replaced by… something else….

"*Монстр.*" "*Monstre.*" "Monster." They thought Yael couldn't hear their whispers, but she did. Yael's mother was quick to extinguish them, hissing, "She's my daughter! Not some creature!" into all corners of Barrack 7. Challenging anyone who dared to voice otherwise with battle-ready eyes.

But even Yael's mother watched her with a wariness that wasn't there before. Her lips pulled in a tight slant every time she returned to the bunk and found her daughter curled up in straw and pain. Brow slick with sweat.

"Fever still," she'd mutter after pressing her frail fingers to Yael's skin, then turn to their bunkmate. "Miriam, get me some snow."

It always melted fast—the snow Miriam brought dripped down her skin in one hundred different ways. Braiding down her throat, into her workdress.

"You're not cold, Yael?" The older girl shivered, tucked her fingers into her armpits for extra warmth.

"She's different from us," Yael's mother answered. Though Yael's hair was short, too short to smooth, her mother ran her hand over it anyway. "She's sick."

But she *was* cold. Chills laced over her skin as she burned from the inside out. Yael was fire and ice. Together. An impossible thing.

"N-Not." Yael coughed the word out. "Not different. I'm the same."

Her mother didn't answer. She kept smoothing her daughter's bristled scalp with fingers so thin that Yael felt the hard of bone beneath their touch.

"You *look* different." Miriam cocked her head.

Same, Yael wanted to yell again. *Same on the inside. Where it matters.* The same girl who proudly recited the *Mah Nishtanah* at Passover seder. The same girl who played ball games with the other children in the ghetto streets. Who wouldn't let go of her mother's coat *no matter what* when they were shoved into the train cars. Who cried when the numbers were needled into her skin, and cried even more when she realized they would never come off.

She wanted to tell them these things, but Dr. Geyer's poison was too strong. Yael was lying down, but her head spun, images flashing like fragments of shattered mirror. Thoughts broken and everywhere, glazed by fever-fire. Prayers ghosted above her—"*El na, refa na la*" (God, please heal her, please)—mother's voice, mother's lips, mother's hope. The lump of the Babushka's dolls under her patch of mattress, curved into her spine: one solid thing. The only solid thing.

Everything else was falling apart. Sloughing off with her skin.

Maybe I'm not the same, came the sudden thought. She didn't cry at the needles anymore (she hadn't since the very first injection session, when Dr. Geyer slapped her wrist and demanded that she stop sniveling). He'd changed that.

You are going to change.

"Babushka?" Yael struggled against the straw, pushed herself elbow high before she realized the voice was a memory. The bunk across from hers was crowded with many wavering faces, but none of them was the Babushka.

No. That was wrong. It was *change things*.

You are going to change
things.

She collapsed back into the scratchy straw.

————

Howls woke her. It was the same chorus she heard every night. Groans of sorrow, wails and loss from every barrack.

Twining together in wild song. During her first weeks in the camp, she'd imagined there were real wolves—just behind the barbed wire and sizzling electric fence—wild and free.

But tonight the howls were different. The song that tugged at the fringe of Yael's dreams felt closer. *Was* closer.

The bunk's wood trembled when Yael sat up. The world around her felt like the swabs the nurse sometimes wiped her arm with—clear and cold. No more creeping chills. No more fire under her skin.

The fever was gone.

Her mother's back was to her. Hunched over so Yael could trace a ladder of ribs through her workdress. They shuddered in time to tears, howls, crooning sobs.

"Mama?" Yael reached out for her mother's back. "I'm better now."

Her mother seized at the touch, her cries all choking into one. Knotting back into silence.

For a moment Yael wondered if she was still dreaming. But her fingers meeting her mother's back. That was real. She felt the shudder of her mother's breath. The scrawn of her starving muscles. The hot, hot, hot of her skin.

"Mama?" she called again, breath hitched tight in her throat.

The woman turned, eyes on her. They were...strange. The same color as her mother's (dark like the shadows in an evening forest). The same shape...but they seemed to belong to someone else. Yael looked deep into them but could not find the woman who'd birthed her. Raised her. Held her close when their cattle car rattled over kilometers and kilometers of track.

"What are you?" Her mother pulled away, voice scraping.

The empty space beneath Yael's fingers was frigid. "I'm—I'm Yael. Your daughter."

"No!" Her mother's eyes wheeled, side to side. "No... you're not my baby. Not her."

Stab, stab, stab. These words were a hundred needles all at once.

"Mama..." she tried again.

"Don't!" Her shriek tore through the barrack, waking the near-dead from their sleep. Miriam jerked awake, stared at her bunkmates with bleary eyes. "Don't call me that! I don't know who—what—you are, but you're not my Yael!"

Whispers cluttered the straw around them. Yael felt the eyes on her. Dozens, scores, hundreds had awoken.

"Rachel!" Miriam grabbed Yael's mother by the shoulders and said her name over and over. Like a spell. "Rachel. Rachel. Be calm."

Every part of Yael's mother shook: her head, her shoulders. She shrank away from Miriam's touch until her back was to the barrack wall. "It's not her! It's not Yael!"

Yael was shaking, too. Pumped full of the poison of her mother's screams. They flowed hot inside her. Not fever, but anger. The helpless kind a person fills themselves with to keep the fear away. "Stop, Mama! Stop! I'm ME! I'm Yael!"

She yelled until she caught Miriam staring at her. The older girl's eyes were as wide and awled as Yael's hidden matryoshka dolls.

"Y-Yael?" Miriam said the name carefully. Her hands

were still set on Rachel's shoulders, but all her attention was on the girl across the bunk. "You...changed."

Yael followed Miriam's stare, down to her own arms. The raw shine was gone, peeled away with all those scrolls of dead skin. No more splotches or spots. Her skin was soft, white as milk. Her fingers danced up, pulled out a single strand of hair. It was shock pale.

The way Dr. Geyer always wanted it to be.

"That's not my daughter! It's a monster!" her mother kept howling, pulling against Miriam's grip. "Yael's dead! Dead! Like everything else here!"

Yael—certain now this was a dream—turned over her arm, upending the crooked numbers. She was still marked. Still Inmate 121358ΔX.

"Look." Yael tried to offer the numbers to her mother— proof that she was who she was—but her mother's eyes kept wheeling. Lost and glazed.

"She's delirious. She doesn't know what she's saying." Miriam's voice frayed with the strain of trying to keep Yael's mother still. "Her skin is burning."

Fever. Yael could see it—now that she looked—shimmering over her mother's face, emptying out her eyes. Yael thought of her own sickness and the coolness of her mother's hand pressed to her forehead. Had she passed it on? Poisoned her mother with her own flesh? Her own change?

"I'm Yael. I'm alive." She said this to her mother and Miriam. To the three speechless bunkmates, who had slid away from the straw mattress and into the aisle. To all the hundreds of women who were watching their bunk.

But most of all, Yael said this to herself. Because the whispers in a dozen languages were coming back to haunt her. *Монстр. Monstre. Monster.* Her mother's voice was the loudest of all. *It's a monster!*

I'm Yael. I'm Yael. I'm Yael, she thought back. *I'm special. I'm going to change things.*

But right now, it didn't feel that way.

Her mother wasn't screaming anymore. Across the bunk Miriam was soothing her down into the straw. Yael's mother curled up. Had she always looked so small? So thin? The fever seemed so much *larger* than her—flaring out of the edges of her skin. Like a spirit trying to peel out of a body.

One of the silent bunkmates came back with some snow and handed it to Miriam. The older girl pressed it to Rachel's forehead, the way Yael's mother had done for Yael only hours ago. But it didn't help. Her mother only whimpered against the cold. Those strange and familiar eyes stopped wheeling, went dull.

Dead. Like everything else here.

The women of Barrack 7 stopped whispering for just a moment, and all Yael could hear was the agony of everything. The death camp's song rose from every corner of the night. Not wolves. Just people. Crying and crying and crying.

She howled with them.

CHAPTER 9

NOW

MARCH 11, 1956
PRAGUE TO ROME

The pack stayed tight. Knit into a delicate formation of wheels and gears. The racers moved as a herd through foothills patched with shy spring grass and jutting crags of rock, through towns lined with cheering, swastika-waving citizens and Reichssender cameras camped for the perfect shot.

As first and second place, Katsuo and Luka led the line out of the Prague checkpoint. Both racers were far ahead, as small as the dirt granules flecked across Yael's goggles. She itched to be with them, to twist hard on the throttle and let the road vanish beneath her. Meters swallowed as fourth gear kicked into place.

But this could not happen for three reasons. Takeo, Hiraku, and Iwao. They were fanned across the road—third, fourth, and fifth place. The exact same racers Katsuo had gathered to his table, Yael noted. Probably to plan this very tactic. It *was* planned. There was no doubt about that. From the moment they'd ripped out of Prague, the trio had formed their blockade, spaced evenly across the asphalt in an unwavering line.

The road was locked.

The boys' pace was sluggish. Yael's motorcycle raged behind them. Trapped in third gear (*too slow, too slow*), her hand pining on the throttle. She'd fought her way through the choked pack, edging out Yamato, Dolf, and Karl for sixth place. They were still close, trailing her by just a meter, as she pulled up behind Hiraku's rear wheel.

The boy was the youngest of Katsuo's three allies. The weakest link in this mechanical dragnet. Sooner or later Hiraku would slip up, and when he did, Yael would be ready.

Watching, waiting, watching, waiting. Kilometers spun through Hiraku's splash guard. The hills swelled, and the air swam with the taste of mountains: fresh fir, the silvery sparkle of snow. Yael's body started to ache, cramped with the tension of being ready and waiting, waiting, waiting....

But the kilometers kept spinning out, out. And somewhere ahead, Luka and Katsuo kept tearing away, away. (She couldn't see them anymore; both boys were lost to the bend of mountain roads.)

Another bike wove up, dangerously close to the lavender smoke of Takeo's exhaust. Its wheels ate away lateral road space. Centimeters Yael needed if she was going to make a pass, break through Katsuo's human barrier.

"I'm sorry, Ad!" It was a testament to how slow they were

going that she could hear Adele's brother. He screamed at the top of his lungs as he half straddled, half stood on his bike.

Yael didn't know how Felix had managed to squeeze up so many places in the airtight formation. The punch he'd thrown at Luka had docked him a whole hour, making him the last rider out of Prague. Though all the racers left at the same time, their formation was determined by their places on the board. Adele's brother was far enough away in the lineup that Yael had been able to ignore him without trying. But he was next to her now. Peeling back her concentration with electric eyes.

"Luka was right! I drugged your soup!" he yelled.

No Scheisse. Yael was half tempted to shout this back, but there was no time. Hiraku was looking over his shoulder, distracted by Felix's loud confession. It was the waver Yael had been waiting for.

A jam on the throttle burst her forward, sent her bike lunging at Hiraku's. His mouth fell into a slack O of surprise, horror. Yael's wheel didn't even touch his, but the aggression alone was enough.

Hiraku's bike swerved off the road. His scream rose as high as his wheel, cutting off in a sick crush of metal. One long scar plowed through minty, newborn grass: tangled bike and mangled boy.

His partners spread wide, trying to repair the crack in their dam. But it was too late. Yael was through the breach, kicking her bike into the highest gear. The road spooled out in front of her, a wide tar ribbon rippling into the jaws of the

Alps. Roadside foliage smudged into a long blur. The sudden end of Hiraku's screams chased her: silent, silent, silent.

She had kilometers to go yet.

———

Gravel and pits. Slopes and bends. Shadow and chill.

These were the mountain roads.

Yael flew on wings of leather and wind, the motorcycle humming beneath her. At every turn, every peel around a large boulder, she expected to see Luka and Katsuo. But the boys had wings of their own . . . speed that carried them through the mountain pass. Even stretching her engine's limit over patches of winter-worn road wouldn't close the space between them.

Evening pooled early in the crevasses of the Alps. Shadows clung to the edge of Yael's goggles, crept through her aching limbs. Even when the mountains were far behind, nothing but ridges and memory against the far horizon, the darkness grew. Her weariness settled in for a long night. But Yael pushed on.

One by one the others fell behind, their headlamps dropping off into the dark. Pulling to the edge of naked twig vineyards to eat and rest. It was a smart, conservative move. Staving off sleep deprivation and utter fatigue. That was what Yael should've done—would have done—if she were a normal racer.

If she didn't have all the red, red territories drowning inside her. If she didn't have five wolves and the fate of the resistance galloping alongside. If she didn't have two boys hounding her with a past she didn't possess. If she didn't have a Roman address she needed to reach before she crossed the checkpoint line.

The stakes were higher than a few hours of exhaustion. A few grams of hunger.

You have nothing left to prove. Everything to lose.

Those words were for Adele. The normal racer.

For Yael it was squared: everything, everything.

So she rode on.

———

Rome was wrapped in a sleep like death, skeletal against the moonlight. Rib-cage shutters clapped over windows. Doorways and arches gaped, as empty as eye sockets. The streets' worn stones reminded Yael of teeth ground to the nubs. Even its heart was made of ruins: The Colosseum rose to meet the pock-faced moon. As Yael rode by, she felt the weight of the place. All the dust and time rolling off its stones.

When Yael was certain no eyes were around to see, she cut her motorcycle's engine and pushed it off the Axis banner–draped race path, into an alley strung with laundry. Clothes and white sheets shuddered and twisted—a hushed dance. Yael lingered beneath them, breathing in the scents of lavender soap and alley-dank. The mouth of the street yawned. Empty.

Part of her wanted to wait. Let the darkness spit out

anything that was lurking. But the checkpoint was still ahead, and every minute she sat was official time lost. Chalked against Adele Wolfe's name on the scoreboard.

The address wasn't far from here. Yael could be there and back in five minutes. Riding straight up to the resistance's door was out of the question. Her motorcycle and riding gear were conspicuous enough as it was, and the city was clearly under curfew. There would be patrols. Yael unclipped her helmet, unnoosed the Iron Cross from her neck. The swastika armband was next to go, crammed like bright guts into her leather pannier. Then, with a final glimpse down the alley's empty spine, Yael changed herself.

It came like a memory, drew out like a sigh. Always painful—switch, click, shift. An Italian face: olive skin, dark hair, shaded eyes. (Non-Aryan by strict standards, though Hitler's racial system was built just as much on politics as it was on weak pseudoscience. Like the Japanese, Italians were "honorary Aryan," because of their pro–National Socialist war efforts.) This appearance would be enough to avoid immediate identification if she stumbled across a patrol. But the cobbled streets stayed empty as she walked through them.

The door Reiniger's coded numbers led her to was small, painted in a splintering oxblood red. Darkness leaned inside the nearby windowpanes. Yael knocked four times—two double staccato beats—just as the protocol instructed.

The shadows stayed, licking behind the curtains. But she heard quick footsteps, the lock sliding back. Italian words whispered through the crack: "What do you want?"

95

"The wolves of war are gathering," she recited the first half of the pass code.

"They sing the song of rotten bones," the voice behind the door answered. Weathered wood pulled back to show a boy not much younger than Yael herself. Skinny, all elbows, with an acne-riddled face. Hair peaked pillow high, eyes heavy with sleep.

"Volchitsa," he whispered her alias. "Come in."

"I can't stay," Yael told the partisan as she stepped over the shallow doorframe. The room beyond smelled of candle wax and basil. "I'm still on the clock. Didn't want to risk a tail from the checkpoint. I need your group to get a request through to Germania. I want all the information Henryka can collect on Felix Wolfe and any additional information she has on Luka Löwe's relationship with Adele Wolfe."

The boy nodded. "We'll send the request straightaway."

"Tell her I'll retrieve the files at the drop in Cairo." The next official checkpoint was days from now. (At the very least.) The thought of what could happen during those sandy kilometers worried Yael, but there was little choice in the matter. She'd just try her best to avoid Luka and Felix until then.

"Is there anything else you need?"

Yael shook her head.

"I must go. Finish this leg of the race." She was already walking when she said this. Out the door, into the dark.

"I'll be watching you on the Reichssender. Our hope goes with you, Volchitsa."

Yael tried to swallow the partisan's words, nod them away

with her good-bye. But they clung, digging their needle claws into her shoulders. *Hope.* A strange word. In her past, it had been a light, wispy thing. Crushed as easily as a finger under a guard's boot. But now...now *hope* weighed so much, as if the Colosseum itself had collapsed on top of her. Mortar and suffering. Brick and time. Pouring into Yael's chest cavity. The place that was supposed to hold her heart.

The streets were still vacant when Yael walked back through piazzas with shimmering fountains and sculptures. A copper statue of the Führer, still gleaming with newness—Yael suspected it had once been a statue of Mussolini, replaced shortly after his assassination at Hitler's megalomaniac commands— watched her pass with blank eyes. Tears of bird waste streaked down his cheeks.

Good aim. Yael nodded to the nearest pigeons, crammed shoulder tight across the window ledge of a basilica. *Keep it up.*

She was just about to round the bend back into the alley when she heard the voices. Yael stopped and shrank against the church's bastion walls, listening as three separate voices spoke hurried German.

A patrol. The alley hadn't been as tucked away as she'd thought.

Yael's fingers dug into the stucco. She edged to the corner, dared a look. The soldiers were clustered around her bike, just as she feared. Prodding its leather and chrome like vultures over a dead thing. Rifles were slung across their shoulders; their eyes were shielded heavily by caps.

The Iron Cross! The swastika armband! The panniers were

sealed, as she'd left them—clipped buckles and leather straps—but the soldiers were still poking. It was only a matter of time before they ripped open the satchels and found her National Socialist gear. Put the pieces together. Ruined everything.

Time was something Yael did not have. Chalky minutes were racking up: *tick, tick, tick*. Seconds she couldn't afford to lose.

She couldn't let them see her as Adele. Victor Wolfe would have no plausible alibi for an abandoned bike in a back alley, so close to a checkpoint. Any story she offered in Adele's voice would be picked apart: meat, tendon, bone. They'd peck, pick, peck until they found the cobweb gaps. Shredded her open.

Her Zündapp had no distinct markings. These men shouldn't be able to track this incident back to Adele Wolfe. Not if it was a brunette Italian woman kicking the guns from their wrists.

She could still get out of this clean.

Herr Hitler's blank copper pupils watched as Yael ducked into the alley. *"Heil Hitler!"*

They jumped when she spoke, as if her salute were an actual gunshot. Yael took the moment to survey the alley in full. Three men. (Two privates. One sergeant. All stocky and built.) Three rifles. (Carcanos. 7.35 mm. Strong punch, dodgy accuracy.) Laundry fluttering overhead. One heavy, heavy Zündapp.

The closest soldier was the first to regain his composure, the only one to return her salute. "You're out after curfew," he said in rough Italian.

—ACT LIKE YOU BELONG NOT A HOLLOW STUFFED GIRL—

"Yes." Yael halted under a wide bedsheet. Doorway gas lamps flickered and fleshed out the air between them. "I'm on official business. I have papers."

The men looked at each other. Both privates had unslung their rifles, but their stances were slack. They weren't expecting a fight. Who would from a lone alley girl?

"Official business?" The sergeant took her bait. Edged closer.

Closer.

Yael's arm swung out, up. Her fingers snagged the cloth and pulled. The sheet fell—an avalanche of cotton on top of the sergeant. The privates yelled, all surprise, rifles pressed back into their shoulders. Yael gave them no chance to aim as she lunged at the sergeant, met his sternum with her fist. He stumbled back, into the first private. Both went tumbling, a white cloth tangle.

The third patrolman was slow, his finger frozen over the trigger. Yael kicked the Carcano from his hands and stole the air out of his lungs with a second roundhouse. He stumbled to the ground, winded.

He was just a boy. Not much older than the partisan she'd just met. Yael could see his pulse fluttering, fearful against the smooth skin of his throat.

Yael's knife rattled against its boot sheath. Her P38 sat hard against her rib cage.

Simple solutions. Permanent silence.

Vlad had taught her the art of killing. The ways to snuff out a man's life were endless: blow to the temple, shot to the chest, twist of the neck. Yael had perfected them all. She knew where the line was—that tenuous string between the land of the living and the twilight of ghosts—and how to cross it.

Yet for all Yael's knowledge and skill, she never had.

The rabbits Vlad had taught her to catch and clean didn't count. Neither did the cases and cases of empty vodka bottles she'd shattered to perfect her marksmanship. Or the straw dummies she'd punched through with knife holes.

People—living and breathing—were different.

Death. The cost of living. Following her as close as wings. Swooping down on all she passed. It had become such a careless commodity. Flung far and wide in the name of progress. But Yael knew from her many, many brushes with it that death was not a power to be wielded lightly.

No. It was a power to fear. A power that swallowed your soul, piece by piece, until there was nothing left.

She would not be like the guard with the flat winter eyes, who kicked the Babushka's frail body again and again. She would not be like the soldiers of Germania, who shot stray bitches and Jews alike. When Yael took a life, it would mean something.

A death to end this death.

So she had lines of her own. Lines before the line. Her bullets and blade were for three things: defense, coercion, and the Führer's chest.

There were no strict lines stopping Yael now as she loomed over the boy-soldier. This scenario could be considered defense, and his blood wasn't exactly innocent. She pulled out her gun. Saw the depths of the boy-soldier's eyes plummet. Deep, deep, deep into a fear she knew well. A fear she still faced every day, every night, when she woke from nightmares of smoke and wolves.

He was *one of them.*

But she wasn't.

Yael brought the gun down—hard—on the private's head. Visions of death rolled back with his eyes, as limp as the rest of him.

The other two soldiers were scrambling out of the sheets. Yael leapt onto the bike, twisting it to life. The second private lunged for his gun, but the Zündapp's wheels were already turning. Yael shot off beneath flurries of laundry, into the twisted freedom of Rome's ancient streets.

CHAPTER 10

NOW

1st: Tsuda Katsuo, 13 hours, 38 minutes, 30 seconds.

2nd: Luka Löwe, 13 hours, 38 minutes, 34 seconds.

3rd: Adele Wolfe, 15 hours, 48 minutes,

53 seconds.

Yael sat in the checkpoint dining area, wondering what unfortunate family had been displaced from their property. Whoever they were, they had expensive tastes. Marble floors, craftsman wrought-iron chandeliers, racks filled with vintage wines, the green bottles gathering dust. Tapestries covered every wall except one, where the scoreboard loomed. Yael sat at the table, studying it. There was a dish full of noodles bathed in rich Bolognese sauce by her elbows, but she wasn't even certain she possessed the energy to pick up her fork.

Two hours. Ten minutes. Twenty-three seconds.

That was how much time she'd lost. Yael took in the difference with a hissing breath. She'd have to do better than that. Third place would not get her an invitation to the Victor's Ball. It wouldn't have her dancing in Hitler's arms, smiling for the cameras, reaching for her weapon....

She needed to claw back into first and stay there.

"Look who finally decided to show up for the party!"

Yael's jaw locked—hate-tight—at the sound of Luka's voice. The boy was still in his riding gear: boots and gloves freckled with mud, his battered brown jacket hanging from his shoulders. He looked as exhausted as Yael felt. His stubble was heavier. Goggle rings (hours old) etched red tracks around his eyes, mingling with the bruises Felix's punch had inked there.

"What are you doing here?" Yael didn't bother keeping the spite out of her voice as Luka took the seat across from her.

"Got the road jitters. Always takes a few hours to get them out." Luka brought a crumbling cigarette to his lips and smiled in a way that made Yael regret saying anything at all. Her words had invited Luka to keep talking when all she really wanted was for him to swagger off. Take his "Blood and honor!" and proud pedigree with him.

Yael started eating her food in hopes that her silence would bore Luka away. But the boy seemed set on watching her eat, siphoning cigarette smoke through his bandaged nose as she slurped her noodles.

Something about him seemed softer this evening, Yael noted between bites. Perhaps it was this smoky film in the air or the tape over Luka's face, but the edge between them was no longer a knife. More wisp and feather. Skin's-breath and late-night whispers.

Don't think I've forgotten. What you did.

After everything that happened between you two…

Adele and Luka. So many sides to their story.

Noodles caught in her throat. She had to cough them down. Luka tapped his cigarette. All of its ash crumbled away. The end glowed raw.

"I see you found a way through Katsuo's little blockade," he said.

Yael followed Luka's gaze to the scoreboard. The sixteen spaces below Adele's name were blank, waiting to be filled by racers who'd taken extra minutes for food, rest. But the list's end was anchored by a struck-through name: ~~Shiina Hiraku~~. She read those letters and heard the squeal of his wheels. His scream. Its sudden, savage end.

"Is he dead?" She wasn't sure why she asked this. Why her throat felt thick and tangled, as if the noodles were still clogging it.

"You know they never bother telling us these things." Luka crushed his cigarette into the table. It left a charred black mark. "Does it matter?"

Did it? After all, she'd followed her rules. Stayed behind her lines. The line through Hiraku's name was an accident. Collateral damage.

Yael swallowed. But the tangle stayed.

Did it matter? One life. A drop in a vast, vast ocean of hundreds, thousands, millions.

Yes, pounded the hollow of her heart. *Yes*, cried her wolves.

It mattered. All of them mattered. All of the hundreds, thousands, millions. Vast, vast…

Would it ever end?

Five, just five. Focus on them. Make it manageable. Babushka, Mama, Miriam—

—STOP—

Now was not the time for gathering her pieces. For becoming Yael. Because she was Adele Valerie Wolfe, and she could not let the boy across the table see anything more.

But Luka was looking, trapping Adele's reflection in his indigo irises. The corner of his lip twitched—in a slippery way that Yael (even with all her training) couldn't read. He was reading her, though, flipping through the files of her eyes. Wordless webs of memories.

Could he see through the cracks?

Did it matter?

"I guess not," she finally answered with Adele's voice, Adele's words. She kept talking, desperate for a change in subject. "You were right. Felix drugged my soup."

"And you're surprised?"

"I'm surprised you warned me," she said.

Luka tugged out a pack of cigarettes, tapped two onto the table. One he jammed between his lips. The other he sent rolling over to her.

Yael eyed it, trying to imagine how something so compact and white could smell so awful. "The Führer doesn't approve."

"Is that how it is now?" Luka's face thinned, eyes, lips, and all. In it Yael saw the truth: Adele would've taken the cigarette.

If Adele had ever smoked, it had been a very good secret. The information wasn't in the girl's file. Nor had Yael ever spied her with a cigarette during any of her surveillance sessions. Her flat hadn't even smelled of it....

"You've done a lot of things I never expected, but going full-on lemming?" Luka pulled a matchbook from his jacket. "Was one waltz with Herr Hitler all it took to melt you into his Aryan-morality lapdog?"

Yael's eyes slid to the Iron Cross around Luka's neck. It was dull with road grime, as dirty as the rest of him. "Like you're not in this race to win the Führer's favor?"

The boy clucked his tongue, his head shaking as he weeded a match out of the book. "I thought you knew me better than that. Then again, I thought I knew *you* better than that.... You're quite the slippery one, Fräulein. Made of lies and vice and things not so nice."

"Come up with that rhyme all by yourself?" she asked.

"Clever, isn't it? Maybe I'll become a poet after all this." Luka struck his match against the table. "I warned you about your brother's little soup stunt because I want you to stay in this race. This road is long and hard, Fräulein. You don't survive it without allies. Like I told Herr Wolfe: I plan on keeping you around."

"You'd trust me as your ally?"

"Trust?" Luka's match went out from the force of his laugh. He didn't bother striking another. The cigarette dangled unlit from the corner of his mouth. "I trust you about as far as I can throw you. But we need each other. Even if you think I'm *not worth it*."

His last words were startling. They made Yael recall the look on his face when she'd said them. The flinch that mixed with his bloodied nose when she pulled a furious Felix away.

She'd hurt his feelings.

Pain like that wasn't inflicted by an enemy. No—the victor's expression was warped with an emotion far cloudier, far grayer.

(Heartbreak?)

Luka Löwe had cracks, too. And through them Yael glimpsed . . . something. . . . This boy was more than just letters and snapshots in a manila-bound profile. More than just jaunty words and smirks. More than just a victor, a poster boy of the Reich.

But what?

She needed that file.

The main door to the checkpoint swung open. A herd of foggy-eyed race officials tumbled into the lodge, their voices anxious.

"There are sixteen racers on the road right now. It's impossible to account for all the Zündapps." The Roman checkpoint operator's accent was mozzarella soft, balancing out the red frustration on his face. "Come back tomorrow and we can give you a more solid answer."

The men with him . . . they were the patrol from the alley. The sergeant and private she'd tangled in a sheet. The soldier-boy whose life she'd spared.

Maybe they had opened her panniers. Maybe they'd seen the Iron Cross and swastika armband. Maybe—against all odds—they *knew*.

Yael's fingers went white around her fork.

"It was a girl." The sergeant's eyes swept through the room, latching on to Yael. "About her age."

The men turned toward Yael. They were all eyes—the way the death camp's officers had been when Dr. Geyer put her on display. Showcased his handiwork of needles and change.

Yael wasn't sure which would break first, her fork or her fingers clenching it. She was all too aware that she wore the same clothes she'd had on in the alley. Her P38 sat in her pocket, heavy with unfired bullets.

They knew. This thought rounded and tore through her chest. *They knew. They knew. They knew.*

"Not her, though." The soldier-boy spoke first. "The girl who attacked us had dark hair. Brown eyes."

"It's night," the checkpoint operator grumbled. "Partisans swarm these alleys like rats. Nothing to do with us."

"Zündapp KS 601 motorcycles aren't so common here." The sergeant's eyes stayed on Yael. "Where were you an hour ago, Victor Wolfe?"

"I was crossing the Tiber." She managed the flattest voice she could. "A few minutes from this checkpoint."

The sergeant stepped closer. "Do you have any proof of this?"

Luka spit out his cigarette and rose from his chair. The breadth of him blocked out the sergeant's stare. "You might be low on Zündapps, but we're straight out of brown-eyed brunettes. If I were you, I wouldn't go around bragging about how you got beat up by a girl. Not such a great bullet point on your curriculum vitae."

The sergeant's face grew red. "Your opinion is noted, Victor Löwe."

"It usually is." Luka crossed his arms. "Now, maybe you can let the girl who's just ridden thirteen hundred kilometers finish her dinner?"

The flush crept—redder, redder—into the sergeant's clenched jaw as he eyed the half-spooled noodles in Yael's bowl. After an agonizing moment he turned. His men followed, the soldier-boy looking over his shoulder one last time before he ducked back into the cool Roman night.

They were gone.

Yael's fingers slid off the fork. She stared at Luka. He faced the door, arms still crossed. Shaggy afternoon blond— too long by Hitler Youth standards—fell around his face, hiding his expression. This boy...was...*more.*

But what?

When Luka finally turned around, his face was twisted. *He should patent that smirk,* Yael thought, *make a mask out of it.* "Better eat up and get your beauty sleep, Fräulein. This next leg is a bitch."

Yael watched him leave, flicking his unlit cigarette into the trash bin. Her heart scattered like buckshot in her throat.

CHAPTER 11

NOW

MARCH 11, 1956
ROME CHECKPOINT

Yael was exhausted, but sleep did not come easily. Her body was all-over sore (no matter how she positioned herself on the mattress, she felt its springs—coil, screw, and stab—against her tender muscles), and her insides were still skittish from the dining hall. It didn't help that every quarter hour the dorm door's hinges squealed, letting in another road-worn racer. It also didn't help that her bunk was directly across from Luka's. He was asleep and not facing her, but his presence still set Yael on edge.

She kept her eyes on the victor's bare back. A silver chain cut around the base of his neck, glowing between hills of vertebrae. His Iron Cross hung from the bedpost. It looked strange apart from him. Or maybe he looked strange apart from it....

Did it matter?

Yael flipped to the other side of the mattress. Everything was so heavy: her muscles, *hope*, the slash through Shiina Hiraku's name. It piled into her chest as she stared at the cracks in the dormitory wall.

Instead of sheep she counted wolves.

1,2,3,4,5. 1,2,3,4,5. 1,2,3,4,5. 1,2,3,4,5. 1,2,3...

———

THEN

THE THIRD WOLF: MIRIAM
SPRING 1945

With the spring came the thaw. With the thaw came the stench. Flowers grew somewhere, but even vast carpets of blossoms couldn't overcome the smell of death.

Besides. Nothing grew here.

In the life before—the life Yael struggled to catch, hold, remember—death had been a shocking thing. A time for tears, a time for rituals and remembering. But when Yael's mother passed, there was no observing the seven days of shivah. There was no grave to pile high with visitation stones. There was no long, low male voice to recite the Kaddish prayer.

There was only this: Yael's mother there, then not.

Miriam tried to honor Rachel's memory by pulling some straw pieces from the mattress, twisting them together, and propping the braided piece against the wall. ("Just pretend it's a candle, burning," she said, looking at the straw with a set jaw.

"We cannot forget the dead, Yael. You must never forget the dead.")

After Yael's mother died, the монстр, monstre, monster whispers of Barrack 7 ceased. Yael found herself surrounded instead by silent, pitying glances. She kept to the corner of her old bunk. Clutching her dolls. Watching. Waiting.

Changing.

She found that if she thought hard enough, felt deep enough, she could control the change. Memories of her mother caught her first, showed her what was possible. Yael would look at the flea-specked mattress space (newly occupied by a woman with a shining, bald head, who still kicked in her sleep as if she had something to fight) and picture her mother there. As she was before, with the velvet fold of her rich hair. With constellations of freckles dotting her forearms.

Her being flared with sadness, beat with a black, black rage. Yael took the burn and pressed it into the hollow of her bones.

Made it hers.

Her hair grew, rippled fresh past her shoulders. Long and thick enough to braid. And one by one the freckles came, splashing across the inside of her arm, threading through the gaps in her numbers.

She was Yael, but not.

Not my Yael. Монстр. Monstre. Monster.

"Rachel?"

Yael's breath snagged. She looked up and saw Miriam. There were only seven (maybe eight) years between them, but the older girl was trying her best to fill the gap Yael's mother had left: reminding Yael to eat, clinging close for extra warmth at night, asking her about her doctor visits. Of all the residents in Barrack 7, Miriam alone did not seem bothered by Yael's topaz eyes or the pale-fire strands of her hair.

But as Miriam stood by their bunk, clutching two chunks of bread and taking in the face of Yael's mother, fear settled into her features. It clung to her jawline, shaded her skullcap curls. Her face was a two-way ghost: seeing one and being one.

"It's—it's me." Yael whispered this because she wasn't completely sure. The whispers had sunk too deep, too many times. "Yael."

Miriam's hands trembled; precious bread crumbs scattered to the floor. Her skin stayed as pale as the dead's when she finally swallowed her shock, crawled into their bunk.

"What are you doing?" Miriam asked Yael, and huddled close. The whole of her was like a wing—hovering over the younger girl, sheltering her in shadow. Yael realized this was so the other women of Barrack 7—who were filing back down the aisles, weary and worn—wouldn't be able to see how she'd changed.

Miriam was protecting her. The way the larger matryoshka dolls snapped over the small. Keeping them hidden.

"I—I don't know," Yael whispered. She kept looking at the freckles. The ones she always stared at when she was sad or scared. When her mother had held her close. It was so strange: seeing something that was gone, yet wasn't.

Her mother's freckles. On her arm.

Yael. But not.

"Can you do it again? Look like someone else?"

Could she? Yael shut her eyes. The first person she saw behind them was the Babushka, with her crow's-feet and piano-key smile.

Change things.

Change.

Yael felt the cold sadness of the snow. The smoke-haunt behind the old woman's eyes. She took these things and wrapped them inside her.

When she opened her eyes, Yael saw new lines in her skin—age and years she had not lived. Fingers worn by whittling knives. Muscles made wiry by jobs she had not worked. Her mother's lush tumbles of hair were gone. Silver now. And short.

Miriam's first question was not *How?* or *Why?*. Instead she frowned and tugged at her stunted black curls with nervous fingers. "Does the doctor know?"

Yael shook her head.

"Can you change back to the way you looked this morning?" Miriam asked.

Yael had seen that pastel Aryan face—the one that was hers, but not—only in pieces. In the polished gleam of the scalpel tray, in the shine of Dr. Geyer's glasses, in the uncertain puddles of the latrine. She shut her eyes and scraped up all these fragments, pasted them together with the burn she always felt when she was strapped to the gurney. Not the one the needles gave her, but the deeper one. The one that writhed and spit whenever the doctor's eyes met hers. The one that wished the smoke would eat him instead of the Babushka, Mama, everything else.

"That's good," Miriam whispered when the change had finished. "Stay that way. Don't show anyone. Especially not the doctor."

"Why?" Yael asked. She thought of the morning her mother did not get up with the rest, the morning Dr. Geyer saw Yael's transformation. He'd smiled so wide she was afraid his face might split apart, and offered her a whole handful of candies—as if pieces of sugar and sweet could make up for everything.

She couldn't imagine what he'd do if he saw this.

"This…" Miriam paused. "This is special. This can get you out of here."

━━━━━

"The host has a marvelous success rate. Over the course of a few months I've infected her with a number of manipulative compounds. It seems her melanin and pigment levels have responded accordingly."

Host. She'd been upgraded. No longer *subject* or *inmate.* She was a carrier, a shelter for disease.

Dr. Geyer and two officers formed a half-moon around the gurney. The newcomers had not introduced themselves to Yael, but she'd gathered their names by listening. One was

Josef Vogt, kommandant of the death camp. And the other was Reichsführer Heinrich Himmler, a man from Berlin who smelled like shoeshine and aftershave. Their faces were as pressed as their shirts, starched of all emotion as they studied the girl on the edge of the table. Blue eyes and blond hair. Shoulder blades and haunt.

"She does look very…Aryan." Reichsführer Himmler—the man with the most bars sewn into his uniform—spoke first. "Disturbingly so. How exactly does it work?"

Dr. Geyer had his arms outstretched, the way they'd been when Yael first saw him. His angel pose. Only this time he wasn't welcoming, but presenting, her. "I've been injecting the host with a compound I created meant to suppress melanin levels. This, of course, affects her hair, eyes, and skin. A chemical whitewashing from the inside."

"And there are no side effects?" Reichsführer Himmler asked.

"The onset is…dramatic. Life-threatening fevers, epidermal shedding. It *is* an infection, after all. But if the host is strong enough to survive the virus taking root, there seem to be no repercussions."

The Reichsführer's eyebrows rose high. "None? None at all?"

Don't show anyone. Yael was glad for Miriam's command. Glad that Dr. Geyer shook his head. Glad she had something none of these men could touch, steal, destroy.

Kommandant Vogt cleared his throat and adjusted his spectacles. "Dare I ask, Dr. Geyer, what exactly is the point of this research? You can dress her up, take her out, but filthy blood is still in her veins. She isn't pure."

Yael's eyes drifted down to the tiles by Reichsführer Himmler's freshly shined jackboots. The floors had been bleached for his visit—scoured white with bristles and prisoner sweat. Only the grout still held traces of darkness, blood long spilled.

She wondered if their blood—"pure blood"—was the same color.

"Agreed, Kommandant Vogt." Dr. Geyer nodded. "But think of the implications! If a Jewish urchin can appear Aryan, then why not the rest of us? What would take generations with eugenics could be accomplished with just a few injections! Those of us with flawless pedigrees who want more desirable traits can have them. Why, even the Führer himself..."

The two listeners went wide-eyed, and Dr. Geyer realized his mistake. He swallowed back the words with a shaking throat.

Reichsführer Himmler saved the room from its sterile silence. "A fascinating application, Dr. Geyer, and one I'm quite interested in, to tell the truth. But we'll need more proof that this host is not an anomaly. You need to test more hosts before you can consider infecting the general public. Perhaps, down the line, if your experiments continue to be fruitful, we can present them to Berlin.

"I think Experiment Eighty-Five shows much promise," he went on. "Keep up the good work."

Yael stared at the floor instead of the men. Not because she was afraid of them, but because she feared that the blackness and burn inside her might spill out. Trigger the change she could not let them see.

Kommandant Vogt's shoes shifted in a way that meant he was eager to leave. "Ah, gentlemen. I'm afraid you'll have to excuse me. It's Bernice's birthday, and I promised my wife I would be home in time for the party."

"Your daughter!" Reichsführer Himmler's voice was lighter now that he wasn't talking about good work and death. "How old is she?"

Yael looked up to see Kommandant Vogt's features transformed. He pulled a wallet from his pocket and held up a portrait of Bernice, tilted so even Yael could see the plum-dip dimples of her smile. Her hair was light—in curls almost as tight as Miriam's. A light mole dotted her left cheek.

Yael memorized the photograph, tucking all its details deep inside her.

"She's turning seven today. My wife is making seven-layer chocolate cake. It's Bernice's favorite."

Chocolate. A whole cake of it. The thought made Yael's stomach stretch, hollow with hunger that was always there. She stared at Bernice's photo and wondered what it was like, the unfenced life. With fathers and parties and seven-layer cakes.

Kommandant Vogt's wallet snapped shut. He'd caught her looking; Yael knew this from the squirm of his lips. The eyes that shunted so quickly from hers.

Perhaps they were harder to stare at, now that they were blue.

━━━

When she told Miriam about the photograph, the older girl actually smiled and Yael could see the pinch on the edge of her eyes. Crow's-feet that would not have a chance to grow.

She put her hands on Yael's shoulders. "You're certain it's Kommandant Vogt's daughter?"

"Yes. Her name's Bernice. She was turning seven. They made her chocolate cake."

"And you remember what she looks like?"

Yael nodded. It was hard to practice changing without a proper mirror, but she had. During lonely barrack days—when the others were off sifting through the clothes of the dead for things too valuable to turn to smoke—she stood over the scummy puddles of the latrine, catching pieces of herself echoed with the daylight. She was getting better at controlling the burn. Yael held other people's faces in her mind, sewed them to her bones with sadness and rage. She could never say *how* she did it. The skinshifts were like walking or chewing or crying—part reflex, half conscious. All pain.

Bernice was her favorite face to imitate because whenever she peered in the puddle and saw the baby-doll curls, she could pretend they really were hers. The chocolate cake, too.

The only thing she hadn't mastered was the girl's dimples. She had to practice grinning. Coax them out.

"Seven years old. She should be your size. Maybe taller. Fatter, too, if she's eating all that cake," Miriam muttered. "I'll ask some of the other women. See if they can help."

It was only the next evening, when Miriam returned from the sorting hall, that Yael realized what she was talking about.

"This should do." Miriam reached under the thin gray film of her workdress, pulled out another dress folded carefully into quarters.

Yael stroked it with barely there fingertips, afraid that if she pressed too hard, the dress would vanish. The fabric was soft, faded. Ruffles laced the edge.

"We got you shoes and a sweater, too." As if on cue, these items appeared on the mattress, offered by a number of hands that emerged from the gaunt rush of workers.

"You should be able to pass. Pretend you've been called to the doctor's. Once you reach the medical barracks, you change when no one is watching. Pretend you're looking for your father, Kommandant Vogt."

A guard's bark tore through the barrack doors. Miriam tucked the clothes quickly into the same mattress cavity the matryoshka dolls huddled in.

"But, Miriam . . . what about you?"

The other girl didn't respond with words. She reached out and squeezed Yael's hand. That was when Yael understood. Miriam was not coming with her.

Yael's chest was frozen—tight with fear, frosted with anger—her words felt stuck inside. She had to tear them out: "I—I can't."

There were wolves beyond the fence. She did not know if she could face them. Not without Miriam, or Mama, or the Babushka…

"Rachel was right; this place is death. People don't walk out of those gates." Miriam's eyes drifted through the door, to the ever-smoky sky. Her hand was still tight around Yael's. "But you can. You are special, Yael. You can *live*."

Live? In a world of fangs and lonely?

Or die. In a cage of smoke and needles.

Yael knew Miriam was right. But excuses still tumbled to the edge of her tongue. "But my arm, it has my numbers. I can't change them."

"Hide the marking under your sweater. They won't know the difference," she said.

"I don't want to leave you, Miriam." Yael felt her lips trembling. "I don't want to be alone."

"You're going to have to be brave." Miriam leaned back into the mattress and pulled out the Babushka's handiwork. She started to take the matryoshkas apart with small, loving twists. The same way the Babushka had. One by one the dolls fell away. Until only the smallest was left. "You won't be alone. I'll be thinking of you. And Rachel and the Babushka and all the others…they're watching."

"You really think so?" Yael was used to watchings: guard towers, medical inspections, the puckered-mouth nurse. It wasn't such a leap to think that the dead's eyes flickered above the smoke, alongside the stars.

"I have to." Miriam took the smallest doll, pressed it into

Yael's palm. "You can't take all the dolls. They're too big to fit in your pocket. I'll keep the others safe for you."

The wooden pea baby was so small, nearly lost in the folds of Yael's hand.

"If you feel lonely," Miriam went on, "you can look at it and know I have all the others."

So small by itself. It would get lost if she dropped it....

But she wouldn't. Yael's fist closed. She held it close to her heart and thought of all the invisible eyes. Watching.

"They'll all be together again someday." Miriam's voice crumbled. It was a promise both of them knew would never hold.

———

Nightfall. A time when the ugliness of the camp shone only in patches of electric light. Darkness oozed between the barracks, pooling into all the cracks the spotlights could not reach. These cracks were Yael's trail, her breathless path from Barrack 7. She walked them quickly, her shoulders stuck close to the barracks' walls.

The fence was her first obstacle—lacing electrified metal and barbed teeth that faced the railroad tracks. Yael had crossed it many times, in the wake of guards. It was the only path to the medical block. Her way out.

Two guards stood in front of the gate, their stares drifting through rows of bread-box barracks. Its bars crossed with giant, bracing X's of metal.

X's barred her from freedom. But it was an *X* that would let her pass, open the way to Dr. Geyer's office.

Yael filled her lungs with ashen air and stepped into the light. Her arm was turned outward so the scroll of numbers shone clearly. All the way down to the *X*.

—WALK STRAIGHT HEAD HIGH WORDS STRONG—

"I need to see Dr. Geyer," she told the guards.

Both men stiffened. Ever since the change, the camp guards eyed her the way the barrack women once had: their irises embroidered with fear.

"I'm feeling funny." She wrapped her arms around her stomach, where Miriam had flattened and bound the new shoes to her ribs. The yellow dress and sweater were hidden under her baggy workdress. "He told me to come and see him if that happened."

—COUGH FOR EFFECT—

The guards shrank back as if she were contagious.

"He'll be angry if you don't let me through." Yael spilled out all the lines Miriam had fed her.

The guards looked at each other, nodded some silent agreement.

The gate opened.

Yael could not breathe as she walked over the tracks. Every piece of her lit bright by the floodlamps. A perfect target for the rifles in the watchtowers, following her exposed frame. Even the hairs on her arm flared. Stolen clothes and shoes lumped under the sheer fabric of her workdress. It was a miracle the guards did not notice what she hid.

She could not see the stars from here, consumed as they were by lamps and smoke, but she felt the watchings. Yael imagined the Babushka just above her, showering magic and miracles.

—WALK STRAIGHT HEAD HIGH BE BRAVE—

Another miracle—she walked alone. Taking her path to freedom with small, uncertain steps. Crossing the tracks, back through the second gate.

Here she faltered. The gate closed behind her with a clang.

The gatekeepers kept their posts as Yael veered left. Toward the infirmary. The lamps were lesser here—strung along an empty walk of poplars and bricks—maintaining the illusion of a town. When she drew close to Dr. Geyer's office, she stopped.

This was as far as she could go as Yael. Jewish daughter. Experiment. Subject. Host. Inmate 121358ΔX.

Monster.

Yael tucked into the shadows, shed her workdress, doffed her wooden shoes, changed her skin. She pulled down the sweater sleeves Miriam had so carefully folded. Her numbers swallowed up by fragile, cashmere threads until even the X was gone.

She was Bernice Vogt now. With rag roll curls, a father who treasured her picture in his wallet, a mother who baked chocolate cake.

Yael looked into the glow of the infirmary window. Tried to imagine a whole piece of cake smoothing through her throat. Swelling her belly with velvet, cocoa rich.

This thought carried her up the steps of the medical block. Through the door.

—WALK STRAIGHT—

The hall's air felt thick, warm. Clotted with smells of salt, red, and iron. Her sweater itched against her skin.

The doctor was in. So was the sour-faced nurse. Both had their backs to the door. They stood over the gurney, over a small, unmoving lump. Red was in rivers on the floor. Veining along the grout. Staining the edges of Yael's stolen shoes.

—STOP—

She halted in the door, unable to peel her eyes off the blood. It looked so different fresh. Still clinging to life and bright.

Most of the children who go into his office do not come back again.

He's saving you.

Passing you over.

The Babushka's miracle, magic words spun in her head. The blood smell crept through her nostrils, clung to her insides. It made her words sticky and hot.

"Is my papa here?" she asked, and tried not to look at the hand that hung limp off the gurney. Its fingers wilted and blue and so, so small.

Dr. Geyer and his nurse looked up at the same time. Mirrored expressions: wide, frozen, horror. There was a scalpel in the doctor's fist and scarlet—dashed and dotted and crackling like radio code—across his lab coat. Only his face was pure white—drained, as if the blood soaking everything were actually his.

Staying Bernice was almost impossible. Imaginary chocolate cake roiled in her stomach, rotten bits of soup scaled her throat. She looked at the gap in Dr. Geyer's teeth and could not forget how much she hated him.

"B-Bernice? What are you doing in here?" It was the fear in the doctor's voice that helped her hold on. She was Bernice Vogt, the camp kommandant's daughter, standing in a red sea, seeing what no child should. These things seemed to upset Dr. Geyer more than cattle cars of families he shredded apart while standing on his apple crate, more than the blood that dripped from his hands.

So Yael stood straighter, ignored the quease in her stomach. "They told me Papa was in the medical buildings. I was sent to fetch him."

"Kommandant Vogt?"

She nodded. "What are you doing?"

Dr. Geyer tucked his scalpel behind his back—as if that could hide the tiny sliced body on the gurney—and scowled under his breath at the nurse, "Take care of her! And be certain she doesn't mention this to her father!"

The nurse set down her clipboard. She approached Yael with careful steps over the slick of tile-blood.

"Come with me, darling," she cooed as she tucked Yael's hand into hers—there were no bones, only the squish of fat. "Let's get you back home."

Yael wondered if she'd been this gentle with the hand

from the gurney. Before the lab-coated angel harvested its life...sliced and spread. She didn't look back as the woman tugged her away. Out into the night where the poplars' leaves rustled against a spring wind. So loud it almost drowned out the song of the barracks. So fresh it almost made Yael forget the sanguine stick in her throat.

Almost.

It was so easy—the nurse's way out. No gunshots. No sizzle of wires and smells of charred flesh. Gates swung open for her without a word, and she walked on through, pulled Yael with her.

"You mustn't tell anyone what you saw in there," the nurse said over her shoulder as she led the girl down the gravel path. A house sat at the end: glowing, cheery windows, a chimney spouting deathless smoke. The whole property was hedged in by a forest. Thick-trunked, glossy-needled pines. Perfect for disappearing into.

"Dr. Geyer, he tries very hard to fix people," the nurse went on. Tugging Yael behind her. "He looks for ways to make things better."

Progress.

But why, why, why? So much blood demanded an answer. Yael was hungry for it. Hungry enough to push one question further: "If he was making that person better, why was there blood everywhere?"

The nurse stopped. Those sausage-link fingers clamped around Yael's arm. Cushy fat crushing into those hidden numbers. The sugarcoating the nurse had tried so hard to keep on her face washed away, revealing the stone of a woman Yael knew so well. "Sometimes people have to die to make things better. It's a sacrifice for the good of everyone else. Do you understand?"

Yael understood these were easy words to say when you're the one standing over the altar. Plunging the knife. She also understood that Bernice Vogt would nod, because the seven-year-old with yellow hair and dimples would never be the sacrifice.

So that's what she did.

"Good," the nurse said.

Blood swam in Yael's memories, clung to her mouth. Her arm was still itching beneath her sweater, under the nurse's tight grip. She tugged her hand away. "I can walk by myself from here."

The nurse didn't argue or linger. She left the girl alone. Standing in the middle of the wide, fenceless road. Yael stood rooted there for a moment, a stump of disbelief, staring at the place that had just spit her out. Death had unhinged its jaws, let her tumble away.

She slipped her hand into her pocket, cradled the wooden pea baby in the crease of her life line, and tried not to think of all the pieces she had to leave behind, even though they left her heart gaping. Were they flesh or wood? Did it matter? Both could burn. . . .

Bernice Vogt's face slipped away. The ghost girl whispered to a smokeless sky, "I'm Yael. I'm alive."

The heavens—full of the dead's eyes and stars—whispered

back: *You are special. You can live. You are going to change things.*

—NO MORE WALKING STRAIGHT RUN NOW DON'T LOOK BACK—

Yael turned and vanished through the pines.

CHAPTER 12

NOW

MARCH 16, 1956
NORTH COAST OF AFRICA

The desert was a thing of beauty. Powder and earth yawned out under a canopy sky. Caramel dunes rippled, edges shimmering under the wind. The air swam—never still—with granules and *heat*.

The road (if one could call it that) ran along the coast, where sands stretched and slid into a glistening sea. The path they drove along was narrow, pitted, strewn with rocks. Speed was not an option here. The sand was too slippery, and potholes gouged the road. Yael's Zündapp shuddered over rocks, rattling her bones until she feared they might shatter. After several days on the bike, every part of her body was sore: calves, gluteus maximus, thighs, shoulders, back, arms, neck, face, even her fingernails and teeth. The day of rest on the ferry crossing the Mediterranean Sea had, in Yael's opinion, only made the pain worse.

She'd made up for it since. Three days of vicious riding with little rest. Rarely stopping, never slowing. It felt like an impossible pace, but even this wasn't enough to overtake Katsuo and Luka. The pair forged ahead. First and second. Neck and neck. Dust clouds spun behind them like angry jinns, clotting Yael's nose, lodged between her teeth. She rode with her armband as a makeshift scarf, straining to see the biggest potholes and swerving to avoid them.

But no matter how hard she swerved, how much she flirted with dangerous speeds, Yael stayed a solid third.

Two hours. Ten minutes. Twenty-eight seconds. The gap between herself and the leaders was growing dishearteningly large. (She'd lost another five seconds on the road to the ferry.) Time Yael was beginning to believe she'd never gain back. Not at this rate—weaving and rattling and choking on Luka's tracks. Yael kept waiting for a slip, a mistake, but Katsuo and Luka were flawless.

And so she must be.

The kilometers rolled on. Sand flayed Yael's goggles, scrubbed her cheeks raw. Thorny thirst twisted around her throat. It had been hours—a high sun—since her last break. And that was only long enough for a few sips of water and a fresh canister of gasoline from a coastal village.

Even the evening did not bring relief. When the sun fell, the sands embraced its fire. The whole world melted amber— trapping Katsuo's and Luka's silhouettes. The pair had slowed. Only whispers of dust peeled off their tires as they tried to navigate the stretching shadows. Darkness washed in fast, flooding the desert and paving the road. The motorcycle's headlamp was useless. It lit the dust—bright golden fog. Hazing everything until all Yael could see were her handlebars and Katsuo's and Luka's taillights. Still riding.

She could not slow. She could not stop.

Now was the time for reclaiming time. While Luka and Katsuo crawled, she would fly. Even tired. Even scoured. Even parched. Even blind.

She could not lose this race.

Yael's bike bucked down, writhing as its front tire clawed up the jagged side of a pothole. Her sand-gagged scarf caught most of her curses as the Zündapp's engine roared. Strained. In the sickening space between heartbeats, she feared it might stop, fall back into the hole. But the tread of her tire held true.

Katsuo's and Luka's taillights kept fading. Away, away. Yael wrenched the throttle. The Zündapp's engine bellowed, and the bike shot forward into the too-bright dust. Her front tire caught the next pothole with a twist. For a moment Yael was flying, through dust and air and dark. Arms stretched wide as wings.

And then she fell.

The road clamped onto her, sliding its rocky teeth along the soft of skin. The tough of leather. *Pain.* That was all there was, for seconds. The road's bite sank—deeper and deeper—into Yael's body. She tried to cry out, but her lungs wouldn't move. No sound. No air.

No air.

No air.

When she finally gasped again, it was a thick, nothing breath. Clotted with dust. Too much like smoke.

Pain.

Yael was afraid to move. Afraid of what she would discover when she did. All her nerves were on overload, frayed. It was impossible to tell where the hurt was coming from. Her leg could be shattered. Her collarbone, bowed. Her wrist, snapped…

It was the sound of another engine that finally stirred her. A roar, then a purr, then a sputter. A bright headlamp. Fourth place was pulling to a stop, leaping off his bike, coming for her. Yael's reflexes worked through the agony. Vlad's training kicked in, twisting her up, drawing her gun, switching off the safety. Yael stared down the sights with a rattling breath.

At least her wrists weren't broken.

The silhouette swept toward her, paper-cut sharp against the glare of the headlamp. She held the pistol steady, aiming it at fourth place's chest. But the boy didn't stop.

"Oh, *Scheisse!*" It was Felix. Kicking breathlessly through the sand. Yael's instincts stayed strong. She held her P38 higher. Adele's brother froze at the sight of the gun, terror glared across his face. His hair was bright and fractured against the glow of the Zündapp's headlamp.

"Ad." He spoke slowly with his hands out. "It's me. Felix. You've had a bad fall. Put the gun down."

There were sparks in Yael's eyes, swimming like her

thoughts. *Would Adele keep the gun pointed at her brother? No? Yes? Maybe?*

Her gun hand shook.

So many sparks. No air.

—KEEP BREATHING—

Maybe? Yes?

No.

She dropped the gun with a gasp.

Felix knelt down in the sand, arms still outstretched. Hovering over her. Frantic but never touching. "Are you hurt?"

Her breaths were coming easier now. In, out. In, out. The sparks faded, but the pain—it was everywhere. Gently, gently Yael tested each limb. Arms, legs. Feet, hands. Left, right. Nothing was broken. It was just pain. And it would pass. The kind that settled in skin always did.

She was shaken, bleeding, raw. But she could still race.

"I'm f-fine." The words crumbled out of Yael. All her strength she saved for pushing against the sand, managing a stand on wobbly legs.

One step. Two. Her knees felt like tinfoil: crumble, bend, crunch.

"Fine? *Fine?*" Felix's white eyebrows flew into his hairline. "*Scheisse*, Ad. You don't just get up from something like that."

I do. Yael clenched her teeth and kept walking.

Felix matched her pace easily. "Where is it, exactly, that you plan on going?"

"My bike…" Where was it? All Yael could see was light

and dust and Felix. She must've been thrown a good distance from the motorcycle. Her unshattered bones were becoming more and more of a miracle.

"No!" Adele's brother snapped, then immediately softened. "No. Look at yourself. You're an absolute mess. We need to clean those wounds before they become infected."

He was right. But Luka and Katsuo were still on the road, and the seconds were turning into minutes....

She kept walking.

Felix kept up, step for step. "These riding conditions are *Scheisse.* Nil visibility, potholes every other second—you wouldn't make it a hundred meters in your condition."

I will. But even as Yael thought this, she was starting to doubt herself. Her tinfoil knees were crumpling fast, and her motorcycle was nowhere in sight.

"Ad, please...don't..." Felix swallowed. His brow furrowed into something sad. "Don't end up like Martin."

No wonder Felix looked so fearful when he first ran up to her. He'd seen that scene before: sibling flung off a bike, lying broken on the road.

The mention of the other brother's name—the *history she did not fully know* behind it—made Yael frantic. The bike, it had to be somewhere. She stopped, did a 360-degree survey of the dusk-crowned road.

Sand. Dark. Sand. There! Seventy degrees back. A lump that was too large, too sharp, too twisted to be a desert formation.

One good look and Yael's heart fell. Her motorcycle had not fared quite as well as her body. The Zündapp lay sideways in the road, contorted, wheel up. Its chrome was fuzzed with scratches, slate paint dented and chipped. One side of its leather seat was shredded. Motor oil oozed like blood into the sands.

Felix walked over to the wreck. "It's probably a good thing you never got around to naming it. I haven't seen you go through a bike that fast since the one you wrecked in '51. You hadn't even had it twenty-four hours, and you cracked the axle. Papa was so mad."

Adele's brother bent down, salvaging the Zündapp's pieces with his eyes. "Axle seems fine this time, though. I'll take a closer look once we get you cleaned up and set up camp."

They were camping together? But—she'd tried so hard to shake him off, keep her distance. Cold shoulders in the refueling stations, scuttling to the opposite end of the Mediterranean ferry, putting in days of full-throttle kilometers...all to end up here. Stranded in the middle of the desert with the person who knew Adele Wolfe best in the world. Bike names and backstory and all...

How long would it take Felix to realize Yael was not his sister?

And what would she do when that happened?

Was that a line she could cross?

Every muscle in Felix's body strung tight as he shouldered Yael's Zündapp, shoved it upright. He was strong—it took him only one try, where Yael supposed it should be two. Were they to fight, she'd have to rely on speed. Take him out before he had a chance to blink. Much less throw a punch.

"Priority one is getting you patched up," Felix called over

his shoulder as he unlatched her panniers. Fished out her first-aid kit and an electric lantern, which he wielded straight in her face. "Your skin looks like schnitzel and pasta sauce blended with gravel."

She'd figured as much. Road rash spread hot over her neck, onto her face.

"Get ready." Felix picked an amber bottle from the first-aid kit and unscrewed the dropper. Yael could mark that smell anywhere: iodine. "This won't feel very nice."

Again, she'd figured as much. But even bracing herself while Felix positioned the dropper over her raw cheeks didn't help. *Drip, plop.* Two tiny splashes of iodine and an entire fresh wave of pain.

"*Schei—serlksm.*" Yael's curse fell apart as she clenched her teeth.

"Sorry." Felix sounded like he meant it. "I'm not the best doctor. Hitler Youth first-aid training only goes so far."

The sting of the iodine plus Felix's purely unironic words added with other doctor memories caused Yael to laugh. Adele's brother was far, far and away from the worst.

If only he knew.

No—if he knew it was "tainted" blood he was touching... who she really was...

Yael's laugh wilted into a shudder.

Felix pulled a pair of tweezers from the kit. "Stay still. I need to pick out some of these bigger rock pieces."

Why did getting better hurt so much? She needed something to distract her, Yael decided when the first gravel bit was yanked from her flesh. "Back in Prague. Why did you drug my soup?"

It took two more rock pieces, another drop of iodine, and a patch of gauze taped to her cheek before Adele's brother started speaking. "You didn't leave me any other choice."

More iodine on the second cheek. Sting and tears.

"You haven't been there, Ad. You haven't seen——" Felix stopped; he sounded like *he* was the one who was getting his skin scraped up and minced. "While you've been cocooned up in that Germania flat, I've been at home, trying to hold things together. Running the garage, trying to get Mama out of bed every day, watching Papa's hair get grayer and grayer.

"I've been trying to hold them together. But I can't." There was a weight behind his whisper. A weight Yael *understood*. Because it was always there. Pressing down, down, down at night. Pressing on, on, on during the day. "I just can't. Not by myself.

"I know why you ran away. Believe me, I've thought of it myself sometimes...." Felix's face grew shame red in patches. As if he'd said something he shouldn't. "But Mama and Papa need me. And they need *you*, Ad. If you die, this will kill them."

"I'm not going to die," Yael said.

More gravel tugged out with tears. A long, smarting silence.

"You asked how I got into the race," he started. "I sold the auto shop. Used the money to bribe Dirk Hermann and the officials."

Yael had never been to the garage, but she'd seen pictures

of where Adele grew up. A house barricaded by mountains of spare tires and car parts. It was the Wolfe family's stake in the ground. A place of generations.

"The auto shop?" She strung out her voice, tried to twine perfect hints of anger, loss. (It wasn't so hard with a face on fire.) "You sold Papa's garage?"

"I'd do anything to keep you safe, Adele. I'd sell the garage a thousand times over if I had to." He patched the second cheek and moved the iodine dropper down her neck. "You need to come home. Before something worse happens."

A last-ditch effort to get a wayward sister home—that's all the drugged soup was. (And, truthfully, all Yael suspected it to be.) Felix was trying to put his family back together. *Snap, snap, snap*, safe. Just like the matryoshka dolls.

Yael couldn't think ill of him for it. Not when the smallest doll sat so lonely in her pocket. Not when the picture of the happy siblings in Adele's flat made her heart crawl. If she still had family, she'd fight for them, too.

She was fighting. Still. Even though the dolls Miriam kept were as gone as the girl herself. Beyond saving.

Yael craned her neck up to the sky, so Felix could patch the wounds there. Above them light broke through the black in thousands: the dead's eyes and stars. The view spoke to the deepest parts of her, gorgeous and hopeful and sad all at once.

"I can handle Luka and Katsuo," Yael told him.

The tweezers trembled at the sound of Luka's name. Jabbed a little extra hard into her neck. "I still can't believe you stood up for that *Saukerl*. After what he tried to do to you..."

When Yael stared down the length of her nose, she could

see Felix's jaw knotted tight, his nostrils flared. Such a sudden, fierce anger. Not for nothing.

"Luka Löwe is an *Arsch*," he said, once he'd regained his composure. "But it's not him I'm worried about. Or Katsuo. Look, I swore on my life not to say anything, which is why I didn't tell you sooner, but something's going to happen during this race. Something dangerous. Something big."

He knows about my mission. It took all of Yael's training for her to stay still. Eyes back to the stars.

"Who told you that?" This might not have been the right question, but Yael wanted its answer. The details of her mission had been kept only to the highest levels of resistance leadership. The rest of the partisans all over the map had simply been told by their cell leaders to *be ready*.

Was Felix part of the resistance? If so, Henryka and her informants had missed this information; there was nothing in Adele's brother's file about partisan activity. More likely the secrets of Yael's mission were slipping, down the ranks, through the cracks.

Neither option was terribly good.

"It doesn't matter who told me. All I know is that we can't stick around much longer. Even if your bike can be fixed, it'll take an act of God for you to catch up on these roads. I know how stubborn you are, but the Double Cross isn't worth your life. Think about the people who *love* you. Papa, Mama, me. Don't we matter?"

Yael shut her eyes, and the stars' brilliant light was gone. Only darkness and the burn, burn, burn of bruises blooming down her arms. Under the road-gnawed leather of her sleeves. Between the markings of the ones who had loved her.

Had. So much of her life was in the past.

"This is worth it," she said, and looked at him.

Those eyes—blue on hurt on blue. It was as if she'd just raised her gun again and shot Felix through the heart. His stare fell down to the dropper. "You should take your jacket off. Some of the road rash got under your collar."

Yael could. But the sleeves of her undershirt were thin, while the bandage over Vlad's wolf was noticeably thick. It was the sort of thing an attentive brother like Felix would not overlook. Just like the patrolman in Germania, Felix would ask. Question would lead to question would lead to question....

There were five reasons Yael could not do this. Five reasons why she stood (her feet were much steadier now). Five reasons she said, "I can fix the rest on my own," and moved to start setting up her pup tent.

There were five reasons, and they mattered the most.

CHAPTER 13

NOW

MARCH 16, 1956

Yael did not take off her jacket. (Changing the bandages on Vlad's wolf could wait. She was too afraid Felix might come bursting into the tent at the wrong moment, see all.) Instead she sat by the tent flap, ate a packet of dried field rations, and listened. Felix hadn't disappeared back into his tent like she'd hoped. Instead he was working. Filling the night with the chokes of a failing motor as he tried to bring her Zündapp back to life.

It was clear now that the motorcycle was past saving, leaking its own oily epitaph into the sand. But despite this—despite Felix's wanting nothing more than for his sister to drop out of the race, go home—he kept working. Knees in the cold sand, shoulders hunched. The wind was picking up, moaning outside the tent. Sand hissed against the tarp. Fuzzed around Felix's lantern. Bit into his tools.

And still he worked.

Partisan or not, Felix was a good brother. Adele didn't know what she had.

Which made Yael even more sorry for what she was about to do. It might take an act of God for her to get ahead, but before that happened she needed a bike.

Felix's perfectly whole Zündapp sat parallel to hers. All Yael had to do was pack up her tent and switch the panniers. If she was lucky, the wind would be enough to mask the sound of the engine crank as well. By the time Adele's brother woke up, she'd be long gone. He'd spend a day or two stranded in the desert until the caravan of supply trucks made its way through. That far behind and he'd be certain to forfeit. Out of race, out of mind.

Simple. No secrets spilled, no lines crossed.

Yael chewed her jerky and waited until Felix packed his wrenches away, walked back to his tent. She waited a few more minutes before she crept outside, her footsteps feather light as she made her way to the motorcycles. Swapping out the panniers should've been easier than it was. Yael's wreck-shocked fingers were clumsy on the buckles. Sand whipped through her hair, stung against the back of her neck. The wind had picked up from gusts to a steady, rushing force. Yael had to shield her face as she turned back toward the tent.

And then she saw it.

Really, it was more what she did *not* see. Where a crescent fingernail moon had hung moments before was only black. And the stars—the stars were being eaten alive, light by light. Swallowed into a darkness that had nothing to do with the night.

It was a sandstorm. Reiniger had warned her about them. He'd seen plenty during his war years: walls of dust that rolled from the horizon, as fast as a swarm of locusts.

Take shelter. Hunker down, Reiniger had told her. *Breathe light so the sand doesn't get in your lungs. You'll be useless until it passes. No light. No air.*

She had to get inside. So many stars were gone now, and she'd ventured out without a lamp, but Yael knew it was eight paces from the motorcycles to her tent. She had no choice but to plunge for it.

The storm—it wasn't just howling. It was an army of noise: threading, twining, roaring all around. Dust seeped through the cracks in her facial bandages, watered the edges of her eyes. She had to push her way against the wind, through the living rivers of sand at her feet. The tent held true as Yael pried her way in, coughing as if her lungs depended on it.

More of Reiniger's advice was coming back to her: *Most times the storms are small. They roll over in an hour or so.* She'd have to wait it out. Make her move for the bike once the hour (or so) was up.

But the storm only grew worse. The hour or so stretched into two. The wind cried louder, and the tent leaned further, until Yael was certain it was only her weight keeping the structure in place. The walls and floor were gone. It was all just a tangle of plastic, cocooning Yael against the sands.

She slept it out, curled up in a fetal position, catching

snatches of dreams. Sometimes it was hard to tell what was sleeping and what was waking, since her nightmares were also made of howls and darkness.

But finally the light came. Morning sun cut through a deep orange haze. The wind dropped, the clouds thinned, and Yael pulled back the tarp.

The land was changed, a desert reborn. Sand as far as the eye could see. Everything was covered in it, Yael discovered as she started to dig her way out of the tarp. Felix's tent was half swamped, and the Zündapps sat hub deep. She'd have to dig the motorcycle out, too—and fast if she wanted to be back on the road before Felix woke up.

It was only when Yael stood and started walking toward the bikes that she noticed the hitch in her plan: There was no road. The potholes, the rocks, the gravel—all of it was gone. The dunes stretched all the way to the sea. It was so silent, Yael realized as she looked out over the tabula rasa landscape. No wind, no engines. The sun was well over the horizon, but no one was racing. Without a road, most of the racers were stranded.

Sand was tricky to drive in, but not impossible. She had a compass and a map. And even if those failed, she knew the stars. Yael could find her way to Cairo. Road or no.

This was her act of God. Her chance to get ahead.

She sprang toward Felix's bike and started digging. Palmful by palmful, she excavated the first wheel. It took longer than she liked. The sand was silky and loose, and kept sliding back into her trench.

She didn't make it to the second wheel.

"Ad! Have you seen this?"

Dread pooled at the bottom of Yael's stomach when she heard Felix's voice. She twisted around, so it looked as if she were examining her own shattered motor. She could see Adele's brother through the gaps in the bike's broken gears—stretching in front of his pup tent.

Oh, how she wished he'd kept sleeping.

"Ad?" he called again. "You awake?"

Yael slid her hand into her P38 pocket and stood. "Over here! Just looking at the engine."

He smiled. (The sight left her amazed and sick all at once. How could he smile at her, after everything she'd said and done? How could she grip her pistol, after everything he'd said and done?) "You really scratched it up," he said, walking over. "There are two big cracks in the engine block, and the carburetor is completely busted. I can fix it, but we're going to have to wait for the maintenance van."

Usually cradling the Walther P38 in her palm centered Yael: life, death, power. But this time she felt her own pulse rattling against the metal. Hard and scattered. Not ready.

Felix pulled out the pocket watch he'd looked at in Adele's apartment. Up this close, Yael could confirm that the watch had seen (vastly) better days. Its edges were blunted and warped, the glass on its face, cracked. Felix clicked it open only a second before shutting it again. "It's late. Not that time really matters out here. Might as well eat something." He moved over to his bike and started to unbuckle the pannier. "I've got some protein bars in here if you want some. Drug free."

Adele's brother was wrong. Time *did* matter out here, which was why Yael lined up like a shadow behind him as he spoke. She slid out her gun, stared at the back muscles beneath Felix's thin cotton shirt. Already spotted with sweat against the morning sun.

He means well. He loves his sister. He doesn't deserve this.

"That's odd. I thought I packed them somewhere in here," Felix was mumbling to himself, digging through the pannier that wasn't his.

Just knock him out, Yael's pulse prodded. *Get it over with. Quick.*

Her hand scabbed around the pistol. She couldn't make it move.

Felix's own hands slowed. His back muscles clenched. "This—this is your stuff."

Too late. Adele's brother was turning. *It's now or never.*

Yael's boots sprayed sand as she launched at the boy. Felix did not fight back. He didn't even try to shield himself as she whipped the pistol—a starburst blow to his temple. He crumpled to earth.

Yael was shaking, and she tasted jerky bile in her mouth, but she worked quickly: gathering the rest of her belongings from the sand, digging out the motorcycle's rear tire, packing her panniers to the brim. Felix stayed motionless, faceup, arms splayed out, so it looked as if he were trying to make sand angels.

The desert's heat was building, layer by cruel layer. Yael knew it would be many minutes, maybe even hours, before Felix woke from the blow she'd dealt him. Too long to lie exposed under a high African sun. So she took an extra minute to drag him into his tent—*Scheisse, he's heavy for such a wiry boy! All muscle!*—trying not to look at the nasty bruise already swelling against his eye socket.

Then she left him there. And rode on.

Driving a motorcycle through sand was like trying to sprint through water or run inside a dream. Impossibly slow. It took Yael several tries to get the Zündapp's tires level and moving. Every time the wheels caught and burrowed deep she had to slide off. Dig it out with strength and painstaking technique. It was exhausting, sweat-glazed work.

Constant speed was key. She slid all the way to the back of the seat, finding the perfect balance so that her weight wouldn't drown the wheels.

The way was long, gritty, hot. But she was moving. Yael let the sun guide her, gauging her path east. She knew she was on the right track when she mowed past Luka's tent. His head popped out at the rumble of her engines. Like every other racer, he was hunkered down, waiting for the supply vans to make their way through with further instructions. He'd been shaving, his jaw half masked in creamy lather. The look on his face was one Yael knew she would treasure—mouth open, stray bubbles dripping from his chin.

She flashed him a grin. Even took the time to wave.

Luka's eyes sobered. He ducked back into his tent.

Katsuo's camp was just two dunes on. He squatted in front of it, his hands covered in glittering scales as he gutted a fresh Mediterranean fish. When he saw Yael's bike, he stood—his

148

catch forgotten in the sand. He made no movement toward her or her bike, nor did he rush back into his tent as Luka had. Instead he tracked Yael's progress with his eyes, knife clenched tight in his fist.

Yael didn't bother waving.

She kept inching furiously ahead, chasing those two hours, ten minutes, twenty-eight seconds. The storm's breadth was massive; its waste stretched on and on. Sand stuck to her wheels and drowned the motor. Yael's only comfort was that Katsuo and Luka were fighting the same forces. Plying their way down the roadless path. Centimeter by centimeter.

And, finally, the road. Yael's goggles fogged with tears of joy when she saw it: the spine of rocks and solid that rose from the sand. When her wheels reached it, she shot forward. No dust clouds, no silhouettes, no well-meaning brothers...

The way was clearer than ever now.

CHAPTER 14

NOW

MARCH 18, 1956
CAIRO CHECKPOINT
KILOMETER 5,742

For two days Yael rode alone. Every town she passed was empty, with the exception of the Axis Tour refueling stations, which housed a few sunburnt Aryan faces. Sand pushed against the dwellings' doors like snowdrifts. No one had lived on this coast for years. According to Reiniger, the villages' native populations had been deported to labor camps within a year of the Great Victory. She was driving through a dead land.

Yael's pace through this final stretch of desert had been a hefty one, fueled by Luka's gleaming stare. Katsuo's knife. Her night camp had been short. She'd stayed on the road until the last traces of light had left, and packed up her broken tent before the dawn-glow lined the eastern dunes. Fuel and water were her only day stops, precious minutes spent in skeleton towns. Every time she refilled her gas tank and her canteens, she studied the road behind her. Scanning the horizon for dust and motion.

They were coming. She felt it in her bones. The urgent need to stay ahead. And she was ahead. Hers was the very first Zündapp to reach Cairo. This city, at least, was thriving. Its air swam with the heady smells of diesel and incense. Dried dung and heat. Its streets were tangled and alive: carts heavy with pomegranates and figs, kneeling camels, impatient jeeps. Yael wove through these as best she could, all the way to the checkpoint.

The Axis Tour officials weren't expecting her. The time-keeper slouched, asleep, in his chair. The Reichssender staff and Japanese journalists sat around a weathered card table, with cooling scarves wrapped around their heads, bottles of mineral water sweating by their elbows.

When Yael rolled into the compound courtyard, their expressions looked as Luka's had: stunned, then resolved as they scurried for their cameras. The timekeeper nearly fell out of his chair as he rushed to record her time.

Adele Wolfe: 5 days, 6 hours, 11 minutes, 28 seconds.

Yael wiped days of dust from her still bandaged face and took in the numbers. Under a week, road time, from Germania to Cairo. It was a good pace. Excellent, actually.

But would it be enough?

She had two hours, ten minutes, and twenty-eight seconds to find out.

Yael's answers to the Reichssender's questions were half-hearted, breathless things. (Yes, the storm was bad. Yes, of course, it felt good to reach Cairo first. No, she'd had no idea her brother would enter the race.) Her attention was on the road as she took off her jacket, replenished the beads of sweat along her brow with swigs of mineral water.

An hour passed.

She watched the street from the card table, making wet O's in the wood with her bottle. Picking at the bowl of dried figs and dates. Twisting the ends of Adele's fair hair (this might have soothed Adele's nerves but did nothing for hers). Anything to make the seconds go faster.

Every engine sputter, every peel of distant wheels, revved Yael's heart. She kept expecting to see Luka's bike rounding the corner. Or Katsuo braced on his Zündapp, determined to keep the number one in front of his name. But it was not them...not them...not them.... The minutes crept by. Hope hitched higher and higher in Yael's throat.

The compound's gate stayed empty. For two hours, ten minutes, twenty-*nine* seconds.

I'm ahead! All those months training on the autobahns, collecting kilometers and road rashes...they were not for nothing. These thoughts fizzed bright as Yael watched the timekeeper chalk Adele Wolfe's name in the top slot. She raised her empty bottle of mineral water, toasting a cloudless sky: *Cheers to that!*

Luka rounded the corner first, the whole of him coated in dust as his bike skidded to a stop. His face was lopsided with hair. He'd never finished shaving.

Luka Löwe: 5 days, 6 hours, 21 minutes, 2 seconds.

"You look ridiculous." Yael, still soaring on her triumph, couldn't help but tease the boy as he approached her table with stiff, saddle-sore steps.

"Says the girl wearing more bandages than a mummy." Luka collapsed into a chair and rested his feet unceremoniously on the tabletop. Boots, dust, and all. "Where's brother-dear?"

Yael fished a spare date out of the bowl. In those long hours when there was nothing but her, sky, and road, she'd tried her hardest not to think of Felix. How he'd crumpled without a fight. How she'd just left him—adrift in a sea of sand, with a throbbing temple, and a broken bike.

The memory was nagging at her. More than it should have. But he was out of the race now. Yael only hoped that he hadn't overheated inside the tent.

"I'm not his keeper," she said, and bit into the date.

"Well, he certainly seems to be yours." The tape was gone from Luka's nose, but he still traced it gingerly. His fingertips raked away lines of dust, showed the bruised purple beneath. "It's fortunate my looks are handsome enough to afford some ruggedness."

"I can keep myself just fine." Yael nodded at the board, where Luka's time was being chalked. Second place.

There was a chorus of horns from the marketplace. A spray of seeds and color as crates of fruit went tumbling to the ground. All this laced with vendors' curses as Katsuo rounded the corner and blew past the timekeeper. His bike cut to a halt at the last possible moment, its front tire shuddering just centimeters from the table. Flooding Luka's and Yael's faces with dust and exhaust.

Katsuo didn't look at his numbers. His eyes honed in on Yael as he stepped off his bike. It was a hunter's stare: thirsty and grim through his goggles. Yael met it, held it, biting down on the date pit so hard she feared her teeth might break.

Finally the boy turned. Walked away without a word.

"You're in the crosshairs now, Fräulein. You might be able to keep yourself, but no one gets through this race alone." Luka uncrossed his legs, leaned over the table. Closer, closer. Until Yael could feel the bristle of his unshorn jaw, smell the rich leather of his jacket. And although the sun broiled hot above them, Yael felt goose bumps singing just under the surface of her skin, threatening to break out. Adrenaline. Fear. Something else.

Something *more*.

The victor's lips were so close to Yael's ear all he had to do was whisper, "Soon, very soon, you're going to need me."

CHAPTER 15

THEN

THE FOURTH WOLF: AARON-KLAUS
PART 1
AUTUMN 1949

Yael was alone.

There were months spent in the forests, where she ate berries and mushrooms and listened to real wolves howl. There were nights tucked away in haylofts, where she munched on horse oats and fell asleep to the lullaby lowing of cows. And weeks of walking, walking, walking. The food was better in the cities—loaves of bread, sausage links, apples as shiny as spit—but it was guarded by so many eyes. Nearly impossible to steal without getting caught.

She stole money instead. Yael found that she liked picking pockets. It wasn't hard, especially in Germania. She was blond and small and went unnoticed in crowds. She hunted by the river Spree, where couples walked hand in hand and flocks of schoolchildren ran amok.

Yael always leaned by the river barrier, her fingers worrying the edges of her sweater sleeve as she watched and waited for money to saunter toward her in the form of gold watches and wallets.

It was best when schoolchildren dashed past. Yael could pretend she was one of them. Misstepping, bumping into some Germanian's shoulder, using that shocked second to fish her fingers down their pockets, cry an apology, and run off. Reichsmarks richer.

She always got rid of the wallets downriver (splash, sink, gone). The bills and coins she tucked in her pocket, alongside the smallest doll. She would change her face and her clothes in a nook under a bridge and go buy bread.

It was a good system. Yael rarely went hungry.

But one day she made a mistake.

The young man was an obvious target. His arms were full of parcels and envelopes. He walked so fast that his overcoat billowed to the sides. Too hurried to notice the beauty of the Spree's currents or the boats that bobbed like hunched gulls along the river wall.

It was too early for the schoolchildren yet, and the river walk was strangely empty. There were no crowds to disappear into.

She should have let him pass.

But it was one of those rare days when Yael was hungry (the crowds had been slim all week, and she'd spent the last of her Reichsmarks on a new sweater with sleeves long enough for her growing arms). The hunger wasn't yet desperate or bone-gnawing, but it was there, scooping hollow pains into her stomach. Desert places, missing pieces.

Yael hated feeling empty.

So, just as the young man moved past, she stepped out, into him.

The collision was harder than she'd expected. The young man's parcels tumbled; his envelopes spun. He fell to his knees and started collecting them before Yael could stammer sorry and slip her fingers into his pocket.

She knelt next to him. Grabbing the nearest envelope with her right hand and fishing into his pocket with the other. Yael was halfway through the transaction when she noticed the stamp on the envelope she was holding.

The bird with the broken cross.

He was one of *them*.

—RUN LIVE CHANGE THINGS GET AWAY GET AWAY GET AWAY DON'T LET HIM SEE—

Yael tore her hand out (walletless) and tried to run. But the National Socialist had been watching. As her arm pulled away, he caught the cuff of her sweater.

Off came the sleeve. Out came her skin. Yael twisted to a stop, and time went still, frozen by the sight of her numbers. They shone blacker than ever in the twilight hour. There, there, there, under the sorrowing blue sky for all to see.

The young man grabbed her wrist, reading the ink as dark as his Reich stamp.

"I see," he said slowly.

—GET AWAY GET AWAY—

She tried, but the National Socialist's grip was too tight.

The young man looked around the riverbank. Still empty except for the scatter of packages at his feet. His fingers

157

loosened—not enough for Yael to run, but enough for his next words to mean something. "I'm not going to hurt you."

This caused her to look at him (really look, not just as a target or an enemy). *Boy* was still traced in his features: the nervous bob of his Adam's apple, the acne sowed in his hollow cheeks. His eyes were blue at first glance, but not quite enough when you really looked. His stare held a softness she did not expect.

"I can help you." The young man let go of Yael's arm. He started rolling up his own sleeve.

This was her chance to run. Escape back to lonely.

The numbers stopped her again. But this time they did not belong to Yael.

They belonged to the National Socialist.

There on his left forearm—between braids of throbbing teal veins—115100AΔ. As black and sloppy and permanent as her own.

"Will you let me help you?" he asked.

Her answer was to kneel to the ground again and start picking up the eagle-stamped envelopes. The young man, not–National Socialist, tugged his sleeve back down and nodded at Yael's bare arm.

"Cover up and follow me," he said.

And that was how she met Aaron-Klaus.

———

Yael was amazed at how much the young man knew. About himself. About the world.

His real name was Aaron Mayer. Born in 1933 to a laundress and a tailor in a small Bavarian town. His childhood was filled with yellow stars—sewn to his clothes, pasted to the window of his father's shop—and broken glass. He was ten when the trains took him.

His fake name was Klaus Frueh. Born in 1933 to a watchmaker and a housewife in Munich. His childhood was filled with swastikas—pinned to his lapel, draped in the window of his father's shop—and "Blood and honor!" He was ten when he joined the Hitler Youth.

Aaron Mayer survived in a death camp for a whole year. One of the officers picked the boy out of the lines to clean his house, weed his garden. The officer's wife grew fond of the boy, to a fault. She hid him in an empty shipment truck.

The resistance found him, fed him, gave him papers.

Klaus Frueh began to exist.

Aaron-Klaus could not be reintegrated like the other children the resistance came across. He would not fit back into a normal life: the war orphan with perfect papers sent to live with his distant relatives in the Alps. His numbers—his Aaron Mayer–ness—would not be erased, so he stayed with the resistance.

Its headquarters were in a Germania beer hall. (Beneath it, actually, in the basement.) The hall was full of brown shirts and swastikas. Yael's numbers flamed under her wool sleeve when she saw the tables full of officers. But they didn't seem to notice her heat, or the young man with an armful of parcels. They were too busy laughing over foaming steins.

Yael followed the young man down into the cellar, into damp darkness crowded with dozens of beer barrels. Aaron-Klaus approached the third-to-the-last barrel of the second row and turned the spigot like a screw until the wooden face swung back. There was no flood of beer, only a passage Aaron-Klaus had to hunch over to fit in. He ushered Yael through first, pulled the door shut behind them. It was a short hallway, made of bricks and other things that carried voices. Yael heard two of them: a man and a woman.

The woman: "A message got through from London. The deportations of their population to the continent labor camps have gotten worse. They're impatient for the new Valkyrie to fly."

The man: "The time isn't right. The forces are spread so far across the globe.... We have to reinforce our contacts."

The woman: "Any news from the Americas?"

The man: "Same isolationist *Scheisse* as always: 'European politics are for Europe.' They think nonaggression pacts and oceans will protect them. They want no part in a second Valkyrie."

They sat in a denlike room. It was a cave of books and papers, with a radio as large as Yael herself. She stopped in the open doorway and took it in: the smells of leather bindings and typewriter ink.

The man and woman stopped, too. They stared at her with misset mouths. The man wore a cross on his chest. Black. Iron. A wide-winged eagle hovered over his right breast, the rainbow chaos of pins above the other.

A real National Socialist.

Fight or flight kicked in again. Pumping hot between Yael's toes. Itching all over her skin. But there was nowhere to run and no one to fight.

—HIDE THEN—

The something else—the monster—crawled inside her, a skinshift begging to be let out.

Yael clenched her teeth together and tried not to think of faces. She was going to follow Miriam's instructions, no matter what. She could not, would not, let them see.

Aaron-Klaus walked past her and set his parcels down on the card table. "Here are the packages you requested, General Reiniger."

"Packages?" The woman stiffened and glared at the National Socialist officer. "You sent Klaus to pick up a file drop?"

"He volunteered for it, Henryka." Reiniger shrank a bit as he said this. A small, un–National Socialist motion that let Yael breathe a little easier. "My usual runners were engaged."

"He's sixteen and untrained!" the woman snapped. "What would happen if he'd been stopped and questioned?"

"I wanted to help," Aaron-Klaus said. "I hate being stuck down here, reading books and doing math. I want to be out there. Doing things!"

"And you will." Henryka rolled her shoulders in a way that reminded Yael of a farmyard chicken. Fuss and cluck: "When you're eighteen. After you've spent some time on Vlad's farm learning how to handle yourself."

The National Socialist officer—Reiniger—was looking at Yael. His true-blue eyes cut across the card table. "Now, who's this?"

Aaron-Klaus welcomed the distraction. He waved for Yael to come into the room. "I found her by the Spree. She's marked."

"Marked? But—" Henryka's voice faded. She looked at the girl: honey-gold pigtails, teeth a little too big for her mouth. An Aryan poster child. (Yael actually *had* stolen the face from a watercolor advertisement for the Hitler Youth.)

"Will you show them?" Aaron-Klaus asked.

Baring the numbers was against everything inside her. Yael did not even show them to herself. When she changed clothes, she never looked to the left. There were a few—few—times when she'd try to take them off. (They'd never really stopped itching after that last night in Dr. Geyer's lab, so she scratched and tore and tried to erase things that could not be.) All she ended up with were bloody fingernails. Scabs turned to scars, wiped clean after her next change.

Aaron-Klaus pushed back his sleeve again. It looked so easy when he did it: soft rolls of fabric and arm stretched out. Numbers boldly bare under the army of tin lampshades.

Yael tried to do the same. But she didn't feel easy or bold when she peeled back her sleeve. She still did not look at her numbers. She let the others glimpse her ink. They did so in silence. When she tugged the sweater back down, they didn't ask to see her tattoo again. They didn't ask why her hair was blond or how she'd escaped.

Reiniger only asked for her name, which she gave him.

Henryka fed her.

162

Life beneath the beer hall was three glorious, fatty-fresh meals a day; a strawless bed she did not have to share; warm-water baths; and a toilet that flushed.

Yael's sleeves stayed down. Her face stayed the same. The монстр, *monstre, monster* inside curled up for a long, long sleep.

She set herself to learning. When Henryka was not busy clattering away on her typewriter or talking in hushed tones with visitors, she taught the girl how to read. Their school was at the steel card table in the middle of Henryka's office. Its tiny surface cluttered with textbooks, cocoa, and laughter. Aaron-Klaus grumbled about something called calculus and ate more than half the plate of chocolate crullers Henryka sometimes baked. The radio in the corner hummed, always on.

It took Yael only four months to master reading German. She started choosing books from Henryka's library and teaching herself what was inside. From there the world was hers.

But not really.

The world belonged to the Third Reich.

This fact was easy to see, plastered across the office wall in the form of a map. It looked so very different from the old atlases Yael sometimes flipped through, the ones that showed a mosaic of countries: Britain, Italy, France, Egypt, Iraq. Orange, purple, green, yellow…dozens and dozens of kingdoms and hues. Republics and shades.

All of these were scarlet now. Territories of the Third Reich, ruled by ruthless *Reichskommissar*s who answered unwaveringly to Germania. Even with the multiple coded thumbtacks that clustered around its borders, the capital city looked so small. Yael found it hard to imagine how the tiny, dark fleck could hold so much sway over the continents.

"There are so many territories, so many people getting shipped to camps.... Why doesn't anyone fight back?" she asked Aaron-Klaus one afternoon. The young man was hunched over the table next to her, twiddling a graphite pencil, scowling at a string of numbers.

"Hitler and his henchmen are the guards of this world. They have the guns. They have the power. If a single territory tried to secede on its own, the Reich would crush it," Aaron-Klaus said. "Everyone is afraid. No one wants to die."

"What if someone killed the Führer?" Yael asked. "Do you think that would change things? Make people less afraid?"

Aaron-Klaus tucked his pencil behind his ear, where the saffron roots of his hair were starting to show. (Yael often found herself wondering what he would look like without the biweekly bleach. Handsome—to be sure. The thought was always followed by a blush.)

"Many people have tried. Valkyrie—" The word had scarcely left his mouth when the door slid open. Henryka, as short as she was, seemed to fill the whole doorway with her crossed arms, her explosive hair.

"Have you finished your worksheet, Klaus?" she asked.

"Almost," he lied. Yael knew he'd spent most of the past hour making faces at the equations and eating crullers.

"Reiniger stopped by this morning." Henryka let out a sigh that was...sad. "It's been decided that you'll be going to Vlad's farm."

Vlad's farm. Yael had only been at Henryka's for a year, but the name held a tinge of legend. Tucked away in the Alps, it was the place you went to learn to fight. To master the art of marksmanship and cracking a man's skull with a single kick.

"Really?" Aaron-Klaus's entire face lit up. As if all this time he'd been a lamp sitting on a shelf, gathering dust, and someone just remembered to plug him in. "Vlad's farm?"

Henryka nodded, but the motion was heavy. "I still think you could use another year here, but Reiniger insisted."

The thought of Aaron-Klaus leaving scrabbled inside Yael. Who would toss wads of graphing paper into her hair while she studied? Who would come and sit by her bed at night when black smoke nightmares made her shake and sob? Who would eat all the crullers?

"I want to go, too," Yael said.

"Absolutely not." Henryka sounded as if someone had hit her. Yael looked closer and realized the older woman was almost crying. "You're *far* too young."

"I'll come back, Yael. I promise." Aaron-Klaus's voice buzzed electric. "And when I do, I'll teach you everything I know."

———

Valkyries: Maidens in old Norse mythology. They are choosers of the slain, who appear on battlefields to decide which soldiers die and which live. Though many paintings depict Valkyries riding to war on horseback, a verse inscribed on the Rök Runestone describes a Valkyrie named Gunnr using a wolf as her steed.

This was what the yellowed pages of Henryka's encyclopedia told Yael about the word. There was even an illustration: Beautiful women made of bare breasts, feathers, and curves stood in the middle of ruin. Deciding. Who lived. Who died. Their gazes combed through fields of snapped spears, broken axes, shattered bodies. The skies above them were inked with battle smoke. Black and etched, line by careful line.

They looked like angels, with those wings. Beautiful, monstrous, something to be feared.

Yael did not think this was the Valkyrie Reiniger had referenced. The one Aaron-Klaus managed to spit out before Henryka interrupted. But the picture sang to Yael anyway. (It was a sad, savage ballad. One that howled angry inside her, stirred the monster's restless sleep.) She liked to imagine the scene: a powerful woman with wings unfurled, looming over the Führer. Making a choice.

Life or death.

CHAPTER 16

NOW

MARCH 18, 1956
CAIRO CHECKPOINT

Riders leaked in: first a dribble, then a pour. The gap between the leaders and the rear of the pack was widening. At this point in the race, names started dropping off. Vanishing with a strikethrough of chalk.

Now she was responsible for two lines. Yael couldn't bring herself to look at the names she knew would be crossed out. ~~Shiina Hiraku~~. ~~Felix Wolfe~~.

Besides, she had other things to worry about. Such as retrieving the files. Felix might be a problem solved, but Luka... he and Adele seemed magnetized. Pulled together, propelled apart. Polarized or fused, depending on the day. There seemed to be no escaping him.

Soon, very soon, you're going to need me.

As much as she wanted to hate the boy, Yael didn't doubt his words. Katsuo's stare still haunted her, hours later.

Alliances weren't uncommon on the Axis Tour, but there was no way she'd walk into a blind agreement with someone like Luka Löwe.

She needed to know that history first. She needed the files.

Even at night Cairo thrummed with life. It wasn't National Socialist patrols Yael was worried about (though there were plenty of those, rumbling about in jeeps, lounging outside cafés), but the sheer number of eyes. There were no curfews here. Night vendors lined the sidewalks, hawking produce and linens under strings of glaring bulbs.

Yael pretended to be shopping. Sifting through crates of shriveled pomegranates and apples—crop leftovers that the territory's *Reichskommissar* decided weren't worth exporting. She bought a scarf and wrapped it over her head so that the fabric hung low, covering her profile as she waded through the night market crowds. She changed faces while she walked, borrowing features from the people she passed. The falconlike nose of a grain merchant, the dark hair of a boy sweeping a café floor, eyes like all the locals: brown, hungry, resigned to dust.

This kind of changing—last-minute patchwork girl, stolen pieces, angry stitches—always made Yael feel slippery. At least when she was someone like Mina or Adele, she had papers, a backstory (no matter how cobwebby). But when she was this...a bit of every stranger in the street...

What was left, besides the wolves? Apart from memories and pretending?

Emptiness.

These hollow spaces were the darkest. Yawning open like Cairo's many alleys, twisting into places Yael did not like to go. Where the whispers of dead women echoed: *монстр, monstre, monster*. Where the rage she always swallowed down smoked and roiled. Waiting, waiting...

Usually Yael ignored it. Always she feared it. Because she knew exactly what this place inside her was capable of. It was the part of her that *needed* lines. The part—if Yael chose to listen to it—that could so easily become like the National Socialists.

But this time Yael did have something solid as she wove through Cairo's maze of streets. The paper of coded addresses in her undershirt. This took Yael all the way to the city's fringes, where dogs roamed in packs and the desert's lonely sands hazed across streetlamps. The address Reiniger had given her belonged to a café, she realized when she stepped up to the door. Tables lined the open sidewalk, cast in an ill, flickering glow. All empty.

Had she read the address wrong? Yael stood for a moment, eyeing the storefront. Inside, a girl washed tables with a dirty rag.

"Can I help you?" A man—older and balding, with sandstone skin—stretched out of the shadows by the door. So suddenly that Yael braced herself. Feet flat, fists tight, ready to fight.

It took her a moment to recover and recite the code words. "The wolves of war are gathering."

"They sing the song of rotten bones," the man replied. "Your Arabic is commendable, Volchitsa. Come inside. I have what you need."

The girl cleaning the tabletops froze when they walked in. The man's "Bring us a pipe!" sent her scuttling into the back rooms. The man sat down at the farthest crooked table.

"I can't stay long." Yael sat as well, but her back stayed stiff. The café's emptiness would not let her relax.

"Business has been slow these days." The man nodded at the quiet around them. "It's hard for customers to appear when they're being shipped off to labor camps. More and more people have been disappearing, stolen in the night. Many in Cairo are ready to fight, but we cannot afford the full wrath of the Reich...." The man trailed off as the girl moved back into the room, set the pipe on the table. Yael's contact picked up the mouthpiece, drew a long breath. Bubbles danced in the glass. The smoke he exhaled smelled of flowers and spring. Nothing like crematorium fumes. "Much rides with you, Volchitsa."

When he offered Yael the mouthpiece, she shook her head. "The package?"

"Ah, straight to business. Very well." The man placed a folder on the table. Yael recognized Henryka's handwriting across the front immediately—mother hen scratchings— worried and illegible. The sight made Yael wish she were back in the beer hall basement, sipping cocoa with the Polish woman, talking about life and poking fun at the terrible act- ing on the Reichssender shows.

She was just slipping the papers into the lining of her jacket (the same place she'd stowed her swastika armband before walking through the market) when the shop door squealed. Yael's contact looked up. His nostrils flared, lips stiff.

She stole a glance over her shoulder, through the fabric of her scarf. Quick and back. What she saw was a punch to the heart.

Black jacket still covered in road dust. Goggles shoved high, helmet in hand. Swastika armband. Crooked nose. Adele Wolfe in reverse.

Impossible. He...he wasn't supposed to come back from that. He was supposed to give up. Go home...

And now he was *here*, of all places.

Hell had frozen over, and Felix Wolfe was the ice. He stepped through the doorway, movements shaking with an anger so hot it burned cold.

"What are you doing here, Ad?" His voice stung at the back of her patterned scarf.

Yael focused on the glowing coal on the top of the shisha pipe. He must have spotted her in the crowd, followed her at a distance, watching from a layer of market stalls and dimly lit crowds. Had he seen her change? Spotted the manila folder? There was only one way to find out.

All too aware of the P38 against her ribs and the knife in her boot, Yael turned to face him.

Immediately she wanted to wince. Her pistol whip hadn't been as neat as she'd meant it. The whole side of Felix's face was swollen: one eye shut. His hairline invaded by dried blood and bruise.

But Yael kept her guilt hidden, her expression straight. "I'm sorry," she said in Arabic, "do I know you?"

Felix's mouth dropped open, but he found nothing to say.

171

His silence mixed with the room's floral shisha smoke. His good eye blinked at odd intervals, trying to erase what he was seeing. Brown eyes, black hair...an Egyptian girl with a few road-rash scabs still dotting her cheeks. (Yael hoped that in this flickering light, with his bad eye, the marks would look like freckles. She thanked the stars she'd removed her bandages before leaving the compound.)

"But—" Felix started backing away. "Apologies. I—I thought you were someone else. I was mistaken."

The last word wasn't even fully out of Felix's mouth before he melted back into the night. The door slammed behind him, as loud as Yael's heart. She sat still, watching his silhouette ripple across the glass.

Yael tore the scarf from her face, left it crumpled by the pipe's base. "I have to get back to the compound before he does."

Whatever the contact's response was, Yael didn't hear it. She was already running, lurching into the street, her mind rattling with thoughts of Adele and what almost happened. She had to skinshift and get back to the compound. Quick. Change her clothes. Act like she'd been there for hours. Do anything she could to quiet whatever suspicions might be scratching Felix Wolfe's thoughts.

Not that he would even suspect. He would trust his good eye above all else.

Wouldn't he?

Shift and *click*. She was Adele again, sliding the National Socialist armband back up her sleeve as she ran. Yael sprinted around a corner, dodging a boy dragging a cart of sad wares. Always her eyes scanned for Felix—tough shoulders, silken gait—but there was no sign of Adele's brother. He must have taken a different way, she decided once she reached the night market, started wading through stalls and shoppers. A (hopefully) longer way.

Yael's lungs were starving by the time she reached the compound gates. She struggled for breath as she strode across the courtyard. Past the line of parked Zündapps. There were sixteen, still. The same number there had been when she'd left. Felix must've seen her from the road. Abandoned his bike to follow her. Which meant he would come rolling in at any moment.

"Keep huffing and puffing like that and you'll give yourself an oxygen high." Luka sat at the table, a perfect imitation of his afternoon self: tilted chair, boots slapped heretically on the tabletop. A cigarette fumed between his lips. "Where've you been skulking, Fräulein?"

"Out for some air." Yael started walking toward the compound entrance. "Road jitters."

"This'll take the edge off." Luka offered up his cigarette.

Yael stepped around the smoldering stub. There was no time for smoking or clever word wars. Felix would be here any minute, and she had to be ready. Ready to face his furious questions. Ready to face what she'd done.

"I did a little digging," Luka called out in a way that made Yael slow, turn. "Found out Hiraku's not dead. He broke both his legs and raked half his skin off. But he's still kicking."

The victor paused, quirking an eyebrow as he reviewed his own sentences. "Poor choice of words. Anyway, just thought you might like to know."

Not dead. One life spared. One life out of millions. Just a drop. But it mattered. It rolled off Yael's chest. Made it one life lighter.

And Luka, he'd remembered her question. He'd *seen* how much it meant to her . . . through the cracks. And he'd tried to find an answer, showed cracks of his own. A *more*ness—

Felix's headlamp swung through the compound gates, such a blinding glare that Luka threw his arms to his face and the timekeeper (who'd been asleep) nearly fell out of his chair again. Yael felt paralyzed, translucent—prisoner under the spotlight, walking past the fence, over the train tracks, through her lie.

Adele's brother pulled her former motorcycle to a stop. The engine cut out midsputter, all light gone.

She could walk through this lie, too.

—MAKE YOUR JAW SLACK BREATHE NORMAL ACT LIKE YOU'VE BEEN HERE—

Her clothes were a problem. Her panther-black jacket. A white undershirt (more orange now with all the days of sand). Leather gloves. The boots. All the same as in the café. But it had been dark there. And she'd been wearing the scarf.

Maybe Felix would think these things coincidence. In truth, he seemed too irate to notice. Felix's movements off the bike were jerky. He flung his helmet and goggles to the ground on his warpath to the card table.

"What in the name of the *verdammt* New Order happened to your face?" Luka's question held more than a hint of glee as he scrunched his still splotched nose.

Felix's wound looked even worse under the courtyard lamps. Jagged with old blood and ooze. Left eye stitched shut at his pale lashes. Red flesh plummeting into blue into purple into a different shade altogether. As dark as what slept inside her.

The sight made Yael sick. But she had to face it because Adele's brother was in front of her now.

"You fixed the bike," she whispered.

"I told you I could," he said. "Only took me three hours after the supply caravan showed up."

Dead silence. Chipping stares. What did he want her to say? Something like this was so far past apologies, and though Yael herself was sorry, she *shouldn't* be. When she got to the end of this race, she'd have to do far worse deeds. . . .

"You left me stranded in the middle of a desert. Unconscious." But this deed did sound pretty awful, the way Felix said it: his voice twisting tight, tighter, tightest until it was as squinched as his wounded eye.

"Your own *brother*, Fräulein." Luka stood. His cigarette fell to the ground, forgotten, as he stepped closer to the siblings. "You've always been a cold one, but this is a new brand of savage. Even for you."

Felix's fists bundled into knots as he turned on Luka. A growl—pure hate, all threat—climbed up his throat. "No one asked for your commentary, Löwe."

"Consider it a gift." Luka's eyes darted to the other boy's knuckles. His lips twisted as if he'd just read something that humored him. "You really should have Nurse Wilhelmina look at your face. She does a wonderful taping job. Tender fingers."

"I'll gift you with another broken nose if you don't get out of here. I've got all the hour penalties in the world to spare." Felix jerked his head over to the scoreboard, where the time-keeper had just finished chalking his official time: *6 days, 19 hours, 40 minutes, 16 seconds.* Last place.

Luka's smile stayed, but a dangerous tightness overtook his jaw. The desert air between the boys swam with testosterone and the smell of the bike's hot motor. Rubber and diesel and fight.

This time, Yael promised herself, she wouldn't stop it. Both boys were too much of a threat to her mission. She'd be better off without them.

But Luka Löwe had no hour penalties to spare, and the timekeeper was watching. The victor dug his fists deep into the pockets of his brown jacket and shrugged. "Far be it from me to ruin your little family reunion. Nice chat, Fräulein. Let's do it again sometime."

Luka strutted back to the door, into the barrack's bright electric lights and the clouds of insects glittering around them. "Nighty-night, Wolfes," he called before he vanished altogether.

The fight was left to Yael.

She thought back to the last night in Germania. How the

twins stood just feet apart, facing off in their ram-horn *CLASH*. Adele's arms had been crossed. Yael crossed hers. Tried to imitate that unfeeling, icy stare as she looked back at Felix.

The anger was still there (lurking in the clench of his fists, flushing pink across the uninjured half of his face), but it wasn't the same temple-throbbing rage that had threatened to dismantle Luka. It was changed and checked. Safety on.

Sister mode.

"Where did you go?" he asked.

Yael crossed her arms tighter. As if the extra pressure could soothe her now explosive heart. What should she tell him? How much of Adele's face had he seen in the market? Enough to make him get off his bike, trail her...., Had he seen the scarf purchase?

Crack, crack went Felix's knuckles. Popping as he waited for her answer.

Lie by omission was the hardest to catch. Yael decided to risk it. "I took a walk through the market to get some air. Then I ran into Luka—"

"No." Felix cut her off. "No. That's not what I meant. Where is my sister?"

Locked in a Germania beer hall basement. Probably getting fat on plates of Henryka's chocolate crullers and cups of cocoa. Plotting a useless escape. Yael's heart pounded—full, full, full—with this knowledge.

"What are you talking about?" she snapped back, the way she supposed Adele would: yell for yell. "I'm right here, you dummkopf!"

177

"Flirting with Luka. Wearing perfume. What you did in the desert... This isn't you, Ad."

Flirting? Perfume? Felix wasn't even talking about the market or his real sister. He was talking about her Adele-ness. The widening gaps Yael was trying not to fall through, clutching to a fraying string of an alias.

"I wasn't flirting with Victor Löwe." She scowled at the thought.

"Fine. Being chummy with him, then." Felix's good eye narrowed. "You should've been dancing for joy when I broke that *Saukerl*'s nose in Prague. But you stopped me. Why?"

Because I thought that's what Adele would have done. Obviously not.

Instead Yael stammered, "I—I didn't want you to get hurt."

"Clearly that's not your top priority." Felix snorted. The motion wrenched his tender face, made him wince. "I'm not a dummkopf, Ad. There's something missing. Something you're not telling me."

Felix glanced behind his shoulder at the timekeeper, who'd gone back to sleep in his chair. His voice dipped to a hush. "What's going on?"

No, Felix Wolfe wasn't a dummkopf. Far from it. He was close. Too close to the truth. Too close to *her* truth. *There's something missing.*

Yael had to steer him away.

So she stared straight at Felix and that terrible, terrible bruise. She did not flinch. "What's going on is I'm trying

178

to win this race. And I can't do it with you clinging to my tailpipes."

"Clinging to your— I'm trying to protect you!" A third knuckle cracked. And a fourth. And a fifth.

"I don't need your help," Yael told him. "Go home, Felix. Go back to Mama and Papa before you end up like Martin."

Flinging the dead's name like a weapon was a low move, but it worked. Their conversation was done.

Felix had no more knuckles left to crack. He turned and slammed his fist into the card table instead. Wood splintered. The bowl of figs and dates went flying, their shriveled sweetness scattering in the dust by Yael's boots as she walked away.

CHAPTER 17

NOW

MARCH 18, 1956
CAIRO CHECKPOINT

There was another paper token beneath Yael's pillow this evening. A tiny crane made out of Arabic newspaper. Yael sat for a moment on her bunk, admiring the handiwork of the bird nestled in her palm. It was the same size as the smallest doll. Whoever folded it had taken time, care.

Yael tucked the crane into her jacket pocket alongside the star (now a bit crushed from her desert wreck). The motion edged her sleeve close to her nose. Yael froze. The dread in her stomach stretched and grew.

Wearing perfume. This accusation had made no sense when Adele's brother had said it. But now...now Yael understood.

Her jacket smelled like flowers and smoke. It smelled like shisha.

And Felix had noticed.

A great fear vised Yael's chest. Crushing down and in, until not even the empty spaces mattered. Her lungs were frozen.

No air.

Memories of the wreck returned. No air. Gravel in her skin. Felix cleaning her wound, spilling secrets he had no business knowing. Adele's brother was here to protect his sister. Not turn her in. He wouldn't go to the racing officials unless he learned the truth: Who she was. Who she was not.

The file was evidence of this secret. It had to be memorized and destroyed before Adele's brother could confront her again. So off to the washroom Yael went.

Its door was latched shut when she arrived, choking sounds seeping through its wood. Uneven breaths, a severe, stifled sniff. Yael's heart panged at the noises, for she knew them well.

Behind the door, someone was weeping. Someone who was trying very hard not to.

Yael had half a mind to slink away. But this washroom was the only place on the compound where she was guaranteed privacy, something she needed if she was going to be reviewing the kilo of pages weighing down her jacket.

She rapped on the door.

All sounds of crying stopped. Replaced with scuffing boots and the rush of a faucet. Nearly a minute passed before the water cut off and the door swung open.

Yael had imagined many different faces—splotched in red, streaked with tears—inside the washroom. Ryoko, perhaps. Or maybe one of the younger first-years: Rolf or Taro.

She'd even, for a fleeting second, pictured Felix bracing himself against the sink. Pale hair, jagged face.

Not once had she considered that the sounds might have come from Tsuda Katsuo.

At the sight of Yael, the boy paused, just long enough for her to pick out the faint pink swell beneath his eyelashes. The rest of his face was damp, not with tears, but faucet water. He'd scoured it clean.

Why would Katsuo, of all people, be weeping? He was a hunter, a victor....

A victor with an entire empire's expectations crushing down on his shoulders. The hope of a people. The need to win. It was a lot to carry, even without the added weight of an impending putsch. Enough to make anyone falter.

But there was nothing faltering about Katsuo now. His eyes, bloodshot though they were, snapped back into the vicious courtyard stare as he shoved past Yael, disappeared down the hallway.

Tsuda Katsuo: Not so easy to read after all.

But Yael had other people to read about, so she pushed her shock aside and entered the washroom. She crouched on the covered toilet by the steady stream of masking incense smoke and opened the envelope. It held sixty-four pages in all. Introduced by Henryka's short note:

VOLCHITSA,
THIS IS ALL THE INFORMATION WE COULD
GATHER. I HOPE YOU FIND IT USEFUL.
—H

This was what she was dealing with.

There were dozens of pages on **Felix Burkhard Wolfe**. Yael kept peeling them back. Fact after fact after fact.

Felix's school records. (He'd been much more studious than Adele.) Physician's notes. (He struggled with acrophobia. And had been admitted to the hospital twice for a broken nose. Otherwise he was a peak specimen of the Aryan race.) Hitler Youth logs. Records of all the cars and motorcycles he'd repaired in his father's auto shop. Yael could see by the flux in dates and the absence of grades that he'd dropped out of school two years ago to run the business. He'd been excused from regular Hitler Youth meetings to tend to this duty and had no social life to speak of. (Which was why Adele had gotten away with posing as him for so many weeks. There was no one to miss the real Felix Wolfe.)

There were enough facts to beef up any future conversations with Adele's brother, which was something. But the information Yael needed most wasn't there. Resistance activity: unmentioned, unknown.

Yael set these papers by the sink, moved on to the next stack: **Luka Löwe & Adele Wolfe**. It was considerably thinner than Felix's file.

No known contact existed between the two before the ninth Axis Tour. They rode in close proximity from Rome all the way to Osaka, where Adele finished the final leg alone. Luka's time was over two hours off, though in the interviews he never said why. There was no known contact between them after the race.

Everything that happened started in Rome. *What you did* ended in Osaka.

And between?

Yael tossed the files to the ground. So much ink and white and *nothing* spread across the washroom floor. She raked her fingers through Adele's silky hair and stared at it all.

There were too many blank spaces. Luka and Felix. Neither boy was what she'd read on paper. Watched on archival films. Expected from swastika-wearing Aryan youth. Things were so different face-to-face. Flesh-to-flesh. So complicated.

Both were so much more.

There was a tightness inside Yael's chest that had nothing to do with pain or fear. She'd trained for ice storms and starvation. Torture and long stretches of desert thirst. Lying with a blank face. Looking straight into the Führer's eyes as she slid a knife into his ribs.

She thought she was ready for this mission. Ready for anything.

But not this. Not *relationships*.

This wasn't something she could fake.

CHAPTER 18

NOW

MARCH 19, 1956
CAIRO TO BAGHDAD

There was more desert ahead.

The road was just as weather-worn as it had been on the tour's third leg. And although she was still in the lead, Yael's pace felt painstakingly slow as she wove her bike through potholes: all crawl, less race. The scenery didn't help—Yael had never been in a place so empty as the wilderness beyond Cairo. Endless horizons, sheer length and grand nothingness. On the first night when Yael cut the Zündapp's engine and set up her camp, there was nothing. Just silence and a heavy dark—the noise she carried inside her. Always.

This was how she knew she was not alone.

The footsteps outside her tent were soft. Not even whispers over the sand. Yael sat up when she heard them—heart strung, gun in hand.

The noise stopped.

She grabbed her electric lantern and slid out of the tent. A pair of eyes gleamed—eerie sea-green stars. Yael raised her pistol, dropped the light. The eyes darted. A glimpse of sandy fur flashed across Yael's patch of illuminated desert. Just a desert fox. Probably drawn to her camp by the tin of beef and prepackaged crackers she'd devoured hours earlier.

Yael clicked the P38's safety back, slid the gun into her pocket, and bent down to get the lantern. That was when she saw them: human footprints, strung across the sand. Spaced too far apart to be her own.

Every single one of Yael's senses ratcheted up as she wheeled around and took in the camp. The smell of cool sand, her tent haloed in lamplight, the shadows stretching long around it… melting into a lonely, lonely night. No sound.

Nothing.

Yael was the only soul left in her camp. But this knowledge hardly calmed her. No racer would go to the trouble to hike all the way to her camp (and forfeit hours of precious sleep) to leave only footprints.

Something was wrong.

She turned to her bike. The Zündapp was where she'd parked it, sporting the normal scuffs and dents. Its tires were full, unpunctured. (Her visitor probably wasn't Takeo, then.) The fuel line was intact. The engine untampered with, starting on the first try.

But the footprints-not-her-own were here, too. Planted just by the rear tire and…

Her canteens.

Yael turned to them with a deflating heart. All four were where she'd left them, lodged by her panniers, but crooked. One of the caps was too loose. When Yael unscrewed it and lifted the open container to her nostrils, she knew.

This was Iwao's work. Katsuo must have sent him to put his **fondness for drugging food and drink** to good use.

The soporific's scent was faint. It would have been undetectable but for all of Vlad's neurotic training (*Smell this! Smell that! One sip of this and you're done!*). Yael's thoroughly schooled nose told her it was a sedative—a single swig and Yael's ten-minute lead would be gone.

She cursed Iwao first, then Katsuo—and to think, she'd almost felt sorry for the victor!—then herself. **Guard your provisions with care.** She hadn't. She hadn't, and now all four canteens of water were compromised.

Yael might not have taken the drug, but the damage was done. Baghdad was well over a day's ride away—all sun, through land where water was scarce. Yael's throat cracked just thinking about it.

She poured out her canteens at dawn, watching as the water threaded crystal in the rising sun, catching glints of gold and orange before vanishing in the sand. She scavenged a pebble from the roadside, let it tumble in her mouth as she drove. It kept the saliva flowing, made the morning bearable.

The refueling stops were no help. There were no limitless wells to draw from, just men camped with drums of gasoline beside the road, guarding limited water rations of their own. (They'd been warned about this drought of supplies in Cairo, given two extra canteens for the leg and ordered to ration them, which was probably *why* Katsuo had sent Iwao to Yael's camp in the first place.) She managed to beg a few swallows of water from an official at the first stop, but this only made her thirst worse. By noon there were cracks inside her, and they were spreading. Yael began to see water everywhere it wasn't. (In the shimmer of heat just down the road. In the shadows cast by rocks.) The Luka in her head kept talking— as smug and smirking as the real one: *Soon, very soon, you're going to need me.*

None of the other refueling officials had been willing to part with their precious water, and by nightfall Yael felt fractured, ready to fall to pieces. She wasn't going to make it to Baghdad

Soon.

Very soon.

Now.

Why did he have to be so right? There was no telling how far behind Felix's camp was or if he'd even be willing to give her a drink. But Luka...his camp was bound to be close to hers. And he would have water to spare.

It took five minutes to walk to Luka's camp. The pebble was still clattering in Yael's mouth, grinding her teeth. She nearly choked on it when she approached the boy's tent, called for him.

He was out before his name left her lips—though it was obvious she'd caught him unawares. His jacket, shirt, and Iron

Cross were nowhere to be seen. The boy was raw muscle and skin under the shine of the half-moon. A silver dog tag rested against his breastbone. A Luger pistol gleamed in his hand, aimed at her face.

Yael was too thirsty, too tired to hold her arms up. She didn't even have the energy to hate him.

"Ah, Fräulein." Luka's arm lowered when he registered her presence, tucking his gun back behind his trousers. His eyebrows flew high and the lines in his abdomen deepened. A not-so-subtle flex attempt. "Like what you see?"

They *were* very nice muscles. Worth at least a thousand German maidens' snared hearts. But Yael would sooner pluck off all of her body hairs one by one than admit this.

"Back-k in R-Rome—" The dryness in her throat felt like rusty razors. Yael cleared it out and tried again. "In Rome you suggested we could be allies. You said we need each other."

"I take it this isn't a social call." His eyes held hers for a long moment. All black, but for the irises. These gleamed—deep sea blue, water blue. Reading in his unreadable way while she crumbled into dry, dry pieces. An arm here. A rib there.

"I need water," Yael said. "Enough to last until Baghdad."

"Water?" Luka turned. His back muscles rippled as he retrieved his undershirt, pulled it over his wild, windtorn hair. His free fingers stroked the bristle on his jaw. "I don't know. I was saving some for a shave...."

"Please." Yael gritted her teeth together, hating how much grovel and thirst crept through her voice. *So much for not sounding desperate.* There was her gun, heavy in her left pocket, and the knife bracing her boot, but she knew she wouldn't be fast enough to take Luka's water by force. Not as drained as she was.

"Beards get awfully hot out here," he went on. "All that itch and hair makes for poor concentration."

He had to be joking. He had to be.

"Katsuo tried to take me out," Yael informed him. "He sent Iwao to drug my water. He'll do the same for you."

"Of course he will! Has the heat spoiled your brain, Fräulein? Did you forget all I taught you last year?" Luka threw up his hands. "Katsuo's pride is everything to him. Why do you think I've been holding back this whole time? Because two is my favorite number? The best way to handle Katsuo is to let him think he's winning."

"You're ahead of him now," she pointed out.

"Yeah. Well. The last time I let you out of my sight it almost killed me, and I lost the race. I'll be damned if it happens again."

The image of Luka, arms outstretched, started to swim. As if he were being swept away by a mirage. The sand beneath Yael was beginning to tilt. She wasn't sure how much longer she could keep standing.

"Katsuo has at least two more allies left," she said. "The Axis Tour isn't even half over. If I fall behind now, you'll be Katsuo's only real threat. He'll come at you with everything he has. You'll be out of the race before New Delhi."

Yael watched the possibilities of her words playing out behind Luka's face. The road ahead: dusty Baghdad, razor rocks threading past caves and mountain passes, so many places to slip or be ambushed.

"I suppose I could stand a bit of scruff. Some girls love the wilderness wastrel look." He rubbed his jawline again. "I'll give you one of my canteens on two conditions."

Yael stood, waiting. Trying her hardest not to collapse.

"The first: You will owe me a favor. One I can cash in at any time."

She nodded. Her world scattered with the motion. "As long as it doesn't involve me letting you win without a fight."

"Fair." Luka held up his next finger. "Second: You will sit right now and have a smoke with me. A *real* smoke. With real words. The way we used to."

Yael's knees were quick to crumple. Even when she was sitting the earth seemed to spin beneath her, silver moonlit sands jumping at her like waves. She spit her pebble out, afraid she might swallow it.

Luka knelt in front of her. His arms were still outstretched. Canteen in one hand, cigarette in the other.

She took them both.

The water was warm and tinny, but it was life. Yael took two deep swallows, and though her throat ached for more, she fumbled the cap back on. She had to make it last.

Luka sat close, leaning against his rolled-up sleeping bag. It was like magic, the way he lit his cigarette. He flicked his match against the heel of his boot. Let the flame's glow flare and fade as the ash lit bright.

Yael's attempt was clumsier. Her match took two strikes.

She blamed the thirsty shake of her fingers. When her cigarette finally lit, Luka sighed, brought his own to his lips.

"I thought I had you all figured out," he said after a lingering draw. The way he watched Yael reminded her of a lion. Eyes brave and visceral. "For nine months I lay awake at night and remembered what you did. But now...now I don't know what to make of you. A girl who leaves her own brother for dead in the desert, but feels a guilt trip for a boy she doesn't even know?"

"I left Felix incapacitated. Not dying." Yael lifted the cigarette to her lips. It tasted awful. She wondered how people could keep inhaling it. Cigarette after cigarette. Package after package. How they could let the smoke live inside them like it was nothing.

"A blow like that to the temple? One kilo too much pressure and bye-bye, brother-dear." Luka made a slick cutting motion across his throat. Embers scattered off his cigarette, bursting to the ground like angry stars. Dying one by one.

"You think I'd kill my own brother?" Yael spit the words out, but the taste of ashes stayed: clinging, rotten.

"I wouldn't put anything past you, Fräulein." Luka's eyes narrowed, still examining her in that lion-smart way of his. "You're an absolute *verdammt* mystery to me. Every time I think I've uncovered the true you, I find a whole new layer of secrets. After the race last year, I always wondered if there was ever an honest moment between you and me."

"Honestly? I think smoking is disgusting."

"The real Adele emerges!" Luka laughed and took another

drag from his cigarette. "So all those nights we sat together under this sky and you smoked nearly half my pack, you were just pretending?"

"Something like that."

"You owe me about two cartons of cigarettes, then. They aren't cheap, you know. Especially since Hitler banned them." Luka huffed out a lungful of smoke. "As our dear Führer tends to do with anything remotely interesting or worthwhile."

"I'll pay you in Tokyo. With part of my winnings," Yael told him, even though she knew it would never happen. While the Iron Cross was presented at a ceremony before the Victor's Ball, the money was awarded later. After her waltz with the Führer and the fall of an empire. She'd be long gone by then.

"I still expect you to finish that one," Luka said.

"A deal's a deal." Yael took another tongue-curdling breath in. She'd need more water after this.

He laughed again. More sparks tumbled to the sand, fading in silence.

Silence. All silence. It screamed between them.

"Sometimes I miss this. You. Me. Secrets. Stars." His words curled out with the smoke—wisps of burning air that actually looked pretty. "I thought I was invincible. Before you."

"Katsuo beat you before I ever competed," Yael said.

"I'm well aware of my losses, Fräulein. Even if I don't show it." Luka's hand went to the back of his neck, rubbed the chain there. "You know I'm not talking about the race."

There were so many versions of Luka Löwe—the National Socialist and the racer, the vicious and the proud, and then this...the *more*ness—all snapped up inside him. Shells different every minute. Faces within faces. Masks within masks. Dolls within dolls.

Which version was the real one? All? None?

But this Luka Löwe, the one sitting in front of her now, had loved the real Adele. Yael could see it in his eyes—where Adele's face was captured in indigo and intimate—in the tremble of his fingers around his cigarette, in the tortured twist of his lips.

He'd loved her enough to hurt.

"When I woke up in Osaka last year, I thought an army had blitzkrieged my head it hurt so bad. But that was nothing. *Nothing* compared to how I felt on the inside—" He stopped short. "I should hate you. I've tried. Sometimes I even think I do. But the feeling never sticks.

"Who knows, maybe you never cared for me. Maybe you were playing me the whole time. Or maybe you just saw your chance to win in Osaka and you took it. But there are two truths I'm sure of."

"What?"

"I care for you." It was the most sincere, unflinching thing Yael had ever heard him say. For a moment she forgot the taste of ash that coated her tongue.

But it was still there. Sticking to the roof of her mouth. Sliding between her teeth.

Yael tapped her cigarette clean. It was down to the nub. Luka's cigarette was fading, too. The amber glow on his face was dying. Pulling him out of her twenty-twenty sight. "What's the second thing?" she asked.

"This race—the Axis Tour of 1956—is mine." There was no threat in his voice. Just a deep certainty. "I will not let you win again."

Yael's cigarette had burned out. Deal done. She buried it in its own sandy ashes and stood.

Luka didn't bother getting up. New shadows grew across his face, closing between them as he watched her. "You're a dangerous breed, Adele Wolfe. But I'm always up for a challenge."

And then the darkness came in full. Snuffing his cigarette with a smoky hiss.

CHAPTER 19

THEN

THE FOURTH WOLF: AARON-KLAUS
PART 2
SPRING 1952

The beer hall basement was a lonely place without Aaron-Klaus. Most days it was just she and Henryka. The contacts who came through never stayed for long. A dinner or two, some talk of distant red-mapped places, and they were off. They never said where, but after they left Henryka always switched the numbered thumbtacks around on her map. P5 to Paris. T11 to London. A32 to Cairo. The numbers hopped like pieces in an intricate game of Stern-Halma. Over former borders, crossing paths, a dance of pinholes through Henryka's wall.

Yael studied as much as she could. Every subject in every language Henryka could get her hands on. The card table buckled under the weight of all her books. The corner radio was replaced with a television screen. (The novelty!) It, too, was always on.

Red still soaked the world.

Months passed, rolling through years.

1950…1951…1952…

Calculus was just as hard as Aaron-Klaus had always groaned it was. Measuring change with numbers and symbols cramped Yael's fingers. Spun her brain. Yael usually got lost in the equations, chewing on her pencil as she tried to make sense of them.

She nearly bit through the soft wood when she heard his voice drifting from the hall.

"It's been six years since the Great Victory. What have we been doing this whole time? Skulking in basements. Scuttling messages back and forth. Hoping every day not to get caught."

Aaron-Klaus was back! But he sounded different. There was a depth in his voice—a rage she'd heard only in hints and jags before, now beached. A leviathan of emotion: whole and rotting.

This kept Yael sitting in her chair, pencil jammed between her teeth. Listening.

"We're building the necessary framework for a putsch. We're getting closer." Reiniger was back, too. It had been months since Yael last saw him. A snowy Christmas Eve. He'd brought her a parcel full of sweaters and scarves. When he left, Henryka had placed his pin (A1) in Rome. It had jumped around a lot since then—Paris, London, Tripoli.

"NOTHING HAS CHANGED! Everything has gotten worse. We've forgotten Valkyrie—"

"The world isn't ready, Klaus." Reiniger's voice was commander cool. "Operation Valkyrie was drafted for a smaller, more concentrated Reich. In the event of the Führer's death, a military emergency would be declared, and the Territorial Reserve Army would secure all government operations. A putsch was difficult enough to accomplish when the Reich was contained in Europe. But the New Order has grown. There are too many variables now. We must continue to build our network of allies and unite the various resistances. This is what you've been trained to do."

So that was Valkyrie. Not a woman of war—bearer of life and death—but a military protocol. Still, the picture stayed in Yael's head. She'd flipped to it so many times that the encyclopedia's spine had a permanent trench.

"And when will the time be right?" Aaron-Klaus kept shouting, but in a terrible, hushed kind of way. "The longer we wait, the more people die."

"If we strike at the wrong moment, we could *all* die," Reiniger said. "Just like the conspirators who implemented the first Valkyrie. Everything we've worked for would crumble to pieces."

"You know what I think? You're scared. You saw what happened to those first conspirators, and it paralyzed you."

"You're angry," Reiniger replied. "You need to compartmentalize."

"Millions of people are dying! I can't just keep hiding in here!" Aaron-Klaus's words stung through walls. Slipped like wasp venom into Yael's veins—all burn.

She dropped her pencil.

"That's exactly what you're going to do until you get a handle on yourself. Stay here. Run drops for Henryka. Cool your head," Reiniger said. "Once you prove to me that you've managed to contain your emotions, then we can talk about your next serious operation."

"But—"

"This conversation is finished." Reiniger must have been wearing his military jackboots. They made distinct sounds on the concrete floor: *tap, tap, tap.* Away.

The door from the hall slid open.

At first Yael thought she'd misheard Reiniger's steps. A man stood in the doorway. He was tall and tight shouldered, with a flushed face and thinned lips. But it *was* Aaron-Klaus, she realized as he stepped into the room. Aaron-Klaus without the boyness she'd seen by the river.

"Yael?" Aaron-Klaus paused. The features of his face softened, remolding into a smile. "You look different."

Don't show anyone.

Yael's heart twisted. Her eyes glanced to the mirror behind Henryka's desk (the one the older woman used to gauge her need for a hair bleach). No, she hadn't changed....She'd kept Miriam's command. Hers was the face Aaron-Klaus had found her in. The face they'd always known her as.

"I'm a teenager now." As her gangling limbs attested. Whenever Yael stood in front of her reflection, she was reminded of the encyclopedia entry on Annam walking sticks. Insects with twig bodies, twig legs. Practically invisible.

"And Henryka's already got you doing advanced mathematics?" Aaron-Klaus sat down in his old seat, across the card table. He smelled like the outside: pine and rain and clouds. "What are you? Some sort of prodigy?"

"How was Vlad's farm?" she asked, because she wanted the time they'd missed to not be between them. She wanted to understand his change. Trace it and solve, like the calculus problems.

"Hard. But I have muscles now." He flexed his arm and grinned. Both actions seemed empty, echoing the shouts Yael had just heard from the hall. The real measure of him.

"What happened?"

Yael was not asking about the farm, and Aaron-Klaus knew it. "I took the train back. There were magazines and coffee. Cushioned seats. A woman across the aisle was flirting with me.

"And then a transport came, on the other side of the tracks. I could see them through the cattle car's cracks. Fingers. Eyes. Just a few, but I knew there were hundreds. Hundreds going off to die. No one else in my car even batted an eye. The woman across the aisle kept talking about how excited she was the Führer had decided not to ban makeup."

Memories of her own cattle car rattled back: days of dark dark, wails, sick, stench. They chugged through Yael. Trackless. Tearing up her insides. It was so easy not to think of it here, with a belly full of spätzle and new sweater sleeves.

It was so easy to pretend she was normal. Not special. Not marked.

But she wasn't. She was. She was.

Memories, words, numbers, monster. All just under her sleeve. Tucked inside her skin. Hiding. Her own leviathan. So, so large.

"Vlad taught me lots of things. Shooting. Lying. Killing. I thought I was training for something important." Aaron-Klaus's face gleamed: anger and sweat. Not a lamp this time, but a torch. Hungry to set something ablaze. "But Reiniger just wants to use me as a messenger boy."

"That's important." Yael looked over at the map, the pins that riddled it like acne. There were more every day. Pushed into all corners of the globe. "The Gestapo reads the mail. Taps the telephones and telegraphs. We need people to deliver things so they stay secret."

The corner television was on, glowing its endless loop of propaganda. An old reel was playing, one Yael had seen many times over. It was the Führer's first speech after the Great Victory. Where he stood in front of "my fellow victors," ushering in "a new era of man." The volume was muted, but every word shone through the tremble of his mustache.

These pictures flickered black and white over Aaron-Klaus's face. "We can't be scared anymore. Someone has to do it. Step up and change things. Kill the bastard."

Not for the first time Yael wished that Valkyries were real. That one would blast through the windows of the Chancellery—all skin, fury, and feathers—and wing the Führer away. Choose one final death.

———

Yael knew it would happen before it did. Aaron-Klaus never told her anything, but she heard it anyway, crammed between the words he didn't say. She saw it in the tight of his fists, the hard of his eyes as he watched the propaganda reels.

When Aaron-Klaus didn't show up for breakfast, Yael knew he wasn't sleeping in. He was not off retrieving files from the drop spot by the florist on Leipziger Street. He was not on an assignment out of Germania; if so, he would've said good-bye.

Yael hoped she was wrong as she hunched over her graphing paper. Working through another list of Henryka's calculus problems. The Reichssender channel flickered, a constant pilot light. There were no propaganda reels today. It was a live recording: Hitler was giving a speech in front of the old Reichstag. The building he torched to secure his power sat in the shadow of the Volkshalle's newly finished behemoth dome.

"The communists thought they would raze our great country to the ground. More than twenty years ago they set fire to this building, the heart of German government. But the Aryan race has arisen victorious. We've left the ruins of old Berlin behind, embraced the monumental splendor of Germania...."

The Führer's words always sounded the same, no matter what he said. His voice was always brassy, laced with fire. Predictably hypnotic.

And then—a different noise. A startling *pop* through the speakers. Two. Three.

Yael looked up from her equations and slopes. There he was somehow, Aaron-Klaus. In front of the stage. His face ablaze—set on the Führer. There was a gun in his hands.

Dark spots bloomed through Hitler's uniform. One, two, three.

He bled like the world.

The Führer crumpled. The silence of the crowd shattered. Jagged, glass-sharp screams stabbed through the speakers. Aaron-Klaus seemed frozen. Unable to run or shoot or speak. Even the SS men seemed to move slowly. They came from every side—like a flower furling in reverse. Ringing in. Tighter, tighter. Aaron-Klaus's gun swung up to his temple.

No one wants to die.

But what was it the nurse had said? *Sometimes people have to die to make things better.*

Someone has to do it.

Another *pop.* So small. So deafening.

A sacrifice.

For the good.

Dusty moon gray flooded her mouth. Graphite. She'd bitten all the way through her pencil.

Yael couldn't spit it out. She couldn't move at all as she watched the SS swarm over the two bodies. The crowd was roaring around them. Roaring. Roaring. Roaring. And then it wasn't human voices at all. The picture cut out, and there was only static. Consuming everything.

She was still staring at it when Henryka walked into the room. The older woman frowned at the screen.

"What's wrong? Did it break?"

For the first time since she'd gotten it, Henryka turned the television off.

There was a death in front of the Reichstag that day (May 16, 1952). But it was not the Führer's.

Three bullets to the chest (though *Das Reich* reported it as four, to make the crime more heinous, the recovery more miraculous) + the finest Aryan surgeons in Germania = a life saved.

Not calculus, though it seemed just as hard to understand. Yael's head swam every time she tried to think about it. Aaron-Klaus was dead, and the world had not changed.

No, that wasn't true. It had changed. A night curfew had been imposed on Germania. Fear of discovery—which had only been a lurking thing before—was thick. Arrests had been made, Reiniger told them. Most of them false connections. Necessary scapegoats, sacrificed on the altar of the Führer's demand for vengeance.

The Gestapo had taken a picture of Aaron-Klaus's dead, unchanging face. They flashed it all over the Reichssender and plastered it all over Germania's alleys and shop windows.

It was only a matter of time before someone recognized him. Before things were traced back to this basement. So they packed up their possessions into empty barrels (boxes would look too suspicious) and moved to another beer hall. Henryka stripped her office barer than a corpse. Shredding piles of encoded letters. Files. Old transcripts. She tore the map off the wall in one furious, fell swoop. Pins went flying: A1, L52, R31... hundreds scattered across the floor.

Yael picked them up. When she found Aaron-Klaus's pin (K15), she slipped it into her pocket. It rattled and poked at the smallest doll as she moved on her hands and knees, gathered up the others. There were tears in her eyes and a burn in her chest. New, yet so, so old.

They left the television off. A lonely, one-eyed prophet in the corner.

"You'll have to leave it," Reiniger told Henryka when he finally arrived. His face was more than severe as he took in the empty room. "Stupid, foolish boy."

Henryka was crying, too. "You should not speak of the dead so."

"He just wanted to change things." Yael exhumed his words, realized how familiar they felt as they left her lips. *Change things.*

You are going to change things. Not Aaron-Klaus.

If only she'd remembered. If only she'd told him. If only she hadn't tried so hard to be normal, to hide the monster inside...

Reiniger's expression curdled. "The only thing he's changed is our chances of a successful operation. We were so close. Weeks from executing Valkyrie. Klaus has unraveled everything. The SS and Gestapo are on a witch hunt. I've told all the cells to lie low, but I have no idea when it will pass."

"We'll wait it out," Henryka whispered. "We'll try again."

"There might not be another chance," the National Socialist general said with a sigh. "There have been too many attempts on his life. The Führer has decided to cease public appearances

205

to minimize risk. He'll address the *Volk* solely over the Reichs-sender. Even if he does go out in public again, the security around him will be impregnable."

"What about his inner circle? Are there any candidates?"

Reiniger shook his head. "Any who showed signs of wavering or weakness were weeded out after the first failed attempt to execute Operation Valkyrie. The Führer only lets the loyal ones close. The ones who would die for him. No one involved in the resistance made that list."

Henryka stared at the television screen—as dead and glassy as her eyes. "There has to be some way."

"For what you're talking about, Henryka, we'd need a doppelgänger. And a sympathetic one at that." Reiniger shook his head. "I'm sorry, but it's over."

Yael's hands were in her sweater pockets, squeezing around the smallest doll and Aaron-Klaus's thumbtack. Its sharp end dug into her palm. She knew there would be blood when she pulled her hand out. But she did not care, she was too busy with other pains. Everything was flooding back—

Chosen by an angel of a different kind.
Marked with an X.
You are special. You can live. You are going to change things.
Yael, but not.
Монстр. Monstre. Monster.
Someone has to do it.
—WAKE UP WAKE UP NOW IT'S TIME—

It wasn't just about staying alive anymore, or being normal. All things were leading up to this.

"Me," Yael said. "I can do it."

All that pain—so fresh, so much, so angry, so old—now awake. Yael took it and wove it through her bones. She shut her eyes and thought of the Valkyrie.

—LET THEM SEE—

She showed them her greatest secret. Her greatest shame. Her change.

CHAPTER 20

NOW

MARCH 21, 1956
BAGHDAD CHECKPOINT
KILOMETER 7,250

Baghdad, a city that really wasn't a city at all. Anymore. Its fringes were only a memory of a town, hollowed shell houses with broken windows, belongings long looted. Mosques loomed. Their walls of mosaics veiled in dust. The spires that had once called all to pray and had guided every eye up toward God now pointed for no one into an empty, washed-out sky.

There was still some life at the center. People spared the horrors of the ever-burning oil fields. Spared to be props for the Reichssender cameras. Spared to be foot servants for the region's *Reichskommissar* and other National Socialist officials. To serve them iced coffee on silver trays and sweep up the dirt their jackboots tracked indoors.

The Baghdad checkpoint was beautiful, much more so than any of the others. Its doorways arched in the most welcoming of ways. Latticed windows caught the day's harsh light, spread it across the floor like a story. Colorful tiles—blue, white, gold—fit together in intricate patterns across the walls. The air bloomed with spices and tea, incense and heat.

The checkpoint's inhabitants were hardly as elegant. The scour of the road was beginning to show on even the most hardened racers. Torn jackets, dented boots, faces scrubbed raw by sand. Language eroded, becoming just as crude as the racers came in, saw their times. (There were more than a few *Scheisse*s and *kuso*s hurled at the blackboard.) The standings hadn't changed much:

> 1st: Adele Wolfe, 7 days, 7 hours, 11 minutes,
> 30 seconds.
> 2nd: Luka Löwe, 7 days, 7 hours, 21 minutes,
> 8 seconds.
> 3rd: Tsuda Katsuo, 7 days, 7 hours, 22 minutes,
> 6 seconds.

Yael was still in the lead. Still a target. The bull's-eye weighed heavy on her back, all eyes aimed at it. No matter where she took her meal of lamb and chickpeas, the stares followed. Katsuo's was the worst: katana-slice sharp. (Yael couldn't be sure, but it seemed that after their washroom encounter, the boy's glares gouged even deeper.) Takeo sat on his right side, flipping his switchblade open and shut. Iwao sat on Katsuo's left, looking particularly miserable. An extra chair sat between him and the victor. The failed drugging attempt must've put Iwao on the outs.

The German boys were watching, too, more closely than Yael might've liked. Taking note of her bruised throat, her scabbed, ruddy cheeks.

It wasn't long before one (or all) of them would strike again. And Iwao had come far too close to ruining her race. Yael needed an ally. A real one—to take night watches and fend off pincer movements.

The options weren't promising. Yael assessed the room like a world-class bettor. Divided the racers into the camps they made themselves:

NAME	STANCE
Katsuo. Takeo. Iwao. Lars. Ralf. Dolf.	*Against her. Point-blank.*
Masaru. Norio. Isamu. Rolf. Karl. Taro.	*Not against her, but none of them would be much help. First-year no-threats didn't make the best allies.*
Yamato.	*Introverted. There was no reading him.*
Luka.	*Who knew, really? She'd thought she had him pegged, but now he was a wild card. Nothing to put her bets on, anyway. Best to keep her distance. Keep the favors owed to one.*

NAME	STANCE
Ryoko.	*Was she the one folding the papers? Yael suspected so. But tiny paper animals and a smile hardly an ally made.*
Hiraku. Hans. Kurt.	*Gone. (Hans Muller and Kurt Stark both withdrew after the sandstorm.)*

There was just one person on her side, in her camp.

Adele's brother sat alone at a table, hunched over the scattered silver innards of his pocket watch. Sleepless purple crescents under his eyes bled seamlessly into his pistol-whipped face. Even after a few days and Nurse Wilhelmina's attentions, the wound looked bad. Blackish, blue, edges of green—still bright enough to shrivel up the words in Yael's throat.

But she needed to say *something* to him. She needed Felix Wolfe on her side if she was to get to the end.

True, he was suspicious. He knew too much while Yael knew too little. But the situation would only grow worse if she ignored it. Like the weeds that always sprang along the borders of Vlad's vegetable garden. She needed to yank his suspicions out by the roots. Plant them elsewhere.

The best way to do this, Yael decided, was to tell Felix Wolfe the truth. Not the whole truth, of course. Felix would do anything for *his sister*, and that was who she had to stay. As for the finer details of her mission…she'd feed him the bread-crumb version. Just enough to lead Adele's brother where she wanted him to go.

It was a risk, betting that Felix's love for his sister was stronger than his fear of the government. But he'd kept Adele's secrets before, staying silent and hidden when she raced in his name.

Why should this one be any different?

Felix didn't even look at Yael when she came to stand by his table. Her shadow stretched over the dozens of metallic cogs and gears. She was close enough to read the letters along the bent casing. Hand-scratched, faded as ghosts: *Property of Martin Wolfe.*

Yael cleared her throat. "Is it broken?"

"Stopped working. Too much sand," Adele's brother muttered. He was using the same tweezers he'd patched her up with so many nights ago to pick through the watch's pieces. "Clogging the gears."

"Can you fix it?" Yael asked.

Felix stared at her the way Adele had just before Yael knocked her out cold. Oh, how those blue eyes could burn! "Do you care? You always hated this watch."

Vendetta against cheap pocket watches owned by dead brothers. Another character trait to add to the list. "I—I just…"

"What do you want, Ad?"

"I thought I should bring you some food." The plate in Yael's hands shuddered as she offered it out. Boiled chickpeas rolled along the rim like lopsided marbles.

"I thought we weren't supposed to accept food from other riders."

"Touché." She set the plate down by Felix's elbow and herself next to it.

Adele's brother turned his stare back to the eviscerated pocket watch.

"I'm sorry for stealing your bike. And…doing that." She nodded to the hurricane bruise that battered his hairline.

Felix kept sorting through the gears with his tweezers. Eyes down, saying nothing.

"I need to win this race," she said again, "and you're right. I need your help. Will you ride with me? The rest of the way?"

He set the tweezers down (it was more of a drop, the way they clattered onto the table, landing awkwardly between the gears) and faced her in full.

"I'm tired, Ad. Tired of sand in my teeth. Tired of having my left eye swollen shut. Tired of being so saddle sore I can barely get up for a night piss. I'm tired of you promising to come home and never being there. I'm tired of your empty apologies, your endless lies. I'm tired of fighting to keep this family together." Adele's brother nodded back at Martin's watch—one hundred timeless pieces of metal and glass. "I'm tired of fixing things that always break."

"I'm tired, too." This was the truth. Yael was exhausted, full of muscle ache and sun-drain. But that was nothing compared to the weariness inside her. The one that began on that train so many years ago. The one that stretched long, long, long down the narrative of her life.

"Then stop," Felix said. "Just stop."

She pictured it for a moment: running from everything. In fact, she'd imagined it before, staring at Henryka's map. She'd decided north would be best, somewhere in the long swath of the Siberian taiga—nothing but snow, animals, pines. No people for hundreds of kilometers. No more death as close as wings. It wouldn't take much to survive off the land, not after all that Vlad had taught her....

But there would be no peace, not even there. Not while the Führer lived on and ashes piled higher, always higher. Too many bodiless souls to count.

No. What weighed inside Yael was something stopping would not fix. There was only one way to end it.

Get to the end.

"I can't," she whispered.

"What do you mean—" Felix stopped short. His spine grew ramrod straight and Yael saw the subtle shift behind his eyes. The *knowing* bursting through him, full throttle.

There was no stopping now. "You're right. I haven't been myself lately, but there's a reason for that. A dangerous, big reason."

Yael watched him carefully as she said this. His tow-blond hair was parted and combed, the essence of order. Its paleness bled down into the rest of his face. Until even his sunburn and bruises were washed out by shock.

She waited for his answer. The muscles in her calves

clenching the same way they had in the closet of Adele's flat. Waiting for attack/truce/retreat. Felix's silence held for another few beats. The cramps crept up Yael's legs, and suddenly she wished she'd picked a less conspicuous place for this encounter.

But all Felix did was whisper, "The secret I told you at camp...it's you."

Yael shook her head in a way that said (screamed), *Not here*. A glance over her shoulder showed her that no one was listening. Not really. Katsuo's stare had migrated to a different corner of the room, where Yamato and Ryoko sat together, the book of poetry open between them. (It was considerably more worn than it had been in Prague: spine cracked, pages dusty and dog-eared.) This time Yamato read the words aloud as Ryoko listened, folding her napkin into quarters. Her smile had grown.

The German boys whose names all sounded the same were archipelagoed around the edge of the room, being interviewed by the Reichssender or napping.

And Luka...he was nowhere to be seen. Probably off flirting with the nurse.

"Will you ride with me?" she asked again.

Felix said nothing. A sharp, sharp silence.

Iwao laughed, too hard, at something Katsuo said. The sound clashed against the tiled walls. Yamato kept reading aloud in a lilting voice, reciting a haiku about the change of season. One of the first-year German boys had started snoring.

215

"Felix...please..." Yael didn't take her eyes off Adele's brother: still wordless, still pale, still elbow deep in pieces of the pocket watch. "I need you."

His answer?

Felix grabbed a fistful of chickpeas. Dropped them one by one into his mouth.

He was in.

CHAPTER 21

NOW

MARCH 22, 1956
BAGHDAD TO NEW DELHI

Yael decided to fall behind. Not in time. She had enough of that (ten minutes was a comfortable lead), but when she kicked her engine to life and started out into Baghdad's streets, she let the herd swallow her and waited for Felix. Luka plumed past, and true to his advice, he stayed just a few meters behind Katsuo's tail. Not losing any time, but not gaining any either.

Yael kept Felix at her side, Luka in her sights, and the end in her heart.

This desert was vastly different from the dunes and sands of the African coast. Its cracked earth stretched far, a devilish, dust-filled landscape. Mountains loomed on the horizon, like the waves of the lie-detector polygraphs Vlad used to hook her up to. The roads were different as well. Less pitted, more amenable to fourth gear.

The first night out they camped in an ancient fort, meters from the road. It was a place long gutted. Riddled with some animal's dried pellets, hemmed by ruined walls. Stars strung across the roofless dark, burning like the oil fields.

Yael sat with her back to the crumbling stones, watching as Felix checked the time with Martin's battered watch (he'd fixed it!) and rooted through his panniers for field rations. He did this with his back to her, she noted, even though the side of his face was the color of spoiled mayonnaise. They hadn't spoken a word since the chickpeas, but words only seemed to be a sliver of the twins' relationship. There was a white flag in the air between them—high and fluttering—tensions off. (At least on Felix's side. Yael had spent much of her time on the road reviewing facts: **Felix Burkhard Wolfe. Anger issues. Lonely, lonely as her.**)

"Dehydrated chicken or dehydrated beef?" Felix broke the silence as he walked up to her, balancing two silver packages in his hands. "Honestly, I can't taste the difference."

The last car he had fixed was a Volkswagen. According to the Wolfes' neighbors, every year on the twins' birthday, Felix visited Martin's grave and held vigil there. Fact after fact after useless fact.

This interaction, this being a sister...it wasn't something Yael could fake.

The solution was simple enough, painful enough.

She just had to treat him like a brother. The way she had once treated Aaron-Klaus.

Above, the starlight wavered from forces long gone, centuries past. Her fourth wolf scorched in skin and memories as Yael reached out and grabbed the closest packet. Chicken.

"Fenrir," she said.

Felix's good eyebrow arched at her.

"That's what I'm naming my bike," Yael explained.

"You mean *my* bike?" Adele's brother slumped down next to her, back against the same decaying wall.

Right. They'd never actually switched motorcycles back after Cairo. The Zündapp she'd started the race with—the Zündapp Felix had limped into the third checkpoint—was long gone. Traded in for one of the few replacements each checkpoint city was stocked with.

"Want it back?"

"After you went to all that trouble?" Felix shook his head. "*Fenrir*'s all yours. Where'd you learn to throw a gun around like that anyway?"

In an alpine valley at a farm that was no farm at all. "Where do you think?"

"Dark alleys? Hidden attics?" His slender shoulders hooked into a shrug. "I don't know. Where do resistance members usually commit sedition?"

The way Felix said this—with tight lips and a snake-slit eye—made it clear he wasn't resistance himself. He must've stumbled across a leak of information.... Yael tore the ration packet open with her teeth and tried not to think of how much

219

intel was puddling all across Europe. Drip, drip, dripping from ear to uncleared ear.

It was time to lay down some crumbs. Divert his suspicions with close enough truths.

"Shisha cafés," she answered.

"I *knew* it!" Felix clenched his fists. Jabbed at some phantom enemy in front of him. "So that was you...."

"Not me," Yael lied. "A double. I saw you following me and had a girl in the café swap clothes. Take my place. I hoped you'd think it was a mistake. Let it go."

Something like anger dawned on Felix's face. "Do you know how much danger you're putting yourself in? Our entire family?"

Yael slipped a piece of chicken into her mouth, buying a few more seconds of silence. *Chew, chew, chew. Swallow chicken down, spit answer out.* "Why do you think I haven't been home? I've been distancing myself on purpose, Felix. To protect you and Papa and Mama. That's why I brained you in the desert. You were supposed to go home," she explained. "I didn't want you getting caught up in this."

"Too late, Ad. It doesn't matter if you're in Frankfurt or a thousand kilometers away! If the Gestapo even caught a whiff of what you're doing, they'll skin you alive. They'll skin *all* of us alive. Whole families have been carted away for less."

Felix's eyes were grave, like he expected her to be surprised. But they'd already carted her family away. Already taken her skin. Alive. She'd watched it slough off like autumn leaves. Everything she was falling away...

"What's the resistance making you do?"

If he thought the race itself was too dangerous, he'd balk at the idea of what Yael had to do in the end. She could not tell him. "They're not *making* me do anything."

"Then what are you choosing to do?" he asked.

She thought of the file Reiniger had given her. The sound of all those thick papers sliding across Vlad's scarred farm table. Adele's life. The Führer's death. Spelled out in no uncertain terms.

A choice.

Was it ever a choice? When every turn and bend of her life twisted to it? When the Babushka told her she would *change things*? When death let her walk away, time and time again? When the stars gave her sandstorms? When she could be anyone, felt like no one?

Yael shook her head. "The world is wrong."

Would Adele say that? Probably not. But Adele wouldn't have joined the resistance in the first place. And it was too late, the words were out now. "We've known it our whole lives, haven't we? But we never say anything because it's easier not to, because someone might be listening. People disappear overnight and are never heard from again. Women are being bred like livestock for the Lebensborn. Husbands, fathers, brothers, sons are all dead—"

She choked on the last word, made herself stop. Because that subject was endless. It held too much of herself. "The world is wrong. I'm just doing my part to fix it."

Wind, still hot and gritty from the desert day, beat against

221

the old fort wall. Accenting their silence. Yael watched Felix from the corner of her eye. He gripped the beef packet, his fingers tight.

"How'd you find out about the mission?" she asked.

"It was the Schuler boy." Felix ripped his package nearly in half as he said this. Dried beef spilled out of the torn plastic. "The one from Wolfsgang Street who always fancied you. He thought you were in danger, so he warned me that something was going to happen on the tour."

"It wasn't his place," Yael said.

"And who says it's yours?" Felix was too flustered to pick up his beef. Instead it just sat in the dust. "For God's sake, Ad, you're just a seventeen-year-old girl! The resistance has no right to ask you to risk everything. Why does it have to be you?"

The boy next to her was so unlike Aaron-Klaus. Aaron-Klaus, who'd found her. Aaron-Klaus, who'd believed in a better world. Aaron-Klaus, who'd left her, forever, because *someone has to do it.*

No, Felix Wolfe was more like a burr. The kind that stuck to your socks after a walk through long grasses. Hooked, stubborn, along for the ride, jabbing if you tried to remove it.

He was jabbing now. Eyes on edge: watching, asking, needing an answer. A reason.

Not *her* reason (four + one + ink + pain).

What would Adele fight for? What would make Felix fight for her?

Yael shoved her hand into her pocket. Felt Aaron-Klaus's thumbtack, the crumpled paper sculptures, the smallest doll.

The answer Adele's brother needed to hear wasn't so far from her own. Lost family. Missing pieces.

Snap, snap, snap, safe. That was what would drive Felix Burkhard Wolfe where Yael wanted him to go. "This world will tear our family apart. Even if I don't get caught on this mission, you and I will get sent to different Lebensraum settlements. Mama and Papa will have no one."

"If we help the resistance, we can change that. We can stay together. Be a family again." These words ached inside Yael as she said them. She gripped the talismans inside her pocket so hard the long-blunted edge of Aaron-Klaus's thumbtack broke skin.

"I'm asking you to trust me," she said. "You can drop out and go home. Or you can help me win this race. Get to the end."

Felix set down his packet. The winds from the wall dipped down, lifted it out of the dust. It danced and fluttered and spun like a living thing through the lamplight. Yael waited for him to ask what the end would be, but it seemed not to matter.

"Remember what Papa said to us the morning of Martin's funeral?"

The old thumbtack dug into her palm. She didn't want to let it go. "I don't like to think about that day."

"Makes two of us," he said, voice changing as he quoted the twins' father, "'There is iron in our blood, and it binds us together. We are Wolfes. We are stronger than this.'"

Felix reached out and touched her arm. There were so many layers—hand over jacket over sleeve over bandage over skin over inked wolves—yet they felt like nothing at all.

"We're Wolfes, Ad. I trust you. And I'm on your side. No matter what."

So many words said through so many more layers—love over the biggest lie of all, over anger, over abandoned, over scared little girl alone on the road. Yet for a moment Yael heard these words skin to skin. She turned her eyes to the crevasses of the night sky—its pits of stars—and imagined that Felix had said them to her, Yael. (After all, there was iron in her blood, too.) That this boy was really on her side. No matter what. That they would get to the end of the race together and that he'd somehow understand why she'd stolen his sister's identity, used it to kill the world's most powerful man. That she would somehow survive what was coming. (*Life or death.*)

It was a nice thought. A nice moment.

But she knew in her heart that Felix would fade like all the others, become nothing but ink in her skin and fragments for nightmares.

He would not walk away. Not like Aaron-Klaus. No—she'd have to tear him out herself, like the burrs on her socks. Show him who she was. What she'd done. What she was about to do.

And it would hurt.

———

Two days passed. Three riders were wiped off the road in a nasty wreck. (Rolf's front wheel caught the sharp side of a

224

rock. The resulting blowout took down ~~Dolf~~ and ~~Norio~~ in a tangle of metal and merciless dust.) Felix stayed at her side, just as he said he would. Together they kept a good pace. Katsuo and Luka stayed in sight, never quite swallowed by the hazed blue horizon. The other ten riders kept on Yael's tail. Hungry engines, famished stares. Every time one of them revved close and tried to clip her, Felix pulled in, edging the offender off the road.

Then came the mountains. They were not as grand and jutting as the Alps, but the roads writhed through them like an angry serpent, edged with fangs of rocks. Sometimes there was no road, only ledges barely wider than their wheels. Felix stayed behind Yael, stalwart and grim-faced as she balanced her bike along the path. Prayed into the heights of the sky that she would not fall.

She didn't. Felix let out a scuff of a breath when they reached the other side, bikes intact, bodies whole. His shoulders shook when he looked back at the drop they'd just skirted. Well over twenty meters. Bone-dashing at best.

And then she remembered: **Acrophobia: an intense fear of heights**.

He faced it for her, without so much as a word.

"You okay?" Yael didn't have to fake the concern in her voice.

"Yeah." He shuddered when he said this. "How do you think the Reichssender crew and the supply vans will get past that?"

"They must be taking a longer route. Around this mountain

range." Which meant they were alone this stretch. No room for error. Poisoned rations or mechanical breakdowns during this leg could mean the end of things.

"Lucky them." Felix's eyebrows twitched under his goggles. "We should go, before Luka and Katsuo get too far ahead."

But there was no fear of that. A few curves and slopes later they found the pair, stopped in the middle of the road. Their engines were off, as were their helmets. Yael brought her own Zündapp to a halt.

They'd reached a dead end.

The craggy brown mountains that rose on either side had collapsed, swallowing the road with dirt and boulders. Some of these were far bigger than Katsuo, who was scaling the mass. Luka leaned against his motorcycle, watching with lazy eyes as he plucked a new cigarette out of his silver case. Yael parked her Zündapp a good distance from his and kept one hand shoved into her P38 pocket as she tore off her goggles, got a clear view.

There was no way past it. It was so steep that Katsuo had to use his hands to steady himself as he climbed. By the time he reached the top, he was in miniature.

"Landslide," Luka grunted.

"We can see that, dummkopf," Felix muttered under his breath as he pulled up next to Yael.

"It looks recent." Yael slipped off her bike. The debris in the road was still churned up. Not pounded down by the elements. Her eyes followed it, scanning the hillsides.

Adele's brother picked up a handful of the loose dirt and

let it sift through his fingers. Katsuo crouched on the mountain above. Luka wedged the cigarette between his lips and hunted for a match.

And then Yael saw it. Her breath hitched.

"Someone did this on purpose," she said. "Look."

Felix followed the plane of her finger. To the high, high mountainside, where the earth had been scooped in chunks that reminded Yael of the bomb scars that pocked Europe's buildings. The signature of explosives.

"But why? Who?" Felix asked.

Yael pulled her pistol out of her pocket. Kept her eyes on the hillsides. There were shadows in the pockets of stone. Too many places to hide.

Luka wasn't leaning anymore. He dropped his cigarette case and reached into the back of his trousers, producing a gun of his own. "*Scheisse*," he muttered, and aimed his Luger into the wounded hills.

But the dark places of the mountains were already rising, pulling apart. Men spilled out, swarming their valley, arms full of Mosin-Nagant rifles (7.62 mm). Soviet-made. More accurate than Yael would like to think with their barrels aimed at her chest.

"Drop your weapons!" This was the solid German command from the man at the front of the pack, followed by a clattering stream of Russian. "Track the boy from the hillside. Make sure he doesn't get away. We can't afford any loose ends."

Two men broke off from the rest, started to climb the unsteady earth. A glance up showed Yael that Katsuo was gone. Only a wisp of dust in his place.

"Put your gun down, Fräulein Wolfe." The commander spoke German again. "It is our preference to keep you in one piece."

Two pistols stood no chance against so many rifles. Yael knelt down, placing her precious P38 in the middle of the ruined road, alongside Luka's gun. They looked so small and useless between the rocks.

"On your knees," the commander barked. "Hands on your head."

She knelt down, studying the group as she did so. There were nearly twenty in all, including the men who had gone after Katsuo. Their uniforms had seen better years (some were not wearing them at all), but it was easy to tell they were what was left of the Soviet army. Specters from the white space on Henryka's map.

Though the Soviet Union had been crumbling before the Axis's double-border invasion, Hitler's Great Victory completely shattered it, claiming every piece of land just beyond the Ural Mountains. Moscow. Leningrad. All the cities and their surrounding farmlands were claimed for the Lebensraum—the necessary eastward spread of the Aryan race. The rest, the Reich claimed, belonged to the Greater East Asia Co-Prosperity Sphere. But Emperor Hirohito had his sights set to the Pacific, so the wilds of Siberia went untouched. It was a wasteland stripped of infrastructure and export, reduced to feudal living.

There were stories of border raids in the Lebensraum east of the Urals, but Yael had never heard of guerrilla fighters this far south. What were they doing so far past the border? And why were they pointing guns at some of the Axis's most prized youth?

Yael listened for answers as the Babushka's language chuffed back and forth between them:

"Where are the rest of the racers?"

"Coming along the ledge. Our comrades will close in behind, make sure there is no escape."

Our comrades. It was a whole platoon.

"Let's get them back to base," the commander's Russian boomed against the valley sides. "Comrade Gromov, once the rest of the racers are detained, you're to radio Novosibirsk. Let them know the first part of our operation is complete. Tell them we're awaiting further instructions."

"Yes, Comrade Commander Vetrov."

Yael kept her face mystified, writ with question marks, as the soldiers bound her hands. Adele didn't speak Russian. Neither did Felix or Luka—a fact that played plainly across their features.

"Up!" the soldier behind her ordered in sloppy German. "Come with."

She stood. Started walking at the prod of his Mosin-Nagant. The rifle herded her toward the hill. The entrails of dirt and rocks they'd eviscerated from the earth.

"What about their motorbikes?" One of the men nudged Katsuo's bike with his rifle.

Comrade Commander Vetrov turned without a glance. "Leave them. They won't need them anymore."

CHAPTER 22

NOW

MARCH 25, 1956

The "base" was an abandoned village. Stone box houses stacked like a child's building blocks along a mountainside. They were a good way from the Axis Tour route, at least thirty minutes of being sardined in the back of a truck. While they'd rattled in the transport—all cussing, jabbing limbs, and dark—Yael closed her eyes and thought of the map in Henryka's office. Officially they were in red-mapped space, Reich territory. In reality it was a no-man's-land made of gutted villages and crumbling roads, just southwest of the white void.

The perfect place for the Axis Tour racers to go missing without a trace.

The soldiers guided them to a house in the center of the village. A single, large room with barred windows. There was more than enough room for the thirteen of them. Every remaining racer except Katsuo.

According to the guards, he'd disappeared. Yael positioned herself closest to the door, where she could hear the guards gossiping in the Russian they thought none of the prisoners could understand.

It was, however, hard to hear when the room around her was crammed with fear, arguments on the brink of exploding.

"Do you think they're going to kill us?" whimpered one of the German boys. (Ralf, maybe? A first-year, no threat.)

"I've heard that communists pull your fingernails out one by one and make you eat them!" Lars said next to him. Ralf's mouth twisted, as if he were about to be sick.

Luka groaned, repositioned his bound arms against the wall behind him. "I'd give all my fingernails for a cigarette right now."

"They have nothing to gain in our deaths." Yamato's Japanese flowed from the other side of the room. Even in their captivity the Germans and the Japanese sat apart. Luka, Felix, Yael, Karl, Lars, Ralf on one side. Yamato, Iwao, Takeo, Taro, Isamu, Masaru, Ryoko on the other. "Not yet."

The German racers blinked at him, their brains jogging to translate. Though most riders took the other country's language in secondary school, it was rare that they actually communicated with one another.

"He says soldiers have no reason to kill." Ryoko's German was slow—syllables stunted and grammar excruciatingly proper—but all who heard understood.

"Katsuo ordered us not to talk to them!" Takeo hissed at the girl in Japanese.

231

"And where is Katsuo?" Ryoko snapped back. "Some leader he is: forcing you to do his dirty work, abandoning you at the first sign of trouble!"

The other racer looked affronted. "Tsuda Katsuo is going to win the Double Cross and bring honor to our nation! I am proud to help him do it! As you should be!"

"There won't *be* a Double Cross if we don't get out of here," Ryoko reminded him. "The Germans can help us escape."

"The Germans aren't our friends," Takeo said. "No matter how many presents you leave under Victor Wolfe's pillow."

The girl's face paled.

"They're going to pull out our fingernails first!" Lars's German escalated to a wail. Drowning out the Japanese conversation. "*Then* they're going to kill us!"

"Will you all shut it?" Yael found herself scowling at the entire room. Her head was pounding, clashing with plans and the impossibility of the situation before them. The knife was still in her boot, but it wasn't enough. From what she'd seen on their way in, the village was well guarded.

None of the racers challenged her. Unsteady quiet blanketed the room, interrupted only by the diesel burps of truck engines and the chatter of their guards.

"We have two hours before the Axis Tour's supply vans complete their detour and realize the racers are missing. We're hoping to find the Japanese boy before we move out."

"He can't have gone far."

"The scouts swear he's disappeared. No big loss anyway. The racers we got should be enough leverage."

232

Two hours. Their time was running out. And Yael very much doubted that Katsuo was coming back to rescue them.

"Do you have a plan?" Felix whispered into her ear.

Not much of one. Reiniger, she knew, had been in communication with Novosibirsk, where the remnants of the Soviet Union's government now sat. She'd seen the messages delivered to him in blocky Cyrillic symbols. But Reiniger never allowed her close enough to see the meat of those letters. These were things not related to her mission, he reasoned. Things she did not need to know, so they could not be tortured out of her if she was captured. Yael suspected that this line of reasoning went both ways. It seemed Reiniger had not thought it necessary to share the finer details of her mission with the Russians.

He never thought she'd be captured by his own allies.

Protocol was this: Reveal nothing. Especially under duress.

But now, Yael did not see any other way. Her skinshifting was no help in a village with only men. And one knife against a whole platoon... The only effective weapon she had was the truth.

Yael wheeled around and kicked the wooden door with her boots. The guards' chatter snuffed short. She yelled to them, "Comrades!"

"Are you mad, Fräulein?" Luka scowled. "They're about two steps away from shooting us as it is!"

She ignored him and kept thrashing at the wood. The door flew open. Afternoon light speared through, along with the muzzle of a rifle. Yael froze.

"Quiet!" the guard ordered with a jerk of his Mosin-Nagant.

"I need to speak with your commander." The German tumbled out of her, blurring and fast, before he could shut the door again. The guard's brow wrinkled; she could see him trying to interpret her words.

"Vetrov," she tried again. "Let me talk to Vetrov."

A second silhouette edged into the door. The other guard. His German was better. "Why? What do you have to say to him?"

The first guard's rifle was still aimed at her chest. But more than this, Yael was aware of the twelve pairs of eyes and ears in the room behind her. If this was to work, she had to maintain her cover. She couldn't make it look like she was collaborating with the Russians.

"The Japanese boy. The one who ran. I know where you can find him." It was the only thing she could think of that might drag her to Vetrov's office without raising the others' suspicions. She only hoped the guards would bite.

("See?" Takeo spit in the room behind her. "The Germans aren't our friends.")

The fluent guard reached out, lowered his companion's firearm. "Where?"

She shook her head. "Take me to Vetrov. I'll only tell him."

The soldiers looked at each other for a moment, conferring in murmurs of Russian she could only catch in pieces.

"Come with me." The second guard pulled her up by the arm, out of the building.

"While you're at it, could you tell them I want my cigarettes back?" Luka's proud voice slipped out of the closing door. She found it oddly comforting as the guard with the good German dragged her through the village, into another abandoned building.

Comrade Commander Vetrov was wilted over his makeshift desk, like a houseplant left weeks to its own devices. Even his eyes were the color of sad celery—watery, tired—when they settled on Yael and her guard. He sat up straight and waved them into the room.

"What's she doing here?" His Russian was snapping, edged with exhaustion.

"She says—"

Yael broke in. Her own Russian was as fluent as it was those many years ago, during her nights with the Babushka. "Many pardons, Comrade Commander, but I had to speak with you in private. Away from the other racers."

"I was not aware you spoke our mother tongue, Miss Wolfe."

"I'm not Miss Wolfe."

And there it was. The truth. All lies stripped back in a single sentence.

She stood—as exposed as the smallest doll—while a mountain breeze licked through the glassless windows. It rattled stacks of papers and curled the edge of Vetrov's map. It blew some of Adele's angel-wisp hairs into Yael's face. She watched through the fringe as the comrade commander's face twisted and turned. Several times he opened his mouth, but no words came.

"I'm part of the resistance movement. I've been assigned to steal Adele Wolfe's identity and participate in the Axis Tour. I've been posing as her for a couple of weeks now."

"So you're saying that you are not Miss Wolfe? You're... someone else?"

Yael nodded.

Vetrov's eyes were no longer drooping. They were more of a biting mint color as they narrowed at her. "You're lying."

She nodded at the gold band on his right-hand ring finger. "Do you have a picture of your wife?"

"Yes, but—"

"Show it to me," she said.

From the bolster of neck veins and the thinning of his lips, Yael expected him to shout *nyet*, but the officer dipped his hand behind his lapel. Pulled out a black-and-white photo— worn and loved. Looked at many times. The woman printed on the paper had dark hair and a sad gray smile. One that matched her eyes.

Yael took this woman's image deep into herself. She folded the sad and gray into her own irises. Pressed it behind her own lips. The hair ruffling against her cheeks turned dark, heavier. Yael had to guess the finer colors, the way she had with Bernice Vogt's photograph oh so long ago. Again, it worked.

Comrade Commander Vetrov took in this uncanny version of his wife with remarkable calm. His hands clasped together over the map. "I see."

The guard behind her did not start or reach for his Mosin-Nagant. Something was not right. Both men had just watched

her change—become *someone else* in front of their very eyes—
and they hadn't even flinched. True, Comrade Commander
Vetrov's eyes looked even more alert (a whole garden of fresh
now), but it was more out of thought than surprise.

Perhaps it was because they were soldiers. Trained to see
the impossible, deal with shock. But the others had been soldiers, too. Like Reiniger, who'd sworn and turned so white he
could have been dead. Like Henryka, whose mouth had hung
open for a good two minutes before she could shut it. Like
Vlad, who'd reached for his drawer of hunting knives before
Reiniger could calm him down. Explain things.

It was all very odd.

"I'm not Adele Wolfe." It sounded strange, saying this
aloud after so many days of telling herself the opposite. Yael
went on, trying to shake the men's apathy. "You're making a
very big mistake, stopping this race. If I fail my mission, the
entire resistance will suffer."

"And what exactly is your mission?"

Lying would be natural, simple. What she was trained
to do. But Yael had also been trained to read situations, and
she could taste the tension of this room—the years of warfare
and guerrilla fighting that weighed on Comrade Commander
Vetrov's shoulders, a bitterness toward the Reich in his eyes.
(Yael recognized these things because they were what she
herself carried.) She knew that only the truth would convince
this man. Only the truth had a chance at setting her free.

"The Third Reich is rotting from the inside. People are
unhappy with the New Order, even some in the Führer's

237

closest circles. The resistance has been growing, connecting under the Gestapo's nose. We're strong enough to change things now. Every cell in every city is waiting for the signal to rise up and destroy the New Order.

"My mission is to give that signal. My mission is to kill the Führer at the Victor's Ball. For all the world to see." The enormity of Yael's words filled the room, pressing into every corner.

This time Vetrov looked surprised. "You? You are going to kill the Führer?"

"Only if I win the Axis Tour, which will be impossible if you kidnap all of its participants," Yael said sharply. "You have to release us."

"That will be difficult," the commander told her as he slipped the photograph of his wife back inside his weathered uniform. "My orders came directly from Novosibirsk. We're to capture the racers of the Axis Tour and use them as political leverage to reclaim our territory in the west."

"Leverage?" Yael couldn't believe the word leaving her mouth. "How does Novosibirsk expect to keep racers hostage without bringing the wrath of Hitler on its head?"

Vetrov shrugged. "As you said. The Third Reich is rotting, on the verge of falling apart. We've been...alerted that a putsch is on the horizon. We're just trying to reclaim the land they took before anarchy takes over."

"But—it won't work. The Reich won't fall apart unless I give the signal. And that can only happen if you let us go."

The commander frowned. "If I released you, it could be considered treason."

Treason. Facing a firing squad and their gun barrel's punctuating ends. What commander would risk that?

"This is all a big misunderstanding," Yael said. "Erwin Reiniger. He's my commander, and I know he's been in contact with Novosibirsk. He's the one who alerted you to the putsch. If you radio them and explain things—"

Comrade Commander Vetrov stood slowly.

"I will radio Novosibirsk. But even then I cannot guarantee your freedom. Also, I would prefer it if you stopped imitating my wife, Miss W—" The officer caught himself, choked back her alias. "What is your name, exactly?"

Yael melded back into Adele's features. The winter-struck hair and eyes that fit as tight as a glove.

"If they ask, you can tell them I'm called Volchitsa." She knew her code name was the only one of worth. The only one Reiniger would have offered to the Soviets, if he'd offered one at all.

"Volchitsa." The officer repeated it in a way that Yael, even with her flawless Russian, could not imitate. With the same crusting lilt her old friend used to use, with the love of a mother tongue. "She-wolf. An interesting choice."

"I didn't choose it," she told him. "It chose me."

———

Yael spent an hour slumped against the far wall of Comrade Commander Vetrov's improvised office. Watching the afternoon sun shift through windows, over the cracks of the forgotten building. Counting the trucks and men and guns that rolled past the window. (Three trucks. Twenty-three men. Too many guns.)

The guard stood across from Yael. It was clear he did not think of her—cross-legged on the dirt floor, hands bound—as a threat. He looked relaxed: shoulders sloped, rifle loose at his side. It would've been easy enough to overpower him—kick his feet out from under him, pin him unconscious, use the knife still hidden in her boot to sever her ropes.

She could even escape the camp, she figured. If she stripped off his uniform, used it with some added height, short hair, and the cap tugged low over her eyes.

But that wouldn't help things. Not really. She needed to win the Axis Tour, and for that she needed the other racers. There was no way she could smuggle twelve racers out from under a loaded platoon with only an hour left.

A long shadow grew in the doorway, materialized into a red-faced Comrade Commander Vetrov. Yael stood, her lungs as full as a hot-air balloon while the Soviet officer walked back to his desk.

"I've spoken with my superiors. They have no knowledge of communiques with Erwin Reiniger, or of the name Volchitsa."

Yael felt the air in her lungs leaking. Down, down, down to earth.

"They've ordered me to bring you back to Novosibirsk," the officer went on. "So they can verify your story."

Back to Novosibirsk? That was thousands of kilometers in the wrong direction. It would mean the end of her race. The failure of her mission.

Not now. She'd come so far, fought too much....

The commander's eyes flashed to the guard. "Aleksei, go resume your post at the prisoners' house. Leave the girl. I'll take care of her."

When the guard bowed out, left them alone, the Soviet officer sighed. It was a sound that pressed him into his desk chair.

"We're no good to you as leverage." Yael tried not to yell this. "If I go back to Novosibirsk, the resistance won't strike. The Reich will be as strong as ever, and once you threaten the lives of their prized youth, they'll invade. Raze Novosibirsk to the ground. It's in everyone's best interests if you let us go."

"The thing is, Volchitsa, I believe you. I believe you, but my hands are tied." He nodded at Yael's arms as he said this. The ones that were actually bound with rope. "If I let you go, my life and my men's are forfeit."

Yael thought there would be an end to her breath. That her insides might stop sinking. But they seemed bottomless.

The Soviet officer put his hand on the desk. It landed harder than it ought have: with a clunk over the splay of papers. When Vetrov's fingers drew back Yael saw why. Her Walther P38 sat on the map—over coordinates and red marks and countries that long ago lost their names.

Vetrov nudged the pistol forward with his knuckles. Over borders. Back toward where Yael stood.

"But—should you escape on your own—that's a different matter entirely."

CHAPTER 23

NOW

MARCH 25, 1956

"Took you long enough." Luka's voice was the first to greet Yael as she was shoved back into the racers' room. Even with his arms tied behind him the boy looked lounging, lionlike. "No cigarettes?"

Yael fought the urge to roll her eyes as she stepped over Luka's outstretched legs. No, she didn't have cigarettes. But she did have the gun Vetrov slipped into her jacket pocket, and a plan. Both of these things sat close to her heart as she settled by Adele's brother.

"What were you doing, Ad? You were gone so long." Felix swallowed. "I thought something had happened."

"Yes, what *were* you doing, Fräulein?" Luka sat up straight. "Chatting about the weather?"

"She was selling out Katsuo to the commies," Takeo said in Japanese, scowling from the other side of the room's shadows.

The ones that grew thicker with every minute the sun dipped lower behind the mountains, swelling their valley with early twilight.

Felix tensed beside her. In the corner of her eye, she could see his jaw working. His own icy stare was locked on Luka, who caught it and smirked back.

This—it occurred to Yael—was the perfect chance to leave the boys behind. She alone had a gun. She alone knew that there was a transport truck parked at the fringes of the village. She alone knew that Comrade Commander Vetrov was calling all his men to a briefing at 1800. The only soldiers between them and that truck would be Aleksei and the other door guard.

But she couldn't finish the race without them. There would *be* no race without them.

"I was scouting." Yael fished her knife out of her boot as she whispered this. It took a few tries. She had to bend her body at awkward angles (which might have been impossible if Yael hadn't used her skinshifting to lengthen Adele's arms a few centimeters), fumbling for the hilt with bloodless finger-tips. Once the knife was out, she twisted around, wedged the blade (edge up) between the soles of Felix's boots, and started sawing.

Every eye in the room watched as her ropes fell away. Yael rubbed life back into her wrists, then started to cut the fat twines of Felix's rope.

Luka's spine strung even straighter, his eyes narrowing. "Scouting *what* exactly?"

Another flash of silver and Felix was free. Yael peered through the window's rusted bars. Light pastelled against the ridge-backed hills—sharp jags and soft glow. They'd have to move out soon; 1800 was coming, dipping low with the sun.

"There are plenty of transport vehicles a few hundred meters from here. We reach one of those, and we've got a chance of getting out of here." She looked straight at Luka and held up her knife. "Do you want to be free or not?"

His eyes whet against the blade, their own kind of sharp. Finally he turned, offering up his hands. "So...what...we're just going to walk out the door and drive away?"

"Most of the men are concentrated at the north end of the village." Yael sliced his bonds as she said this, passing the knife along so Luka could do the same for Lars. "If we can take care of the two guards at the door, we should be able to sneak down the western side streets without being seen. We get to a transport and steal it. We'll be kilometers away before they realize we're gone."

Ryoko, Yael realized, was busy translating her German. Explaining the situation. The Japanese racers listened quietly, their faces still. Betraying nothing.

"And what if we get caught?" one of the younger Japanese boys (Masaru, 14, no threat) asked Ryoko once she'd finished explaining. "Has Victor Wolfe thought of that?"

"They'll kill us!" Takeo said this twice. Once in Japanese. A second time in German, so the whole room could understand what was about to happen.

All eyes turned to Yael. Waiting for her to tell Takeo he was wrong.

Unfortunately he wasn't. This was one thing Vetrov had made clear. If his men saw them running, they'd shoot. And the commander would do nothing to stop them.

This would be a real escape. A real game of life and death.

"We might not be friends, but we don't have to be enemies. If we work together, we can escape. All of us." Yael looked at Ryoko as she said this. A mayfly smile flickered over the girl's face as she turned to translate.

Takeo said nothing. When his own ropes were cut free, he waved Yael's knife off in a different direction, pulled his Higonokami from his boot, and flicked it open. The knife's edge had been sharpened so many times that its slightest touch melted through the next racer's ropes. He gave Yael a pointed look (much, much blunter than any of Katsuo's) and passed his prized weapon to Yamato. Brass hilt first.

Both blades made their rounds through the room, slicing racers free. When Yael's knife finally reached her again, she stood and walked to the door. The lock between them and the guards was simple enough. It would take only seconds to pry open.

"If you want to stay, fine. I'm leaving," she told them. "If you want to live, I suggest you do the same."

Every single racer stood. Yael waited until they were all pressed close to the door. She sank the blade into the wedge with all her strength.

Splinter, pull, *pop*.

Felix flew, shoulder first, into the wood.

CRASH.

Aleksei didn't even have the chance to yell before Luka was on top of him. Pulling the guard down in a flash of leather and speed. (Those abdomen muscles, it seemed, weren't all for show.)

Adele's brother handled the other guard. Two uppercuts later, the soldier was on the ground. Gunless.

"Let's move!" Yael hissed. Both guards were out. Luka bent over Aleksei's still form, the Mosin-Nagant tucked under his arm, fingers dancing through the unconscious guard's pockets.

True to Vetrov's word, this section of the village was empty: littered with abandoned, crumbling houses. The transport sat at the bottom of the hill, a few odd meters past the last forgotten building. Yael led the way—knees jarring down the steep slope. Her boots slid through layers of gravel as she tried her hardest not to fall.

They were halfway down the hill when the first shot sounded. No yells, no warning. Just a rifle's thunderous cry. Ripping through the crown of wild mountains. Tearing Yael's breath out of her throat.

The wail that followed it was thin in comparison. "They're escaping!"

Another shot. The wall by Yael's head cracked and cratered. She stopped worrying about the gravel, ran faster. Until her feet weren't even touching the ground. She was skidding down the hill, tumbling on a riptide of rocks.

Above her, behind her was all noise. Luka swearing. Boots and boys skidding. Shouts and shots.

Finally, *finally* she reached the bottom of the hill. Another few lunges brought her to the truck's cab door. Yael threw it open, saw the scene behind her.

Vetrov's squad gathered like a storm at the hillcrest. Pouring over. Their rifle muzzles flared lightning bright in early dusk. Raining lead core and pain on the escapees below.

Boys were already piling into the back of the transport. Bursting through their own dust cloud. Ralf, Lars, Masaru, Iwao, Karl...

Felix ran up next to her. "Hurry, Ad!"

Taro, Ryoko, Isamu...

Ten. That's how many had made it to the truck. Ten out of thirteen. There were no more silhouettes breaking through the thick, thick dust. Just rifle cracks and men running down the hill.

"We have to go! Now!" Adele's brother screamed. Vetrov's soldiers were halfway to the transport. Tumbling at the same speed as the rocks.

—HE'S RIGHT GO GO SAVE WHAT YOU CAN—

Number eleven appeared: Takeo, Higonokomi blade in hand, throwing himself into the back of the transport. The cloud behind him was starting to thin, enough so that Yael could see the final two. One: smaller and stumbling, hurt. The other: just behind, trying to hold back the deluge with his own single rifle.

And an army pouring down the hill.

They weren't going to make it.

Not alone.

"We have to leave them!" Felix was already inside the cab, fumbling with the dashboard, searching for the keyless ignition.

—GO GO SAVE WHAT YOU CAN—

The lines in Yael's soul dug deep as claws. Her third wolf howled (all guilt, all regret), and the road in front of her was full. Too full. With the boys who would not make it. With the army behind.

Did it matter?

—SAVE WHAT YOU CAN—

I can save them all, Yael thought back. Against herself.

"Start the truck!" she screamed at Adele's brother, and tore away before he could stop her. "I'll be back!"

She ran back toward the gunfire and saw Nagao Yamato's mouth knotted tight in pain, his steps limp and uneven. When Yael drew closer, she saw why: His right foot was bent, twisted. Every time his weight fell on it, he screamed, but he kept pushing.

Just beyond, yelling the injured racer forward, was Luka. The victor was a terrifying sight. Wild and torn; his face smeared in red like war paint. He had his back to Yamato, the stolen rifle pressed into his shoulder. Aim and *BOOM*. A soldier above them crumpled, fell still on the hillside.

One out of a dozen.

"Move your ass, Yamato!" Luka screamed in clumsy Japanese as he twisted back the bolt, slid in a second cartridge.

The earth spit around her: rock, metal, death. But Yael

kept running, straight to Yamato's side. She threw his arm over her neck, started to pull him forward.

Six meters. Five. Four. Yael could see all the faces of the other racers—pale and anxious, strung like misshapen pearls. Exhaust spilled out the truck's tailpipe.

Luka's gun went off a second time.

Three meters. Two. The other racers' hands reached out from the truck. White arms. Ghost fingers. Reaching, reaching...

One meter. None.

Yamato's weight rose off her shoulder. Yael clawed onto the transport's bumper. Already it was moving, pulling away under Felix's lead foot as she heaved herself up. Yamato slid in beside her, dragged by Takeo and Taro.

Luka.

Yael pushed up on the truck bed's rough floorboards and saw him running, face grim through the mask of exhaust. Arms windmilling. Behind him, the first of the soldiers. So close Yael could see the stars embroidered on their uniforms— as red as Luka's bloody face.

Luka was fast, but the soldier behind him was faster. Closing the ground between them with black-booted lunges. His arm outstretched with hungry claws of fingers.

He's not going to make it.

Yael reached into her jacket, pulled out the pistol Vetrov had returned to her. She held it high, lined up the sights, tried to ignore how the truck was shaking beneath her. Yael held her breath and pulled the trigger.

She was done leaving people behind.

There was an explosion of fabric and red by the soldier's knee. He fell screaming as Luka ran, ran, ran. Launched himself into the back of the transport. He landed so close to Yael that she felt his bristle and scruff brush her cheek. Smelled the stick of his blood.

She lifted her gun again and peered down the sights. But there was no need. The truck's engine howled in the octave of highest gear. Wheels churned faster than any mortal could run. Vetrov's men became silhouettes, blurred shadows, then nothing.

Yael tucked her pistol away. Her hand still shook, but this time it wasn't the truck's fault.

They were all here, not one left behind: Yamato in the farthest corner, cradling his twisted ankle. Ryoko next to him, already examining the injury. Takeo, Isamu, Lars, Masaru, Ralf, Taro, Karl, Iwao—all sprawled and breathless on the flatbed's boards. Felix in the cab, foot on the pedal and hands gripping the wheel.

And Luka, still leaning hard against her. With heaving breaths and a face full of blood. His cheek smeared red all over Yael's clothes. She didn't have the heart to push him away.

"They're going to follow us! They're going to follow us and kill us!" Lars watched the dark road behind them. The terror in his eyes was fresh, startling. The fear of the never-hunted.

Yael envied it.

Takeo, who sat next to the German boy, shook his head. "They won't."

"Like *you'd* know!" The panic had spread from Lars's eyes to the rest of his face.

Takeo lifted his Higonokami knife. He handled the blade like a sacred thing; there was an art to his movements as he guided it through the air. Too fast for Yael or any of the other stunned riders to react. But Takeo was not cutting, or stabbing. Just showing.

"I would, actually." He looked at Lars down the length of the blade and spoke in perfect German. "There were only two other transports, and they were parked quite close to our prison. I slashed their tires."

CHAPTER 24

THEN

THE FIFTH WOLF: VLAD
APRIL 1955

"You are thinking too hard." Her trainer's words shot straight past Yael's shoulder. Over the long alpine field, to the row of empty vodka bottles. He spoke Russian this time—a language he tended to favor. "Squeeze the trigger on the bottom of your exhale. The P38 will do the rest. Try again."

Yael lifted the pistol. One-handed, fencing stance. Her arm was sleeveless, and the April air was still a bitter thing in the mountains. A minefield of goose bumps washed over her bare skin and the numbers lined there.

She was shaking too hard. There was no way she'd make the shot.

"You know"—she let the gun fall to her side and faced Vlad—"if you'd let me use my right arm, all of these would be gone in thirty seconds."

Vlad smiled, and the crags of his face softened. (Even the deep knife scar that ran over his empty eye socket. The one he never talked about.) It was a genuine paternal expression. So unlike the way Dr. Geyer had looked at her... "And then what would we use for targets? Even I can't drink that fast. Besides, the point of this exercise is for you to use your weak side. There will come a day when you'll need to shoot with it."

Yael knew he was right. Reiniger was the one who sent her here, but it was Yael herself who first asked about learning how to shoot. She liked the idea of power in her hand. The same power the guards at the death camp carried every day, the same power Aaron-Klaus had tried to use against the Führer.

The power of life and death.

She wanted to harness it, make it her own.

But it was harder than it seemed. It wasn't just finding a shiny gun. Point and shoot. It wasn't just hours standing in front of fence posts, aiming at imaginary enemies. It wasn't just the mornings of sixteen-kilometer runs through the woods. It wasn't just afternoons of martial arts and knife work and skinshifts. It wasn't just evenings of language study and lie-craft.

It wasn't just becoming strong. It was about becoming not weak. And this process was something else entirely.

"It's cold," Yael said. "I need my sweater."

It wasn't the cold making her shake. Yael knew it. And Vlad knew it, too. (After three years of continual lessons, Yael often suspected that her trainer understood her better than she did herself.)

"No," he told her. "Shoot."

Yael aimed at the vodka bottle again. The numbers on her arm were so close: 121358ΔX. She couldn't not look at them.

"Look down the sights. Straight ahead," Vlad growled. "That's where the danger is."

Yael breathed in the mountain-fresh air, breathed out—to the end of breath itself—and squeezed the trigger.

She missed.

The pistol shot echoed around them. Off in the distance an avalanche answered, cracking down thunderous, spiny slopes.

"Better." Vlad switched to Japanese. As always, it took Yael's brain a half second longer to register the change. "You were actually looking this ti—"

Her trainer stopped speaking and held up his palm (this, too, was scarred, struck through the center), shorthand for silence. Yael held her breath and listened: gravel grumbling under tires. She turned to look down at the valley's only road. A battered Volkswagen churned along, working up a cottontail of dust.

Someone was coming.

No one came to Vlad's farm. Most people had no reason to—it was too far in the Alps for idle country drives or hikers—and the few who did were preceded by an elaborate series of radio signals.

"Change faces. Get to the third arsenal," Vlad ordered her. "Wait for my signal."

The third arsenal was the far wall in the barn loft. Behind stacks of last season's graying hay. The two cows Vlad kept for milk nosed their stall doors as Yael rushed in, switched her face to match the papers of a girl named Liesl Gehring, climbed the ladder, chose the Mauser Kar98K, and lay by the loft's open window. She watched the road and waited.

Vlad stood at the edge of the drive, hands shoved into his pockets where his own gun sat. Ready.

The Volkswagen pulled up, its engine wheezing from the long climb up the mountains. A man in a long, dark coat stepped out. His face was shaded by the brim of his hat.

Yael took a long breath. Her index finger hovered just above the trigger.

"Where is she?" The man slammed the car door shut.

Vlad took his hands out of his pockets just as Yael exhaled. They were empty. No gun.

"What are you doing up here, Erwin?"

Reiniger! Yael's finger slid off the trigger, but she stayed where she was.

"We have an assignment for Yael."

The last of Yael's breath left her lips. For a moment she forgot to inhale again. The hay bale prickled against her stone-hard lungs.

An assignment. Doing something. Changing things. She'd dreamed about this moment for months now—every night, lying on her bunk, staring at the knots in the pinewood ceiling, before the real dreams (nightmares, always nightmares) set in.

Vlad shook his head. "Her training isn't complete. She's not ready."

"You've had her almost three years. That's longer than most operatives we've sent here. Besides, I've seen her test results. What part of her isn't ready?"

"There's more to going in the field than just performance. I will not make the same mistake I made with Klaus. Yael needs more time here."

Klaus. Three years and that name still carved at Yael's heart like a potato peeler. Scraping off angry, raw, battered, bloody bits. Pain she could not fully face, so she pushed it into other things. Shooting. Running. Lying. Fighting.

Reiniger removed his hat. The face under it was weary, grim. It matched his sigh. "If I could give it, I would. But this isn't just any assignment, Vlad. It's *the* assignment."

This time Yael's heart froze along with her breath. Her trainer seemed just as stunned.

The assignment: Kill the Führer, resurrect Operation Valkyrie.

"All the more reason she shouldn't take it," Vlad said when he found his voice.

"No one else but Yael can do this. Now, where is she? I'd like to speak with her."

Vlad signaled her. Yael sat up on the hay bale, the Mauser propped on her knee. Reiniger didn't look surprised.

"Come." Her trainer turned toward the house. "We'll talk about this in the kitchen."

———

Yael grabbed her sweater as soon as she arrived in the kitchen. Vlad was filling the teakettle, and Reiniger sat at the farm table, his hands folded on top of a manila folder.

"It's been a while, Yael." He smiled as she scuffed off her boots and shrugged the wool over her shoulders. "You look well."

Yael sat down at the table and thought that he looked older. It had been only a year since Reiniger was last at the farm, but the time between seemed tolling. His hair was weeded thin. His crow's-feet had spread, nearly as deep as the Babushka's used to be.

Vlad turned from the stove. There was a vodka bottle in his hand, mostly empty. A soon-to-be target. He set it down on the table between the three of them and nodded at Reiniger's folder. "What've we got here?"

"Five days ago the ninth Axis Tour came to a close in Tokyo."

"Propagandist bullshit," Vlad muttered in Russian as he unscrewed the vodka cap, unleashing a smell that made Yael want to gag (it always reminded her of the nurse and her cold, cold cotton swabs). He poured it into his teacup.

"Who won?" Yael asked. There was no television on Vlad's farm. The only radio was shortwave, meant for emergencies. Not distractions.

Reiniger slid the file across the table. "Open it," he told her.

She did.

Name: Adele Valerie Wolfe
Age: 16
Birthplace: Frankfurt, Germany

The photo clipped to the paper showed a pretty, smiling girl. Angelic.

"I thought they didn't let girls race," Yael said.

"They don't," Reiniger told her. "She took her twin brother's papers and raced in his name. It wasn't until she won that her true identity was exposed."

Yael studied the photograph more closely. There was a hardness to Adele Wolfe's eyes she'd glossed over before. And her smile stretched just a bit too tight. Anger, maybe? Something...something strong and desperate enough to push her over twenty thousand kilometers, three continents, and two seas, past nineteen muscular boys.

Not an angel, then. Something fiercer.

Like a Valkyrie.

"The Führer took quite a liking to Fräulein Wolfe at the Victor's Ball," Reiniger said.

"She's pretty and blond." Vlad sipped from his teacup, straight-faced. "Just his type. Not that they ever last long. Geli, Eva...all the women he's interested in have a nasty habit of dying."

Reiniger went on, "The Führer and Fräulein Wolfe shared a dance together."

"A dance?" Her trainer frowned. "Hitler never dances."

"He did at the Victor's Ball. The Führer let Fräulein Wolfe close enough to touch in a public place. Where the Reichssender cameras were airing everything on live television. It's the opportunity we've been waiting for."

"You want me to race as her?" Yael stared at the picture.

"And win." Reiniger nodded.

Adele stared back. Eyes black and white and daring.

"But why her? Can't I just take any girl's face? Create a false identity?"

"It has to be Adele. Any new girls entering next year's race will be subject to Gestapo scrutiny, which we simply can't risk. Adele already has established qualifying times, plus she's acquired the Führer's blessing. The Gestapo won't touch her. If she wins the Axis Tour next year and attends the Victor's Ball, she's guaranteed to be able to get close enough to Hitler to execute him.

"You have eleven months to memorize Adele's life and learn to race motorcycles. You'll have to come back to Germania, so you can observe Victor Wolfe up close. Also, we have a man who works on Zündapps. He's agreed to teach you mechanics and riding techniques."

Back to Germania. Yael looked over at Vlad. Her trainer's good eye was nearly as slit as his empty socket. He sat dangerously still. Watching Reiniger. The National Socialist general was staring at her. She realized he was waiting for an answer to a question he'd never actually asked.

Behind Vlad the teakettle whistled, spewing white-hot steam. Shrieking and shrieking and shrieking like a trapped beast. Like the answer inside her.

—*SOMEONE HAS TO CHANGE THINGS KILL THE BASTARD YOU ARE SPECIAL YOU YOU YOU ARE A MONSTER A VALKYRIE*—

"I'll do it," she whispered.

Vlad's chair clattered—hard—as he stood. He turned to the stove and silenced the kettle's tinny screams.

"Yael stays with me one more month. Then she can return to Germania."

Reiniger's eyebrows rose up to his receding hairline. "That's time we can't spare, Vlad. She has to learn to be a completely different person. That's thirty days of study time down the drain."

"She has to learn to be who she is first." Her trainer poured their cups full. "She won't be ready for this mission otherwise."

Reiniger looked so, so tired. As if he were the one who'd run sixteen kilometers under the alpine dawn. He sighed and ran a hand through his thinning hair. "What do you think, Yael?"

She thought she always wanted to shoot with her right hand. Even now her left arm was swaddled in sweater and tucked by her side, like a broken bird's wing. The other was strong and capable and ready.

But it was not all of her.

Vlad was right. There would be a day when she would have to shoot with her left, fight with her weak. That day would come on the Axis Tour. It could even be the day she had to face the Führer.

On that day Yael wanted to shoot straight. She wanted to be ready.

Yael shut the folder. "I can study here. Nothing will be lost."

"One month. Thirty days. That's all you're getting, Vlad."

"That's all I need," he said.

———

DAY 3

There were no more survival scenarios. No more identifying bottles of poisons by smell. No more flinging knives at long-dead tree stumps.

What Vlad tasked her to do was harder than all these things. He had her sit at the farmhouse table, her left arm stretched out over water stains and coffee rings. All sleeves gone. He made her stare at her own skin.

121358▲X

...

121358▲X

...

121358▲X

Vlad sat with her during the long, silent hours. He watched not just her arm, but her fingers, her eyes. Yael knew he was looking for tremble and tears. She tried her hardest not to give them to him. (What kind of Valkyrie cries?)

"When you look at those, what do you see?" he asked on the third day.

It wasn't so much seeing as feeling. Feeling the tattooing

needle pressed to her skin. Feeling Dr. Geyer's eyes on her as the final *X* marked her as his. Feeling the deep and dark of the crematorium's endless smoke inside her, waiting for the day it would face *other* monsters. Devour them.

She told Vlad this.

"I didn't ask you what you feel. I asked you what you see."

What did she see? These numbers—they were hasty, scrawled things. Full of crooked imperfections. The eight slanted too far. The ones were different lengths. Three was on the prowl, with tips like fangs.

"I see someone else's writing," she said finally.

Vlad kept looking at her, waiting for more.

"I—I see what they did to me."

Still silence. Pulling answers out of her.

"I see what they did to all of them."

The Babushka kneeling in filthy snow. The small blue hand on the gurney. Her mother's fever eyes and faded whimpers. Miriam clutching all the other dolls. (For years Yael had held out hope that her friend had somehow lived, that the dolls *would* be together again. She'd even been deluded enough to start planning a rescue mission until in her research she discovered the unbearable: Barrack 7 had been gassed not long after her escape.)

All of them. Dead.

Yael's jaw clenched so hard she thought her teeth would break. Her empty-hole heart echoed, so hungry. Full of gone.

The past was always there: running the trail beside her, ringing through her gunshots, searing through her skinshifts.

But there was always another kilometer to run, another target to hit, another face to perfect. Things Yael could cram the pain and anger into. Fuel herself forward.

But Yael's arm on the table, so sacrificial, so bare—this was different.

Alongside, she could stay a step ahead.—*KEEP RUNNING DON'T LOOK BACK*—

Face-to-face, all she could do was step into it. $121358\Delta X$. Remember and be rended.

She was in pieces as it was. How much more could she be torn?

—TOO MUCH—

Yael pulled her arm off the table. She was shaking.

Vlad did not scold her or tell her to put her arm back. His voice was strangely soft, so unlike the gruff of his face. "This is the final stage of your training. It is the hardest and the most important."

"Why?" Yael felt winded, broken. As if every kilometer she'd ever run had collapsed back on her body all at once. "What good does this do?"

Vlad put his own arm on the table. Hand splayed. Scar up. It was a shiny, punched thing. As if a nail had been driven through the center of his palm.

"This I got the same day I lost my eye. The same day my wife and daughter were killed because the Gestapo discovered I was double-crossing them."

In her three years at the farm, Yael had never asked about Vlad's scars, and he'd never offered. But she knew they had something to do with the gold ring he held in front of midnight fires and the sad sting of vodka on his breath. (All this when he'd thought she'd been asleep.)

"I'd just returned from a mission in Moscow, and I found"—Vlad's palm closed into a fist—"SS men waiting for me. My girls were dead. I was supposed to die, too.

"I lost everything that day. My family. My name. My life. I was only half blind. This eye had crystal-clear vision, but I couldn't even look in a mirror for two years. Every time I tried, I saw my scars. I saw their faces: my Therese and my little Katja. Asking me why I stood there and they did not. Why I couldn't save them. I couldn't answer their questions."

He opened his palm again. Let the old hurt show.

"But the more I did not look, the more I knew I had to face them. The more I did not hear, the more I knew I had to listen."

"Why?" Yael asked again.

"Because I woke up one morning and realized I'd become a man who wouldn't walk into rooms with mirrors. Who wouldn't use polished spoons or look through windows at night, when I might see myself staring back. By pretending the pain was not there, I had let it root. I'd given it power over me.

"I decided I couldn't be afraid of my own life. My own reflection. So every morning I make myself look in a mirror for five minutes. Face it all."

Yael looked down at her lap, her trembling arm. "So I'm just supposed to make things better by staring?"

"Better?" Vlad choked on the word. "It never gets *better*.

It just gets less. It becomes something you can face. If only for five minutes."

"But what about compartmentalizing?" It was a word Reiniger used a lot. A word Aaron-Klaus had sworn by. A word Vlad himself had said during their early training sessions. A word Yael had come to write her own definition for:

Compartmentalizing: Taking something full of pain and burn and pushing it back to the darkest place of yourself. The place even you're afraid to go.

"Compartmentalizing is good. Especially when you do what we do. But it isn't a permanent solution. If you keep pressing things down, never letting out any true feeling, you turn into a volcano. BOOM!" Vlad's scarred hand became a fist again, slammed down on the old battered wood.

"Like Aaron-Klaus…" Except that hadn't been a *BOOM* but a *pop*. Too quiet. All for nothing.

"Yes." He nodded. "Like Klaus. I made a mistake and didn't teach him how to vent. All his pain came out the wrong way. Sloppy."

Blood and static everywhere. Thumbtacks on the floor. The wrong death.

"I can't watch that happen again. Not to you, Yael." His scarred, daughterless hand grabbed her marked, fatherless arm. "This is what you are stronger than. But you must learn to see it that way. And you will only see it if you let yourself look."

"So what? I'm supposed to just stare at it? Every minute of every day?"

"You remember where you came from and what you came through. But you stare straight. Down the sights. Even if you've only got one damn eye left."

Yael looked, yet again. Her arm shook less, now that Vlad held it.

"The ghosts will stay. Just like your numbers. Just like my scars. Just like our pain." Vlad pulled his hand away. "But you don't have to be afraid of them."

Remember and be rendered.

She put her arm back on the table.

———

DAY 29

Inhale.

Exhale.

Stare down the sights. With two damn eyes.

See the ghosts lined up in a neat little row.

Between the numbers that cannot be erased.

12, BABUSHKA, 13, MAMA, 58, MIRIAM, ΔX, AARON-KLAUS.

You must never forget the dead.

Remember and be rended. Be rendered.

Look straight, where the danger is.
Inhale.
Exhale.
Reach the bottom of the breath
        And shoot.

———

DAY 30

Good-bye. It was always good-bye, wasn't it?
   She never could say it out loud.

CHAPTER 25

NOW

MARCH 25, 1956
BAGHDAD TO NEW DELHI

There had been a flash flood during the Axis Tour of 1951. Just on the outskirts of Dhaka. A wall of muddy water had raged over the leaders of the pack, taking one racer's life and drowning the bikes of five others. One rider—future victor Kobi Eizo—salvaged a farmer's rickshaw and pushed on, making it to the sixth checkpoint with only a thirty-minute loss. The move was contested by some (could you compete in a motorcycle race without a motorcycle?), but in the end the officials praised Eizo's resourcefulness. The Axis Tour was about strength, survival under even the worst of circumstances. In scavenging the rickshaw, hadn't Eizo displayed these very traits?

Thus, Rule 27 was added to the Axis Tour's conditions: "In the event of undisputed motorcycle loss due to external forces out of the racer's control, said racer may finish the leg of the race by alternative means of transportation."

According to Rule 27, the race was still on.

Felix certainly drove as if it was, pressing the gas pedal all the way to the floor. The truck's headlamps carved through the wilderness, kilometer by kilometer. Yael, who'd climbed into the cab through the rear opening, navigated with her head out the window. Trying to make sense of the star instructions that streaked over them.

"Gas isn't going to last." Felix nodded at the fuel gauge, where the needle sloped dangerously to the left.

Yael studied the light-speckled sky. They'd been driving— mostly south, a bit east—for hours. It was only a matter of time before they came across a settlement. The question was, would the needle hold out? Or would they sputter and die on the side of the road, become sitting ducks for any men Vetrov sent after them once they'd patched their tires?

"Keep going," she said.

Felix obeyed, throttling the steering wheel. "Luka wouldn't have gone back for you. You know that, right?"

She did. Didn't she?

The whole thing surprised Yael now that she thought about it—so many kilometers away from the adrenaline and heroics. Luka Löwe was one of her strongest threats. Logically, tactically, she should have left him behind. Eliminated the risk. (After all, he—blond-haired, blue-eyed National Socialist—deserved it. Didn't he?)

Yet there he was, curled in the back of the truck with his undershirt wadded against his ear. Yael's own under- shirt was smeared with his blood; her gun was another bullet lighter; and her hand still shivered from another brush with *almost-death*.

Neither of them—it seemed—was invincible.

Yael looked back out the window, where the stars flickered like dying cigarettes.

Felix guided the truck around a hairpin bend, and suddenly the night was broken. City lights shimmered against the far hillsides. An electric wildfire eating away the base of the mountains.

No, Yael realized as they pulled closer, not a city—a camp: laced in barbed-wire fences. Studded with watchtowers. Webbed with train tracks.

Numbers and needle memories burned in her arm as Felix wheeled them closer. Her nails dug into the truck cab's upholstery. By the time they reached the fence, she'd stabbed holes in her seat, and the truck was sputtering, choking on its final few fumes.

The watchtower floodlights had turned their way. Seeing all. National Socialist soldiers swarmed around the Soviet-marked vehicle with guns raised. All Yael could see for a moment were the searing lights, the swastika armbands, and rifle muzzles. Her heart squeezed, and her nails dug into her seat. Scraping springs.

But Adele Wolfe was their darling. Not their prisoner or prey. As soon as they caught sight of her face, their guns lowered, and their leader stepped forward, stammering apologies.

The racers poured out of the flatbed—jostled and dazed. A man with a medic kit made his way to Luka. (His face was still all blood, even with the red he'd left on Yael's clothes and his own crumpled undershirt.) The boy swatted him off to where Yamato sat at the back of the truck.

The first thing Yael asked for was a radio. She feigned ignorance of its knobs and buttons, relaying a conversation through its operator to the New Delhi race officials. It was a short session, fuzzed with static. But the gist was this: Kidnapped. Escaped. Okay now. Is race still on? Yes. Get to New Delhi.

Roger that.

The second thing Yael asked for was gasoline: "Enough to get us to New Delhi."

"Fuel's sparse out here." The overseer—a squat man with a square jaw—waved at the fenced land behind him. It was not a death machine—Yael could tell that much from the smokeless smells—but a labor camp. Mining, from the looks of it. "All of it's rationed for generators and scheduled transports. Besides, if you drive *that*, you're certain to get shot."

"When is the next transport to New Delhi?"

"I have some men driving out tomorrow afternoon; they'll get to New Delhi by nightfall."

"Tomorrow afternoon?" Not fast enough. Not with the race still on and Katsuo still in it. Logically, tactically, Yael knew that the boy was probably still on foot with no chance of catching up. Yet she couldn't shake the feeling that the victor was somehow ahead. "Is there any other way?"

"There's a cargo train being loaded. It leaves for New Delhi in ten minutes. There will be room in the ration cars."

A train...
    dark,
        swaying,
closed space,
        hot bodies.
(and under it all: *yah-ell, yah-ell, yah-ell*)

"Victor Wolfe? Is something wrong?"

Her eyes were closed, she realized. Yael opened them, found the overseer looking at her. Chin tilted. Eyes narrowed.

"It—it's the fastest way?" she managed.

"The shipment should reach New Delhi by midmorning," he told her.

Twelve hours. A time difference that could make or break the race. If Katsuo wasn't out there—somewhere—she would've waited. Taken any other way. But she would not, could not, risk it.

"We'll take it," she said.

———

The train was mostly coal. Cars and cars of it: dark mined out of dark, piled high. There were two ration cars at the end, stuffed with empty food crates, spray-painted with labels like RICE and BEANS. Basic laborer's rations—back to New Delhi to be refilled. The racers wedged into the cracks. Ralf and Lars throned themselves on top of the hollow boxes. Yamato and his freshly bound ankle leaned in an empty corner. Ryoko sat next to him, her head nodding into his shoulder, off to sleep. Felix curled on top of the closest stack of crates.

272

He was snoring.

Yael could not rest. She sat near the open door, where her name rushed past with the night. *Yah-ell, yah-ell, yah-ell.* Memories mushroomed up with the sound: the stench of urine and sweat, how her mother's wool coat felt like sparrow claws against Yael's cheek, how Mama's heart thudded a terrified tattoo into Yael's ear as the train slowed. Stopped.

Her own heart nearly burst when Luka slipped into the corner of her vision. He settled beside her, not far enough away.

"You look like you've just seen a ghost, Fräulein."

If only Luka knew how right he was. Not one ghost. Hundreds. *Thousands.* There was not enough sadness, enough anger, enough *her* for numbers like that.

"I don't like trains." It was Yael speaking—not Adele. She realized this too late, before she could clip her words short. Her weary, wired mind started flipping through Victor Wolfe's file. She couldn't remember anything about trains. Maybe Adele really did hate them.

Luka seemed doubtful. "The girl who races motorcycles and breaks out of a Soviet compound hates *trains?*"

Yael glanced over her shoulder, to see if Felix had heard, but Adele's brother stayed asleep on the boxes. She looked back at Luka. There was still blood on his face. Dried, flaking into its own jagged design. "You're not looking so stellar yourself."

"*Verdammt!* It's the hair, isn't it?" Luka spit into his palm and slicked back his hair. It was a vain motion—doing nothing

273

to unknot the tangle of matted blood. What it *did* do was give Yael a view of his wound.

"Your ear!" she gasped. The top lip of his cartilage was gone. Torn off and sealed with clumps of dark blood.

"Commie clipped it when we were running. I'll live." He shrugged, his stiff hair flopping back over the site. "Symmetry's overrated."

"Maybe, but infection isn't." Yael studied the boy again. He didn't *look* feverish. Yet. His face was cool blood and moonlight. "You should've had that looked at."

"There will be better medics in New Delhi." The boy's hand fell to the dog tag around his neck. His thumb polished over its letters. An absent, habitual motion. His Iron Cross was nowhere to be seen. Yael suspected that—like hers—it was a wilderness away, tucked in his lost pannier.

"Like Nurse Wilhelmina?"

There were quirks all over Luka's face: eyebrows, nostrils, half smile. His dog tag flashed as he let it fall back to his chest. "Is that jealousy I detect in your voice?"

"You should probably have your hearing checked," she quipped back.

Luka's smile became a full one. He said nothing.

"You're incredibly skilled at pretending to be an *Arschloch*," she said.

The victor laughed. "Who says I'm pretending?"

"You went back for Yamato," Yael pointed out. "That was selfless."

"Just trying to get even with the commie who ruined

my looks. An ear for an ear." Luka's response was as fast as the train, lying speed. "But let's talk about you for a minute, Fräulein."

"What about me?"

"I suppose"—his voice dropped to a whisper only she could hear—"I could talk about how you knew exactly where the transport would be. Or how your pistol magically re-appeared in your pocket."

Yael took a deep breath. The P38 pressed hard against her rib cage. Its metal met the frantic flash, *thud, verdammt* of her heart.

"But the thing that interests me most…the thing I can't figure out…is why you saved me. The girl I knew last year, the girl who tore my heart out with her bare teeth…that girl would have driven away. No looking back."

The train clattered and swayed. Luka's eyes tried to pin her, but Yael wouldn't meet them. She looked out the door instead. At the empty, moonstung wilderness.

"I'm not the only one pretending to be someone else." Luka was still whispering, but his words were so, so loud. So close. *He* was closer, Yael realized when she looked back. Close enough to stab or toss her out the door, onto the tracks.

He kissed her instead. A motion made of the same fluid lion-grace that had felled Aleksei.

She'd been trained to survive many things: Starvation and bullet wounds. Winter nights and scouring sun. Double-tied knots and interrogations at knifepoint. But this? A boy's lips on hers. Moving and melding. Soft and strength, velvet and iron. Opposite elements that tugged and tore Yael from the inside. Feelings bloomed, hot and warm. Deep and dark.

Yael pulled against them. Back and away. Every part of her body was awake, her skin glaring with goose bumps.

Luka exhaled, more sigh than breath. It sounded like a note in a tragic symphony. He was still close, leaned in so his dog tag dangled between them. Yael could see the story punched into the metal: 3/KRADSCH I. 411. (Kradschützen, his father's old war unit.)

"You've changed," Luka said. It was eerie. How clever, cunning, and close he was. It was as if she weren't wearing another face at all.

Now it was Luka pulling back. The dog tag beat against his chest as he jumped to his feet. "You may have saved my life, but I never asked you to. You still owe me a favor."

Before Yael could answer, Luka disappeared behind a stack of crates. Kiss and run.

She sat motionless for a long moment, watching everything else move and streak and rattle around her. The mountains on the long horizon peeling back. Dry, cracked earth pulling out like yards of fabric. The boys on their boxes. Still sleeping.

Except one. Felix's eyes were open. Staring in a way that suggested he'd seen. His arms were tense and bare in his white T-shirt. Clenched like his fists as he sat up from his jacket pillow.

"Want me to punch his face in?" He slid off his box. His halo-blond hair was plastered flat with sleep. It would have been comical if not for the snarl on his lips.

Lips. The feel of Luka's still clung to hers. The taste of sand and savage, howling through her insides like a storm.

Yael shook her head. Brought her arm to her lips and wiped.

As if a leather sleeve could get rid of it.

"I'd like nothing more," Adele's brother muttered.

She couldn't help but remember the fireplace throwdown in Prague. The fury on Felix's face, the blood and threat that covered Luka's. So much uneven emotion... *What you did* against *what he tried to do to you.*

Whose anger was righteous? Any? All?

"I can handle Victor Löwe," she said.

"Be careful, Ad." Felix's thumb began popping his other knuckles. "Luka isn't someone you want to mess with."

He wasn't. Was he?

She thought she knew him. **Luka Löwe. Born February 10, 1939. Pompous, proud Grade A *Arschloch*.**

But people were more than crooked type and swastika-stamped documents. No number of bullet points and biography facts could pin the soul behind the eyes. The many versions of Luka she'd seen.

There was the Victor Löwe who swore all allegiance to the Führer, shouted, "Blood and honor!" and *"Heil Hitler!"* And then the Luka who sat in the sands, polishing his father's dog tag, breathing outlawed fire and smoke, scoffing at Hitler's policies. The Luka who stayed behind, got his ear shot off for an injured boy.

The Luka who kissed her.

277

The *more*ness of him was beginning to show. The way ruins were excavated by an archaeologist. Brushstroke by brushstroke. Bit by bit. And slowly, she was beginning to see beneath the goose-stepping pedigree. Yes, Luka Löwe was a National Socialist. But so was Erwin Reiniger (for the sake of an alias and so many lives). And hadn't Aaron-Klaus been wearing all the trappings of an Aryan elitist when Yael met him? Wasn't she wearing those very things now?

Yes, Luka Löwe was a National Socialist, but he was different on the inside.

Where it mattered.

"If he gives you any more trouble, any at all..." *Snap, crack, pop*, went Felix's knuckles. A twisted, breaking countdown...

"Stop that." Yael emulated Adele's scowl, swatting at Felix's fist the way she once batted Aaron-Klaus's hand from her share of crullers.

"Why?"

"Arthritis. Grape-sized knuckles. My general sanity," she added.

"Lost causes. All of them." Adele's brother laughed (and again Yael was reminded of Aaron-Klaus: jokes across the card table, teasing, hair ruffles, feeling like a normal child, if only for a moment). A smile broke out on Felix's face. He unfurled his fists and patted the wooden pallet. "You should get some rest. It's no feather bed, but it's not too bad."

The wood was still warm when she rested on it. Felix leaned against the crate. So close that Yael could hear the *tick, tick, tick* of his fixed pocket watch, see the paprika dusting of freckles on his cheeks. He stared off and off through the car door, out to the fullness of the moon.

Yael wondered, as she closed her eyes, what he was thinking about. Martin, maybe? She wondered, too, which car Luka had disappeared to. That ear needed treatment soon....

Tick, yah-ell, tick, yah-ell, tick...

━━━━━

When she opened her eyes again, it was to a clear blue morning. Sweating air and city outskirts crept outside the train car's open door. Children and dogs and chickens. Wobbly shacks with laundry strung between them like signal flags, their tin roofs already beating back the heat of the sun. Rutted red earth roads, stirred with the hum of motorbikes.

Felix leaned against the open door, looking out on the shantytown.

Yael sat up on the crate, felt the deep imprints of the wooden slats on her cheek. She hadn't slept so hard in—days, weeks, months, years?—Yael couldn't remember when.

Adele's brother looked over at her. "Ad, come see this."

Outside was a whole crowd of people—earthen skin, even darker hair—dancing in a way that reminded Yael of sea waves. People leapt to the music and tossed fistfuls of powder into the air above their heads, where it blossomed.

Colors. Bright, bright, and everywhere. Lush purples, sunset magenta, green like lime rinds, pollen yellow, lava orange, blue as light as the Wolfes' eyes. The sky overflowed with them.

"What do you think they're doing?" Felix asked.

Yael didn't think. She knew. What they were seeing was Holi: a festival welcoming the arrival of spring. She'd read about it in one of the books Henryka rescued from the National Socialist bonfires. Its battered pages were full of dry English sentences describing the "native peoples in the British Empire." The writer described Holi in only a paragraph: music, dancing, fires, and brilliant, powdered pigments. When she'd read about it, slouched in the chair in Henryka's office, she'd tried to imagine what it looked like.

But Yael never thought she'd actually see it. So many colors all in one place. Dust that meant something other than decay and death.

"They're celebrating." Yael couldn't hide her surprise. She'd thought that this day—like so many other things—had been wiped away. But they were past the Seventieth Meridian now. Out of the Reich and into the Greater East Asia Co-Prosperity Sphere, where words like *Aryan* and *Untermensch* had no meaning. It seemed Emperor Hirohito let the people celebrate their traditional festivals.

The whole city was blooming, she realized as the train kept on. Kilometers passed by their open door—colors and crowds—until the train finally started to slow, groaning along the metal tracks. Felix stuck his head out of the car. "Looks like we're almost to the station."

Yael stood. Her eyes were still on the powdered clouds (so bright, so beautiful!), but her mind was as tense as her leg muscles. In the corners of her vision she could see all the other racers standing. Readying themselves for the mad dash from the train station to New Delhi's checkpoint.

The race wasn't over yet.

"You ready to run?" she asked Felix.

He nodded. Stood beside her.

NEW DELHI JUNCTION STATION. The sign was written mainly in kanji, with tiny German subscript and an even tinier Hindi scribble (hand-etched, like graffiti). Yael's calves cramped and screamed as they rolled past it. The freight train ground like furious teeth:

Slow.

Slower.

Stop.

She started to run.

CHAPTER 26

NOW

MARCH 26, 1956
NEW DELHI CHECKPOINT
KILOMETER 11,541

The checkpoint wasn't far from the train terminal. At least, that was what the stationmaster informed Yael when she lunged up to the ticket window. It was only a couple of kilometers south, he told her in choppy Japanese, listing off road names along with haphazard instructions: Out of the station. Down this side street. Past the bazaar. Through some square. Along another street. You'll know it when you see it.

Men, women, and children milled so tight in the station's front road that there was hardly any room for traffic. Yael fought her way through the jostle of shoulders. Looking, looking, looking for the right street signs. Trying to read their kanji through the butterfly haze of powder and crowd of too-tall heads.

Felix, at least, was easy to keep track of. His hair glowed white in the colored cloud as he pointed to a far-flung street sign. "This way!"

Yael pushed through the layers of revel: children's laughter, the chime of ankle bells, "Happy Holi!" cried and crowed, fingers that smeared powder against her cheeks as she passed. There was something electric about the colors that exploded in the sky, reminding Yael that not everything was gray ashfall, yellowing weeds, withered blue hands, crimson rivers of blood....

There was still beauty in this world. And it was worth fighting for.

So Yael ran all the faster.

The crowd thinned and tendriled into the side streets, where Yael could run without stopping. Felix wasn't the only one running with her. Others had followed from the train. Takeo and Masaru ran furiously close to her heels. And on the other side of the street—ducking through a scatter of bazaar stalls and brilliant-neon women—was Luka. The victor's face was swirled with dried blood, yellow powder. He looked like one of the old Norse gods from the engravings Yael used to study.

He moved like one, too: lightning fast, thunder strong. He looked over when he drew even with her, snagged her eyes, and winked.

Then he pulled ahead.

They poured back into a square thick with celebrating crowds. Yael ran as fast as she could. Her movement was silvery as she threaded Adele's svelte form through the slim canyons between dancers' muscular backs. Luka was not nearly as graceful. He bulled his way through, stumbling over saris and sacks full of powder.

Yael reached the other side of the square first. Through the aqua, golden, orange haze, she saw the Axis banners flying high. Japan's brash sun. The Third Reich's broken cross. Marking the street in even lines.

The checkpoint was close.

The crowd was clearing as were the colors. Every lunge Yael took brought the banners into better view. She could see the finish line now, stretched white across the red dirt road.

Luka loped past, trailing dust like sun motes. His words didn't even sound winded as they floated back over his shoulder. "Don't strain yourself too hard, Fräulein!"

He crossed the line first. Takeo burst past, just as Yael dragged herself over the line. Felix jogged up behind her, not even trying to keep up with the others.

It didn't matter that two boys crossed the line before her. They'd gained only seconds. She was still ahead.

"Scheisse!" Luka swore as he kicked at the dirt. It clouded the air as red as Holi dust. Yael followed his stare to the scoreboard, where an official was calculating their times. Etching them in order.

The first name was already there.

**1st: Tsuda Katsuo, 11 days, 6 hours, 55 minutes,
6 seconds.**

She stared at the numbers and the name in front of them, stunned, as her own time was chalked out.

2nd: Adele Wolfe, 11 days, 10 hours, 20 minutes,
12 seconds.
3rd: Luka Löwe, 11 days, 10 hours, 29 minutes,
20 seconds.

Not by seconds or minutes, but by hours. Three and a half hours.

Katsuo had beaten them all.

———

The news got worse.

It was delivered to them at dinner. All the racers were exhausted, both from the last leg of the race and the intense questioning the racing officials imposed on every single one of them. (Who kidnapped them? Why? How did they escape? Over and over and over until all their answers were streamlined and written down in an official report. The Reichssender crew and the Japanese journalists were instructed to record a highly edited version of the story: LANDSLIDE DECIMATES RIDERS' ZÜNDAPPS. The Axis Tour was a display of ultimate victory. Guerrilla kidnappings didn't fit into this narrative.)

Yael had eaten her fill of chicken curry and basmati rice. Instead of chewing, she was glowering at the scoreboard— working Katsuo's lead between her teeth.

Three and a half hours and no sandstorms in sight.

The Japanese victor attained this lead by evading the Soviet soldiers and holing up in a cave until the heat of their search died down. "It wasn't hard to double back and steal my own bike out from under the commies' noses," Yael heard him bragging to Takeo and Iwao. Both boys still sat next to Katsuo at dinner, though they seemed much less enthused by this story than they had by his earlier ones. Iwao did not laugh. Takeo jammed his knife so hard into the table that he had to use two hands to wrench it out.

Katsuo, as he went on to tell them, drove back to the detour road the supply trucks had used to skirt the mountains. By the time he caught up to the supply caravan, the other riders had radioed in. So he blasted his way through the night, to New Delhi and the first slot on the scoreboard.

There were over nine thousand kilometers between New Delhi and Tokyo. Gaining back the time between them would be hard, but not impossible. Yael would have to push: sleep in bursts, ride through the night, pray for a merciful road.

The New Delhi checkpoint official—a lean, fierce man with the rising sun wrapped around his arm—made his way to the end of the dining table. The room fell silent.

"We were unable to recover the Zündapps." He spoke in Japanese first, then repeated the words in clean, stilted German. "And we don't have enough replacements for every racer."

RIP, Fenrir. Yael frowned down at her leftover curry. *You had a good run.*

"In all ten years of the Axis Tour we've never been faced with a situation quite like this: racers without bikes. We've been in communication with Germania and Tokyo, and it's been decided that the race will go on with new bikes."

"However, your Zündapps were specially fitted for the tour's hardships, and there are no motorcycles of cross-country-racing caliber in New Delhi. Officials in Germania and Tokyo have agreed to a revised racing plan."

The table was not just silent but dead still. Even spoons had stopped scraping. Fourteen sets of eyes (eight brown, six blue) stared at the official.

"You'll be flown to Hanoi, where a shipment of Rikuo Type 98s fitted in Tokyo will be waiting. The race will carry on from the Hanoi checkpoint. Your times will remain the same."

New Delhi to Hanoi. That was over 4,800 kilometers of race.

Four thousand eight hundred kilometers. Gone. Just like that.

Yael felt her heart falling, falling, falling. The curry in her stomach bubbled and churned.

Katsuo smiled.

"Hanoi?" Luka, who'd kept an uneasy seat at the end of the table, stood. He'd obviously been to see Nurse Wilhelmina; an absurd amount of gauze was wrapped around his head. As if he'd lost a whole ear and not just the tip. "You're sending us all the way to Hanoi? That's almost a quarter of the race! That's unacceptable!"

He smacked the table. Fourteen plates rattled. The red in Luka's cheeks flushed deeper as he went on, "Why not ship them here? Or even to Dhaka?"

The checkpoint official stayed cool, almost surgical in his

delivery. "The decision has been approved by the Emperor and the Führer themselves. To question this decision is to question them."

Luka's palm stayed flat on the tabletop. He sat back down.

"We find it very acceptable." Katsuo didn't even try to hide the smug in his voice. It oozed from his pores, widened his smile.

"That changes things," Felix murmured beside her.

It did. From *hard* to *impossible*. Hanoi to Tokyo was only 4,433 kilometers. Close to 3,600 of those would be on an unfamiliar bike and 800 over the East China Sea, out of Yael's control altogether. Sleepless nights and fourth gear would not be enough. And she couldn't simply wait for another miracle.

Yael looked down the table. Every racer's face—except Katsuo's—was stunned, crumpled. Lars seemed close to tears. Masaru's eyes were hollowed out, his lips edged paper-straight: the look of the lost. Because they all knew the truth—they had no chance of catching up. None of them did. Unless...

Her eyes found Luka's. He was watching her—a frustrated stare through wads of bandages—passing something between them. Something different from the kiss, but still dangerous. Still knowing.

Allies?

Yael nodded.

It was time to play dirty.

CHAPTER 27

NOW

MARCH 27, 1956
FLIGHT FROM NEW DELHI TO HANOI

The kilometers looked so different from above. An easy span of centimeters: rivers sprouting like nerve endings through lush jungle hills. Days of mud, malaria, and muggy misery. Nights of tiger calls and howling primates.

Yael watched it all pass through the airplane window. Part of her was glad for the respite. The tropical portion of the tour was historically the hardest, collecting the highest number of crossed-out names, with its mosquito-stab diseases and countless river crossings. It was a rare year indeed that thirteen riders made it to Hanoi. (~~Yamato~~ was out of the race, his ankle too severely sprained to keep riding.) In fact, Yael couldn't remember the last time it had happened. If ever.

The plane cabin rattled as if every screw and bolt were coming apart: bouncing and roaring through clouds. Even with cotton stuffed deep into Yael's ear canal, the propellers drowned out everything else. She didn't even hear Luka approach until he tapped her on the shoulder.

She jumped, looked over to find him standing in the aisle, leaning into Felix to get close to her. Adele's brother's face dialed from scowl to sour. He swatted the victor's hand: *Go away.*

"Mind if…take…seat, Fräu…" Luka's tilted dark eyebrows filled in the gaps of his question.

He wanted to make plans here? They'd have to scream to be heard. Katsuo was seated only two rows and an aisle away, a smile still carved into his face. Luka leaned in farther—so his dog tag dangled onto Felix's nose—and held out a notebook and a pen.

Felix glared at Yael as she nodded. She didn't need the years of sibling history to read the warning behind his eyes: *Don't do this; don't trust him.* She kept nodding until Felix finally rolled his eyes and stood.

As Luka settled into the seat, Yael was aware of his nearness. Their elbows grazed together on the shared armrest. Brown leather sticking to black. When he pressed the notebook in his lap and began writing, his elbow jostled. Every letter he created nudged against her hidden wolves.

It was nice writing: stout, but not too blocky. Strong without being strict. *If either of us wants a chance of winning this tour, we need to take care of Katsuo.*

Yael nodded and looked back to Katsuo. The boy was still sky high, gloating into his window. Paying no attention to the rows of racers behind him.

Luka kept scrawling. *Remember what happened outside Hanoi last year?*

He handed the writing tools to her. Yael tried to look calm as she splayed the notebook against her lap. Newsreels and pages of transcribed interviews whipped through her memory as she pressed pen to the paper.

Hanoi. Hanoi. Hanoi.

What happened outside Hanoi?

A seventeen-year-old German rider had slipped off the road into a rice paddy. Shattering both his bike's front axle and his leg beyond repair. But that couldn't be what Luka was talking about. He and Adele had been far ahead of that accident. There was something—something else—about a fight on a ferry crossing? It had been a mere blip in that day's recap. Squeezed between gruesome reports of the German rider's amputation and the *Chancellery Chat* where the Führer praised his great sacrifice for the immortal glory of the Fatherland and the Third Reich.

It had to be the ferry. Yael pushed the pen so hard the ink started to blot before she replicated Adele's writing. *The ferry?*

Luka flipped to a new page after she handed the book to him.

We need to keep on Katsuo's tail so all of us cross the Li on the same boat. Give him a little dose of history. But this time we'll get the job done.

These words did not help the turbulence nausea in

Yael's stomach. What had happened on the Li River ferry? What did Luka expect her to do? Push Katsuo off? Sabotage his bike?

Whatever it was, she'd have to improvise.

Luka kept writing. In any case, we need to stay together. Ride close.

Riding together. Yael nodded again (she was beginning to feel like a jack-in-the-box: bouncing, nodding, bouncing, nodding), but her toes clenched inside her boots. It was risky enough having Felix alongside, all the time watching. But Adele's brother—while he threw a good punch, stuck burr-tight to her side—was interested in one thing: his sister's safety. Her alliance with him was good for protection, but aggression... aggression was Luka's specialty. The victor had a fire, a plan to make sure Katsuo never reached the finish line.

They'd just have to part ways before he turned that fire on her.

She fished the notebook from Luka's hands. How far will we ride together?

He grinned when he read this. A burst of white teeth through peeling, chapped lips. Strange, Yael thought, they hadn't felt rough at all when they were touching hers that night on the train. They'd been more silk and shock. Tingling like winter-dry air.

Yael caught herself and looked away. Luka's fingers feathered against hers—slowly, slowly—as he slid the notebook from Yael's grasp.

Her toes clenched so hard a few of them actually popped.

It was just a touch. Just a kiss. Just a chemical reaction flaring under her skin, changing things. It meant nothing—not when Yael was not Yael and the world was dying and he was one of *them*. (Wasn't he?)

Luka handed the book back: As far as we need to go.

Yael looked at the words for a moment. So open-ended, begging for questions or a response: *How far?* Or *Let's go.* Or *Blot, smudge, smear, and spilled-ink secrets.*

She snapped the notebook shut and handed it back to him. There was nothing else to say.

CHAPTER 28

NOW

"What do you think you're doing?" Felix's question melted with the rustle of palm fronds in Yael's ears. She stood under the humid watch of Hanoi's sun, trying to breathe through the leather of her jacket, air as thick as hurt. The other racers had stripped off their riding gear, down to bare muscles and undershirts as they strolled through the sweltering courtyard, toward the line of Rikuo 98s. Thirteen motorcycles fresh from the plane: virgin shiny, no dust or dents. The riders approached them slowly—the way a trainer might face a feral beast—inspecting the gears and deep-tread tires from every angle.

Felix was the only one not paying attention to the new motorcycles. He watched Yael instead, frowning as she moved toward her bike. "Luka's playing you."

"How do you know I'm not playing him?" Yael knelt

down to get a closer look at the Rikuo's specs. Drum brakes—front and rear. A hand-operated three-speed gear change. A wider, heavier frame with less horsepower than its Zündapp counterpart. Even at its highest gear, she could tell, the Rikuo would offer only a fraction of her old bike's speed.

It would be like riding a draft horse after weeks on a thoroughbred.

(Luka put it more succinctly, shouting, "These bikes are complete *Scheisse!*" from three Rikuos away.)

"The way things are now, Katsuo is going to win this race." Yael kept her voice low. The other racers seemed just as preoccupied with their bikes as she was, but there was no guarantee who might be listening. "He's over three hours ahead on his home turf, riding a model of bike he's almost definitely trained on. We've only got three, maybe four, days of actual riding left.

"Luka has a plan"—whatever it was (Yael, digging through her memory the entire remainder of the flight, could recall nothing about the Li River ferry)—"and he needs my help."

"He's not a part of…that thing"—Felix's pointed stare spelled out *resistance*—"is he?"

Yael shook her head.

"Then you can bet his plan doesn't involve letting you win." Felix stood over her, arms crossed, blocking some of the sun's swelter with his lanky frame.

"If Luka and I don't work together, it's mutually assured defeat. Once Katsuo's eliminated, we'll go our separate ways."

Adele's brother kicked her Rikuo's tire.

All the reasons she'd pumped herself full of kept leaking out in a hiss. "Besides, Luka won't try anything as long as you're watching my back."

Yael looked up after she said this, trying to gauge the pressure behind Felix's face. But there was too much light behind him, too many shadows rubbed into the Nordic geometry of his features. He was unreadable.

"Why did you let him kiss you?"

It took Yael a moment to process his question, ingest it word by word. *You. Him. Kiss. Let. Why.* It took her another few heartbeats to work out possible answers.

Because I am Adele Valerie Wolfe.

Because I wasn't expecting it. Because I'm different on the inside. Because I was on a train. Because he needs to think I trust him. Because I'm alone.

Because I'm not Adele Valerie Wolfe.

Too many answers, all of them clogging her throat. None of them just right.

"I just ask," Felix went on, "because I wonder if maybe your judgment has been clouded."

Yael bristled at this and stood, so the light was even between them. Shadow for shadow. Shine for shine. "This isn't about me and Luka," she whispered. "This is about winning. This is about—"

Her wolves sweated under the leather, begging for air. And her heart felt so weak, so heavy—always breaking off at the edges, smaller, smaller, smaller. Into pieces she tucked under her sleeve. Was there even anything left?

Felix raised his eyebrows, waited for her to go on.

"I have this under control," she told him finally. "We just have to ride with Luka for a day. Then the race will be even again."

"C'mon, Ad. You can't trust him...."

"I don't," Yael said. "But as far as I can tell, this is the only way. If you have a better solution, I'm all ears."

Felix's jaw knotted as he chewed back his temper.

When it was clear he had no answers, Yael turned and slid onto the bike. She turned the ignition into a smooth start, got a feel for the humming motor, the tension of the throttle and brakes. Within the first ten seconds, Yael knew the ride would be clumsy—sheer size and unwieldy gears.

Her practice laps on the streets around the checkpoint were wavery. The engine burned her calf, and she kept reflexively trying to change the gears with her foot. All the while her conversation with Felix beat at the back of her skull. A migraine of questions, unsaid answers.

Doubts started sliding in when Yael mixed up the gear change for the fifth time, got flustered, and let go of the throttle. The bike shuddered beneath her. Katsuo passed her just as the engine stalled out, his own riding flawless.

It took Yael a moment to collect herself. Breathe in, push it all back.

It was just a kiss. And it meant nothing.

It was just one day, one ferry, one strike through a name. And it meant everything.

Yael cranked the Rikuo back to life, luring it into a steady speed down the street.

She had everything under control.

They started off the next morning, lining up according to time as they did at every checkpoint—thirteen racers stacked under the sweltering sun, calves cramped and waiting to push off. Muggy, tense silence stretched out among them, punctuated by crickets and idling motor hum, finally severed by the gunshot.

BOOM and go!

Katsuo was off. It took Yael two wobbling seconds to balance, crouch, be on her way, and see that he was already meters ahead. She coaxed the engine to its highest speed. Hanoi's humid air whistled over her goggles and smacked against her face. Asphalt ripped beneath her, and rich colonial architecture blipped through lines of palm trees, flag-waving crowds and ever-camped Reichssender cameras.

But it still felt so *slow.*

Yael kept her eyes on Katsuo's taillight. Their speeds were matching now. Equidistant as the city thinned from French-era buildings into shacks and rice paddies. Long kilometers of flat fields—their waters mirrored the pale burn of the sun through the green of growing rice. She followed him close, just as Luka had instructed. The other victor was tailing her. Yael hadn't seen him yet (she couldn't risk looking over her shoulder and misaligning her bike), but she heard the gnash of his engine just behind.

She'd hoped Katsuo might ease up once they were firmly in the countryside, out of the memory of the starting gun. But the victor kept going—raging into the open road, tugging a few more seconds out of his three-and-a-half-hour lead.

It didn't matter, she told herself. All she had to do was stay close. Get to the ferry.

The sun climbed high into a clouding sky, and the landscape changed, transforming into something out of a fairy tale. Dramatic, sudden mountains jutted from waterlogged fields. Like the fingers of an underground giant, hungry for sky. Hundreds of tree-capped heights and hundreds of valleys braided with rivers and mists, rice paddies and lean-tos. Ancient tombs hugged the road—less dramatic mounds of earth marked by poetic stones, overgrown with tattered offerings of money and liquor bottles.

All this and a taillight.

They tore through this watercolor scenery of limestone hills and quiet farms. The afternoon hours were swallowed by sterling clouds, and the mists grew. Their second fuel stop was in a small shack of a town, where Yael crammed down several protein bars while race officials siphoned gasoline into her tank with makeshift hoses. Children watched from matchstick doorways as Katsuo got back on the road first, scattering a group of chickens in his haste.

The Li River wasn't much farther, just two villages more. Its waters wound around the mountains, green and much too deep to forge without drowning their new engines. The bridge that once spanned it was in remnants (destroyed—like so many other things—in the war, never rebuilt). Two crumbling cliffsides facing each other. The road leading to the bridge was

crossed out by an X of boards and red kanji: WARNING: DO
NOT CROSS.

A dirt path redirected the racers to the shoreline, where
a narrow line of stones edged with cormorants stabbed into
the river's shallows. The ferry was moored at the end. At first
Yael thought there was a mistake. The structure Katsuo was
pushing his bike toward couldn't possibly be the ferry. *Boat*
was hardly the word for it. *Raft*, perhaps, was a better term
for the fat stalks of bamboo that had been chopped down,
lashed together in layers.

But Katsuo pushed his bike all the way to the end of the
dock and began to board. The ferry operator—a gaunt man
with a bell-shaped hat and a bamboo staff in his hand—didn't
seem to argue.

Yael wasted no time dismounting her bike and guiding it
along the narrow dock. Behind her she heard Luka's motor
cutting off, and ahead Katsuo's command to the ferryman,
"Cast off before the others get here!"

Either the old man did not understand Japanese or he did
not care. His joints were rusted and slow as he set down his
pole and unknotted the mooring ropes. He wasn't even done
with the first knot when Yael managed her bike down the
ramp, onto the raft.

Katsuo stared at her from the ferry's bow end—fierce,
fierce, cut and carve.

She stared back.

"Get off." It was the first time he'd spoken to her, Yael
realized. He didn't even bother using German.

Yael let go of the Rikuo's handlebars.

Katsuo didn't move. (It was an unnerving stillness. The kind a cobra holds before the strike.) The raft shuddered as it was boarded by new wheels, sinking a few more centimeters. River water crept through the gaps in the bamboo, up the edges of Yael's boots.

Luka had made it aboard. Yael could tell from the shift in weight that he'd taken the stern position. She was sandwiched between them.

Now what?

"It's too late to get off," Yael said in German, staring at the furrow in Katsuo's forehead, made even deeper from the pull of his goggles. It was easier than getting dissected by those eyes.

His Japanese response: "Not really."

They understood each other perfectly.

The water was seeping through her soles, prying cold into the space between her toes.

"Three! Enough!" She heard the ferry operator yell in parcel-Japanese and looked over to see the man jabbing his pole into the fourth rider's chest. A pair of slick cormorants perched at the dock's end watched on as the rider swore, fenced the bamboo away.

That voice, that golden hair edging (too long) from his helmet, the broken brown leather of his jacket…the racer on the dock—watching as the ferryman pushed them out into the swirling emerald currents—was Luka.

So who was behind her?

A boy, for sure. German according to the armband on

his uniform. These were the only two details Yael's frantic glimpse gave her. All others were lost when Katsuo started speaking again, his voice filled with a venom that made her turn. "You think you can rob me of the Double Cross again, girl? You should have gotten off!"

She found him holding a blade—the same one he'd used to gut that fish, now aimed high and at her throat. He was only three steps away (a lunge, really, but there would be no lunging on this pile of sticks). Technically Yael could disarm him in two moves, but the raft was narrow, the river deep, the current strong. One slip, one stab meant the end.

—DON'T MOVE HE MIGHT STRIKE—

Yael stayed frozen, but that didn't stop Katsuo from moving forward. The raft buckled too much with the movement; Yael had to clutch her Rikuo's seat to keep steady. The victor in front of her froze, midstep. His knife curved out of his fist. Both shores, Yael realized, were absent of Reichssender cameras. Katsuo could stab her and get away with it.

"STILL!" the ferryman snapped behind them.

Just two more steps now. Half of a lunge.

—BE STILL BE READY—

"If you move much more, you'll swamp the raft." Her German was slow and insultingly loud, but she couldn't help herself. The glint in his eyes, the shine of his blade, the very real possibility that he was about to take that next step (hell or high water), that she would fall into the river, into the knife, that it was all for nothing...

Every one of these things was getting to her, seeping through the cracks.

"There's too much weight," he said, and raised his blade higher. "I should get rid of some."

They were a third of the way across the river, edging into its deepest part. The bamboo dipped and bowed, and the ferry operator yelled, "STILL! STILL! STILL!" as Katsuo sloshed forward, centimeter by centimeter.

"Look out!" a voice called behind her in frantic German.

Yael braced against the raft. Katsuo conquered the second step. Started his lunge. Vlad's training burst through Yael's veins, pushing her limbs into autopilot.

—DEFEND ATTACK BE THE VALKYRIE—

She jumped back, bending her hips and vitals away from the blade, blocking its path with crossed-X arms. The bamboo under Yael's boots shuddered, and there were two voices behind her screaming; river water sloshed up to the hem of her riding pants. But Vlad's instructions were louder, more present than any of this: "Grab your attacker's elbow, twist it toward you. Now his blade is at your mercy. You can use it to finish him."

Life? Or death?

—BE THE VALKYRIE WHAT IS YOUR CHOICE—

Not yet. Not him. (What would it mean, anyway?)

Yael threw the boy back, over, off.

SPLASH! The river swallowed Katsuo: hungry water, greedy currents. He was already a ways from the raft when he resurfaced, gasping with shock, anger, cold. Floundering in all the constraints of his riding gear.

The raft was floundering as well. Wild, dipping rebounds from the sudden shifts of weight. But the ferryman knew his craft, knew the waters, knew how to make peace between these things. He muttered in his native tongue, something along the lines of *crazy riders*, and pushed them on.

After a stunned moment Yael finally looked over her shoulder in full, saw the rider in the stern position: crooked nose, twisted mouth, whitish hair peeking out from under his helmet. Felix—magical, sticky-burr Felix—always showing up in places he wasn't supposed to be.

He'd been the last rider out of Hanoi. Not *so* far behind in terms of distance, but everyone had been striving at the same speed, the highest gear. How did he pass ten riders? Beat Luka to the raft? She hadn't even seen him at the fuel stop....

"How are you here?" she asked.

He dodged her question. Volleyed it back. "You think there was any way I was letting Luka Löwe get on this raft with you? What would've happened if it was him behind you and not me?"

Yael's eyes trailed the leaf-littered currents, curving around the closest peak.... The Japanese victor was nowhere to be seen. Her gaze snagged the dock's end, where Luka stood, watching. A string of riders gathered behind him.

Had that been his plan? Shove her between himself and Katsuo? Let his two biggest competitors duke it out, then shove the winner in the water? No, he'd tried his best to board. And he wouldn't have risked upending his own motorcycle, endangering his own place in the race.

What did it matter, anyway? Yael was at the front of the pack again. Poised to win.

Felix looked over his shoulder, at the sliver of Luka, pulling away, away. "That's that, then."

Their raft scraped against the rocky shore, beached to a stop. And because no one was ahead of her, because no one could move, Yael stood a moment more, watching Luka, surrounded, yet so alone at the end of that dock.

The river hushed and tore between them.

She couldn't help but wonder if maybe she was leaving something behind.

"That's that," she said, and turned away.

CHAPTER 29

NOW

MARCH 28, 1956
HANOI TO SHANGHAI

She was ahead.

And it was good.

They made excellent time from the river, driving down the dirt road as fast as their bikes would let them. Hours passed and the mountains vanished, dropping back into the earth. The fields of rice stretched on, farm after farm after farm. Village, village, town, city. The road's dirt changed to asphalt, and their Rikuos made even better time, ripping away from the orange haze sunset, into the nightrise.

When the darkness swallowed all, Yael flicked on her headlamp and kept going. (There was no dust to stop her.) She would not risk her lead for anything. Not camping, not food, not sleep. Her only breaks were hasty yet necessary refuels.

Felix kept steady at her side. Not complaining or yelling

when she chose to keep on through the twilight. He simply switched his own light on—lit the road double.

Yael couldn't help but let her thoughts turn to what would happen next. After Shanghai, after the barge across the sea, after the finish line in Tokyo.

Would she tell him the truth?

Of course not—he wouldn't understand.

Would she say good-bye?

No, that would be giving too much away.

Just leave him, then? The way Aaron-Klaus had left her—wordless, hanging on an edge she never really could climb back from.

That was the best option. But it felt so wrong to just disappear.... Maybe after everything was over—the assassination, the escape, the manhunt, and the war that was certain to follow—she could find him again.

Find him again and tell him what? *I'm a pseudoscience experiment gone wrong who kidnapped your sister, skinshifted into her face, and killed the Führer while wearing it. Sorry about that. Oh, and sorry again for the pistol whip. It's healed nicely, though.*

She could only imagine how well that would go over, given Felix's record.

No—the good-bye that was not a good-bye was best. It was all she was capable of, really.

These thoughts cycled—round and round and round—and the road gaped dark in front of her, open as a wound. Its edges were beginning to smear: tree branches stretching out too far, flitters like bats around the edges of her eyes. There was a sparking in her stomach, too, reminding Yael that protein bars swallowed at refueling stops were not proper sustenance.

It wasn't until Yael pulled to the side of the road and started rummaging through her pannier that she realized how heavy her lids were. Dropping in a way that demanded sleep.

Felix was yawning, too, as he flipped open Martin's pocket watch and read the time through the glass face's spidery cracks. "We've got four, maybe five more hours of riding left. Five hours until the sun comes up."

Yael dug out a pack of dehydrated meat, struggled to open it. Her fingers were fumbling and all over, drunk from seventeen hours on the bike.

Felix watched pointedly as she gave up and attacked the wrapper with her teeth. Swallowing pieces of dried chicken straight from the bag. "It'd be best to stop and nap. That's probably what the other riders are doing."

Yael looked back at the road. No lights. Just a darkness that swam in front of her eyes, holding so much (as all dark does): days mixing with lifetimes, swirling with dreams. She could almost hear the howls from her nightmares, pressing into her ears.

Felix was right. She needed sleep. But this was the *ride or die* stretch of race. It was not speed that determined the victor now, but endurance.

And Yael had always endured....

The howling only grew louder. Yael was chewing down the final pieces of chicken when she saw the headlamp, rising like a miniature sun. A wrong dawn from the west. The howling grew and grew and grew, not nightmare screams at all, but an engine, raging toward them at the highest speed.

Yael dropped the food. Her helmet? Where was it? No! Goggles first!

—GO GO GO HURRY GO—

Slip. Clip. Snap.

Too late. The headlamp was here and it was—slowing? The engine's rabid chorus clicked to a hum, a stop. Her sleep-starved eyes barely had time to process the brown jacket and chapped lips, before Luka Löwe was off the bike, coming toward her, stride by angry stride.

"YOU! What were you thinking?"

Felix darted between them, hound-quick and bristling. Luka stopped, but his eyes kept on, over Felix's shoulder, into her.

"Your little river stunt didn't do much good. Katsuo's still in the race." He lost no time explaining.

"What do you mean?" Yael asked.

He pointed at her. "I mean second place"—and then he jabbed his finger into his own chest—"third. By a long, long shot. The ferryman unloaded Katsuo's bike from the raft once you left. Katsuo swam to shore and had it started by the time I'd crossed because *someone* didn't have the foresight to cut the fuel lines."

"Oh," was all she could manage. Katsuo. Ahead. Still. Swimming. Of course. Why hadn't she thought of that? (Because she'd been too busy thinking about a victory not yet won and what-might-have-beens and staring across the river.)

Felix didn't seem convinced. His shoulders were rolling, oiling up for a fight. "Where's he now, then?"

"Five kilometers back. Having a *verdammt* picnic on the side of the road," Luka growled past Adele's brother. "I would've handled him myself, but he's got his posse with him. We need to knock Katsuo out before Shanghai. We can use the pincer move from Germania—"

"The one you tried to wipe her out with?" Felix cut in. His knuckles popped into fists. "I don't think so. My sister's endured enough from you."

"Endured?" Luka snorted the word. His dark eyebrows vanished under his helmet line. *"From me?"*

Felix broke. (Safety off. Hammer cocked. Trigger pulled.) He flew at Luka; his elbow hooked viciously around the victor's neck. Crushing him in a headlock.

"Don't act like you didn't attack her in Osaka!" Felix hissed into Luka's ear. His nostrils wide, his neck vined with veins. "When you found out she was a girl!"

It was hard to tell in the dark, but Yael was fairly certain Luka's face was growing purple: dusk to violet to eggplant as he wheezed and scuffled. "Felix, let him go! We need him!"

"NO!" His yell carried all the force of that first Prague punch. "This is for your own good, Ad. I'm protecting you!"

Felix's anger was a match, but hers was a barrel of gasoline. All that roiling blackness sealed shut, waiting for the right moment (that right, ballroom moment, in front of the Führer and the world) to explode.

Yael had to shove him away if she wanted to accept Luka's

alliance and reach the ballroom at all. "I don't *need* your protection, Felix! I never needed it."

Felix's face went slack, stunned at these words. His arm loosened just a little too much. Luka leapt on the moment: heel to the shin and fist back up to Felix's nose. There was a crack and a swear, and Luka stepped free. Massaging the base of his throat.

"Is that what she told you?" he rasped at Felix, then turned and looked at Yael. "Is that what you told him? That *I* attacked *you*?"

If only she knew what Adele had told Felix. If only she knew what had really happened in Osaka. Yael's truthless heart pumped full of adrenaline and not knowing.

Blood—dark and worming—started to creep out of Felix's nose. He didn't seem to notice the red or the pain. He stared straight at the girl he thought was his sister. "So that was a lie, too?"

"That's rich." Luka cleared his throat and spit at the ground. "I'd expect a little less surprise from someone whose sister hijacked his identity and left him for the vultures in the desert a year later."

Felix Wolfe's face turned savage: snarling, blood around the muzzle. "Shut your *Scheisse* face!"

"Or what? You're going to put me in a headlock again?" The victor smirked and turned his back to Felix, all his focus on Yael. "Look, as much as I'd like to continue this little sibling bonding session, Katsuo will be finishing up his food any moment now. And we need to be ahead of him for the pincer

311

move to work. Katsuo will think we're playing chicken, and he's too proud to bow out like you did. We'll be able to reach his handlebars. You in, Fräulein?"

"Reach his handlebars and what?" She stared back into those blue-storm eyes, too hard to navigate without getting lost in. "How do I know you won't steer him at me? Crash us both?"

"I'll let you do the wrenching if it would help you feel better. Ladies first and all that," Luka added. "I'll herd Katsuo in your direction and slam on my brakes at the last moment. You grab his handlebar and steer him off the road."

"And what happens after that?" she asked.

"Then we have a fair race. Just us and the road." He smiled. The action split his dry lips. "I have to say, I'm looking forward to it."

And behind him, Felix was shaking his head, giving her the same look he had on the plane: *Don't do this; don't trust him.*

But what choice did she have? With Katsuo so far ahead and Tokyo so close...

The howls were rising again in the distance. No longer the stuff of nightmares, but waking danger. Here, real, now.

Katsuo was coming. She was out of time.

Yael started walking toward her bike.

"Don't do this, Ad," Felix called after her. "You're risking everything."

Not everything. For her it was still squared: everything, everything.

"I have to," she told him.

"There are other ways—"

312

"Like what?" She cranked the Rikuo's engine.

Felix's blood trailed like ellipses: out, out, out, dripping off his chin, into nothing. He looked so at odds in the dark, staring hard at Luka's back as the victor hopped onto his bike. Revved his own motor.

"Don't go with him. Please, just—just trust me," he offered pathetically.

But Yael was a girl long past trust (the needles had flushed it out of her, along with so many other things), and it occurred to her that—maybe, really, still—Felix Wolfe just wanted his sister safe. That—maybe, probably, actually—there *was* no other way. This was it. If she didn't follow Luka now, all would be lost.

The howls swelled. Katsuo's headlamp broke over the horizon, carving out their silhouettes. Until they were nothing more than shadows themselves.

"We're Wolfes," Felix pleaded. "We have to stick together."

But the iron in Yael's blood did not bind her to Felix. No. She was bound to so much more: a people, a world.

All must not be lost.

Luka pulled out onto the asphalt and looked behind his shoulder. His bike idled, waiting for her. Yael took a deep breath and followed.

CHAPTER 30

NOW

MARCH 29, 1956

Every nerve, every molecule that was her, felt electric, frying at a hundred thousand watts, as Yael urged her bike into the road. Luka drove on the left shoulder—fast enough to use his highest gear, but slow enough to let Katsuo catch up to them. Yael rode parallel (but a bit ahead, so Katsuo would not spot the trap), her wheels shredding through the dew. Meter by meter, minute by minute, the headlamp behind them grew brighter, and the roar of Katsuo's engine swallowed all.

His posse (Takeo and Iwao) rode behind him. Close enough to reassure him, too far away to do much good when it came to it. Their lights were bits of stardust while his was a meteor: blazing, ready for impact.

Here came the tricky part. Yael needed three sets of eyes: one for Katsuo, one for Luka, another for the road ahead. Instead she settled for fractions of each view through her smeared goggles:

A bend in the road. Katsuo revving forward, past Luka. Luka closing in, just centimeters from Katsuo's chrome tail-pipe. Another bend. Luka again, jerking away from Katsuo with a roar of his engine, baiting him, just as he'd done with her outside Germania. Katsuo, attention fastened on Luka trying to decide whether or not to crowd him off the road. Too distracted to notice Yael making calculations of her own in front of him.

It was time to strike.

Yael tapped on the handbrakes, shaving a kilometer or two off her speed. At the same time Luka fed his own fuel line, herding Katsuo in. The chrome of his handlebars flared. Yael could see it perfectly—the place her hand was supposed to clench, push, let go—so bare and silvery.

Luka kept pushing, closer and closer.

Air carved into her cheekbones. The road ripped beneath them: skin-shredding fast. Kilometers, cool darkness, and speed threaded through the gaps between Yael's fingers as she reached out. Out…

So many things happened in one moment. Her fingers wrapped around the handlebar's chrome. Luka's brakes squealed, and the hiss of burning rubber filled the air. Katsuo's head turned and his eyes found hers.

There was no more blade in his gaze. No more hunter's stare. What Yael saw when she looked into his eyes was something far more animal…far more human: fear.

And it cut her—bone deep, marrow deep—all the way to the little girl belted on the gurney, her eyes white with terror as the needles burned through her, one after the other after

315

the other. Who walked under floodlights and stood in a river of blood and heard every one of her heartbeats. Who had her sleeve grabbed, her life exposed by the National Socialist who was not a National Socialist.

The girl who was hunted. The girl who was afraid.

She'd wanted for so long to be the hunter. The predator. The Valkyrie—chooser of life and death—above it all.

But not like this. What was she doing? Dancing between the lines, forgetting them altogether.

They rode for another two seconds. Side by side. Paralyzed and flying.

Two seconds too long—the raw in Katsuo's eyes reloaded into something desperate. Something dangerous.

The commandments of tooth and claw were kicking in. Kill or be killed.

This was not a world for lines.

He grabbed Yael's wrist. Fingers clamping down, trapping her. If she pushed Katsuo's handlebars now she'd be dragged off her own Rikuo. Twisted into the pretzel wreck of metal and flesh. If she let go, backed off, Katsuo would shove her anyway. Send her off the road and ride on.

Another second ripped between them. A bend was coming, leaping into their headlamps, only moments away. They couldn't go on like this for much longer. Katsuo's grip loosened. No longer gurney strength, but enough to hold her. Unless...

Yael twisted her hand, as if she were trying to jerk open a lock, and pulled. Katsuo's fingers clenched, but too late.

Catching all glove, no skin. He pulled so hard the leather lost its cling, snaking off her hand, snapping free, flying—hollow, empty—away. Katsuo watched the formless leather fall into him, his eyes shifting through so many emotions: ferocity → disbelief → fear again →

The glove kept falling. *He* kept falling. So far back that Yael lost sight of his eyes.

But she saw everything else in full, agonizing twenty-twenty detail.

The laws of physics took over. Gravity, momentum, force...boy and bike meeting ground. Sparks fizzed across the pavement, and the light of Katsuo's headlamp spun wild. Stabbing too-bright light into the lump of road that was not road but a body. Splayed and stilled in a way she knew only too well.

He would not be getting up from that.

Katsuo was stopped, but the laws of physics kept on. The bend in the road came, and Yael swung into it. Seeking out the centripetal force, trying to stay even, fighting against the change. The curve was sharp, and by the time she rode it out and looked back, there was nothing behind her. Just the outlines of trees, stark against Luka's headlamp.

Wind howled up her gloveless wrist into her jacket's sleeve, biting the skin of her left arm. Rushing at her, again and again, until she couldn't feel it anymore. Until she was numb.

CHAPTER 31

NOW

MARCH 29, 1956
SHANGHAI CHECKPOINT
KILOMETER 18,741

1st: Adele Wolfe, 12 days, 10 hours, 37 minutes,
5 seconds.
2nd: Luka Löwe, 12 days, 10 hours, 37 minutes,
10 seconds.

It was hard for Yael to tell if she was awake or in a dream by the time she reached the Shanghai checkpoint. The race markers guided her through the city's hazy post-dawn roads—teeming with electric streetcars and teetering rickshaws, the smells of fresh fish and salt—all the way to the splintering wooden docks that zigged and zagged into the sea. The finish line was a ramp onto a boat named the *Kaiten*. The profile of the ship's command deck was warlike, sketched by a sun not yet high. Its hull—all fresh paint and smooth rivets—dwarfed every other ship at the dock, rusted fishing rigs and houseboats.

Yael wheeled her way on board, let her engine shudder and die. Twenty-four hours and seventeen minutes. That was how long she'd been on the bike. It should've been shorter— but after the crash she just *couldn't* keep going. She'd pulled to the side of the road and tried to breathe. She took the glove off of her right hand and slipped it onto her left, but it was all wrong. She threw it into the bushes just as Luka passed, driving into the heavy dewed air without looking back. She waited a few more minutes (she wasn't really sure what for . . . Takeo? Iwao? Felix?) until she couldn't stay still any longer. She had to keep moving, stay ahead, win.

She had to make all their deaths matter.

Even Katsuo's.

His name was already crossed out when she got to the board. (The supply caravan found him hours ago, the time-keeper told Yael when she asked about it. There was nothing the medics could do but radio the fatal wreck in.) Yael stared at the chalked line until her eyes smeared with sleep, and it all became one big white blur. As fuzzed as her thoughts.

~~*Tsuda Katsuo*~~. *(No: Tsuda Katsuo. I should think it without the strike. What use are lines anyway?) Seventeen. Born in Kyoto. Victor of the eighth Axis Tour. Dead. Like so many others. So, so many others . . .*

Five seconds. Not much of a lead. But there's just one more stretch. One final stretch.

Where are my gloves? Oh, right, back there on the road. Lost. Gone.

Gone, gone, gone.

319

There was no dormitory on board the *Kaiten*. The racers were provided with their own cabins for the voyage. They were utilitarian quarters, not much more than a washroom and a bed. When Yael reached Adele Wolfe's room, she crumpled into the fresh linen sheets and slept like the dead. Unmoving, dark, and dreamless.

This time when she woke there was no daylight. And there was no Felix, smiling at her, waving her over to see colors. Her tiny porthole window was crowded with gloom. (Dusk maybe? Or dawn? There was no way of telling.) And Felix…he would be shut away in his own room, if he was even on the boat at all.

At first Yael thought her head was spinning when she sat up, but she soon figured, as she stood on rubbery legs, that it was the movement of the boat. They were already at sea. The other racers must have made it on board during the time she'd slept.

All except Katsuo.

The thought, the name, hit her with the cold, terrible clarity of morning. No more blurring, no more numb.

The memory of him, hitting the road so hard, dashing limbs and joints and life, seemed like a nightmare. Larger than life, clinging to her like an oily film, making her feel sick, dirty.

Too many of her nightmares were real.

"Tsuda Katsuo is dead," she said aloud to the crackless, metallic wall. The words echoed back to her faint, fainter, faintest….

The reasons inside her grew frenzied. Dancing around

320

her lines. *It was either my life or his. It wasn't my fault. Not in the end. If he'd let go, if he hadn't pulled back so hard, he wouldn't have lost his balance. I did not choose his death. But I caused it....*

And the voice that whispered loud, louder, loudest— the oldest whisper of all—said only a single word: *Monster.*

She feared it was right.

———

The sea grew worse, its waters writhing, bucking, lashing every which way. The *Kaiten*'s crew seemed unfazed, walking around the corridors with mountain-goat surety. But Yael and the other racers spent much of the time off their feet, trying to keep the contents of the messdeck from painting their cabin floors. The messdeck itself was sparsely populated when Yael made the wall-clinging journey for sustenance. She was more than thankful for it. She didn't think she could stand the other racers' stares—real or imaginary—stabbing her just as Katsuo's had. One hundred times over.

The stare she dreaded most was Felix's. (According to the scoreboard he *had* reached the ship, in the twelfth and final place.) But Adele's brother and his frostbite eyes were nowhere to be seen. Lars (who looked a little green faced) and Ryoko were the only diners, nursing bowls of *kake udon* and clinging to their bolted chairs.

Yael kept her head down as she retrieved her own bowl and sat at a separate island of a table. The rock of the boat made tiny waves in the broth, rippling through Adele's sad reflection. Yael stared and stared at the tangled noodles, trying to work up the stomach to eat. The last leg of the Axis Tour was just over twelve hundred kilometers from Nagasaki to Tokyo. Twelve more hours of driving in highest gear. Twelve hours of Luka coming after her with everything he had... trying to close that five-second gap between them.

Yael needed all the strength she could get. And though she was not full, she wasn't hungry either.

Just empty and sick.

She was still staring when the chair beside her rattled. It was Ryoko, joining her table. The girl's short, satiny hair brushed her jaw as she bowed. "Hello. I am called Ono Ryoko."

"I'm Adele." Yael nodded back, dared to meet the girl's gaze.

There was no glare behind Ryoko's eyes. No cutting accusation. Dimples appeared on her cheeks instead. "Thank you, for helping us get away from the Soviets. And for helping Yamato. He is very grateful."

Yael did not know what to say. *You're welcome* seemed like a heresy. Saying nothing would be an insult. So she latched on to the final subject. "How is Yamato?"

"He is happy to not be driving anymore. Yamato is skilled at racing, but that is not where his heart lies." Ryoko's cheeks reddened: rosy to plum. She went on quickly. "He wishes to study literature and become a teacher."

Yael thought of the boy's worn book. How he read the haikus aloud in the perfect tone and tempo. "He'll be a good teacher."

Ryoko nodded. "I think so."

Yael shoved her hand into her pocket, drew out the paper sculptures. The star was squashed flat and the crane's neck was bent back, broken. "Thank you, for these."

"You did not open them." Ryoko frowned and fished the papers from Yael's palm. Her deft fingers pulled their crumpled shapes apart, smoothed out the creases.

Both slivers of paper held handwritten notes—neat cursive woven between German propaganda and Arabic newsprint.

On the star: *Katsuo is planning a roadblock with Hiraku, Takeo, and Iwao. Get ahead of them as soon as you can.*

On the crane: *Katsuo is planning to drug your water. Keep your canteens close.*

The truth was inside. Always inside. (And it made Yael wonder, if she unfolded herself, what she would find. The monster of Dr. Geyer's making? Or the Valkyrie of her own design?)

She did not know.

She did not know.

How could she forget her own self?

"You were trying to warn me," Yael thought aloud, because this question was easier to face: "But why?"

"I watched you race last year. You rode very well. Better than the boys. It made me glad. It gave me..." Ryoko paused, searching for the German word she wanted. "Hope. Hope that I, too, could race, even though I am a girl. And in Prague, when I sat alone, you smiled at me, gave me hope again. I wanted to give some back to you."

Hope. Gottverdammt hope. Yael really needed some right

now. She looked down at the wrinkled papers. They'd never be smooth again. Too much had happened to them. But perhaps they could be refolded....

"Do you think you could show me how to make the star?" she asked. "And the crane?"

The girl across from her smiled. "Of course."

Ryoko was a good teacher, too. They spent an hour leaned over the table, creasing paper with their thumbs, talking about motorcycles and boys. (The conversation somehow kept steering back in Yamato's direction. Each time Yael mentioned the boy's name, Ryoko's face dipped into another shade of red.) When the lesson was over, Yael could craft a steady star and a crane that actually looked birdlike.

It is, she thought as she pocketed the two papers, *a good start.*

———

When the seas finally calmed, Yael found that her stomach did not follow suit. It was still turning, tumbling previous meals of *kake udon*, rice, fish, and dried plums inside her gut. She went onto the deck for air, a trick she'd learned from the seafaring heroes on Henryka's shelf of banned novels.

She wasn't the only one. The whole boat had turned itself inside out: racers and crew alike draped themselves over the railings, basking in sea breeze and morning.

Yael scanned for Felix as she moved up to the *Kaiten*'s bow, but he was nowhere to be seen. She hadn't seen him at all during the voyage. She lacked the courage to knock on his door, and she didn't really know what she would say if she did. What did twenty-four more hours matter anyway? The goodbye that was not a good-bye was still best.

The bow was sequestered, walled off by the command tower. The best place for her to stand and stare off into the blue-on-blue horizon.

"Girding your loins, Fräulein?" Luka—another face she'd missed on the initial count—leaned into the railing next to her. "We've got quite a day ahead. Captain said we're only a few hours from port. We should be able to see land soon."

He looked nice. Prepped for the horde of cameras they were getting ready to race into. His hair was freshly washed and slicked back. All the stubble had been scraped from his cheeks. His lips were no longer peeling; he'd smoothed them over with petroleum jelly. The ear tip he'd lost saving Yamato was cuffed in a clean piece of gauze.

It made Yael all the more aware of how grungy she was. She hadn't had the sea legs to stand under her washroom's trickling showerhead. She'd settled instead for a few splashes of water to get the dirt off her face.

But the oily feeling was still there. All across her scalp, soaked into her skin. It would take more than a shower and soap to get rid of it. A lot more.

Yael stared back out at the sea.

He took her silence in stride. "Is this about Katsuo?"

Was she that open? That obvious? Or had he just gotten that good at cracking through her shell and reading her?

"He's dead." She said this just as she'd told the wall. Only this time it didn't echo back.

She yelled again into nothing. "He's dead and it's my fault."

"*Scheisse.*" Luka swore and leaned farther over the rail, his toes balancing on the lowest rung. It struck Yael how easy it would be to push him overboard. Instead she just watched as hull winds and sunlight streaked through his hair.

"You *have* changed." He looked back at her, lips crumpling into a frown. "Don't get me wrong. I like the new you, but I'm not sure I completely understand her."

"It doesn't bother you?"

"What? That Katsuo's dead?" He hopped back off the railing. "I'd be lying if I said it didn't.... But better him than me. Or you. And it would have been you, Adele, if you hadn't pulled away.

"You shouldn't go beating yourself up about it," he went on. "You did what you had to do. If he'd had the wits to let go in time, he'd still be here."

Blunt Luka words, full of ugly truths. Despite everything, despite herself, they made Yael feel a little bit better.

The first traces of land were sprouting out of the sea. Hillsides poking up like spring seedlings. Growing and growing as the minutes stretched silent between them and the boat churned on.

"I'm glad Felix was wrong about you," she said to the rising hills.

He leaned into the railing again, hanging daredevil far

into her vision. "Apparently you gave him quite the wrong impression of me."

"I lie a lot."

"I noticed. You're good at it, too." He turned into her, so close that Yael had to look. Had to see how somber his face was, how tightly he gripped the railing. "Adele—was it ever real? Was there ever a sliver of a moment that you cared for me?"

Yael's thoughts flooded with cracks and trains and *more*ness. There seemed to be slivers of emotion—true and bright—tangled up in this mess of aliases. Luka + Adele. Luka + not-Adele. Yael + this boy who was a National Socialist and yet so much more.

Was it ever real? Were any one of *them* ever real?

"I'm not really sure anymore," she said.

Luka Löwe chuckled to himself. The corner of his lip turned tight. "You're a torturous creature, Adele Wolfe."

He was going to kiss her again. She could see it in the slight five-degree tilt of his head, in the way he drew closer.

What did it matter? The sun was shining and not everything was a lie.

In less than forty-eight hours she was never going to see him again.

Couldn't she just have this? A feeling that wasn't sadness or anger or guilt or weight? A good-bye that wasn't all tears and silence and screaming?

He leaned into her. She let him.

This kiss was much like the last, with the world moving

around them and his lips telling a story to hers. It tasted like one of the Greeks' epic poems: Warring. Heroic. Vast. Full of so many loves and births and deaths.

It tasted wrong.

She realized it as soon as the flavor passed from his lips to hers. Silvery chemicals sliced into her taste buds, stabbed down the back of her throat.

It was a flavor Yael knew well. Vlad had tested her with it so many times, always slipping it into the row of concoctions she had to smell and identify. She could hear him now, holding up the amber pharmacy bottle, explaining what was inside: "This knocks a person out in under a minute, keeps them under for a few hours. Impossible to wake them up. The antidote has to be applied ahead of time to do you any good."

Yael gasped, choked on the feeling of the drug seeping into her. Luka pulled back.

The shine on his lips was still there, and it was not petroleum jelly. The victor swabbed his jacket sleeve across his mouth.

"Yooou saaaid—" Her words were already slurring. So was her vision. "F-Fair race."

Luka shrugged off the words. (Or, at least, she thought he did. He was little more than a brown stain against the daylight.) "Well, you know what they say about love and war."

Yael's hand fumbled for the railing. Missed. The tranquilizer was lead-heavy in her veins, threading through every part of her, melting with the rest of the weight. There was no keeping things together.

Luka caught her midcollapse, whispering into her ear as

he laid her to rest on the deck, "Sorry, love. I really am. But even just five seconds apart you're too good. And I will not let you win again."

Darkness like smoke was swirling in, flushing out the last of Luka's soft words: "I'll see you in Tokyo."

And just like that it was all slipping away. Away, away...

CHAPTER 32

NOW

APRIL 1, 1956

The world around Yael was pitch-black and shaking. A voice hissed. "Wake up! You have to get up now!"

Why? It was so nice here, in the warm dark.... If only the quaking would stop, she could rest here forever. But the shaking grew and grew. Until it buzzed under her teeth and jolted the edges of her fingernails. Rattling everything inside her—words, visions, memories—like dice in a cup.

A long, long train. Holi colors bursting out of a smokestack. The too-yellow-haired woman in the beer hall basement crying and crying as she ripped the world from the wall. Thumbtacks raining down, red as blood. Blood on her jacket. Blood between the tiles on the floor, soaking deep into the grout.

"Wake up!" the voice hissed again. This time Yael hung on to it, tried to remember why it sounded so familiar.

The shaking continued, but the memories that floated back to Yael this time were more solid: Japan's ragged shore drawing close. The morning sun so warm on her face. Luka Löwe leaning down, touching poisoned lips to hers... a kiss that meant everything.

—*WAKE UP WAKE UP NOW IT'S TIME*—

Opening her eyes meant sharp, painful LIGHT. Yael found herself staring into the bottomless afternoon sky. Then a different, sharper shade of blue appeared in the form of Felix's stare.

"Get up!" He did most of the work for her. Pulling Yael into a sitting position by her elbows. She could see she was still on the *Kaiten*, though she'd been dragged from the bow back to the midship portion of the deck. The swallowing stretch of sea was gone. In its place were a crowd of ships and the buzz of Nagasaki's port at the end of the ramp.

Two motorcycles sat close: hers and Felix's. The ten other Rikuos were nowhere to be seen. The sun beat down on them from much too high.

—*PAST TIME*—

It took Yael's body another second to react to these horrible things. First it produced a scream. Then a frantic clawing to get to her bike. Felix moved in synchronized motions beside her as she lunged toward the Rikuo.

"How long have I been asleep?" she wheezed, slipping the goggles over her grease-flat hair.

"I didn't find you until all the racers had been lined up. You weren't there, so I went looking—"

"How long?" She turned and found herself shouting in Felix's face. Some spittle landed on the bruised bridge of his nose. He didn't even flinch.

"I couldn't wake you up," he went on. "Nurse Wilhelmina said it seemed like you'd been drugged. I tried everything. And I tried to get the officials to hold the race, but they wouldn't. That was two hours ago."

The helmet Yael grabbed slipped out of her hand. Tumbled onto the *Kaiten*'s deck.

She didn't bother picking it up.

Two hours. Luka and the rest of the pack would be well past Fukuoka by now. Crushing her five-second lead. Third gear, driving without stopping, all the rage and reason in the world could not get her to Tokyo in time.

It was over.

A part of Yael felt like crying, but the tears weren't there. There was a hollowness instead, scraping the pit of her stomach. Pushing out, expanding, threatening to devour every next moment.

Felix retrieved the helmet, held it out. "Put it on."

Yael's arms hung useless beside her.

When she didn't move, Felix placed the helmet on her head himself. Fastened the strap firm to her chin. "I told you there were other ways. These Rikuos, they've been fitted more for endurance than speed. Luka was right. They're *Scheisse* for a race like this, but machinery-wise, they're capable of so much more. When I was test-driving it in Hanoi, I passed a garage and decided to do some tinkering.

"I switched out the sprockets in Hanoi, to improve the gear ratio and take full advantage of the bike's rpm. It gets better top speeds now."

He'd rigged his bike in Hanoi? Of course, it all made sense now. How he'd reached the ferry so quickly...

"Why didn't you tell me?" she asked.

"There didn't seem to be much point after you pushed Katsuo into the river. You were all set to win. And then on the roadside...I tried. But I couldn't say it out loud. I thought Luka might steal the bike if he knew."

Luka. The name sent a shudder through her. Not fear. Not *all* rage.

(But mostly.)

Yael swallowed it back. "How much faster?"

"About twenty more kilometers an hour. But I had to forfeit some of the acceleration power. It takes a bit longer to get going."

The calculations whirred through Yael's head. Twenty added kilometers an hour...It was twelve hundred kilometers from Nagasaki to Tokyo. If she pushed hard enough, she could get to the Imperial Palace in just over ten and a half hours.

Two hours ahead of schedule.

If she left now, she might catch up with the other racers on the capital's outskirts. There was still a chance....

"Go," Felix said. "Keep our family together. Beat the *Saukerl.*"

A different drug was pumping through Yael's veins. The one she'd been craving in the mess hall. The one she'd tried to build out of crumpled paper and foolish kisses. The one this

Wolfe had given her, in the name of blood and iron: *hope*. It was as heavy and powerful as it had always been. Only now, instead of crushing Yael down, it was pushing her forward. Sliding her onto Felix's Rikuo, kicking the engine to a roar, urging her down the *Kaiten*'s gangway, into Nagasaki's streets.

———

Japan smeared past Yael in solid strokes of color, like pieces of an impressionist's oil painting. Brown-green for rice paddies. Sterling blue for mountain passes. Glittering silver for swathes of seashore. Pale pink for rows and rows of blossoming cherry trees. And—once the night fell—neon bright for shop signs.

It was a beautiful string of shades and earth. Sights that begged for you to slow, look at, savor. Another face, another life, another time Yael would have. But she kept her stare straight, down the sights, at the road ahead. This asphalt was the smoothest she'd encountered the entire race, and once she'd coaxed Felix's Rikuo to its top speed—and it took some coaxing (he was right; the acceleration had been diluted, no longer the powerful rumble that shot her out of Hanoi)—the ride passed like a dream.

She couldn't yet tell if it was a nightmare or not.

Her time was good. She reached Hiroshima just over the three-and-a-half-hour mark, Osaka at the six-and-a-half-hour mark. Stretching the Rikuo's engine to its maximum potential.

She'd just reached the fringes of Tokyo when she spotted the first taillight. The last in a long line of eager Rikuos, weary racers. Yael didn't dare slow as she weaved around the first two stragglers. She blew past their motorcycles with all the extra speed Felix's adjusted sprockets had to offer. Too fast for the city's many turns. Yael rode them relentlessly. She caught up to another taillight and passed it, slingshotting into the heart of the capital.

The wheels of her Rikuo whined, carrying Yael past the next rider. And the next. The streets had been cleared of all traffic, made sacred for the racers. Axis banners lined the way, lording over spectators and cameras alike. The crowd roared like walls of water on either side of her: a sea of red flags and white. It was only a few kilometers now—until the Imperial Palace. The finish line. She could taste it on the neon-lit air, feel it in the rumble of her engine, hear it in the wild screams of the crowds.

Three more taillights; the middle of the herd. Yael threaded needle-tight through them.

Dream or nightmare? Either way she was flying. Throttle twisted all the way down. Fueled by screams and *hope, hope, hope*. She found Takeo and Luka riding close. The knife-wielder's front tire overlapped with the victor's rear. The main gate to the Imperial Palace wasn't far. Its spotlights glared over the crowd's heads. And though Yael could not yet see the finish line, she could envision it (thanks to the final racing shots of prior Axis Tours). A stone bridge lined with orb lanterns, ending in a yawn of black iron gates. The threshold would be marked with a thick white line, flanked by a swastika banner on the right and the rising sun on the left.

The end. Almost there.

The victory. Almost hers.

In a heartbeat Yael was at Takeo's side. Past him. She could hear the boy yelling over the gnash of the engines, but she did not look back. Her focus was on the rider just ahead. She stared hard at the brown jacket as her Rikuo flew: closer, closer, there.

Slowly—centimeter by centimeter—she passed him. The finish line was not much farther, and she had five seconds to Adele Wolfe's name.... Five precious, wonderful, *hope*-filled seconds that would crumble an empire. Heal the world.

The path to the Main Gate bridge was not a straight shot, but a pair of ninety-degree turns—around squares and a mass of spectators—too sharp to take on the highest gear. Yael nearly skidded out on the first one, pumping the brakes just enough to stay upright. The Rikuo growled beneath her—its racehorse gallop faltering. Yael swore at the throttle, pushing it with her gloveless hand, remembering Felix's warning: *It takes a bit longer to get going.*

How much is a bit? Four seconds? Five seconds? More?

The motorcycle chugged desperately toward the second, final turn. The bridge and the victory. Its engine plodded draft-horse slow, clopping forward in sleepy jolts.

And it was not enough.

Luka, his engine fully recovered from the same turn, ripped past—a brown leather blur—crossing the finish line to the crowd's earth-trembling roar. Yael tried not to let the sight, the sound shake her as she spurred the engine forward.

Pop. Pop. Pop—went her Rikuo's acceleration. Too tired, too angry, too helpless to go on.

The seconds crawled like hours, like lifetimes. Each its own small death.

1, 2, 3, 4, 5.

She did not reach the line.

6, 7, 8. (Another death, and another and another.)

Yael rolled through the Imperial Palace gate and pulled her motorcycle to a stop. The engine jerked, sputtered, died when she let go of the clutch, but the cheers would not cease. They roared and fuzzed and ate through the night like television static.

Takeo was the next to wheel through the gate, all burning gears and disappointment. (He hadn't stood a chance, really, but that was the power of hope, the utter cruelty of it.) More racers piled after. Iwao, Taro, and Ralf shot through in quick succession. Masaru, Ryoko, and Karl followed a few minutes later. And then there were the stragglers: Lars and Isamu. But it didn't matter.

It didn't matter.

There was only one winner, and it was not Yael. They wouldn't officially announce the victor of the tenth Axis Tour until all the times were in. Until Felix and her old Rikuo came along two and a half hours later to claim twelfth. But Luka was already being swarmed—Reichssender cameras and racing officials flocked to him. The Reich's golden boy wore a smile made of straight white teeth as he looked into the lenses.

Yael could not move (she was static, all static). She sat on the dead Rikuo and watched as Luka Löwe stripped off his riding gear and breathed loudly into the microphones. All around her the remaining racers parked their bikes and dismantled themselves: helmets, goggles, gloves. But she could not seem to take her eyes off Luka. The boy who was now at the center of everything.

She should have kept hating him.

But all she could feel now was ... nothing.

The empty spaces inside her were opening again—cobweb weak and wide. Yael was falling through them, grabbing on to only snatches of thoughts and words. She could only hold on to three:

All.

> *For.*

>> *Nothing.*

All of it. For nothing. She'd failed her mission. Failed Reiniger, Henryka, Vlad. Failed Aaron-Klaus, the Babushka, Mama, Miriam. Failed the young partisan behind the oxblood door in Rome. Failed the old balding man at the shisha café. Failed too many to count.

She'd changed nothing.

Yael's mind was scrabbling, trying to find a loophole. Something. Anything.

She could steal one of the serving girl's faces and kimonos, slip into the Victor's Ball with a tray of poisoned hors d'oeuvres. But that would not work. The Führer's security was too tight. The SS guards who mushroomed around Hitler always delivered his meals themselves, food flown in from select Reich farms and prepared under the strictest supervision.

Perhaps she could disguise herself as one of the officials' wives. But the Führer had never danced with any of them. Not even Empress Nagako. Adele Wolfe had been the only exception to this rule. The only face he'd ever let close.

If she tried to cut down his life from afar—throw a knife, pull a trigger, and hope that it pierced his ever-alert human armor, hope that it hit his nothingness of a heart—there was little chance of success. Probably, definitely she would end up surrounded by SS and tortured slowly for information. Carved to slow pieces in a dungeon while she shrieked out the names and addresses of the resistance.

Besides, now that she'd lost the race, Reiniger and Henryka wouldn't be ready... they would assume she'd boarded a flight back to Germania (as mission protocol instructed her to do in such an event). If Yael tried to infiltrate the ball now, the resistance would be caught off guard, their element of surprise and unity lost.

Going to the Victor's Ball as Adele Wolfe had been the only way.

"Seems we're both full of surprises today." The voice that pulled her out of her plotting was like a shot of rum—warm, stinging all the way down. Yael looked up to see Luka in front of her bike, both of his hands on her handlebars, leaning in over the front wheel. A wall of Reichssender cameras stood a good way behind him, their bulbous lenses pointed at the pair.

Yael wondered if Henryka was watching this, or if she'd already turned the television off.

"You..." What could she say? What words were there

for a loss this huge? An anger this deep? "You tricked me," was all she could manage.

"Come now, Fräulein, don't act like that." Luka snorted. "Don't pretend you didn't do the exact same thing last year, leaving me with a bloody head and a bloodier heart while you went on to win. All I did was make things fair: Take back what you stole from me. A betrayal for a betrayal. A win for a win. Only I did it with a lot less blood."

"And I'm supposed to be grateful?" Yael hissed. The burn she felt at the very first sight of him was back: catching, growing. Close, too close to her gasoline-tank rage.

"I might not go *that* far," Luka said with a twitch of his too-dark eyebrows. He was practically hooked over her handlebars, straddling the front wheel. Yael couldn't help but fantasize about starting the engine, letting it ride, watching that *Scheisse* smirk slide off his face.

He went on. "Don't you see? You and I, we're even now. Well, almost even." He caught himself. "You still owe me a favor."

A favor? A FAVOR? If only he knew how close she was to actually revving the motor. Letting the blackness out. Yael crammed the rage into her reply instead. "You're a *verdammt* dummkopf if you actually think I'll give you a—"

"Come to the Victor's Ball with me," he said.

It took Yael a minute to process his invitation, since he'd said it so calmly, dousing her own coals of words.

"It was such a bore last time. All those officers and officials and speeches..." Luka sighed and leaned back. His hands still clutched her steering, twisting the lifeless throttle and squeezing the useless brakes. "We could have fun. It'll be a fresh start for us."

Yael stared at the boy. This strange, magnetic boy who didn't blink at leaving his first Iron Cross with the Russians, but fought so brutally to gain his second. Who kissed her like he meant it. (Both times.) Who lost his ear tip to save Nagao Yamato, and hardly shed a tear at Tsuda Katsuo's demise. Who made her want to choke him and hug him all at once.

Arschloch, hero, National Socialist, saint.

He made no sense.

But this time Yael didn't have to figure him out. She didn't have to sift through mask after mask after mask to figure out which one was real. All she had to do was say *yes*.

And she meant to, but she could quite believe it. "You—you want me to be your date? Is that allowed?"

Luka shrugged. "I'm the first double victor of the Axis Tour. I can do whatever I want."

Ah, so they were back to the Prague version of Luka Löwe: puff-chested, proud, who'd been all swagger and brag before Felix's knuckles roughed up his face.

They'd come full circle.

But circles didn't end. Another hit was coming. All thanks to him.

Yael slid off her bike and walked up to where Luka perched. The Reichssender cameras had drawn closer, catching every movement, every angle, every word between them in live time.

"I'll go to the Victor's Ball with you." Yael looked into the cameras as she said this. Even if Henryka had switched off the screen, someone in the resistance would be watching. Word would get back to Henryka and Reiniger and the rest of the cell leaders that the mission was still on.

The crowds kept cheering behind them, though they had no reason to.

Luka stood straight and stepped off the wheel so they were close. Face-to-face. Shoulder-to-shoulder. There were still a few centimeters between them (tense, taut, trying to tease her with smells of leather and musk), but to Yael it might as well have been kilometers.

"It'll be our first proper dance." He smiled with his teeth again. "I look forward to it."

Instead of nothingness and rage, all Yael could feel was the press of her knife inside her boot. The extra weight of the Walther P38 just below her chest.

He wasn't the one she planned on dancing with.

"Me too," Yael said, and smiled back.

CHAPTER 33

NOW

APRIL 2, 1956
THE IMPERIAL PALACE
TOKYO, JAPAN

Late afternoon light poured through the open windows and sliding doors of the Imperial Palace. Warm wafts of air followed, threaded with the sweet scent of cherry blossoms. Yael breathed it in with a weightless chest.

So many things were new. Or about to be.

She'd been a wreck when she first took inventory in the washroom mirror. Though all the dirt and greasy hair had been washed away with her morning bath, there were still faint pink goggle rings around her eyes—shadows of exhaustion scribbled into them like a child's illustration. Road rash scabs smattered her cheeks, so that the freckles she shared with Felix were nearly invisible. Her lips were as cracked as Luka's had been before the not-petroleum jelly.

Yael addressed these things one by one with the makeup kit she'd found sitting in one of the washroom drawers. (One of the few skills Vlad *hadn't* trained her in. Lipstick and foundation and mascara had been Henryka's area of expertise.) Until every trace of the road was gone. Until it looked as if she'd been through nothing at all.

The rest of her body felt just as battered. Every limb stiff, every ligament overstretched. She'd soaked them for hours in a second afternoon bath, staring at the painted wooden panels of the washroom ceiling. Imagining the night to come, over and over again.

There was an official itinerary, which had been proffered to her as soon as she'd been shown to her room:

6:00 – Presentation of the Guests
6:30 – Hors d'oeuvres and Cocktails
6:45 – Toasts
7:00 – Dinner
8:00 – Dancing
8:15 – Murder
8:16 – Escape

Of course, the final two hadn't been on the list, but that was where they fit in the timetable. It would be better to make an escape on a full stomach, Yael reasoned. Who knew when she'd be able to stop running?

She'd taken a stroll around the grounds that morning. She knew it all from blueprints Henryka had gathered, but it helped having a physical survey of the palace complex. Getting a feel for the copper-roofed buildings and methodical garden paths.

By the end, Yael had a solid route mapped out: Get out of the ballroom as fast as possible, grab the survival pack she'd hidden in the gardens, swim across the moat (bridges were out of the question—too many guards and gates), and disappear into Tokyo's night. Leave Adele Wolfe's face and name and life far, far behind.

Her room had been fitted for Western guests. It held a raised bed and windows framed with lush velvet curtains. There was even a television in the corner—bigger and prouder than Henryka's had been. Yael flicked it on as she prepared for the ball, listening to the stories-in-gray as she freshened her makeup, pinned up her hair.

Unlike Henryka's, this television had more than a single channel, but every station in the Greater East Asia Co-Prosperity Sphere was airing the same thing: recaps of the race. There were shots from every stretch of road, every checkpoint city. Though Yael had seen similar recaps before, this one was mesmerizing.

It looked so strange, so apart, behind the glass. Like a dramatic play, not the last three weeks she'd just survived. The channel's narrator detailed the racers' adventures in rapid Japanese—even the ones she did not know about (Lars had almost been bitten by a snake in the Sahara. Norio had had a fit of panic attacks on the ferry from Sicily to Tunis).

The narrator had only made it to Baghdad by the time Yael was ready to get dressed. Along with an itinerary, she'd been given a gorgeous *homongi* kimono to wear to the ball. The silk was a bright teal that made Adele Wolfe's eyes look almost faded. It sported a red lacy pattern that Yael supposed was meant to be roots or branches. To her it looked more like veins.

She drew the window curtains, casting the room into a flickering darkness as she shouldered off her robe. Behind her the television pumped out the tale of the racers' miraculous, motorcycle-less appearance in New Delhi. (The narrator had clung to the landslide cover story.) There were shots of them running through Holi dust to the finish line. The screen had sucked away all the colors. No more joy, just ash pouring over their foreheads, clinging to their necks and arms.

The kimono fit well when Yael tied it into place. Its sleeves were loose but lengthy enough to cover her marked arm. Though Vlad's wolf was almost healed, Yael opted for new bandages. A roll of gauze sat on the bed, waiting to be bound over each and every tattoo, but Yael couldn't bring herself to cover them just yet. She'd removed her dirty bandages before the first bath and it was nice to have the ink out and breathing for a change.

Then there was the matter of weapons. While the kimono's sleeves were loose, its skirt was floor-length in the most constricting way. Even if she *could* wear her boots to the ball, it would take too much time to bend down and retrieve the blade there. While the knife and its sheath fit easily around her thigh, there was no way she could reach it. She'd already found a way to conceal her Walther P38 in the silk obi tied around her waist—just a quick snatch and pull away. But Yael felt naked without the blade, so she skinshifted just enough to make Adele's hair longer, lusher, thicker. She repinned the pale locks into a pile and slid the blade inside, sheath and all.

Easy to hide, easy to reach.

The narrator kept speaking through the dark, telling the story of Hanoi. Yael sat on the edge of the bed, unable to tear her eyes from the screen as the camera panned to Katsuo. Driving through long kilometers of rice paddies. Lazy face and limbs at ease, soaking in the luxury of his long lead.

One of the last shots of him alive.

The camera panned back to Adele Wolfe—hot on the victor's tail, her lips wrapped tight around her teeth. The look on her face was almost feral. The crouch of her body over the Rikuo was definitely predatory. As if she were gauging the right moment to leap and sink her claws in—

It was easy to see now, from the other side of the glass. From pixels and kilometers and a sobering death away.

She'd gotten lost again. Adrift in a life not her own. Entangled in smiles and histories and secrets and relationships she could not fake. She'd forgotten who she was for a moment. For more than a moment. And Katsuo had paid the price. She'd lost the race because of it.

A light rap on the door brought Yael back into the present. It wasn't time yet, was it? The ball wasn't for forty-five more minutes. True—she was armed and dressed, but not *ready*. She felt too scattered, too dismembered. The roll of gauze still lay on Yael's bed, but there was no time to wrap her arm. She shoved the bandages into the band of her obi, tugging the left sleeve of her kimono extra low, before answering the knock.

When she slid the door open, it was not Luka she faced, but Felix. She could see Adele's brother had spent his day similarly to hers, scrubbing away the filth of the road. His hair was trimmed, and his nose had been taped. Instead of leather riding gear he wore a uniform. A brown button-down shirt with party markings in all the right places: Hitler Youth symbol on the lapel, swastika band choking his upper arm. A black necktie draped over his chest.

He looked like a different person in these things. It took Yael a moment to sort his name from his appearance. "Felix—"

He seemed just as startled at her flowy kimono and the makeup on her face. "So it's true. You're going to the ball with Luka Löwe."

Yael nodded and moved aside to let him into her room. This wasn't a conversation for the hallway, where servants dashed back and forth and ears listened through too-thin doors.

"I tried to find you this morning, but you weren't here." Felix stepped inside. His eyes landed on the screen, where Takeo was giving a breathless interview on board the *Kaiten* about finding the wreck that was Katsuo—using words like *tangle* and *broken* (the same way she felt inside).

Yael shut the door. "I was walking the grounds."

Adele's brother didn't look away from the screen. They were showing the scoreboard from the *Kaiten* now; the shot was focused on Katsuo's struck-through name. The narrator had transitioned into a sort of eulogy. Talking about the racer's early life, achievements, family, love.

All gone now.

"Thank you for giving me your bike." She could not fake it. Even now. Felix Wolfe was pale against the light of the television. The way he stood, with his fists tight and his eyes hard and the pictures of the world-as-it-was flickering over his face . . . it was Aaron-Klaus all over again.

Only this time Yael was the one who was leaving, who could not say good-bye.

All these things rooted into her voice, impossible to sift out.

"Thank you for everything."

He spun around. And Yael knew she'd said too much. Fear crept back into Felix's face, as thick and full as it had been that night he found her wrecked on the road. The look she imagined his eyes held when Martin crashed on the Nür-burgring track, watching death, destruction, loss fold out in slow motion.

"This is the end—isn't it?" he asked in a way that made Yael suddenly aware of the entire layout of her room. The heavy curtains, perfect for the sheet-tangle move she'd applied in Rome. A bronze lamp by the bed, blunt enough if it came to it . . .

She really, truly hoped it wouldn't.

Felix crossed his arms, so that the armband throbbed crimson in place of his heart. "What they want you to do . . . I'm guessing it's supposed to happen tonight? At the ball? Isn't that why you accepted Luka's invitation?"

The television filled her silence with fresh shots of the live awards ceremony. The one currently taking place somewhere on the palace grounds. The one Yael and the other racers had not been invited to. (Why honor weakness?) Luka stood on the platform, hands tucked behind his back. Mount Fuji rose up in the long distance behind him. Emperor Hirohito stood to his right. And next to him...

Hairs prickled all across Yael's skin as she watched the Führer—live in black and white. He held two Iron Crosses in his hands. Two SS bodyguards hovered next to him.

Adolf Hitler was here. On the grounds. Within reach.

Yael's hands itched for her gun.

Felix noticed. He shifted his body to block the screen. So all she could see was his outline.

"If your mission is what I think it is...what you're about to do." He picked through these words like a soldier in a minefield. "There's no coming back from something like that."

Yael almost smiled when he said this, because he was right. Because there were so many things she had not come back from. Because all those versions of her were scattered across her arm and she was just starting to piece them together again.

"Maybe the world is wrong...but you don't have to be the one to save it," Felix said.

"Someone has to do it," she echoed back.

But he was not Aaron-Klaus. Not even a little. He did not understand. "Maybe. But not *you*."

You are going to change things, the ghosts of herself whispered. *You, Yael.*

"I've trained for this, Felix," she tried to explain. "I can fix things. I can make the world right. I can keep our family together."

"I wanted to trust you, wanted to help. But now that it's actually here...you could die, Ad. You could get our whole family killed." The fear was in Felix's voice now—fear on fear on fear—as he stepped forward. It made Yael's legs tense beneath the folds of her kimono. Kept her mind working through the physics of the room.

Everyone is afraid, her fourth wolf growled, *even him.*

She should not have opened the door. She should not have let him in.

"Felix." Her voice was low and full of warning.

"Some things are too broken to be fixed." He took another step when he said this. Because this was a wreck he thought he could stop. Because he would do anything to keep her—no, his sister—safe.

When he launched himself at her, Yael was not surprised. Only sad.

Speed was what she had to rely on. It wasn't so simple in a kimono, but she managed to deflect his swiping grip. Twirl just out of reach. They'd switched places, so it was his back to the door, hers to the curtains.

"Please, Ad. Even if you succeed, what do you think the Gestapo will do to Mama and Papa? You'll destroy them...."

She could've told him that there were resistance operatives waiting outside their residence in Frankfurt. Ready to whisk the Wolfes away to a safe house as soon as the deed was done.

Explain that their real daughter was safe and not a world-class assassin.

But there was no time. Felix was lunging again. Because he only wanted to restrain his sister, his movements were hesitant, slow, easy to dodge. Yael let him barrel toward the window and its burgundy curtains.

She doubled back, sank her nails into the heavy velvet, and pulled. The curtain rings popped, and the room filled with light again. Felix stumbled under the fabric: blind and confused. Yael worked quickly, pressing him to the floor and wrapping him tight. When she was finished, she folded back the fabric so Felix could breathe.

Yael knew what she had to do. She used her right hand to keep the fabric pinned. (He was already wiggling, struggling like some furious chrysalis.) Her other hand reached into her obi, for the gun.

Felix stopped thrashing, went stiff-still under her. His eyes fixed on her left arm. But it wasn't the P38 he was staring at. When Yael followed his stare, she could see her wolves. All five of them—unbandaged and running, running, running into the kimono silk gathered at her elbow.

Loose *Scheisse* sleeves!

Adele's brother didn't even look at the gun. He was too mesmerized by the ink. Swirling black beasts clawing up his sister's skin. "What are those?"

Not what.

Who.

Who, who, who, who, who.

"You should've gone home." Yael felt like crying when she said this. She was working the pistol around in her palm, butt first.

Felix watched her do it. His eyes were so much like Adele's, full of the same ice and slit and slow-cooked knowledge that something was not right.

"I don't understand," he said finally.

"You will," Yael told him. "And when you do, know that I'm sorry. You're a good brother."

She didn't have the heart to make this pistol whip as hard as the last (or maybe she had *too* much heart). When the deed was done, she couldn't bear to look at Felix too much. She unrolled him from the ruined velvet, tore her bedsheets into strips, and made them into ropes. Three around his legs, two around his wrists, one as a gag. Even if Felix woke up before the ball was over, it would take him hours to work himself free.

Once Adele's brother was secured and hidden under the bed, Yael tried her best to drape the curtain back over its rod, repin her hair, touch up her makeup. Restore things to the way they were before.

Some things are too broken to be fixed.

Was Felix right? About his family? About the world? About...her?

How broken was too broken?

A glimmer of silver caught Yael's eye. Martin's pocket watch lay on the floor by the television. It must have slipped out of Felix's pocket when he was lunging. Yael knelt down and scooped the timepiece into her palm. Felt the cool warp of its metal, the scratchings of a dead brother's name, the watch's pulse still *tick, tick, tick*ing against her skin. Yael shut her eyes and remembered all of its dozens of shiny parts spread out on the table. Adele's brother sorting through what looked like an impossible mess with his tweezers. Taking all these pieces, putting them back into place.

The watch in her hand was not pretty, nor perfect, but it was whole. The hour read quarter to six through the cracks in its glass. Soon, very soon, *she* would be on the television screen.

She had to make herself ready. Whole.

Yael turned down the television's volume so there was only silence, sat on the bed, and pulled her sleeve back one last time. The wolves. It had been so long since she'd even looked at them, much less traced their forms, said their names. So long that Vlad's wolf was no longer a wound, but scabbed over. So long because she'd forgotten to remember. She'd gotten so caught up in living.

Miriam's wolf whispered from their bunk, over a flameless, waxless candle: *You must never forget....*

So Yael traced them all. One by one. Life by life. Wolf by wolf.

———

THEN
LUISEN STREET
GERMANIA, THIRD REICH
NOVEMBER 1955

Every night, before Yael curled under her sheets (before they became tangled in her frantic, dream-fleeing legs), she stared at her arm. She faced her own skin and the ink the National Socialists had put there. She let the ghosts settle next to her and whisper. And she was not afraid.

But the numbers were starting to wear on her.

She could not erase them. And she could not forget.

Memories and ghosts belonged to her. The numbers didn't.

She would remember (who they were, who she was), but it would be on her own terms, through her own ink. This was why she went looking for the man on Luisen Street.

He was not at all what she'd expected a black-market tattoo artist to be. He was a delicate man—all willow and blond—who kept his flat clean. It was a small, white-walled space: bare wood floors, sketchbooks in neat piles, charcoals stacked beside them.

No sign of needles, but Yael knew they were there. The needles were the reason she'd come—followed the rabbit trail of Germania's black-market contacts.

"What kind of piece are you looking for?" the man spoke slowly. Even his steps were cautious as he paced the cramped room. (Everyone in Germania walked on eggshells. Whether their transactions were legal or not.) "I have some landscapes. Portraits. Charcoal, acrylic, oil."

He was a real artist. Most of those did not exist anymore. The Führer—still high and bitter from his artistic failures in Vienna—had quickly gutted the Reich of any true masterpieces. Yael could see this man's talent in the nearest open sketchbook. A nude sat, bare-backed, looking over her shoulder. There was care in the artist's lines—they swooped and curved gentle as a lover's touch.

"I was looking for something more...permanent. Something in ink." She recited the words her last contact had instructed her to say.

"I see." The artist stopped pacing. "Follow me, then."

It was little more than a closet—covered up by a false panel and a rack of heavy coats. Inside was a chair, bottles of ink, a tray like the unsmiling nurse's: full of gauze and swabs and sterile.

And the needle. It was more complex than the one that stabbed Yael's numbers in: with springs and screws and a long, steady grip. It almost didn't look like a needle at all. But the point was still there. Waiting to dig and pierce. Slide into her skin.

"What is it you want?" The artist walked over to the tray and picked up the needle. It must have been heavy, yet he held it the way he might handle a brush. Graceful.

Yael took off her jacket. Peeled back her shirtsleeve. She held her left arm out, just as she had so many times on Vlad's table. She stared at the artist and his needle.

The artist looked at her numbers. His slight face tilted to the side. As if he were inspecting a painting, every brushstroke and highlight. Every sloppy, wavering, permanent line. He stared so long that her arm started to ache.

But Yael kept it straight. Her hand did not shake.

"I've seen these before," he said finally, "but never on such a pretty blond."

"Can you cover it?" she asked.

The artist shoved his wire-framed glasses up the slightness of his nose. "Of course. Have you thought about a design?"

She had. The decision hadn't been hard.

"I want wolves." The animal that carried the Valkyrie Gunnr into battle. Creatures made of freedom and fierce. Who could survive alone, but howled—always cried for their pack.

"How many?"

"Five." Four for her ghosts and one for Vlad. So she would always remember to face down the sights.

"That will take a good deal of time. Several visits." The artist frowned and held the needle high. It glinted in the closet's bare bulb light, like some cursed fairy-tale spindle. "There will be a lot of pain involved. And then there's the matter of money."

"I'll pay it all," she said.

Yael dug a wad of Reichsmarks from the depths of her jacket. Months' worth of stipend, still held together with the brass clip Reiniger had slid on when he handed it to her and said, "Don't spend it all at once."

It was a lot of money. Even by black-market standards. The artist didn't even count it. Just the thickness of the bills was enough. He gestured to the seat.

"Wolves. Five wolves," the artist said, mostly to himself, as Yael slipped into the chair. He set the needle down for a moment, replacing it with a sketchbook and charcoal. His hand sketched the creatures with quick care. Five wolves. Swooping, wild, elegant. Made up of many, many, many lines. "You're certain this is the design you want?"

Yael nodded.

"Just let me know when to start."

Yael looked at the numbers for the last time. She looked at the artist's hand—tense with future wolf-lines—as he retrieved the needle and held it just above her veins. Sharp but steady.

Just like her arm.

"I'm ready," she said.

————

NOW

Remember and be rended.
(You must be broken to be fixed.)
Remember and be rendered.

Babushka—the one who gave her purpose.
Mama—the one who gave her life.
Miriam—the one who gave her freedom.
Aaron-Klaus—the one who gave her a mission.
Vlad—the one who gave her pain.

These were the names she whispered in the dark.
These were the pieces she brought back into place.
These were the wolves she rode to war.

CHAPTER 34

NOW

APRIL 2, 1956
THE IMPERIAL PALACE
TOKYO, JAPAN

Why is this night different from all other nights?

This was a question from another time, another place. Living in one of Yael's rare-photograph memories. The scene was traced in black and white—the dark ghetto night warded off by the stubs of candles her mother lit. It was a desperate Passover, Yael's last. (The train came that autumn.) Gray faces lined the seder table, taking in a meager meal. All was not right, but they sat anyway. Filling the night with stories of Exodus and freedom.

Yael was the youngest at the table, and the duty of reciting the *Mah Nishtanah* fell to her. Its first words were *Why is this night different from all other nights?*

This was a question from another time, another place, but it rose up in Yael now, as she stood at the entrance to the ballroom. Met with an answer from the wholeness of herself.

Tonight death is at Hitler's door. And I am the one to bear it.
I have always been the one to bear it.

Yael could not find her breath as the announcer called out their arrival, "Presenting the victor of the tenth Axis Tour, Luka Wotan Löwe, and his escort, Miss Adele Valerie Wolfe."

Luka offered her his left arm, like some lost gentlemanly soul from Prussia's Junker class. He even looked the part: smooth chin, hair tied back, uniform starched. He wore his jacket, but even that had been treated—conditioned and oiled so the cracks were hardly visible. The leather of his sleeve felt butter-soft as Yael wrapped her fingers around his inner elbow and stepped into the ballroom.

A quick sweep of the area showed Yael her target had not yet arrived. The world might be dying, but the ballroom of Tokyo's Imperial Palace was very much alive: woven through with color and music and laughter. Its ceilings flowered like a garden above them, each golden tile painted with a different plant. Red camellias, lilies with petals like fire, hives of purple erica, pink peonies, stars of edelweiss. Crystal chandeliers lit the crowd of dress uniforms and silk kimonos below.

Emperor Hirohito and Empress Nagako were the first to greet them. With highest honors and smiles. The meeting was brief, the duty of gracious hosts.

As soon as Yael and Luka left the emperor and his wife, the racers were swarmed with humanity—the edited version. Only the finest of features and genes. It was brownshirts for the most part. Men whose names were pinned like an afterthought at the end of long, involved military titles. Their swastikas danced around the pair as they shook Luka's hand and nodded admiringly at the Iron Crosses around his neck. (*X* over *X*. Crossing each other out.)

For men who'd done such horrible things, their conversation was as mundane as mud. ("The weather here is delightful, isn't it?" "So, Victor Löwe, what are your prospects after this?" "You've never been to Lake Zell in the summer? You absolutely must!") This made it easy for Yael to tune out their voices as she watched the doorway for new guests. Her heart thudded taiko drumbeats at every fresh name the announcer called. There were couples from Tokyo's high society and Japanese generals. There were racing officials and more brownshirts.

But never him.

The room was getting crowded. Yael made note of every camera lens. (There were six, set up in a star formation from various points in the room, meant to catch every moment of the Victor's Ball, every angle.) She'd have to time the event just right...in view of most cameras, but close to the edge of the room. By a door, or even a window. There were two main exits (one south end, one west end), but that was where most of the guards would be. The row of windows on the ballroom's east side would be her best bet.

"You look like you're about to cut and run." Luka leaned close and whispered in her ear, "Am I such a terrible date?"

There was a break in the swarm around them, Yael realized. The general buzz of the ballroom had faded.

Luka didn't seem to notice. He kept talking to himself, via her. "I won't lie. I feel the same way. Not really my scene." He tugged at his uniform's collar. The crosses jangled heavy around his neck. "God, I want a smoke."

The announcer had been silent for over a minute now. And the ballroom doors, Yael noted, were shut, which meant something, someone, was brewing behind them.

This was it. She could feel it in her bones, leaking, rising, lava-hot.

She could feel *him*. Just on the other side. His presence was so powerful that it preceded his body, entrancing the room. Most of the crowd was silent now. Staring at the door, expectant, waiting...

"I'd appreciate if you let my arm survive the evening." It was only after Luka hissed this that Yael realized she was still hanging on to his elbow, her fingernails punching deep into his jacket.

When Yael let go, she did not know what to do with her hands. They were itching, itching, twitching for a weapon, but it was not time yet. So she folded her palms into themselves. Still her nails dug deep.

"Seems like you could use a smoke, too," Luka muttered.

"No smoke," Yael said. "No more smoke."

The room was so quiet, so *ready*, that they could hear the breath the announcer took before his next brazen words. "Presenting the Führer of the Third Reich, Adolf Hitler."

The doors opened.

He was so wreathed by SS that Yael could hardly see him

at first. The bodyguards surrounded the Führer like a quarantine. An impenetrable wall of black uniforms and guns, shielding him from the diseased populace. But the ring widened as Adolf Hitler stepped into the room.

And there he was. Not black and white. Not some disembodied voice. Not a face on a poster. But the man himself. Monster in the flesh.

Most people applauded his arrival. Yael's nails only dug deeper.

The Führer walked straight toward them.

He was not a large man. In fact, Yael stood a couple centimeters taller than him in Adele Wolfe's body. Their eyes were almost level, colliding when Yael looked at him. His irises were blue. The shade of a sky scraped bare and a skeleton soul. The color of veins just beneath skin, needle-ready. A current like blood ran through them—something sparking, which spoke of red, red words.

The rest of him seemed almost dull in comparison.

During his *Chancellery Chats* the Führer was all brimstone and blazing fire. But here, in front of her, under the golden shimmer of the ballroom ceiling, he looked faded. There were so many things the Reichssender cameras did not show. Silver bristled through his mustache, frosted his hairline and its neat part. The kind of gut that comes with age pressed against the buttons of his brown shirt. Lines creased and crept and webbed along his eye sockets.

He was an old man now: sixty-six. He'd lived so much longer than so many.

Yael's stomach churned. Her bones leaked acid like a busted battery.

"My congratulations again, Victor Löwe," the Führer said as soon as he stopped, keeping some distance and guards between them. "The Double Cross is no small feat. You are a fine specimen of the Aryan ideal. Strong, resourceful, cunning. The New Order needs men such as yourself as leaders of the next generation."

Luka's head dipped in a way that could be interpreted as a nod. His crosses clashed against each other, into his chest. "It was my duty to race, *mein* Führer."

Deeper, deeper dug Yael's nails.

"Perhaps your next duty is at the Chancellery. Once you return to Germania, I'll have my people get in touch with you regarding a position."

This time Luka did not nod. He did not smile at all. "Yes, *mein* Führer."

Adolf Hitler did not smile back either. It wasn't until he turned to Yael that his thin lips even hinted at emotion.

"Victor Wolfe. I'm very pleased you're here. I hope to see much more of you this evening." His words weren't red or rough when he spoke to her. He sounded civil, even friendly, even *more* than friendly.

She's pretty and blond. She could hear Vlad now, grumbling over his cup of spiked tea. *Just his type.*

It took all of Yael's training not to stab the Führer there and then. (Not that she hadn't thought about it. It would have been impractical; there were still SS guards between them and too many faces blocking the cameras.) She did the impossible instead: She smiled and fluttered her pale, pale eyelashes, the way she supposed schoolgirls did when they caught sight of their sweethearts.

"It's an honor to see you again, *mein* Führer. I quite enjoyed our evening last year."

Now he smiled. His lips formed a perfect bell curve—a whole distribution of emotions, intent.

"Will you dance with me tonight?" he asked.

Yael opened her palm—she had to stop digging before she hit blood, before everything spilled out at the wrong time—and replied, "It would be my greatest pleasure."

Beside her, Luka fell victim to a coughing fit that twisted his face and rattled his lungs. Yael could hardly tell if it was real or not.

"Are you all right, Victor Löwe?" The Führer's concern fell flat. As if he was reciting lines. His eyes glinted something feral while he watched the boy.

"Too many cigarettes," Yael said.

Luka stopped coughing. The look he gave her was brilliant, a masterpiece of wrath and emotions: *That-was-our-secret* mixed with *hell's-frozen-over* and a dash of *go-to-hell* and *fine-be-his-Aryan-morality-lapdog-for-all-I-care.*

That should teach him not to cheat.

The Führer looked disgusted. "The vice of lesser races, planted to sabotage the bodily purity of the Aryan. I do hope *you* aren't partial to smoking, Victor Wolfe."

Yael stared straight into those witching eyes and wondered

if he'd ever seen it—the billowing black being pulled out of the death camp's smokestacks like intestines. A never-ending gutting.

"I find it repulsive," she told him with a smile (even though her own insides felt drawn and quartered).

The evening moved along, into hors d'oeuvres and cocktails, toasts waxing poetic on Victor Löwe's strength, a formal dinner in an adjoining room with adjoining cameras. Luka maintained a sour expression throughout all of these. The Führer kept his bodyguards close. And the acid black in Yael's bones kept bubbling, rising.

Then finally the dancing.

The first dance belonged to the victor. Luka's arms were stiff around her when they took to the floor. Yael gripped the edges of her left sleeve as she placed that arm on Luka's shoulder (she did not want the silk falling away again, exposing her fresh bandages). It wasn't really a proper waltz (it *couldn't* be with the constraints of the kimono). More of a spinning around on the floor in tiny, awkward steps. They danced for over a minute before Luka finally spoke.

"So, when's the wedding?" There was a taunt in his voice that was a little too vicious. Too real. "Am I invited?"

He was talking about her and the Führer, Yael realized. At least it meant her flirtations had come off as genuine.

"You're jealous." She laughed.

"Are you really so surprised?" He was dead serious. Those lion-smart eyes were softer than she'd ever seen them. His hand was light, light on her waist. "Do you really not know?"

Yael did know. And it amazed her that, even though there

366

was a sorceress's boil of anger and hurt in her chest, the boy in the brown jacket could still find a heartstring. Tug it. Make her feel something else…

—STOP—

—THIS IS NOT WHY YOU'RE HERE—

She was slipping away again. Becoming someone she wasn't. Someone Luka cared for long before Yael stole her face.

She tried to tell him as much. Let him (and, in many ways, herself) down easy. "Luka. I—I'm not someone you'll ever be able to love."

But *no* was not an answer Luka Löwe was used to swallowing. "I know you've sworn off marriage and the Lebensborn, but I promise it would be different with me. I tried moving on after last year. But every girl I met was boring, dull as a bovine. You challenge me, Adele. You always have."

As soft as Luka's eyes were, his face was even softer. The features that could make *one hundred* thousand German maidens swoon were molded by so many emotions, so much hardness melting away.

"You're wrong," he whispered. "There is no one else."

Scheisse! Was he…*proposing?*

She needed to put a stop to this. Quickly. Before the Reichssender cameras caught whiff of it. Before the entire ballroom *ooh*ed and *aah*ed and any chance she had at dancing with the Führer was ruined.

"We'll never be able to trust each other," she said.

"Nonsense." Luka shook his head. "We're even now. Remember?"

Her *no* had to be stronger than this. Hope-shattering.

Something Luka would not come back from. At least for a few minutes.

"I do not love you." Yael didn't have the heart to look at Luka when she said this. (Or maybe, once again, she had *too* much heart.) She looked at the ring of spectators instead. Found *him*. The one she was heartless for. "And I never will."

Luka's arms grew rigid, but he kept moving. Performing the choreography of the dance. He spun her around so she could no longer see the Führer. Yael stared up at the ceiling instead, studying the bonsai cypress tree painted on the tile directly above them.

"You always did have your sights set high." His voice stung. A maskless hurt.

The music slowed. Their steps stopped.

Their dance had come to an end.

Across the room, the Führer stepped away from his bodyguards, into the center of the dance floor, to claim the waltz she'd promised him. He moved like a fighter entering the ring: ignoring all spectators, rolling his shoulders, eyes on the prize.

"Looks like your dreams are about to come true." Luka didn't bother removing the bitterness from his voice. He let her go. "I'm going out for a smoke."

"Good-bye." The word clawed out of her before she even thought to stop it.

The victor acted like he hadn't heard. He turned his back on her and walked toward the door.

Yael turned her back on him and faced the Führer. His hand curled like a meat hook around her waist. The current in his eyes thrived and flashed. He was not quite smiling, but his lips were hungry and tight beneath his mustache.

The music started anew.

Adolf Hitler was a much better dancer than Luka Löwe. Though his movements were brutish, more forceful. He seemed to take no mind of the limitations of Yael's kimono, pushed her through them.

All six cameras were crowded on the edge of the floor. Six clear shots.

There was a small break in the crowd, by the windows. The world outside was dark, and the lights against the glass showed Yael herself. In miniature—being spun around and around by the man she hated most in the world. He was steering her closer and closer to the gap. Closer and closer to his own death. Just a few more steps now.

Her right hand was clasped tight in his, caught up in the traditional waltz stance. She'd have to use her left.

"You're quite the woman, Victor Wolfe," the Führer said. "Beautiful, smart, brave. You are one of the highest compliments to our race."

She didn't know if she could keep the hot inside her anymore. Her blood boiled and rose: up, up, up, until she imagined it seeping through her kimono. The same red that ran through its silk. The same red that poured out of every vein everywhere. The same red she was about to tear out of *him*.

But before Yael did all this, she wanted him to *know*. Not just why, but who. Who, who, who. Because if she couldn't be herself now, what was the point of it all?

She'd forgotten who she was so many times. She would never forget again.

Nobody would. After this.

Every version of her rose up with the blood. The smallest doll and the Jewish girl marked with an *X*. The feral pickpocket and the girl who ate crullers, studied calculus. The girl who ran without looking back. The girl who stopped and did. The monster and the Valkyrie.

So many lives behind one solid voice: "I am Yael. I am Inmate 121358ΔX. I am your death."

Yael's left hand dove into her obi as she said this, taking hold of her P38. She had to act fast. The room, the *world*, had heard her, and the bodyguards were already moving.

"You were the first...." The Führer's voice trailed to a whimper, but the swimming in his eyes only grew—a fear as frenzied as sharks who've caught their first scent of blood.

She did not inhale. She did not exhale. But she did look straight.

Life and death. Power in her hand and wolves on her arm.

—KILL THE BASTARD—

The fear flashed loud, louder, **loudest** through Adolf Hitler's irises. And just like that they shifted: blue, green, gold, brown, gray, black... into a *brightness*. Yael saw all these colors pass through his eyes, just as she squeezed the trigger. Just as the bullet tore through the P38's barrel, bridged the nothingness of space between them, tore through his brown shirt, his thin skin, his fleshy cardiac muscles.

This is how empires crumble. This is how tyrants fall.

Like everyone else.

For a moment, he was flying. The wings of death bearing him back, plowing his body to the ground. Red sprouted like moss around the buttons of his shirt. His eyes stared—empty and impossibly bright—seeing nothing of the gold ceiling above.

Adolf Hitler, the Führer of the Third Reich, was dead.

But something was wrong...not just his eyes...the silver of his hair was frothing out, spilling white along every hair. Even his skin turned a shade paler.

He was dead, yes, but he was changing. Changing in a way she'd seen before. In the death camp, Barrack 7. In the shadows of Germania's alleys. In mercury-spotted mirrors.

You were the first... not the only.

It was not the Führer who'd just died. The body at her feet belonged to a skinshifter. Someone like her.

Someone she'd shot and killed.

Yael's seconds were up, spinning back into real time. Bodyguards lunged from all sides and she had to—**MOVE OR DIE**—There was still a rage inside her, and she used it to accelerate her motions. Full throttle.

Yael hitched up her kimono and ran for the window. The glass was antiquated and fragile, taking only one shot to shatter, crumble, make a way for her. Yael lunged through it; more bullets bit the side of the window, followed by the bodyguards' brute screams and a chaos of emotion, rising, swelling from the ballroom.

The grounds were not well lit, and there were more than

a few pools of darkness to melt into. Yael shed her kimono, planted it under one of the few lamps, and sprinted off in the opposite direction. Her body moved to the instruction manual of Vlad's relentless training, but her mind was stuck on one line of thought.

Not him. Not him. It was not the Führer I killed, but an innocent decoy. The cameras caught it anyway, and the resistance will be rising, moving, not knowing that the real monster still lives on ... still sits fat on the bones of the world.

A monster I've poked, very viciously.

The thought made Yael want to retch as she reached the bushes with her survival pack. Changed her clothes, changed her face, pulled her boots back on.

She had to find a telephone, a telegraph, something to message Reiniger and Henryka, warn them....

But it was already too late.

The shot had been heard around the world.

The fuse had been lit.

And there was no extinguishing it.

CHAPTER 35

NOW

APRIL 2, 1956

The Angel of Death sat in front of a television. His glasses had slid to the end of his nose. Everything was blurry, but he didn't bother shoving the spectacles back.

There was nothing left to watch. He'd already seen it all. The happy crowds, the elaborate dinner, the pretty blond girl waltzing with the Führer's doppelgänger, killing him.

It wasn't the sight of blood that rattled Dr. Geyer. (He was a surgeon, after all. It was what he waded through every day—filthy, dirty, red. Blood was just blood was just blood.) No—it was the words that slid under Dr. Geyer's skin, filled him with dread beyond dread.

I am Yael. I am Inmate 121358ΔX. I am your death. That was what the girl had said, with a wrath like hellfire. With the kind of judgment reserved only for gods.

Yael. Inmate 121358ΔX. She went by other names in Dr. Geyer's head: Patient Zero. Lost Girl. Deepest Secret.

She'd always been one of his favorites. Strong, hard to break, unwilling to die. It was a quality he never really could define until he saw it. Iron will, iron soul. It was rare that he saw these things in the eyes that poured from the cattle cars. Even rarer in the children he had to sift through.

Patient Zero had been easy to spot from the apple crate—even though a river of ragged humanity threatened to drown her. Like so many other children, she clung to her mother's coattails. There was fear in her eyes, too, but it wasn't the same animal terror that blinded the others. No—it was calculating, stripping her down, exposing the iron inside.

As soon as this girl stared back at him (and kept staring, through the fear and the pain and the wails of those so much older), Geyer knew she was something he could melt down. Something that might survive the forging.

He was right. She'd been the beginning of everything, his first real success. It wasn't until after she escaped that Dr. Geyer realized what he'd stumbled upon: camouflage—ultimate, endless potential. The escape itself he'd covered up as quickly as possible: firing the nurse (he'd never liked her anyway) and ordering the gassing of Barrack 7. (He'd told Vogt it had been infected with lice, which wasn't exactly a lie.) He stamped DECEASED on 121358ΔX's folder and filed it away. When Himmler asked about her months later, he'd said the girl was dead.

Then the Angel of Death moved forward. (Progress waited for no man.) He tested the compound on more subjects, making sure to lock them up in observation cells as their symptoms manifested. Most died from fever and infection.

Others tipped to the other side of sanity and had to be disposed of. But a few survived. And a few was all he needed to show Himmler the world he'd unlocked, the possibilities. Himmler was all he needed to have the results of Experiment 85 presented to the Führer himself. The Führer's permission was all he needed to test the compound on soldiers and establish the Doppelgänger Project, a top secret initiative to design decoys for important political figures.

Even though he'd closed the file eleven years ago, he sometimes wondered about the Lost Girl. Logic told him she'd starved in the woods, or had caught a stray bullet and bled out (all that glorious research gone to waste). He never expected her to show up again. And certainly not like this.

She'd survived too well. Been forged into something too strong.

The television was off now, but the girl's iron voice kept ringing in his ears. *I am, I am, I am.* Stripping back the Führer's secrets, and his own lies, for all the world to see.

Her judgment was not in vain. Dr. Geyer knew the blame for all this would tumble down the ranks. Land on his shoulders with all the thunder of Thor's hammer. Already he was shuddering....

If only he hadn't lied to Himmler. If only he'd kept her locked up in an observation cell like all the others. If only he'd chosen someone else that night on the apple crate...

But it was done now, and there was no use squirming about it. A girl had lived and a doppelgänger had died, and all Dr. Geyer could do was shove his glasses back up the bridge of his nose and wait. He sat at his desk, staring at the shiny black rotary phone.

It stayed silent for a long, long time. He supposed the Chancellery had its hands full trying to patch up the incident (after all, *everyone* had seen it). Himmler was probably getting the whipping-boy earful that came with screwing up. A verbal flaying that would be passed on to Geyer with exponential fury.

The Angel of Death hoped that was all he would receive.

This girl was the beginning of everything, and as the phone began to ring, Dr. Geyer couldn't shake the feeling that she was also the end of it all.

CHAPTER 36

NOW

APRIL 2, 1956
THE RED LANDS

This was what the world saw: the Führer, dying millions of times. The screaming girl, the shot, the fall flashed across millions of separate screens in millions of separate moments.

And then there was static, all static, screeching, NO SIGNAL FOUND.

But the signal had already been sent. One by one the people turned off their televisions. And they started moving.

In Rome, a door the color of oxblood opened. Partisans ran the streets like rats. Only this time it was a plague instead of a scurry. An acne-riddled boy made the sign of a cross on his chest and blessed the Volchitsa.

In Cairo, a man put down his shisha pipe and picked up the carbine he'd kept hidden since the Great Surrender. All across his city others did the same. They had a meeting to keep at the *Reichskommissar*'s compound.

In Germania, General Erwin Reiniger finished convening with all the officers he'd won over to the resistance's cause. Some of them were nervous: with sweaty lips and darting eyes. Others were unshakable. All of them had itching consciences. Together they represented over half of the Reich's army, and their regiments were already surrounding the city. Ready to devour it whole.

In a basement, Henryka tugged at her too-bleached hair and shuffled pins on a map. With every other breath, she prayed for the girl who might as well be her daughter. With every breath between, she prayed the red away.

Twenty thousand kilometers away (give or take), Yael limped through Tokyo's streets, her short black hair still damp with moat water, facial features blending perfectly with every pedestrian she passed. She kept her ears sharp as she walked, eavesdropping for news—any news at all—of what was happening back west. But the only words out of people's mouths were *Adele* and *assassination*. Everyone's attention was on the shot fired at the Victor's Ball. Just as Reiniger had planned.

Her mission had faltered, yes, but it had not failed. She'd done everything that had been asked of her: rode across continents, attended the Victor's Ball, pulled out her gun, shot straight. A man had died to make the world better, and though it was the wrong sacrifice, there was no taking back the blood.

The red was spilled. But this time, *hope* ran with it.

Operation Valkyrie the Second was a go. All around

the Reich, the web of the resistance was working, spreading. London. Paris. Baghdad. Tripoli. Prague. Vienna. Amsterdam. Cities upon cities were rising up.

The world was not just moving. It was alive.

And it was ready to fight.

AUTHOR'S NOTE

As a writer, I try to examine all facets of life through a single question: *What if?* This question tends to lead to more questions, which lead to more questions.... It's not uncommon for me to try to answer these in book form.

History—such a fluid, fragile collection of dates and events—has always fascinated me. It holds a countless opportunity for *what-ifs*. What if Hitler had made the decision to execute Operation Sea Lion, invading Britain in the summer of 1940? What if, instead of attacking Pearl Harbor, the Japanese aided Hitler's assault on the Soviet Union, causing Stalin to fight a two-front war? What if the Americans had held fast to the isolationist policies that were so popular in the United States during the 1930s?

What if the Axis had won World War II?

Entire books and Internet forums explore the technicalities of this possibility. (A particularly good book is a collection of essays called *If the Allies Had Fallen: Sixty Alternate Scenarios of World War II*, edited by Dennis E. Showalter and Harold C. Deutsch.) Though historians disagree on the likelihood of an ultimate Axis victory, most concede that it was, at some point or another, possible.

The world you've glimpsed within these pages could have been our own. For a time and in a place, it was.

Hitler's New Order was to be built with the sweat and blood of the Slavic peoples. Their cultures were to be stamped out, their lands seized for Lebensraum (territory for what

Hitler believed was the Aryans' divine right to expand eastward), their populations used for slave labor. By autumn of 1944 over nine and a half million foreigners and prisoners of war were being worked to death in factories, fields, and mines all across Germany.

Hitler, who'd held a special hatred for Jews ever since his days in Vienna, sought not just to enslave them, but to annihilate them altogether. His "Final Solution to the Jewish Question" was implemented with firing squads, gas vans, and extermination camps. It's estimated that six million Jews lost their lives by the time the Allies won World War II.

The Reich's women were discouraged from pursuing education or taking jobs outside the home. Instead, women were encouraged to produce as many children as possible for the spread of the Aryan race into their newly seized lands. Mothers who bore four or more children were even rewarded with the Cross of Honor of the German Mother. However, as in the case of this novel's very own Adele Wolfe, there were exceptions. Among the most notable of these was Hanna Reitsch, a female Nazi test pilot who was awarded the Iron Cross by Hitler himself in 1941.

There were over forty documented attempts to assassinate Hitler, but the most infamous of these was the "July Plot," a plan put together by high-ranking officers in Hitler's own army who—like this novel's own Reiniger—felt morally obligated to end his reign of terror.

On July 20, 1944, Colonel Claus von Stauffenberg reported to a meeting at the Wolfsschanze (Hitler's Eastern Front military headquarters) with a time bomb in his briefcase and every intention of killing Hitler. Hitler's death was an essential part of the conspirators' plan to execute a coup d'état against the Nazi government using Operation Valkyrie: a military protocol (designed by conspirator General Friedrich Olbricht and approved by Hitler himself) that allowed the Territorial Reserve Army of Germany to secure Berlin in case of civil unrest.

Only when Hitler was announced dead (and all German soldiers were freed from their oath of fealty to him) could Olbricht and the other conspirators initiate Operation Valkyrie, take control of the Wehrmacht (armed forces), and establish a new anti-Nazi government.

When Stauffenberg's bomb went off at 12:42 PM, the explosion killed four people. Adolf Hitler was not one of them. Unfortunately, Stauffenberg, who'd fled the scene, thought differently and convinced the conspirators in Berlin to initiate Operation Valkyrie. As soon as news of Hitler's survival reached the capital city, the carefully planned coup failed.

The Gestapo's response to the July Plot was ruthless. There were seven thousand arrests and close to five thousand executions following this assassination attempt.

For a time and in a place, this was our world.

Alternative history is a genre composed of educated guesswork and speculation. Some elements of this story are more speculative than others. Despite the fact that Hitler and Mussolini's relationship was temperamental and that Hitler was not known for honoring alliances, there is no evidence that

Hitler intended to betray Mussolini for his territories. There is also no evidence that Hitler intended to extend his Lebensraum policy into Africa and the Middle East. Historically, his projected Lebensraum was contained to Eastern Europe, though there are historians who theorize this acquisition of territory was only his first step to world domination. Hitler did, after all, name his plans for Berlin's architectural rehaul Welthauptstadt Germania, or World Capital Germania.

There are other, more obvious creative liberties I took with this story. The long-distance motorcycle race from Berlin to Tokyo was an event purely of my own design, though there was a specialist group in the Hitler Youth called the Motor-HJ, which was dedicated to training Germany's young men to ride motorcycles. The German army also made heavy use of motorcycle troops, known as the Kradschützen, who were valued for their speed and mobility.

The biggest departure from reality, however, is Yael's skinshifting. One might wonder why I chose to introduce such a fantastic element to such a sobering backdrop.

Racism was inextricable from Hitler's policies. His belief that Aryans were the master race, destined for world domination, fueled his determination to invade other countries and seize their land as Lebensraum. His twisted racial ladder, along with the desire to keep the Aryan race "pure," led to evils such as eugenics, forcible sterilization, euthanizing the elderly and handicapped, and eliminating all of those Hitler deemed unfit for life.

What if, in such a setting, race became irrelevant?

This book, at its heart, is about identity. Not only in how we see ourselves, but also about how we see others. What makes people who they are? The color of their skin? The blood in their veins? The uniforms they wear? I gave Yael the ability to skinshift to address these questions, as well as to highlight the absurdity of racial superiority. By taking creative liberty with this surreal element, I hoped to push readers out of their own comfort zones and into Yael's many skins and, by doing so, to impart a deeper understanding of what humanity is capable of. Both the good and the evil.

By the time this book is published, seventy years will have passed since the Allies won World War II. Some might consider dwelling on history-that-never-was a macabre and upsetting activity. After all, Adolf Hitler did not emerge victorious, and the horrors of the Holocaust were brought to an end. What purpose does it serve to imagine anything otherwise?

For many, it's tempting to dismiss the Nazis and their policies as evils locked away in history. But racism and anti-Semitism are hardly things of the past. The European Union Agency for Fundamental Rights reported in its 2013 survey on anti-Semitism that 76 percent of the respondents believe anti-Semitism has increased in their countries over the past five years. In fact, at the time I wrote this author's note, both the *New York Times* and *Newsweek* had published articles on the rise of anti-Semitism, detailing incidents of mobs attacking synagogues.

It's my hope that Yael's story will not only remind readers that all people are created equal, but also challenge people to educate themselves on the history behind the fiction and to use this knowledge to examine our present world.

The world within these pages could have been our own. For a time and in a place it was, and we should do our best not to forget that.

ACKNOWLEDGMENTS

This book was a big, scary, intimidating project from the start, but I had plenty of help, even before I began writing. My friend Nagao brought me armfuls of research books on World War II motorcycles and weaponry, answered my random questions about panniers, and let me stand in Yael's shoes by teaching me to shoot a genuine Walther P38. My father-in-law spent hours sitting with me at the kitchen table, talking about World War II *what-if*s and *would-be*s. My husband, David, took me on a surprise dirt-biking date, where I got the tiniest taste of the bruises and sore muscles I was putting my characters through. Kate Armstrong and Megan Shepherd both honed this story with their razor-sharp critique skills and led me through many thoughtful conversations on what this book was supposed to be. Anne Blankman let me mine her wealth of World War II–era knowledge. Jacob Graudin introduced me to Hitler's plans for a Berlin-turned-Germania.

I could not have asked for a better editor for *Wolf by Wolf* than Alvina Ling, who understands my stories in the best of ways. I'm also forever indebted to my agent, Tracey Adams, who believed in this book when it mattered the most. Nikki Garcia, Hallie Patterson, Kristin Dulaney, Victoria Stapleton, Andrew Smith, Megan Tingley, the NOVL team—you all make working with Little, Brown a phenomenal experience! Thank you. Amber Caravéo, Nina Douglas, and the rest of the Orion team—thank you for giving my stories a wonderful UK home.

To my readers—thank you for making it possible for me to live out my childhood dream. To my family—thank you for loving me and nurturing this dream. To my God— thank you for giving me this dream in the first place. *Soli Deo Gloria.*

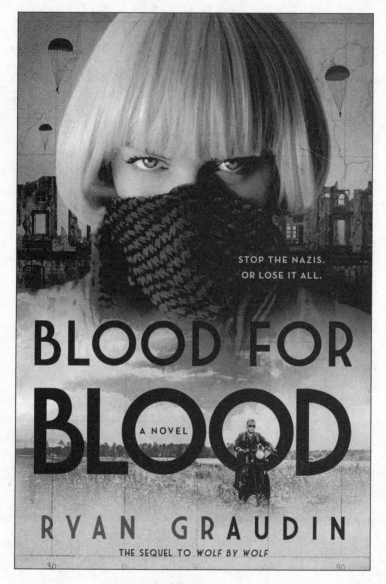

PRELUDE

THREE PORTRAITS OF CHRISTMAS EVE 1945

I

The family room was cramped. Too small for a mother and her three children and the crooked branch the oldest son had sawed down for a Christmas tree. Everywhere Felix Wolfe turned there were pine needles, tinsel, and the faces of his family. Each child stared eagerly at the trio of modest parcels under the spindly branch, waiting for their mother's blessing.

"Make sure you don't tear the paper," she instructed them. "We need to save it to use again."

Martin, as the oldest, went first. His package was the smallest, and held a secondhand pocket watch. Felix opened his own parcel with delicate fingers, carefully unfolding corners and smoothing out creases to find a toy car. It wasn't new—there was a dent in the far right door and some scratches on its bright red paint—but Felix didn't mind. New toys, his schoolteacher had said, were selfish and took away materials the Führer needed to win the war. Metal was needed for Mausers and bullets, not child's play.

Adele tore at the edges of her parcel. Inside lay a doll, with yellow yarn hair and eyes made from the blue buttons of one of their mother's old silk blouses. The doll's dress was made from scraps of its cobalt fabric, sewn with cramped stitches and care.

Felix knew, as soon as his twin stopped and stared at the gift, that she was unhappy. He always knew these things.

"I made other dresses," their mother said. "You can change her clothes every day. And I'll teach you how to braid her hair."

Adele's own plaited pigtails whipped her cheeks as she shook her head and shoved the box away. "I don't *want* a doll! Why can't I have a car like Felix?"

Their mother's mouth pinched. Her eyes went all shiny, the way they sometimes did when she read their father's letters from the front. The sight twisted Felix's stomach.

"Here." He pushed his own present toward his sister. "You can play with my car."

Adele's eyes lit bright as she grabbed the toy. She started making motor sounds and pushing it across the floor. Martin was busy winding his watch. Felix wasn't really sure what he should do, without his car. At least his mother was smiling again, wiping her eyes as she watched her children playing.

"There's one more gift," she said.

All three Wolfe children froze. Felix looked under the tree, but there were no packages left. Perhaps they were getting oranges. Or *maybe* their mother had saved enough rations to bake gingerbread!

Their mother made her way through the room, dancing through bent paper and children's limbs and forgotten toys. She reached the door to her bedroom and placed her hand on the latch. Her smile was wider than Felix had seen it in a long time.

The door opened. Standing at the edge of the bedroom, arms outstretched, was their father, still wearing his army uniform. His field cap slouched over sun-pale hair as he knelt down to greet his children.

Adele was the first child to barrel into his arms, with the delighted shout of *Papa!* Martin—since he now owned a pocket watch and was practically a grown man himself—tried to contain his excitement to a firm handshake. Felix hung back, taking in the sight of his whole family together: Mama grinning by the doorway, Papa pulling both Adele and a not-really-reluctant Martin into a bear hug. Felix's heart warmed while he watched them, brighter than the cinders in the wood-burning stove.

He wanted to capture this moment, hold this feeling inside him forever.

"Felix! My little man!" His father smiled. Even with two children in his embrace, his arms were long enough to reach out for his son. "Did you look after this lot? Keep them out of trouble?"

Felix nodded as he joined the hug.

Their father explained that he was home for good. The war was winding down on the Eastern Front, and the army no longer needed him. He didn't have to say good-bye to them anymore.

No more good-byes. The warmth inside Felix stoked and flared. After years of letters from the front—and Felix always fearing that the next would spell out his father's death—the Wolfe family was together again.

II

———

Luka's father had been home for many months, compliments of the artillery shell that ripped his left arm off. The Kradschützen, elite motorcycle troops who'd been a key part of attacking the Russian front, had no use for limbless drivers, so Kurt Löwe and his remaining arm were shipped back to Germany with a Silver Wound Badge and a second-class Iron Cross. Scars and medals: the marks of a war hero. Luka was awed by both.

There were no hugs or smiles involved in the greeting, just a stern nod on his father's part. Luka's mother told him later it was because his father was tired. (After all, he'd been at war for six years.) He just needed time to rest.

Luka's father rested. He sat in a chair for hours and days at a time, staring blankly at the portrait of the Führer that hung over the mantel. When he spoke, it was never to ask Luka how his classes were going or to praise his wife's cooking, but about the war. He told them about the endless, snowy kilometers he drove on his motorcycle. The firefights he and his fellow soldiers endured. How many Soviets he shot and killed. All for the sake of *mein* Führer.

Kurt Löwe rested for months, but the smiles and hugs Luka's mother had promised never appeared. Not even for Christmas Eve.

The Löwe family sat around the small table, eating roasted carp in silence. It wasn't the contented, holy-night type of silence that filled the holiday's church services, but a strained one—full of chewing and scraping forks. It made Luka squirm in his chair.

"Stop fidgeting," his father growled from the other side of the table.

Luka's mother shot her son a meaningful look. He stopped moving. He felt as if he were sitting on eggshells. As if something was about to break...

His father was dividing the carp into neat little pieces with his fork. "When I went on night patrols on the front, we had to be quiet as ghosts. We moved without a sound. Had to, or else we would've been shot."

His mother cleared her throat. "Kurt, I'm not sure this is very good table talk—"

"Good table talk?" Luka's father set his fist on the table. He was still holding his fork, tines up, tattered fish meat hanging from the metal. "Losing my *verdammt* arm for the Fatherland earns me the right to talk about whatever I want at the table."

His wife didn't reply. Instead she set down her own fork and looked at Luka. "Would you like to open your gift now?"

Luka straightened in his chair, nodding. He'd been waiting for this moment for weeks. A bicycle (shiny and red) was the only thing Luka wanted. Sometimes Franz Gross let him play with his. Both boys took turns pretending to be Kradschützen motorcycle troops, revving imaginary engines as they stormed lines of invisible communists.

"Your gift is by the Advent calendar," his mother said. "Go and fetch it!"

There was no tree this year, but Luka's mother had set up the family's Advent calendar on the mantelpiece. Most of its twenty-four paper doors hung open, revealing a hand-painted Nativity: Mary and Joseph and the Christ Child all gathered in a barn, surrounded by curious animals and poking hay. Blue-eyed angels hovered over the Holy Family. Above them hung a single brilliant star. And above the star...

The Führer's immortalized face loomed, its painted eyes following Luka as he ran to the package by the hearth. The box was much too small for a bicycle and wrapped in old newsprint. Dated headlines told of the advance of the Wehrmacht through Russia, the Reich's impending, undeniable victory. Inked across the package was a picture of the Führer giving a speech about the future of the New Order. Luka ripped through it all to find a set of new shoes and a toy pistol. He stared at them, disappointment bitter in his throat.

"What do you say, Luka?" His father had followed him into the sitting room, watching the whole affair in silence.

"I know you wanted a bicycle"—his mother's voice was soft in the doorway—"but the ones at Herr Kahler's shop were too expensive. Maybe next year, when the war is over."

No bicycle. After weeks, months, years of waiting, still no bicycle. A crying feeling crept up Luka's throat.

"What do you need a bicycle for?" his father asked. His hand strayed up to the second-class Iron Cross that hung from the button on his tunic. "You walk to school."

"I—I want to play Kradschützen with Franz." As soon as the words left Luka's mouth, he wanted to swallow them back. But they were out, along with his tears, swimming through the sitting room.

"Play?" His father's face went hard. Something in his eyes reminded Luka of the painting above the fire. Blue and lifeless. "You want to *play* Kradschützen?"

"I want to be like you."

In a single blitzkrieg movement, Luka's father dropped his Iron Cross and grabbed the boy by his collar. Nina shrank against the doorway as her husband dragged their child past, into the kitchen, out of the house.

It was a snowy evening. Luka's father plowed through the spinning flakes, into the street. His knuckles stayed tight around Luka's collar as he stopped in the middle of a growing snowdrift. "You want to be like me? I spent more nights than you could count in weather far colder than this. Curled up in a *verdammt* foxhole while the commies tried to put a bullet through my skull. You think I spent that time sniveling?"

Luka shook his head. There were more tears now, blurring against his eyelashes.

"Don't show emotion." Kurt Löwe gave his son a rough shake. "Don't you ever show emotion. Tears are weakness. And I won't have any son of mine being *weak*. You're going to stand here until you stop crying."

Luka tried, but the squeeze in his throat only grew worse. The tears that had already fallen were starting to hurt his cheeks: burning cold.

His mother shivered barefoot in the doorway, on the verge of tears herself. "Kurt! He'll freeze!"

"You've let our son grow soft and ungrateful, Nina. Filling his head with art and fanciful *Scheisse*! If I could endure an entire winter in this snow, the least he can do is stand ten minutes in a drift."

"You had a uniform to keep you warm! Luka doesn't even have a coat."

Kurt Löwe took another look at his son: hunched over, teeth chattering, shin-deep in the snowdrift. He stepped back into the house and returned moments later with his prewar brown leather riding jacket and his dog tag. Both items were shoved into Luka's arms. "Put them on."

The jacket was far too big; its sleeves dragged far past Luka's fingers, into the piling snow. The dog tag hung all the way down to his belly button.

"A German youth must be strong. Tough as leather, hard as steel." His father pointed at the jacket and the dog tag in turn. "Stand your ground. Don't bother knocking on that door until the tears are off your face."

Kurt Löwe's arm cut like a scythe through the falling snow as he marched back to the house, hooking around his wife's waist to usher her inside. When the door shut, Luka tried to wipe his cheeks with the oversized sleeve. His father was right. The leather was hard, too tough to blot the tears.

So Luka stood staring at the glowing kitchen window— minute after frigid minute, while his legs grew numb and his heart grew hard—waiting for his sadness to dry on its own.

III

___

A fresh pan of gingerbread sat on the ledge of the farmhouse window. The glass was cracked a few centimeters, just enough to let the cold in. The confection's heat clouded into steam, carrying scents of clove and ginger and molasses all the way across the snow-covered yard, into the barn.

Yael tried her hardest to ignore the smell. She'd already settled down for the evening, taking shelter in the scratchy piles of hay. The barn was warm enough, and the handful of oats she'd scooped out of the horses' feed bin kept the gnaw of her hunger away.

But the gingerbread...

Never in her seven years of life could Yael remember eating anything as good as that dessert smelled. Food in the ghetto had been scarce. Food in the camp had been scarce *and* rotten. (Bits of gruel, spoiled vegetables, moldy bread.) Ever since Yael escaped those barbed-wire fences by using her skinshifting abilities to look like the camp kommandant's daughter, her diet was substantially better. During summer the woods burst with blackberry thickets and mushroom caps. Orchards were so fruitful by autumn that the farmers' wives never seemed to note how the trees on the borders of their property lacked apples. Now that the weather was harsher, Yael took shelter in barn lofts, sustaining herself with horse feed, hoping the owners wouldn't notice that their horses seemed to eat twice as much without getting fat.

She'd lurked in this particular barn for a week. It was an unusually generous length of time, but the family who lived in the house had been too distracted by holiday festivities to pay much attention to clues of her presence. Yael had watched the whole process from the safety of the loft. The decorating of the Christmas tree, the singing of carols, the baking...

She'd watched the mother stir the gingerbread together into a deep brown dough. One of her blond daughters (the same one who trudged across the yard every morning through blank-slate snow; whose breath frosted the air as she sang "Silent Night" to herself and milked the cow; who had no idea that Yael was listening in the loft above) popped the pan into the oven. The other daughter peeled potatoes. Their two brothers played Stern-Halma at the kitchen table—a game full of laughter and elbows.

The family was off in the dining room now, eating dinner and waiting for the gingerbread to cool. The oats in Yael's stomach did not feel like enough as she watched them. She wanted to be in that house. Chuckling, full, and not alone.

That, of course, was impossible.

She was not one of them. She could never be one of them.

But she *could* snag a piece of that gingerbread.

The milking cow gave Yael a lazy, low greeting as she crept down the loft's ladder. She made certain before she stepped out of the barn that her sweater sleeve was rolled down to hide the tattooed numbers on her arm. Her hair, tangled though it was, was as golden as the straw. Her eyes were bold and blue. No one would recognize her for what she truly was.

Snow was falling thick enough to cover her footprints for a short trip to the kitchen window and back. After a few minutes there would be no sign she was even there. Just a cracked window and an empty pan.

Yael slipped across the yard, ignoring the sting of the snow through her thin shoes. The smell of gingerbread was stronger now, the family's laughter louder. She could hear one of the boys telling a joke—something about talking cows riding bicycles. The youngest sister giggled so hard she snorted.

Yael hunched under the window, reaching for the pan with hungry fingers.

"And then the first cow turned to the second cow and said—"

"OUCH!"

Yael, who was always so quiet, so careful, had not taken into account that a steaming pan meant the metal was still hot. She clamped her mouth shut, but it was too late. The youngest sister stopped laughing. Five different chairs scraped across the farmhouse floor as the family leapt to their feet.

"What was that?"

"Eric," the mother said to one of the boys, "go get the rifle."

Yael was off, sprinting across the field, leaving a whirl of footprints behind her. The farmhouse door opened to a yell. Yael did not stop. She did not look back. And it was a good thing, too, because—

KA-BOOM.

Silent night. Holy night.

All is buckshot. All is bright.

She was not one of them. She could never be one of them.

Yael could not go back to the barn (trigger-happy, cow-joking Eric would only follow the footprints, find her there), so she did what she always did.

She kept running.